IN THE DARK

IN THE DARK

Mark Billingham

McArthur & Company
Toronto

First published in Canada in 2008 by
McArthur & Company
322 King St. West, Suite 402
Toronto, Ontario
M5V 1J2
www.mcarthur-co.com

Library and Archives Canada Cataloguing in Publication

Billingham, Mark   In the dark / Mark Billingham.

ISBN 978-1-55278-740-3

I. Title.
PR6102.I44I5 2008   823'.92   C2008-903477-5
Cover design by Duncan Spilling
Printed in Canada by Webcom

10 9 8 7 6 5 4 3 2 1

For Katie and Jack

2 AUGUST

It's a dry night, but the road is still greasy from the shower a few hours before; slick as it's sucked under the headlights, and there's not too much traffic rattling across the cracks in a main drag that's probably the worst maintained in the city.

It's morning, of course, strictly speaking; the early hours. But to those few souls on their way home, or struggling out to work in the dark, or already about business of one sort or another, it feels very much like night; the middle of the bastard.

The dead of it.

It's a warm night too, and muggy. The second of what's shaping up to be a pretty decent August. But that's not why the passenger in the blue Cavalier is leaning his head towards the open window and sweating like a pig.

'Like a kiddie-fiddler on a bouncy castle,' the driver says. 'Fuckin' *look* at you, man.'

'There no air-con on this thing?'

'Nobody else sweating that much.'

The three men in the back are laughing, shoulders pressed together. Staring out between the front seats at the traffic coming towards the car. When they light cigarettes, the driver holds out a hand, demanding one. It's lit for him, and passed forward.

The driver takes a deep drag, then peers at the cigarette. 'Why you smoking this rubbish, man?'

'Friend got a few cases, man. Owed me.'

'So why not pass a couple my way?'

'I was thinking, you smoke that strong shit. Marlboro, whatever.'

'Yeah. You was thinking.' He yanks at the wheel, taking the car fast around a bin-bag that has blown into the middle of the road. 'Look at this shit up here, man. These people living like pigs or something.'

The shuttered-up shops and restaurants slide past the passenger window, Turkish places, or Greek. Asian grocers', clubs, a one-room minicab office with a yellow light. The shutters and security doors are all tagged: letters swooping against the metal; red, white and black; indecipherable.

The territories, marked.

'We got no beats?' One of the men in the back starts slapping out a rhythm on the back of the head-rest.

'No point, man.' The driver leans down, waves a hand dismissively towards the audio controls on the dashboard. 'Pussy-arsed system on this thing.'

'What about the radio?'

The driver sucks his teeth; something small dropped into hot fat. 'Just men talking foolishness this time of the night,' he says. 'Chill-out shit and golden oldies.' He reaches across and lays a hand on the back of the passenger's neck. ''Sides, we need to let this boy concentrate, you get me?'

From the back: 'He needs to concentrate on not pissing in his panties. He's shook, you ask me. Shook, big time.'

'*Se*-rious . . .'

The passenger says nothing, just turns and looks. Letting the three behind him know they'll have time to talk later, when the thing's done. He shifts back around and faces front, feeling the weight on the seat between his legs, and the stickiness that pastes his shirt to the small of his back.

The driver pushes up tight behind a night bus, then pulls hard to the right. Singing something to himself as he takes the Cavalier past, and across the lights as amber turns to red.

She'd turned onto the A10 at Stamford Hill, leaving the bigger houses behind, the off-street Volvos and the tidy front gardens, and pointed the BMW south.

She takes it nice and easy through Stoke Newington; knows there are cameras ready to flash anyone stupid enough to jump a light. Watches her speed. The roads aren't busy, but there's always a job-pissed traffic copper waiting to spoil some poor sod's night.

Last thing she needs.

A few minutes later she's drifting down into Hackney. Place might not look quite as bad at night, but she knows better. Mind you, at least those slimy buggers at the local estate agent's had to work to earn their commission.

'Oh yes, it's very much an up-and-coming area. Gets a bad press for sure, but you've got to look behind all that. There's a real sense of community here; and, of course, all these misconceptions do mean that house prices are very competitive . . .'

I mean, however the hell you pronounce it, De Beauvoir Town *sounds* nice, doesn't it? Just talk about Hackney Downs and Regent's Canal and don't worry about little things like knife crime, life expectancy, stuff like that. There's even the odd grassy square, for heaven's sake, and one or two nice Victorian terraces.

'Stick a few of them, what d'you call it, leylandii at the back end of the garden, you won't even be able to see the estate!'

Poor bastards might as well have targets painted on their front doors.

She's across the Ball's Pond Road without needing to slow down; Kingsland to one side of her, Dalston spreading like a stain to the east.

Not long now.

Her hands are sticky, so she puts an arm out of the window, splays her fingers and lets the night air move through them. She thinks she can feel rain in the air, just a drop or two. She leaves her arm where it is.

The Beemer sounds good – just a low hum, and a whisper under the wheels; and the leather of the passenger seat feels smooth and clean under her hand when she reaches over. She's always loved this car; felt comfortable from the moment she first swung her legs inside. Some people were like that with houses. Whatever the sales pitch, sometimes it just came down to that vibe or whatever when you walked inside. Same with the car; it felt like hers.

She sees the Cavalier coming towards her as she's slowing for lights. It's going a lot faster than she is and pulls up hard, edging across the white lines at the junction.

It has no headlights on.

She feels for the stalk behind the steering wheel and flicks it twice; flashes the BMW's top-of-the-range xenon headlamps at the Cavalier. Better than the landing lights on a 747, she remembers the salesman saying. They talked even more crap than estate agents.

The driver of the Cavalier makes no acknowledgement; just stares back.

Then switches on his lights.

She urges the BMW across the junction and away. The first drops of rain are spotting the screen. She checks her rear-view mirror and sees the Cavalier throw a fast U-turn a hundred yards behind; hears a horn blare as it cuts across oncoming traffic, pulling in front of a black cab and moving fast up the bus lane towards her.

Feels something jump in her guts.

'Why that one?' the man in the passenger seat asks.

The driver shifts the Cavalier hard up into fifth gear and shrugs. 'Why not?'

The three in the back seat are leaning further forward now, buzzing with it, but their voices are matter-of-fact. 'Fool selected her-*self*.'

'You interfere with people, you asking for it, proper.'

'She was just trying to help.'

'The way we do it,' the driver says.

The passenger seat is feeling hot beneath him as he turns away, like it's all OK with him. Like his breathing is easy enough and his bladder doesn't feel like it's fit to explode.

Fucking stupid cow. Why can't she mind her own business?

They pull out of the bus lane and swing around a motorbike. The rider turns to look as they pass, a black helmet and visor. The man in the passenger seat glances back, but can't hold the look. Drags his eyes back to the road ahead.

The car ahead.

'Don't lose her.' Urgent, from the back seat.

Then his friend: 'Yeah, you need to floor this piece of shit, man.'

The driver flicks his eyes to the rear-view. 'You two boying me?'

'No.'

'You fucking *boying* me or what?'

Hands are raised. 'Pump down, man. Just *saying* . . .'

The eyes slide away again, and the foot goes down, and the Cavalier quickly draws to within a few feet of the silver BMW. The driver turns to the man in the passenger seat and grins. Says: 'You ready?'

The rain is coming down heavier now.

His chest thumping faster than the squeaky wipers.

'We doing it,' the driver says.

'Yeah . . .'

The Cavalier eases to the left, just inches away now, forcing the BMW across into the bus lane. The three on the back seat hiss and swear and snort.

'Any fucking second, we *doing* it.'

In the passenger seat, he nods and his palm tightens, clammy around the handle of the gun against his knee.

'Lift it up, man, lift that thing up high. Show her what you got.'

Holding his breath, clenching; fighting the urge to piss right there in the car.

'What she *gettin'*.'

When he turns he can see that the woman in the BMW is scared enough already. Just a couple of feet away. Eyes all over the place; a twist of panic at the mouth.

He raises the gun.

'Do it.'

This was what he wanted, wasn't it?

Kissy-kissy noises from the back seat.

'*Do* it, man.'

He leans across and fires.

'Again.'

The Cavalier pulls away at the second shot, and he strains to keep the silver car in sight; leans further out, the rain on his neck, oblivious to the shouting around him and the fat hands slapping his back.

He watches as the BMW lurches suddenly to the left and smashes up and over the pavement; sees the figures at the bus stop, the bodies flying.

What he wanted . . .

A hundred feet from it, more, he can hear the crunch as the bonnet crumples. And something else: a low thump, heavy and wet, and then the scream of metal and dancing glass that fades as they accelerate away.

THREE WEEKS
EARLIER

PART ONE

LIE, LIKE BREATHING

ONE

Helen Weeks was used to waking up feeling sick, feeling like she'd hardly slept, and feeling like she was on her own, whether Paul was lying beside her or not.

He was up before her this morning, already in the shower when she walked slowly into the bathroom and leaned down to throw up in the sink. Not that there was much to it. A few spits; brown and bitter strings.

She rinsed her mouth out, pressed her face against the glass door on her way through to get the breakfast things ready. 'Nice arse,' she said.

Paul smiled and turned his face back to the water.

When he walked into the living room ten minutes later, Helen was already tucking into her third piece of toast. She'd laid everything out on their small dining-table – the coffee pot, cups, plates and dishes they'd bought from The Pier when they'd first moved in – carried the jam and peanut butter across from the fridge on a tray, but Paul reached straight for the cereal as always.

It was one of the things she still loved about him: he was a big kid who'd never lost the taste for Coco Pops.

She watched him pour on the milk, rub at the few drops he spilled with a finger. 'Let me iron that shirt.'

'It's fine.'

'You didn't do the sleeves.' He never did the sleeves.

'No point. I'll have my jacket on all day.'

'It'll take me five minutes. It might warm up later on.'

'It's pissing down out there.'

They ate in silence for a while. Helen thinking she should maybe go and turn on the small TV in the corner, but guessing that one of them would have something to say eventually. There was music bleeding down from the flat upstairs anyway. A beat and a bassline.

'What have you got on today?'

Paul shrugged, and swallowed. 'God knows. Find out when I get in, I suppose. See what the skipper's got lined up.'

'You finishing six-ish?'

'Come on, *you* know. If something comes up, it could be any time. I'll ring you.'

She nodded, remembering a time when he would have done. 'What about the weekend?'

Paul looked across at her, grunted a 'what?' or a 'why?'

'We should try to see a few houses,' Helen said. 'I was going to get on the phone today, fix up a couple of appointments.'

Paul looked pained. 'I told you, I don't know what I'm doing yet. What's coming up.'

'We've got six weeks. *Maybe* six weeks.'

He shrugged again.

She hauled herself up, walked across to drop a couple more slices of bread in the toaster. Tulse Hill was OK; *better* than OK if you wanted to buy a kebab or a second-hand car. Brockwell Park and Lido were a short walk away and there was plenty happening five minutes down the hill in the heart of Brixton. The flat itself was nice enough; *secure*, a couple of floors up with a lift that worked most of the time. But they couldn't stay. One and a bit bedrooms – the double and the one you'd fail to swing a kitten in – small kitchen and living room, small bathroom. It would all start to feel a damn sight smaller in a month and a half, with a pushchair in the hall and a playpen in front of the TV.

'I might go over, see Jenny later.'

'Good.'

Helen smiled, nodded, but she knew he didn't think it was good at all. Paul had never really seen eye to eye with her sister. It hadn't helped that Jenny had known about the baby before he had.

Had known a few other things, too.

She carried her toast across to the table. 'You had a chance to talk to the Federation rep yet?'

'About?'

'Jesus, Paul.'

'*What?*'

Helen almost dropped her knife, seeing the look on his face.

The Metropolitan Police gave female officers thirteen weeks after having a baby, but they were rather stingier when it came to paternity leave. Paul had been – was *supposed* to have been – arguing his case for an extension on the five days' paid leave he had been allocated.

'You said you would. That you *wanted* to.'

He laughed, empty. 'When did I say that?'

'Please . . .'

He shook his head, chased cereal around his bowl with the back of the spoon as though there might be some plastic toy he'd missed. 'He's got more important things to worry about.'

'Right.'

'*I've* got more important things.'

Paul Hopwood worked as a detective sergeant on a CID team based a few miles north of them in Kennington. An Intelligence Unit. He'd heard every joke that was trotted out whenever *that* came up in conversation.

Helen felt herself reddening; wanting to shout but unable to. 'Sorry,' she said.

Paul dropped his spoon, shoved the bowl away.

'I just don't see what could be . . .' Helen trailed off, seeing that Paul wasn't listening, or wanted to give that impression. He had picked up the cereal packet and was still studying the back of it intently as she pushed back her chair.

When Paul had gone, and she'd cleared away the breakfast things, Helen stood under the shower for a while, stayed there until she'd stopped crying, and got dressed slowly. A giant bra and sensible pants, sweat-shirt and blue and white jogging bottoms. Like she had a lot of choice.

She sat in front of *GMTV* until she felt her brain liquidising, and moved across to the sofa with the property pages of the local paper.

West Norwood, Gipsy Hill, Streatham. Herne Hill if they stretched themselves; and Thornton Heath if they had no other choice.

More important things . . .

She thumbed through the pages, circling a few likely-looking places, all ten or fifteen grand more than they'd budgeted for. She'd need to go back to work a damn sight quicker than she'd thought. Jenny had said she'd chip in with the childcare.

'You're an idiot if you rely on Paul,' Jenny had said. '*However* much free time he gets.'

Blunt as always, her younger sister, and hard to argue with.

'He'll be fine when the baby comes.'

'How will *you* be?'

The music was getting louder upstairs. She'd tell Paul to have a word when he got a chance. She moved through to the bedroom, sat down to try and do something with her hair. She thought men who described pregnant women as 'radiant' were a bit weird; same as people who thought they had the right to touch your belly whenever the hell they felt like it. She swallowed, sour all the way down, unable to remember the last time Paul had wanted to touch it.

They were well past the 'goodbye kiss on the doorstep' stage, of course they were, but they were well past far too many other things. She wasn't feeling a lot like sex admittedly, but she would have been well out of luck if she was. Early on she'd been gagging for it, like a lot of women a month or so in, if you believed the books, but Paul had lost interest fairly quickly. It wasn't uncommon; she'd read that, too. Blokes feeling differently once the whole motherhood business came into it. Hard to look at your partner in the same way, to *desire* them, even before there's a belly appearing.

It was much more complicated, their relationship, but maybe there was some of that going on.

'Poor little bugger doesn't want me poking him in the eye,' Paul had said.

Helen had scoffed, said, 'I doubt you'd reach his eye,' but neither of them had really felt like laughing much.

She pushed her hair back, and lay down; trying to make herself feel better by remembering earlier times, when things weren't quite as bad. It was a trick that had worked once or twice, but these days she was having trouble remembering how they'd been before. The three years they'd been together before things had gone wrong.

Before the stupid rows and the *fucking* stupid affair.

She could hardly blame him for it, for thinking that there were more important things than her. Than a place for them to live. The two of them and the baby that might not be his.

She decided that she'd go and have a word about the music herself; the student in the flat above seemed nice enough. But she couldn't rouse herself from the bed, thinking about Paul's face.

The looks.

Angry, as though she had no idea at all how hurt he still felt. And vacant, like he wasn't even there; sitting at the table a few feet away and staring at the back of the stupid cereal box, like he was reading about that missing plastic toy.

★ ★ ★ ★

As Paul Hopwood drove, he tried hard to think about work; singing along with the pap on Capital Gold and thinking about meetings and stroppy sergeants and anything at all except the mess he'd left behind.

Toast and fucking politeness. Happy families . . .

He turned right and waited for the sat-nav to tell him he'd made a mistake; for the woman with the posh voice to tell him he should turn around at the earliest possible opportunity.

The ghost of a smile, thinking about a lad he knew at Clapham nick who'd suggested they should make these things with voices designed for men with 'specialist interests'.

'It'd be brilliant, Paul. She says "turn left", you ignore her, she starts getting a bit strict with you. "I said turn left, you *naughty* boy." Sell like hot cakes, mate. Ex-public school boys and all that.'

He turned up the radio, switched the wipers to intermittent.

Happy families. Christ on a bike . . .

Helen had been turning on that look for weeks now, the hurt one. Like she'd suffered enough and he should be man enough to forget what had happened, because she needed him. All well and good, but clearly he hadn't been man enough where it had counted, had he?

Mrs Plod, the copper's tart.

That look, like she didn't recognise him any more. Then the tears, and her hands always slipping down to her belly, like the kid was going to drop out if she sobbed too hard or something. Like all this was *his* fault.

He knew what she was thinking, secretly. What she'd been telling her soppy sister on the phone every night. 'He'll come round when he sees the baby.' Right, of course, everything would be fine and dandy when the sodding baby came.

Baby make it better.

The sat-nav woman told him to go left and he ignored her, slammed his hands against the wheel in time with the music and bit the ulcer on the inside of his bottom lip.

Christ, he *hoped* so. He hoped it would all be fine more than anything, but he couldn't quite bring himself to tell Helen. He wanted so much to look down at that baby and love it without thinking, and *know* it was his. Then they could just get on with it. That was what people *did*, wasn't it, ordinary idiots like them, even when it seemed as if they had no chance at all?

Those looks, though; and that stupid pleading tone in her voice. It was killing off the hope a bit at a time.

The voice from the sat-nav told him to take the first exit off the upcoming roundabout. He bit down harder on the ulcer and took the third. Kennington was programmed in as the destination, same as always. It didn't matter that he knew the route backwards, because it wasn't where he was going anyway.

'Please turn around at the first possible opportunity.'

He enjoyed these trips, listening to the snotty cow's instructions and ignoring them. Sticking his fingers up. It got him where he *was* going in the right frame of mind.

'Please turn around.'

He reached across, took a packet of tissues from the glove compartment and spat out the blood from the ulcer.

He hadn't been doing what people expected of him for quite a while.

TWO

'Fore!'

'Fuck was that?'

'You're supposed to shout, man. I sliced the thing over onto the wrong hole.'

'So *shout*.' He raised his hands up to his mouth and bellowed. 'Fore mother-*fuckers*.' Nodding, pleased with himself. 'Got to do these things proper, T.'

Theo laughed at his friend, at the looks from the older couple on an adjacent green. They hoisted up their clubs and trudged off down the fairway. There was no point taking the shot again; he'd drop one near the green. They'd lost half a dozen balls between them already.

'Why you need all that, anyway?'

'What?'

Theo jabbed a finger into the bag slung over his friend's shoulder: soft leather with loads of zips and pockets; dark blue with PING embla-zoned on the side and along the shaft of each of the brand-new clubs inside. Big, furry covers for the woods. 'It's a *pitch and putt*, man. Nine holes.'

His friend was a foot shorter than he was, but solid. He shrugged. 'Got to look good, whatever.' Which he did, same as always. Diamonds in both ears and a tracksuit to match the bag, with light blue trim and co-ordinating trainers. The plain white cap he always wore; no logo, same as everything else. 'I don't need to wear no tick,' he'd say whenever he had the chance, 'to tell me I look *right*.'

Ezra Dennison, sometimes known as 'EZ', but most of the time just 'Easy'.

Theo sauntered along next to him in jeans and a light grey zip-up jacket. He glanced over to see that the older couple were walking in the same direction on a parallel fairway. He gave a small nod, watched the man turn away quickly, pretending to look for his ball.

'This is nice,' Easy said.

'Yeah.'

The shorter boy threw a few waves to an imaginary crowd, messing around. 'Easy and The O, coming up the eighteenth, like Tiger Woods and . . . some other geezer, don't matter.'

Theo couldn't think of another golfer either.

Theo Shirley, or 'The O', or just 'T'. One letter or another. 'Theodore' at his mother's house, or when his friends were taking the piss.

What's the score, Theo-dore?

'So many names you all got,' his father had said once, laughing, same as he always did before he got to his punchline. 'What's the damn point when you ain't even signing on?'

Then that look from his mother. The same one he always got when she was bursting to ask him why he didn't *need* to sign on.

Easy dug into his bag, took out a new ball and tossed it down at Theo's feet. 'Your shot I think, old boy.' He raised a hand. 'Hold the cameras please.'

Theo pulled out his club from the thin, ratty bag he'd been given at the hut and knocked the ball up a few feet short of the green.

Ten yards further on, in the rough, Easy found his ball. He stood over it, waggling his arse for an age, then smashed it twenty yards over the back of the green into the trees. 'The putting thing's boring as shit anyway,' he said.

They walked towards the green. It was bright, but the ground was still heavy underfoot. The laces on Theo's trainers were brown with muddy water, and the bottom few inches of his jeans were sopping from the long grass where he'd spent most of the previous half hour.

Almost a fortnight into July and it was like the summer had got held up somewhere. Theo couldn't wait for it to kick in. He hated the cold and the wet; felt it in his bones, making it hard to stir himself sometimes.

His father had been the same.

Sitting out ten floors up on the tiny balcony, in jackets and sweaters, the old man sneaking him sips of barley wine when his mum wasn't looking.

'We're not cut out for the cold weather, you see? For the breeze and the bitterness. Why you don't see no black men skiing.'

Theo would always laugh at shit like this.

'We're from an island.' Well into the wine by this time. 'Sun and sea, that's natural.'

'Not too many black swimmers, though,' Theo said.

'No . . .'

'Don't make sense then.'

Nodding, thoughtful. 'It's a question of natural buoyancy.'

His father didn't have too much more to say about that. Certainly didn't bring it up when Theo was winning all those races in the school swimming gala. Just stood on the side shouting louder than anybody else; making even more noise when the tight-arsed woman behind tried to shush him.

'Jus' 'cos her boy swim like he's drowning,' he said.

The old man was always talking some shit until Mum told him to stop being so foolish. Even at the end, lying on the sofa, when it was the drugs making him ramble.

Easy marched across the green, began crashing about in the trees while Theo chipped up and putted out. Looking back, Theo could see people waiting on the tee behind. He was starting to walk off the green when Easy emerged, strolled over and started talking, throwing the flag from hand to hand: 'What you doing later?'

'Not much. See Javine, whatever. You?'

Easy threw the flag. 'Some business in the afternoon.'

Theo nodded, glanced back towards the people waiting.

'Ain't no problem, just bits and pieces. You better come along.' Easy looked for a reaction. 'Call your girl.'

'Bits and pieces?'

'*Little* bits and pieces, I swear.' A grin spread slowly across his face. 'Seriously teeny-tiny, man, I swear to God.'

Theo remembered that smile from school. It was hard to remember sometimes that Easy wasn't a kid any more. He was darker-skinned than Theo, his olds from Nigeria, but it didn't matter. Both from the same ends, the same part of Lewisham, knocking about with all sorts most of the time. There were plenty of mixed-race boys in the crew; though most were Jamaicans, like him. A few Asians too, and even a couple of white boys drifting around. He got on fine with them, as long as they weren't trying too hard.

There was a whistle from the tee behind. Easy ignored it, but Theo walked off the green and, after a few seconds, Easy followed.

'So, you up for it later?'

'Yeah, long as we talking teeny-tiny,' Theo said.

'Definite. It'll be safe, T. Besides, stuff comes up, you *know* I always got everything under control.'

Theo saw that smile again, and watched his friend patting the side of the golf bag like it was a puppy. 'What the fuck you *got* in there?'

'Shut up.'

'You high, or what?'

'Here's the way I see it.' Easy laid down the bag. 'A pitching wedge for knocking the ball on the green, yeah? Putter for putting it in the hole. And other things . . . for other things.' The smile spread even wider. 'Know what I'm saying?'

Theo nodded.

It was hard to remember sometimes that Easy had *ever* been a kid.

Theo tensed when Easy drew back a zip and began digging around inside the bag. Tried to let the breath out slowly when his friend fished out half a dozen more balls and dropped them one at a time.

Easy yanked out a wooden club, pointed with it to a flag in the far corner of the course. 'Let's smack a few at that.'

'That's the wrong hole, man. That's not the next hole.'

'So?' Easy took his stance, biting his lip with concentration. 'I just want to whack some of these little fuckers.' He swung hard, missing the ball by an inch, sending a huge, soggy clod flying several feet.

'Yeah. Tiger Woods,' Theo said.

Easy swung again. This time the ball went marginally further than the clump of mud and grass.

They both turned at the shout; saw an elderly man waving at them from outside the small hut near the entrance.

'What's his problem?'

Theo listened, waved back. 'You got to replace your divots.'

'My what?'

Theo walked over and retrieved one of the clumps; came back to where it had been gouged out and stamped it down. 'That's the *eti-quette*, you get me?'

'Fuck sort of a word is that?'

'The way you do something. The proper way, yeah?'

Easy's face darkened. Never the best at being told.

'What they call it, OK?' Theo said.

Easy spat and hitched up his tracksuit bottoms. He reached for another club and marched across to where the rest of the balls lay scattered.

'Fuck you doing?'

Easy turned and swiped at the ball, sending it low and hard towards the old man. 'This is the way *I* do things.'

The old man shouted again, but more in alarm than anger, jumping to one side as the ball clattered against the side of the hut behind him. Easy took aim again, was wider of the mark this time, but seemed happy enough to keep on swinging. Another ball smashed into the hut as the greenkeeper disappeared quickly back inside.

'He's going to call somebody, man.'

'Fuck him.'

'Just saying.'

Easy was already trying to find more balls, swearing under his breath as he reached deep into the bag.

Theo stood and watched. Thinking that his friend was mental, but laughing like a drain all the same.

THREE

Jenny lived north of the river, in Maida Vale, and Helen drove across to meet her in a coffee shop opposite the station. It was not a cheap trip, with the congestion charge and a greedy parking meter on top of teas at nearly two pounds each, but Helen hadn't been able to stomach the tube since she was a couple of months in.

They sat at a table next to the window, watched people beetle past under umbrellas. Jenny waved at a couple of women as they came in; chatted briefly about the upcoming holidays. She had two boys at a school near by, and this was a place where she often met other mothers either side of the school runs.

It had only been a couple of hours since breakfast, but Helen put away the best part of two almond croissants before she'd finished her first cup of tea. Jenny pointed at her sister's belly. 'You *sure* there's only one in there?'

'I think there were two, but he's eaten the other one.'

Always 'he', even though Helen did not know the sex of her baby. They'd been asked if they would like to be told at the twelve-week scan, but Helen had said she wanted to be surprised. She'd realised immediately it was a stupid thing to say; had turned to look at Paul, staring stony-faced at the monitor, and squeezed his hand.

There was only one thing he wanted to know, and no scan was going to tell him.

'It suits you,' Jenny said. 'I thought you were getting a bit thin before. Honestly.'

'Right.'

Jenny usually had something positive to say, but lately it wasn't making Helen feel a hell of a lot better. There was a thin line between looking on the bright side and talking bollocks. Jenny had said that hormonal mood swings made you more interesting and kept men on their toes. She'd told Helen how rare it was to be throwing up all the way through, like it was something that should make her feel special.

Recently, though, she hadn't been quite so positive when it came to Paul.

'How's it going?' The serious face, like doctors slapped on sometimes, and newsreaders.

Helen sipped at her tea. 'He's finding it hard.'

'Poor baby.'

'Jen . . .'

'It's pathetic.'

'How would *Tim* handle it?'

Jenny's husband. A building contractor with a passion for fishing and car maintenance. Nice enough, if you liked that sort of thing.

'What's that got to do with anything?'

'I'm just saying.' Helen felt a little ashamed at her thinking. Tim *was* nice; and even if Helen herself didn't like that sort of thing, Jenny certainly did, which should have been good enough. 'I don't think you can possibly understand how Paul's feeling,' she said. 'That's all. *I* sure as hell don't, so . . .'

Jenny raised her eyebrows. She asked a waitress for more drinks, then turned back to Helen with a smile that said: Fine. Whatever you want. But *you* know, and *I* know . . .'

Helen thought: You're younger than me. Please stop trying to be Mum.

They moved briefly on to other stuff – Jenny's kids, some work she was having done on the house – but it seemed impossible to talk to anyone for more than a few minutes without coming back to babies. Breast pads and pelvic floors. It was like being a womb on legs.

'I meant to say . . . I spoke to a friend who says she knows some good mother-and-baby groups in your area.'

'OK, thanks.'

'It's good to get out and meet other mums.'

'*Younger* mums.'

'Don't be daft.'

Helen had thought about this a lot, and it made her uneasy. All the other pregnant women she'd met at antenatal classes and check-ups had seemed so much younger. 'There's women my age who are grandmothers by now, for God's sake.'

Jenny sniffed. 'Women with no lives, you mean. Two generations of pram-faced basket cases.'

'I'm thirty-five,' Helen said, knowing how ridiculous she sounded, saying it as though it were a terminal disease.

'So? I wish I'd had my two a bit later. A *lot* later.'

'No, you don't.'

Jenny beamed. Even though there'd been no career to put on hold, Helen's sister had embraced motherhood with frightening ease. The piss-easy pregnancies, the figure she'd got back without even trying, the stresses that were just problems to be solved. A fantastic role model, albeit a depressing one.

'You'll be *fine*,' Jenny said.

'Yeah.'

If there are two of you. The unspoken thought that filled the pause brought them back to Paul . . .

'You know you're welcome to come and stay for a while afterwards?'

. . . To his absence.

'I know, thanks.'

'Be lovely to have a baby round the place.' Jenny grinned, leaned across the table. 'Don't know what Tim'll say when I start getting broody, mind you. I say that, but you should have seen him last year with his brother's baby. Wouldn't put the thing down.'

Helen said nothing. She'd called Paul on her way over. Got the answering machine at his office and the voicemail on his mobile.

'I don't want to bang on about this, but have you thought any more about the birth-partner thing?'

'Not really.'

'I'd love to do it, you know that.'

'Jen, it's all sorted.'

'Can't hurt to have a back-up plan, though, can it?'

Helen was grateful when a friend of Jenny's loomed suddenly at their table; drifted off as the two younger women talked about a campaign to ban four-by-fours from the roads around the school. She rubbed at her chest as she felt the heartburn starting to flare up. It was something else she'd grown used to over the last eight months. She thought about how she was going to fill the rest of the day. She could kill some time in Sainsbury's; try to sleep for a couple of hours when she got home. As it went, she'd have been happy to stay where she was until it started to get dark.

When she realised that the woman was talking to her, Helen smiled and tried to look as if she'd been listening all the time.

'. . . Bet you're gagging to squeeze that out, aren't you?' Nodding towards Helen's belly. 'At least the summer's not been too hot, has it? Bloody nightmare when you're that far gone.'

'Reckon there might be a heatwave in the next few weeks,' Jenny said.

'Sod's Law,' Helen said.

Yes, of course, she was desperate to give birth; was sick to death of carrying a space-hopper around; sick of the interest and the advice.

Christ, talk about the weight of expectation . . .

She wanted a baby that would draw a line under things. Wanted its newness.

Right now, though, more than anything, she wanted the company.

Paul left the car in an NCP in Soho, then waited for five or ten minutes in the rain for the taxi to arrive. The black cab's light was off when it swung around the corner and stopped for him. It was already carrying a passenger.

The occupant looked serious as he held the door open and Paul stepped in, but it became obvious that, so far, it was only the weather that was pissing off Kevin Shepherd.

'Fucking shocking, isn't it?'

Paul dropped onto one of the fold-down seats. He ran his hand through his short hair, shook away the water.

'I thought global warming was supposed to sort this shit out,' Shepherd said.

Paul smiled, was jolted forward as the cab lurched away and turned left onto Wardour Street.

'I've got a little place in France,' Shepherd said. 'Languedoc. You been?'

'Not lately,' Paul said.

'Days like this, I remember why I bought it.'

'Decent investment, I would have thought.'

'Aside from that.' Shepherd looked out of the window, shook his head sadly. 'Only reason I don't go more often is the food, tell you the truth. Terrible stuff, most of it. I'm not just saying that because I don't like the French. I mean, I *don't*, obviously.' He laughed. 'But I swear it's overrated. Italian, Spanish, even the Germans, God help us. They all piss on the French when it comes to food these days.'

The accent was almost neutral, but there were still Barrow-boy burrs around the edges he hadn't quite filed off.

'There's a French place round the corner from me,' Paul said. 'Sauce all over everything.'

Shepherd pointed at him, delighted. 'Spot on. And white spuds. *Really* white, you know? Sitting there on your plate like an albino bull-dog's bollocks, with all the taste boiled out of them.'

Shepherd had collar-length, blond hair; looked a bit like that actor in the *Starsky and Hutch* movie, Paul reckoned. The smile wasn't quite so charming, though. He wore a light pink shirt with one of those oversized, trendy collars and a mauve tie. The suit had to be four figures' worth and the shoes cost more than everything Paul was wearing.

The taxi drove west, heading along Oxford Street. Shepherd hadn't said anything, but the driver seemed to know where he was going. It was one of the newer cabs, with a fancy speaker system in the back and a screen showing trailers for forthcoming movies, adverts for per-fume and mobile phones.

'Can I see your warrant card?' Shepherd asked. He watched as Paul dug into his pocket. 'Make absolutely sure who's getting the free ride.' He reached across and took the small leather wallet in which Paul also kept his Oyster card and stamps; examined the ID. 'Intelligence, you said on the phone.' Paul nodded. 'Heard all the jokes, I suppose?'

'All of them.'

The cabbie leaned on his horn, swore at a bus driver who'd swerved away from a stop as he was about to overtake.

'So, tell me just how intelligent you are,' Shepherd said.

Paul sat back, left it a few seconds. 'I know that in the middle of February this year, you were approached by a Romanian businessman named Radu Eliade.' He watched Shepherd blink, adjust his tie. 'He came to you with three hundred thousand pounds, which he'd acquired through a series of credit- and debit-card scams, and which needed a little "cleaning up". "Placed", "layered" and "integrated" into the system. I think those are the technical terms.' A smile from

31

Shepherd. *Definitely* not as charming as his film star lookalike. 'I know that you and several associates rented a yard and a warehouse in North Wales and spent the next few weeks at auctions buying industrial plant equipment for cash, which you sold on a week or so later. I know that Mr Eliade got his money back, nice and squeaky clean, and that you didn't even have to charge him commission, because you made a tidy profit selling your diggers and JCBs on to small businesses in Nigeria and Chad.' He paused again. 'How am I doing?'

Paul had watched Shepherd's expression change as he was talking. It had hardened immediately, as the man sat trying to decide if Eliade had been nicked and done the dirty on him, or if one of the associates Paul had mentioned had been the one to roll over. Then the change: the sweet wash of curiosity as Shepherd asked himself why, if one of the Met's intelligence officers really knew all these things, he was still walking around.

Why he hadn't yet had his oversized, trendy collar felt.

They drove on in silence for a while, the cab rumbling north along the Edgware Road towards Kilburn. The shop-fronts getting that bit scruffier, the Mercedes count dwindling.

'Looks like it's brightening up,' Shepherd said.

'That's good.'

'What about the long-term forecast, though?' Shepherd was trying to find Paul's eyes, to make sure he understood the implication. 'Maybe I should be thinking about spending a bit more time in Languedoc. What d'you reckon, Paul? You're the one in the know.'

'Depends,' Paul said.

The cab pulled over suddenly, stopping outside a parade of shops on Willesden Lane to let two men in.

'That's Nigel,' Shepherd said, nodding towards the man who was taking the fold-down seat next to Paul. He was a big man; fifty or so, with greased-back grey hair and an expression that looked as if it had been kicked into position. Paul grunted a greeting. Nigel, who all but spilled over the edges of the seat, said nothing. Shepherd patted the seat next to his own. 'And this' – he beckoned over the second man, a rather less confident individual in a shit-brown overcoat – 'is Mr Anderson. He's a bit friendlier than Nigel.'

Anderson squinted across at Paul from behind thick lenses. 'Who's this?' A soft Irish accent. Not a whole lot friendlier.

Shepherd leaned forward, shouted to the driver: 'On you go, Ray.'

The chat started as the cab eased away. Shepherd and Anderson talked about a black-tie bash they'd both attended a few nights before; a blue comic who used to be on TV but was now well past his best.

'Just filth, you know?' Shepherd grimaced. Dirty jokes were clearly up there with French food. 'Lowest common denominator.'

He asked Paul if he had a family. Paul said it wasn't any of his business and Shepherd told him that was fair enough.

'Nothing but bloody trouble anyway,' Anderson said.

The cab moved expertly through heavy traffic as Kilburn gave way to the more affluent streets of Brondesbury. Then, further, the houses shrinking and getting closer together as they entered Cricklewood.

'How do you two know each other?' Anderson asked.

Before Paul could answer, the cab turned sharply off the main road, and, after a few minutes of zigzagging down side streets, rattled onto a rutted path and slowed. Paul craned his neck and saw that they were approaching a huge complex of old buildings, dark against a sky that was just showing the first faint traces of blue. He could see the graffiti and the lattice of cracks and holes in all the windows.

The disused waterworks at Dollis Hill.

The cab drew up outside gates fastened with a heavy chain and padlock. Ray killed the engine and took a newspaper from the passenger seat. Nigel moved every bit as casually and Paul watched Anderson's head drop when he saw the Stanley knife appear in the big man's hand.

The Irishman sounded tired as much as anything else. Said: 'Oh Jesus, Kevin. Do we have to?'

Nigel was already bending down to pull out a small piece of wood, a foot or so square, from beneath Shepherd's seat. Shepherd shifted to make room as Nigel grabbed Anderson and dragged him onto the floor of the cab, yanking his arm across and pressing his full weight down on to the back of the Irishman's hand, spreading the fingers on the board.

'Fuck's sake, Kevin, somebody's been winding you up,' Anderson said.

Nigel pressed Anderson's face down harder and looked up, all set.

'An inch should do it,' Shepherd said.

There wasn't a great deal of blood, and the noise was pretty well muffled by the carpet. Shepherd leaned down afterwards and passed a handkerchief to Anderson, who pressed it to his hand and slowly pulled his knees up to his chest.

'That's one finger you'll be keeping out of the till for a while,' Shepherd said. He drew back his feet to avoid making any contact with the man on the floor, and looked across at Paul. 'Like he's not doing well enough. Three new cars he's had in the last eighteen months. Silly bugger.'

'Most people want a bit more,' Paul said. 'Only natural.'

Shepherd thought about that for a few seconds, then looked at his watch. 'You don't mind making your own way back from here, do you? We need to crack on. Don't want this one bleeding all over Ray's upholstery.'

Paul guessed that he could walk to Willesden Junction in about twenty minutes. At least it wasn't raining. He waited.

'Look, I'll be honest with you Mr Hopwood,' Shepherd said. 'There's still plenty I'm in the dark about here. Plenty about *you*. But I am a touch clearer about one or two things. What you know, or *think* you know, for example.'

'It's understandable.'

'Here's the thing, though. I know a few coppers pretty well, and watching you while Nigel got busy was pretty bloody interesting. See, some coppers, whatever they were doing or *supposed* to be doing, wouldn't have been able to stand by and let that happen. They'd have been jumping about, shouting the odds and making arrests, what have you. See what I'm saying?'

'What if I had?'

Shepherd shrugged. 'Pain in the arse, but not a problem. I don't think Mr Anderson would be making a complaint. Nigel keeps himself to himself and Ray's going to say fuck all.' He leaned forward. 'That right, Ray?'

Ray said fuck all.

'A couple of hours wasted at some police station and a couple of days' paperwork for some idiot who could be out catching suicide bombers. That's about it.'

Paul couldn't argue.

'Then there's the copper who can't be seen to give a toss, because he's playing some smart-arse game. Trying to ingratiate himself, whatever. All the same, something like that's going to get a reaction, right? He doesn't just sit there like he's watching Jamie Oliver cutting up a fucking parsnip.' Twice, it seemed as though Shepherd were about to smile, and twice it died at the corners of his mouth. He looked like someone trying to see the joke but not quite making it.

At the nod from Shepherd, Nigel moved across and lurched out of the cab, holding the door open for Paul.

'We should talk again,' Shepherd said.

'If you like.'

'Definitely, because I don't quite get it yet. I *will*, but not yet.' He pushed at the knot of his tie, picked at something on his lapel. 'Because *you're* a different sort altogether, Paul. You sat there and you watched . . . *that*, and you didn't even flinch.'

FOUR

Javine was feeding the baby when Theo got in. Cradling him in the crook of her left arm, reaching around to keep the bottle where it should be, and flicking through the pages of a magazine with her free hand.

Theo stood in the doorway, held up the takeaway he'd picked up on his way back.

'Let me get him off first,' Javine said.

Theo carried the bag through to the kitchen, then came back and sat next to his girlfriend. Dug around the sofa cushion for the TV remote.

'OK day?'

He flicked through the channels. 'Weather was good anyway. Something.'

Something, when you're spending eight hours standing on one corner or another. Looking out. Running backwards and forwards.

'Yeah, it was nice.' Javine stroked her son's cheek with the back of her fingers. 'I took him over the park, met up with Gemma.'

Theo nodded, watched the baby guzzling for a minute. 'He's seriously hungry, man.'

'The powder's not expensive,' Javine said.

'I know.'

'You get it in bulk, same as nappies.'

'I didn't mean that.' Theo turned back to the TV. 'It's good, you know? A good sign.'

They watched most of *EastEnders* while the baby finished, and when Javine took him through to the bedroom Theo put the food in the microwave and took out the plates and forks. King prawn and mushroom for her; chilli beef for him. Egg fried rice and prawn crackers, cans of lager and Diet Coke. Some other soap on Sky Plus while they ate off their laps; that one up north with the farmers and shit. Theo couldn't keep up.

'Gemma was talking about going out one night next week,' Javine said. 'Some new club in Peckham. Says her brother can get us in.'

'Yeah, OK.'

'Sure?'

'I said.'

'I'll leave the bottles in the fridge.'

Theo pushed some rice around. 'Maybe I could ask Mum.'

Javine sniffed and said 'fine', meaning that it wasn't.

'Only if something comes up, you know?'

'Whatever.' Javine let her fork clatter onto the plate. 'But I don't think one night would hurt you, and I think it would be a good idea to save the babysitting up with your mum a bit more, until we really need it, yeah?' She stood and started to gather up the plates. 'Like if the two of us ever go out together, you know?'

'I get it, it's cool, OK?' He finished his beer. 'No need to get riled up, man.' It wasn't cool, not really, but what else was he going to say? Nearly six months since the baby had arrived and he knew that the park or the playgroup was as exciting as her life got. Gemma was the only friend she'd made since he'd brought her back here and he knew she'd left plenty else behind.

Javine carried the plates into the kitchen. 'You want tea?'

Theo and his family had moved from Lewisham to Kent five years before, when Theo was twelve. The old man had swapped his job on the Underground for one on the buses and they'd upped sticks to a place in Chatham with an extra bedroom for Theo's little sister, Angela, and air that was a bit less likely to aggravate her asthma. Everyone was happy. It was near the sea, which the old man had liked, there was bingo and a decent boozer over the road, and though there was a bit of trouble at school to start with, Theo and his sister had settled down quickly enough.

He'd met Javine at one of the big arcades. She and a mate had started giggling when he'd bent over a pool table. Later on they'd shared a joint or two outside and talked until chucking-out time.

Then, the previous summer, when Javine was three months pregnant, they'd had to make the journey back the other way. Theo's grandmother on his father's side had refused to move with the rest of the family, and when the stubborn old mare suffered a stroke, there was nobody else around to look after her. One day the air had tasted of salt; the next they were all back in the same shitty low-rise they'd been living in four years earlier.

Stupidest thing of all, the old woman was as fit as a fiddle now, had started to perk up as soon as she had her family around her again. It was Theo's old man who had got sick. Coughing up blood in their front room, and dying one afternoon in front of the horse racing, while Lewisham Hospital tried to find him a bed.

'Theo?' Javine was shouting now, from the kitchen.

'Yeah, tea sounds good,' Theo said.

Javine wasn't the only one who'd left friends behind when they'd come to south London. Theo still thought about Ransford and Kenny a lot, and Craig and Waheed from football. They'd stayed in touch for a while after he'd moved back, but things had just seemed to drift after the baby. Since he'd caught up with Easy and the others again.

Not that he'd caught up in every sense.

It was because he'd gone away; that's what Easy told him. That's why he'd lost his place; why Easy had a better slot with the crew even though Theo was older. Just bad luck, bad timing, whatever.

Theo's mobile chirped on the table.

Javine shouted through from the kitchen: 'That'll be Easy or your mum.'

'You reckon?'

'Who else?'

Theo hadn't seen Easy for a week or so; not since their afternoon at the pitch and putt. Not properly at any rate. He'd seen him go past a couple of times in that sick Audi A3 he'd taken to driving around. He'd had it for a year, sitting in a lock-up. Polished the fucker every week, changed the Magic Tree air freshener, all that. But he'd done the decent thing and waited until he was only one year below the legal driving age before actually getting behind the wheel.

Theo had his dad's old Mazda, but the piece of shit had been falling apart for years and there didn't seem much point in getting it fixed. The buses were pretty good as it was, and all the shops were within spitting distance.

Didn't really need a car anyway, not how things were going.

That Audi was one sweet whip, though.

Javine stuck her head round the kitchen door and blew a kiss. 'A pound says it's your boyfriend.'

Theo threw his empty beer can at her as he moved to pick up his phone. He looked at the screen. 'You can owe it me.'

When he'd finished talking to his mother, he grabbed his jacket and told Javine he wouldn't be more than a couple of hours. He told her to wait up and squeezed her backside as he kissed her goodbye.

'This is getting ridiculous,' she said.

'I can't hurt her feelings, man.'

'You should think about starting. You're getting a belly on you.'

Theo turned side on, looked at himself in the mirror by the front door. 'That's all muscle,' he said, rubbing it. 'And dick, obviously, all wrapped around.'

Javine grinned and said she'd do her best to stay awake, but that she was feeling wiped out. Theo watched her walk into the bedroom, heard her murmur something to the baby just before he closed the front door behind him. Then he walked down two flights of stairs to the first floor, and three doors along to his mother's flat, to eat his second dinner of the evening.

They sat in a small, crowded pub behind the Oval cricket ground. The conversation competed with quiz and fruit machines, a jukebox that specialised in eighties stadium rock, and a braying bunch of city types on the adjacent table.

'There's a decent Indian round the corner,' Paul said.

'As long as I can have a korma or something.' Helen grinned at the short, blonde woman opposite her. 'Anything too spicy, this baby could come a few weeks early.'

Her friend laughed. 'You know, if your waters break in Marks & Spencers, they give you a hamper.'

'That's bollocks,' Paul said.

'If they break in a curry house, maybe you get a year's supply of poppadoms, or whatever.'

The man next to her grimaced. 'Not too keen on Indian.'

'I'm not fussed,' Helen said.

'Somebody else decide,' Paul said. 'I'll get some more drinks in.' It was only supposed to have been a quick one before they ate dinner, but Paul had already put away three pints in twenty minutes. His voice was louder than it needed to be.

'If we don't go now, we might not get a table,' Helen said.

Paul ignored her and downed what was left of his pint.

Helen looked across at her friend, who shrugged back at her. Helen and Katie had been at school together, and the four of them – Helen, Paul, Katie and her boyfriend Graham – usually got together for a meal out every few months. Paul liked Katie well enough, or said he did, but the boyfriend usually ended up irritating all three of them.

'Says in the paper they might have a serial killer up in Glasgow,' Graham said.

Paul groaned into his glass.

'Oh, don't start,' Katie said.

Helen sniggered, reached for her glass of water. This was usually how it kicked off.

'Nasty one, by all accounts.'

'Aren't too many nice ones,' Paul said.

Graham shuffled forward on his chair, leaned in close to Paul. 'I know you've never had, you know, *dealings* with one, but you've met *ordinary* killers, right? What about that one last week in Essex, got off his tits and cut up his mother? Did you have anything to do with that one?' He waited. 'You must have *heard* something, surely. Seen the reports or whatever.'

Paul stared at him for a few seconds. 'Why do you get off on this stuff?'

'I don't . . .'

'Have you got a hard-on under the table?'

Graham swallowed. It looked for a second or two as if the evening was about to end prematurely, but then Katie piped up: 'Well, if he has, for God's sake give him a few more juicy details, will you? We need all the help we can get and it's a damned sight cheaper than Viagra.'

Graham leaned into her, reddening. 'It's interesting, that's all.'

Paul got up, grabbed his own empty glass and Katie's, waited for Graham to oblige. 'Same again, is it?'

Nobody argued, and as Paul inched out from behind the table, Helen gave him a look that said 'go easy'.

Got back a big, fat 'fuck off' smile.

Paul placed his order at the bar, then slid into the gents'. There was a man at the urinals and Paul loitered by the sink until he had left. Then he took out his phone and punched in a number; pressed the handset between his shoulder and his ear and moved across to piss.

The man answered the phone with a grunt, as though he'd been woken up.

'It's me.'

'What do you want, Paul?'

'Can I come and see you tomorrow?'

A pause. The distant clatter of machinery.

'Why not?'

'Two-ish OK?'

'I've got a bit of restoration work on at the minute. You got a pen?'

'I'll remember it,' Paul said.

'Where are you? Sounds like you're in a bloody toilet.'

'Just tell me.'

Paul listened to the address. 'You thought about what I said?'

'I've *thought* about it, yeah.'

'I need this.'

'Tomorrow . . .'

Paul sighed. Zipped himself up.

'Bring us a bit of lunch, will you? Something nice.'

Paul turned just as the door opened and Graham walked in. Paul saw him clock the phone and held it up before he put it back in his pocket. 'Checking out local restaurants on the WAP,' he said.

Graham just nodded and walked quickly into a cubicle.

Paul stared at himself in the mirror as he smacked the soap dispenser and moved his hands under the tap. He splashed cold water on his face before he walked back out into the pub.

Theo could manage only half a portion of spicy shepherd's pie made with sweet potatoes and a mouthful or two of green beans.

'What's wrong with it?' his mother asked.

'It's fine. I'm just not very hungry.'

Hannah Shirley moved around the table, collecting her own empty plate, and her daughter's. 'I'll leave yours there,' she said. 'You might fancy a little more in a minute.'

'Thanks, Mum.' Theo winked at his sister. 'It's really nice.'

'So, how's my gorgeous boy?'

'I'm pretty good.'

His mother shook her head and tutted. It was the same game they always played. 'You're *far* too big and ugly. I'm talking about my grandson.'

Theo sucked his teeth, shook his head like he was upset. 'Yeah, he's doing OK, too.'

'Just OK?'

'He's doing great.'

'Angela drew something for him at school today. Go and get what you drew.'

Theo's sister raised her eyebrows, didn't move until she was told a second time, then hauled herself into the bedroom.

'How's she doing?' Theo asked.

His mother sat down on the edge of an armchair, began to clean her glasses on her sleeve. 'Pretty good,' she said. 'Better, anyhow.'

Angela wasn't coping as well academically as she had been at the school in Kent; was maybe a year or two behind where she should have been as a ten-year-old. They were thankful that at least her asthma was no worse.

'She's got a real talent for art,' Theo's mum said.

On cue, Angela came back in and pushed a drawing across the table to Theo. A blue sky, a fish-filled sea, and a baby being thrown into the air.

'That me and Javine?' Theo asked.

'You can hang it over his cot,' Angela said.

Their mother put on her glasses and came over to look at the picture again. 'A *real* talent,' she said.

Theo's phone rang and he got to it a second before his sister.

'Yeah?'

'You need to keep tomorrow night free,' Easy said.

'Might be tricky, man. I got Halle Berry coming round.' Angela pulled a face and Theo grinned. 'She's been begging me for weeks, you know?'

'I'll pick you up about nine, yeah?'

'I don't know.'

'You can drive if you want. I *know* you been looking at my whip, man.'

'What's up? Where we driving?'

'Just a favour.'

Angela was still staring at Theo. 'Let me think, all right. Call you later.'

'I'm the one doing *you* the favour, T, you get me? It's a nice bit of business. Just a couple of hours.'

Theo stood up and moved to the far side of the room; lowered his voice a little. 'What business? How comes you always pull this mystery shit, man?' He glanced back to see his mother turning away, stepping into the kitchen, and he knew that it wasn't about respecting his privacy. She didn't want to know was all; *never* wanted to know.

'About nine,' Easy said.

'What a twat,' Paul said. He threw his jacket at the back of a kitchen chair and missed; opened the door to the fridge and stood staring into it, like he was unsure what he was looking at. 'Major, *major* . . . twat.'

Helen rushed straight through to the toilet, bursting, and talked through the open door as she relieved herself.

'You made me laugh tonight, Hopwood,' she said.

Paul closed the fridge and walked out of the kitchen. Looked, grinning, along the corridor at Helen on the toilet. 'What?'

'Taking the piss out of Graham.'

'Wasn't difficult.'

She stood up, wiped and flushed. 'When you said that talking to him was probably the closest you were ever going to get to a serial killer, and Katie laughed, I really thought I was going to wet myself.'

They'd settled on an Italian around the corner from the pub, and despite the awkwardness earlier on, the evening had gone pretty well. Helen had enjoyed herself as much as she had in a long while and she thought that Paul had as well. He was certainly drunk, but she thought it was a good sign. She couldn't remember the last time he'd let his hair down. He'd been singing in the car as she'd driven them back.

He leaned against the wall and started to giggle; said 'twat' again, which set Helen off.

She led him back to the fridge and poured out two large glasses of water. As she was screwing the top back on the bottle, she felt his arms move around her waist; his cock pressing into the back of her.

'Hello,' she said. She could feel him humming against her neck.

In bed, they tried to find a position that worked, but she was too heavy and he was too drunk and rough. He started to swear and slap his hand against the mattress.

She reached for him and told him to shush. 'Let me,' she said, stroking him harder as the moan rose up in his throat; faster, until he pushed her hand away suddenly and rushed, heaving, for the toilet.

Helen stumbled after him, wrapping a dressing gown around herself. She stood in the corridor and watched him on the toilet floor, knowing that he wouldn't want her too close. When he'd finally finished throwing up he looked round at her. He pulled his knees up to his chest and cupped a hand around his genitals. Stayed looking at her as he leaned over the bowl again, spitting and spitting.

FIVE

'Your destination is just ahead on the left-hand side.'

Paul pulled over behind a skip. Took the sat-nav from the windscreen and pushed it into the glove compartment. 'Snotty bitch.'

The pub was set back from a road that ran between Charlton Park and Woolwich Dockyard, in deepest, drabbest south-east London. The river bowed a few minutes to the north. You could probably see the Thames Barrier from the roof; and the Millennium Dome, like a wok with legs, a mile or two beyond. There was scaffolding along one side of the building. The windows had been whited out from the inside with opaque swirls, and there was a sign on the door that said, 'CLOSED FOR REFURBISHMENT'.

Paul tapped on the frosted glass with his car key. There was a school at the end of the street and he could hear the noise from the playground; the kids like squawking gulls.

'Can't you read?'

Paul pressed his face close to the glass. 'I've got an appointment.'

It was getting warmer. He took off his leather jacket and tossed it across his arm as the bolts were slid back.

Inside, there was dust in the air, dancing around the electrical cable dangling from the crossbeams. Paul could feel it on the backs of his hands, taste it when he spoke. 'How's it going, Clive?'

The huge black man who had opened the door nodded as he lifted the trap at the end of the bar. He could barely squeeze through the gap; had to turn and shuffle in sideways. 'Get you something, Mr Hopwood?'

'You got the pumps hooked up *already*?'

Clive laughed and shook his head. 'We've got a few cans under here. Soft drinks and all that for the workmen.'

Paul showed him the plastic bag. 'I've brought stuff.' He walked over to the bar and lifted the protective sheeting. It looked highly polished, but the wood wasn't solid. Half a dozen old-style radiators were stacked in line, waiting to be installed. MDF had been laid down, ready for a new floor, and several boxes of tiles were piled up against a wall alongside sacks of plaster and ceiling roses. 'I know he's had you doing all sorts over the years, Clive, but now he's got you lined up as bar staff, has he?'

'Just keeping an eye out,' Clive said. 'Same as always.'

A man walked in through an open doorway at the far end of the room, drying his hands with a ball of toilet paper. He was a little shorter than average, with dark eyes and darker hair that was thinning on top but still long and curly at the back. The face was fifty-something, but the clothes told a different story: a powder-blue V-neck over a patterned shirt, designer jeans and training shoes.

'What are we eating then, Paul?'

Paul hoisted up the bag. 'I stopped off at that fishmonger's you like in Greenwich.'

The man nodded, pleased, and asked Clive to toss a rag across. A couple of grubby-looking stools had been placed next to a trestle table covered in a thin sheet of polythene, and he used the rag to wipe the dust from it before he settled down. He watched as Paul produced a French loaf, fresh prawns wrapped in newspaper, large tubs of whelks and cockles. He sent Clive across the road to fetch pepper, vinegar and the rest of it, then laughed when he caught sight of the smoothies Paul had produced from the bag: '"Innocent"? You taking the piss?'

They ate with their fingers, flicking shells onto the plastic-covered tabletop and dipping prawns into a catering-sized jar of mayonnaise. Paul listened while his host brought him up to date.

'It's all about bringing boozers like this back to the way they were. Near as you can get, anyway. Brass rail along that bar, Victorian-style lights, all that. Nice Italian-type beer garden out the back.'

'An old-fashioned pub with an Italian garden?'

The man ignored him. 'These places had the guts ripped out of them years ago, got bought up by chains. You ask me, people are sick to death of all the noise and the awful food and everything being the same. Wankers' bars with Belgian beer and Paddy MacFuckerty's theme pubs, all that.' He licked the ends of his fingers, spread out his arms. '*This* is going to be as close as you can get to a proper old pub. A local. I told you on the phone it's a restoration job, didn't I? But it's not just about restoring the features and what have you. It's about an abiding faith in something. About restoring a bit of . . . what d'you call it . . .?'

'Community spirit?'

He pointed. 'Smack on. Plus, it's a decent earner, tell you the truth. Half a dozen of these places, turn each of them round in a month or two, flog them back to the brewery. Can't go wrong.'

'Still got the flats, though? I thought you had the contract to do up that block in Deptford.'

'Oh yeah, never busier.' He leaned back on his chair, looked around. 'Just had to take on a few more chippies, sparks, painters, whatever.'

'And . . . other business?'

The man rubbed his hands against the sides of his jeans, sucked at something in his teeth. 'Come on. Since when do we go there, Paul?'

'Only asking, mate.'

The man picked up his smoothie bottle and held it close to his face with the label facing Paul. He smiled. 'Until proven guilty, Paul. You know that.'

Paul swept the discarded shells and inedible pieces of prawn into the plastic bag; dropped in the empty bottles. 'You said you'd thought about it,' he said. 'What I was asking.'

'I did. I have.'

'So, what can you give me?'

Clive was back loitering behind the bar. He was asked to take the rubbish away and keep himself busy.

'You're not going to like it, Paul.'

'Why is this such a big deal? I'd've thought you'd be only too happy to give me some names. You've got no love for any of these bastards.'

'It's not about love. It's about honour.'

'You serious?'

'You're asking me to grass.' He held up a hand as Paul started to protest. 'End of the day, that's what it boils down to.'

'It's a favour,' Paul said.

'That's never been how it worked with us.' His face asked the question before his mouth did. 'Has it?'

Paul sat back, smoothing down the plastic sheeting with his palms, taking a breath. 'What about some smaller stuff, then? Just bits and pieces.'

'Same thing applies.'

'I've got to give the brass *something*, for Christ's sake. Let them think I'm still doing some work.'

'There are no gradations with this stuff.'

'Fine. I get it.'

'You can't be a *bit* of a grass; same as you can't be a bit pregnant. All you can be is a bit of a cunt.' He waited until Paul looked up at him. 'I'm sorry, but that's how it is.'

Paul nodded, but he'd stopped listening. He knew he wasn't going to get what he wanted. He suddenly found himself thinking about

Helen, about where she was going today.

The door from the street banged open suddenly and a kid walked in; sixteen or thereabouts and out of it. He looked around, confused.

'Can you get a drink in here or what?'

The man at the table turned towards the back room, but Clive was already on his way over to the door, shaking his head and waving his arms in front of him. 'Sorry, mate, the place isn't open yet.'

The kid started shouting about how the door was open, asking if he could just use the toilets, then threatening all sorts as he was pushed back out onto the street.

Clive threw the bolts top and bottom and turned back to his boss. 'My fault. I never locked it after Mr Hopwood came in.'

The apology's acceptance was lost in the explosion of glass as the brick came through the window and the scream of chair legs against the wooden floor. Clive moved quickly for a big man: he was halfway out of the door before the brick had crashed into the base of the bar.

Paul stood up and walked to the doorway to watch. He saw Clive get hold of the kid's jacket as the kid tried to dodge between parked cars.

The man at the table picked a piece of glass off the plastic in front of him. 'What can you do?'

Paul continued to watch as Clive pushed the kid up against a wall on the other side of the road, pressed his face into the grey brick and talked, close to his ear.

'I'm sorry, Paul.' The man stood up from the table and smoothed down his sweater. 'I can't be somebody else.' He took a few steps in Paul's direction. '*You* can. You can make other people think you're somebody else. You have that gift. It's not me, though.'

Across the road, Clive pushed the kid slowly down to his knees, maintaining the pressure on the back of the head so that the face scraped every inch of brick as it went.

Paul could see the red stain from forty feet away.

'Lunch on me next time, then.' The man joined Paul at the door-way. 'What about a bit of dim sum, up west? I know you like all that.'

Paul said that sounded good, and nodded towards the street. 'I think you've just lost a potential regular, Frank.'

When Paul left, the kid who had thrown the brick was sitting on the pavement spitting out sticky strings of blood and moaning. Feeling around inside his mouth. He watched Paul unlock the car and stood up; asked if he could have a lift to the hospital.

Paul tossed his jacket into the car. 'I saw what happened,' he said. 'He didn't touch your fucking legs.'

SIX

Helen had been in her pyjamas and dressing gown since she'd got back from the health centre. She'd padded from room to room tidying up, had made a desultory effort to reorganise the kitchen cupboards and then given up. Decided she'd be far happier trying to eat her own body weight in crisps and Dairy Milk, letting the hand that worked the TV remote get all the exercise.

She half-watched *Deal or No Deal*, losing interest when the big-money boxes were opened, and thinking about that afternoon's visit to the doctor.

Everything was ticking along very nicely, apparently . . .

The head was not engaged as yet, but that could happen any time from thirty-six weeks onwards, so there was nothing to worry about on that score. The baby's weight was almost exactly where it should be. Tick. Her blood pressure was fine, he said. Tick again, well done. She nodded as the doctor rattled off the figures and wondered about *his*: he looked a little red-faced and she couldn't help wondering if he had a bottle of something in a desk drawer. The baby's lungs were almost fully developed now, he said, taking a good-sized breath as if to demonstrate what it was that lungs did. And he could survive unaided if need be, the clever little sod. In fact, all he would be doing in Planet Womb from this point on was lying about and putting on weight.

Helen reached across and took a second slice of cheese on toast from the tray next to her. The least she could do was pitch in.

All ticking along *very* nicely then, until the doctor had asked how *she* was. Until he took off his little round glasses, turned away from his computer screen and asked her that.

'In *yourself*,' he'd said.

She could tell by the look on his face that he'd seen tears at this point in proceedings plenty of times before. That he was putting hers down to the hormone fairy overstaying her welcome. He proffered the box of tissues and asked if there was anyone she'd like to talk to. She shook her head and blew her nose, wondering how he'd react if she looked up and said, 'I don't suppose you could get my boyfriend in here, could you? There's plenty *we* should be talking about . . .'

Helen hopped through the channels without finding anything she fancied. Decided that when Paul got home she'd tell him that, if they were strapped, they could save thirty-odd quid a month by getting shot of the satellite TV.

She brushed away the crumbs from her pyjama top and realised that it was wet. She pulled the back of her sleeve across her face, unwilling to get up and fetch tissues. She had no idea when Paul would be getting home, or where he would be getting home from, and acknowledged that this was the way things were now, more often than not.

Only so much any doctor could tell.

Every box ticked, except one.

The journey north took them the best part of an hour, and Theo only got the Audi above forty for about one minute of it. He enjoyed the thump of the extra bass-bins Easy had put into the back, though, and the leather seats, and the green LEDs on the dash.

Just beyond Highgate Village they cruised past a large house set well back from the road on the other side of a pond. Turned and cruised back again before parking up two streets away.

Theo turned down the music. 'Place has got *pillars*, man.'

'Yeah, and a proper damn alarm,' Easy said. 'You not see that thing flashing?' He took a piece of paper from his pocket and studied it, shaking his head. 'We just going in and out, man, five minutes. Don't need safes and antiques and all that.' He jabbed at another of the addresses on his list. 'Let's try the one in Southgate.'

As Theo took the car back down towards the North Circular, Easy explained how it worked. He told him about his friend who worked as a baggage handler at Luton airport, and helped himself to the odd camera, MP3 player and the like. Who copied down home addresses from luggage tags which he passed on to Easy for a few quid and a wrap of something nice every now and again.

'Everybody's happy,' Easy said.

'Does Wave know about this?'

Easy drew his head back and stared. 'What does that matter?'

Wave. Top man in the street crew. Plenty *he* was answerable to, of course; plenty nobody ever saw. But round the estates and on a few square miles of Lewisham streets, Wave was the one asking the questions.

'Wave' because of the hair: the Afro that sort of fell from one side of his head to the other. And for other reasons of his own invention: *'Because sometimes a wave can be there for everyone to enjoy. To ride on or to splash about in as they choose, you check me? Other times that thing can get big and come down like a tsunami or some shit. That wave can fuck you up if you don't watch out.'*

'Said what the fuck does that matter?'

'Just asking.'

'This is *my* thing.'

'Not a problem,' Theo said.

'Wave got far too much else to worry about,' Easy said. 'Plenty poking up his arse, remember?'

Theo nodded. Yeah, he remembered.

He finally got a chance to put his foot down on an empty stretch through Finchley, catching a couple of green lights on the bounce. He remembered Easy taking him through it all one night, a few weeks after he'd got back from Chatham. Sitting in a KFC with a Coke and nuggets, and Easy sketching out his world on a napkin.

Three triangles, one on top of the other.

'This top one's like the upper distribution,' Easy said, stabbing at the highest triangle. 'Import, smuggling operations, all that. Serious money, and most of it going in white pockets, you ask me.' He drew a line down to the middle triangle. 'This is the warehousing and the factory, yeah? Breaking the gear up and cutting it. Them in white coats and what have you, chopping in the lactose and the caffeine powder and the rest of it.'

'And laxatives, right?'

'All that, yeah. Get off your face and shit your pants at the same time, whatever.' He moved slowly down to the bottom triangle and drew a line hard around the sides, the pen cutting through the napkin as he went over and over it. 'This is where *we* are, which is the crucial part, you get me, T? Down here at the bottom you got your lookouts, that's important. And then moving up a bit there's the runners and the sellers going back and forwards all day from the street to the house, one in one out, with the money and the packages . . . And then right up near the tip of this triangle there's the men who are holding the cash and whoever's in charge of the stash, you with me?'

Theo turned the napkin around and stared at it.

'And here's the beauty part,' Easy said. 'Everyone can move up.' Now he demonstrated with his hands, moving them through the air. '*Everyone*, you listening? Moving up the sides of the triangle and further up from one fucker to the next.' He took the napkin back and pointed. 'Right here, just below the tip of the bottom triangle, that's me, you get that? Number two and still climbing, OK?'

Theo nodded, seriously doubting it.

'Up there at the top, that's Wave. He's like a pig in shit, for real, but there's serious pressure up there too, man.' Easy finished his Coke and sat back in his chair; started tearing the napkin into tiny pieces. 'Plenty pressing down on you from up above, and *plenty* poking you in the arse . . .'

They pulled the same casual drive-past at a smallish semi in Southgate, and Easy told Theo to park at the end of the road. The house was between street lamps, with no sign of an alarm.

'Sweet and simple,' Easy said.

He went to the boot and dragged out an empty suitcase. Pissed himself when Theo asked what it was for. 'Well, it's handy for bringing stuff out, you get me? And I'm thinking, you know, *theirs* will be in Majorca or Lanzarote or whatever, same as they are.' He kissed his teeth and grinned. 'And you're supposed to be the clever one . . .'

Once they were in the house, Easy had the DVD player in the case within a minute or two. He told Theo to stay downstairs and grab whatever else he could, while he went through the rest of the place.

Theo knew the house was empty, but it still scared him to see Easy charging about so full of himself. He crept around the kitchen and the living room, poked through a pile of magazines on a low table. There was a small office built in under the stairs; a computer tucked under the desk, a keyboard and large monitor on top. Theo nudged at the mouse with a gloved finger and a picture appeared on the screen: a woman and three children, beaming from a swimming pool; a multi-coloured lilo and the sun bouncing off the water behind them.

A different holiday.

Easy came thumping down the stairs and Theo stepped away from the desk. He looked at the suitcase which Easy was now carrying with both arms. 'Decent pickings?'

'Another DVD in the kids' room, digital radio.' Easy slapped the suitcase. 'Brand-new iPod in a box, man.' He nodded to Theo. 'You?'

Theo pointed at the computer and shrugged. 'Nothing portable, man. I reckon we're done.'

Easy looked around, then nodded and leaned in close to Theo. 'I pissed on the bed up there.'

Theo stepped away, grimacing. 'That is so completely rank, man.'

Easy was enjoying himself. 'I never, man, fuck's sake, what do you think?' He hoisted up the suitcase. 'Gonna start calling you "Toy", T. Like one of them kid's things . . . robots or whatever. You are *so* easy to wind up.'

Helen woke at the noise of the key in the door and lay there listening to Paul coming in. The coughs and sniffs. The grunt as he dropped on to the sofa to take off his shoes.

She heard him going into the kitchen, heard the squeak of a cupboard door, and hoped that he was making himself something to eat. With luck, she might be asleep again by the time he came to bed.

He came into the bedroom a few minutes later and she stayed turned away from the door, knowing he was getting undressed as quietly as possible so as not to wake her. Laying his watch down nice and gently. She could smell garlic when he climbed in next to her and she knew that he'd been out to eat.

People from work, most likely.

It wasn't the first time that she'd asked herself if he might be having an affair, and she was still thinking about it when she heard his breathing shift, and knew he was asleep.

Not the first time, but as always there was one thought that nagged harder than the 'Who?' and the 'Where?' Harder even than the 'How could you?'

One thought.

What right have I got to complain?

He could feel the cash in his back pocket when he sat down. He reached around and took out the notes, dropped them on the coffee-table.

Two hundred in tens and twenties, Easy had given him. Passed them across when he'd dropped Theo off; before he'd pointed his fist towards Theo's and walked back around to the driver's side of the car.

'What's this for?'

'You helped out,' Easy said.

'I did nothing.'

It was way too much. Theo knew that Easy wouldn't be getting anything like that for what they'd just lifted from that house. He guessed that his friend was just showing off.

But still . . .

'This the kind of paper you could be getting,' Easy said. 'If you moved up.'

'And how's that happen?'

'I talk to Wave and make it happen.'

'Simple as that?'

'You just need to move up that triangle, T.' Easy made that gliding motion with his hand again. 'Spend a little more time indoors, get some of these kids running around for *you*. Come out on a few more trips like this with me, yeah? Fun *and* cash, what more d'you want, man?'

Theo thought briefly about waking Javine to show her the money, but he knew it was a stupid idea. She was like his mum: she didn't want to know. Right, Theo thought, but she liked the money well enough when she had it. She'd be trying to decide which shoes to buy while she was shaking her head and telling him she didn't want to know where the cash had come from.

But it had to come from somewhere, didn't it?

When the Audi had roared away, he'd seen a group of kids watching from the shadows near the garages; their looks eating up the car.

Now, he moved the cash to one side and put his feet up on the table. Sat there listening to the noises of the estate – to the rhythms and the raised voices that sang against the concrete – and tried not to think about a picture on a computer screen.

SEVEN

Paul had left home before seven, beating most of the traffic through Brixton and into Kennington, but he had clearly not been the only one hoping to get the office to himself for an hour or two. Quite a few early birds were wearing pinched, Monday-morning faces when he got in. Not that most of them didn't look every bit as pissed off on any other day of the week.

Happy coppers were the ones in sitcoms, or breathing in the funny-smelling smoke at music festivals.

The conversations over coffee and the first fag in the backyard all tended to meander back to the same topic: the fact that Paul hadn't been seen around the place a great deal of late.

'Whose arse you been licking, you jammy sod?' was the friendliest of the comments. 'Why should we sit here doing all the donkey work while you skive off and swan around, you lazy bastard?' was more typical.

Paul produced the same smug look as usual, and told them nothing. He knew they all had better things to worry about than what he was doing with his working day. He bonded and schmoozed where he needed to; drained the coffee and stamped on the fags so they could all get on with it.

By mid-morning he'd made a decent stab at clearing his desk, though there were still a good many 'shit waiting' folders bulging in drawers or sitting on his computer. He'd fired off a dozen emails, completed the paperwork on as many requests for mobile-phone records and typed up surveillance logs for which he was being pestered by three different units. It was hard enough keeping up with the paper-chase when you were doing what you were *supposed* to . . .

'Want to grab some lunch later?'

Paul looked up as DS Gary Kelly pushed aside a box file and leaned against the edge of his desk. 'I can only pray you're not talking about the canteen.'

'I was thinking about that Chinese place opposite Waterloo Station,' Kelly said. 'Cracking all-you-can-eat of a lunchtime.'

'Sounds good.'

'I mean, you know, only if you're still *here*, obviously.' Kelly was short and sandy-haired, with a smile that changed his whole face, squashing his features. When Paul had first met him, he wasn't sure if people called Kelly 'Spud' because of the Irish name or the potato face. 'I know you've been *hugely* busy.'

'Yeah, sorry, mate. Bits and pieces to sort out. You know how it is.'

Kelly leaned down, lowered his voice. 'No, I don't, to be honest.' He nodded towards the nest of workstations. 'I can understand you not wanting *this* lot knowing your business, but we go back a bit.'

Paul laughed. 'There's no big mystery, I swear.'

'So, let's have it then.'

'I'll fill you in at lunchtime, all right?'

Kelly nodded. Seemed happy enough with that.

'Not that there's anything too dramatic.'

It would give Paul a couple of hours to come up with something. A fuck-up on an old case that had come back to bite him in the arse; some mess he was trying to get himself out of on the sly; maybe a few personal odds and ends he needed to deal with.

Kelly was a good friend, meaning he was easy enough to bullshit.

'How's the missus?'

'She's fine,' Paul said, looking back to his computer screen. 'Huge, but fine.'

'You still excited? Or have you hit the "scared to death" stage?' Kelly had two kids and a wife who had just fallen pregnant again. 'Seriously, mate, it's hard work, but you'll love it, I promise you.'

A good friend, but there was plenty Paul hadn't told him.

'By the way, I need to get fifteen quid off you.'

'What for?'

Kelly stuck out a hand. 'They're organising a leaving do for Bob Barker, a week on Friday.'

Paul dug into his wallet for the notes. 'Where is it?'

'Still arguing about that.' Kelly took the cash. 'Be handier for us if it was round here, but some of those old buggers he worked with on the Flying Squad are pushing for somewhere north of the river. I'll let you know.'

Paul looked past him, saw Detective Inspector Martin Bescott heading his way; pointing, open-mouthed, in mock-surprise at seeing him.

'Oh yeah, he wants a word,' Kelly said.

The DI wouldn't be quite as easy to deal with as Kelly, but Paul knew he could handle it. He stood up and walked around his desk, smiling. Said, 'I don't suppose a note from my mum would be any good, would it?' Fifteen quid down already, and a tricky ten minutes with his boss on the cards; but still, not *too* much that was going to piss him off this morning.

Not with what Kevin Shepherd was offering.

Shepherd had called a few days before: full of it, like they were old friends or something; tossing out an invitation to dinner that night at some new Italian place with 'properly cooked spuds' and no 'fucked-up French sauces'. That was how it usually worked: a meal and a few decent bottles of wine; maybe a day out at the races or an evening in some club or casino; and *always* on them. '*No, no, you keep your hand in your pocket, mate . . . don't be daft, mate, my treat.*' Nothing changing hands, though; not at the beginning.

Just making the intentions clear from a safe distance.

The taxi had picked him up in the same place as before. Ray every bit as garrulous, giving it Marcel Marceau all the way to Shoreditch. Flashing a dangerous look when Paul stepped out of the cab and told him how much he'd enjoyed the chat.

Shepherd was waiting at a table in the corner. He was texting someone on his mobile phone and getting stuck into a generous glass of something. Very relaxed, or making a good job of looking like he was. 'You'll enjoy this, Paul.' He passed the menu across, poured a second glass of wine. 'I could tell when we met that you'd have a taste for places like this. Mind you, we enjoy egg and chips in a greasy spoon when someone else is stumping up, don't we? Human nature.'

Paul enjoyed every mouthful of a wild mushroom risotto, and linguine with clams in a spicy sauce. Shepherd complained that his pasta was overdone, smiling sadly at the waiter, then winking at Paul as his plate was rushed back to the kitchen. He was suitably gracious when a replacement arrived, and when coffee and tiramisu were provided on the house. Paul tried to look ever so slightly impressed while he was thinking that Shepherd was even more of a twat than he'd first taken him for.

They talked about Shepherd's place in Languedoc, and the converted warehouse in Docklands; the cars he drove, and those he kept locked away as investments. Shepherd tried to worm a few more personal details out of Paul, and Paul saw no harm in letting him.

He told him about his flat in Tulse Hill, about his girlfriend and the baby that was just a few weeks away. Shepherd looked genuinely pleased and raised a glass. Joking about how everything was going to change: the nights out on the piss, the sex life, and not least how much money Paul would have left in his bank account at the end of every month.

They both let that one hang in the air for a few seconds.

Obviously, not a great deal was said about money laundering or carousel fraud. No in-depth exchanges about Stanley knives and staff discipline. Just casual conversation, chummy and unbusinesslike – par for the course at this most delicate stage of a relationship. Until they were outside, at any rate; waiting at the kerb for the taxi to swing around.

'This stuff you know all about,' Shepherd said. He had lit up a large cigar and waved it around as he spoke. 'My theoretical business dealings with Romanians and what have you. This is *specialised* knowledge then, is it?'

Paul looked at him. 'That's right,' he said. He toyed with using the same kind of round-the-houses language that Shepherd seemed to enjoy and talking about 'intelligence that had been independently acquired'. In the end, though, he couldn't be arsed. 'It's just down to me, for the minute.'

Very important, that last bit.

Shepherd blew smoke from the side of his mouth. 'I work with a number of police officers and staff, and I suppose they're all specialists of one sort or another.'

'Sounds like you don't need any more,' Paul said.

Shepherd shook his head. 'You'd be stupid not to broaden your network of associates whenever the chance presents itself. Everyone brings something different to the table, don't they? Some kind of expertise.'

'Experts don't usually come cheap.'

'You get what you pay for, Paul.'

The cab pulled up and Shepherd opened the door for him. Paul said thank-you for a good night, then nodded towards Ray. 'You need to tell him to keep the chat down, though. That constant yap-yap-yap's starting to get on my tits.'

'You're a funny fucker as well, which is good.' Shepherd dropped his cigar into the gutter. The skin around his mouth was white. 'Not sure Ray's going to be pissing himself, though. See, some arsehole took his tongue out with a pair of secateurs a couple of years back.'

Paul looked at Ray, who had turned round in his seat. 'Jesus . . .'

'Mind you, laughing isn't *quite* as tricky as yap-yap-yapping.'

'Sorry.' Paul opened his mouth and closed it again. 'I didn't . . .'

Ray almost gave it away then, turning round before his face betrayed him; enjoying the joke as much as he clearly had on any number of previous occasions.

'I'm winding you up,' Shepherd said. 'Look at you.'

Paul clapped a hand to his chest and hacked out a laugh. 'Oh, thank Christ.'

'Your fucking face . . .'

Paul reckoned he was doing the relief thing pretty well. Every bit as well as he did shock and gullibility. He was good at letting the likes of Shepherd think that they had the upper hand, even before they handed over any money. Five minutes later, in the back of the cab on the way into the West End, Paul decided that the whole evening had gone well. And he knew that Kevin Shepherd would be thinking exactly the same thing.

EIGHT

There appeared to be at least one crossword and a couple of sudokus on the go. Several puzzle magazines lay open on the small table next to the sofa, alongside a dictionary, a *Daily Express* and two paperback thrillers with bookmarks inside. Helen was pleased to see that her father was keeping busy, though part of her suspected he laid it all out on display when he knew she was coming round.

He came through from the kitchen with two mugs of tea on a tray, and a plate of muffins he'd made that morning.

'Date and pecan,' he said. 'I've got some cranberry ones in the freezer if you'd prefer.'

She started eating. 'This is gorgeous, Dad.'

'They're dead easy,' he said.

Whether he was putting on a show or not, Helen was pleased that he was looking after himself so nicely. She polished off her muffin and reached for another. Better than I am, she thought.

Her father had moved down to Sydenham five years earlier with his second wife, as many years again after Helen's mother had died. Robert Weeks had been understandably devastated when breast cancer had taken his childhood sweetheart at forty-nine; and, among a slew of mixed feelings, both Helen and her sister had been amazed when he had appeared to find happiness a second time. The marriage had lasted eighteen months.

Nobody quite knew why wife number two had packed her bags so quickly, and their father had never been keen to let on. Helen and Jenny had agreed that he probably wasn't the easiest man to live with and left it at that, but they were once again surprised at his resilience; at the speed with which he'd steadied himself. He'd taken early retirement at sixty-two and dug into the small pot of money he'd put away. He'd joined clubs, taken up hobbies with boyish enthusiasm, and now, to complete the rejuvenation, it looked as though there might be another woman on the scene. Helen and Jenny were still giggling like schoolgirls, months after the old man had revealed the existence of the 'nice lady over the road who sometimes lets me park in her slot'.

The small road was neat and well kept; an army of terracotta pots in its front gardens and its parking spaces guarded as fiercely as children. There were Neighbourhood Watch stickers in most of the windows and a residents' association of which Helen's father was an active member. Jenny said that was how he had met this new woman. Probably wooed her with a muffin.

'You can take a few of these with you,' her father said. 'Straight out of the freezer, thirty seconds in the microwave. Give one to Paul for his breakfast.'

Helen grunted. It sounded a nice enough idea.

'Jenny took some last time she was over. She puts one in the kids' lunchbox.'

Of course she does, Helen thought.

'She was here last week, matter of fact. Did she say?'

'Having a good go, was she?'

'Sorry, love?'

'Slagging Paul off?'

'Why would she do that?'

'Doesn't matter.'

He looked confused, stared into his tea. 'She knows how much I like the lad,' he said. 'I mean, *maybe* she's same as me, thinks Paul should have married you by now, but I know that's just me being an old fart who should mind his own business.' He shook his head. 'No, I don't see any reason why she would do that, love.'

'She wouldn't,' Helen said. 'Sorry. I was just . . .'

Of course she wouldn't. The tawdry private life of big sister and unstable other half was territory that had been firmly deemed off limits months before, and Jenny knew better than to overstep the mark. Helen had a temper that was quite bad enough, even before the hormones kicked in.

'She worries,' her father said. 'But I can't see too much wrong with that.'

Nor could Helen; not when she was being rational. She knew for the most part that Jenny was just doing what sisters always did – taking her side whatever the rights and wrongs might be. Sometimes, though, Jenny's true feelings seemed clear enough: in a judgemental sigh at the end of a telephone call, or a look as she nodded sympathetically and carried on cooking her kids' tea.

Helen was a stupid slag who'd had it on a plate and then screwed up her life at the worst possible moment. Which was fair enough, and precisely what Helen thought herself.

A bad temper, and a bad habit of pressing the self-destruct button.

'You all right, Hel?'

She took a deep breath; could feel the sweat between her shoulders and the flush spreading across her chest. 'Can we open a window? It's baking in here.'

'Most of these buggers are painted shut,' her father said. He stood up. 'I'll open a door.'

Her father's cat, a permanently moulting black and white tom, swaggered across from beneath the window. It showed Helen its arse and wandered away again.

'You and Paul had a ding-dong?' He put a hand on the back of her chair as he walked past; held it up when she turned to look up accusingly. 'I told you, Jenny didn't say anything.' He sat down and began to rearrange the books and magazines on the table next to him, even though they were already neatly lined up. 'You've not really mentioned him for a while, that's all, and I've hardly spoken to him.'

'He's up to his eyeballs.'

'That's not what I meant.' He sat back in his chair. 'If I call and he answers the phone, we normally have a bit of a natter. About the cricket or something on the TV. Now, he just passes the phone over to you, quick as he can. It's . . . awkward.'

'He *is* really busy,' Helen said. 'I barely get the time of day out of him myself.'

It had been an attempt at jokiness, but something in her face must have given her away. Her father nodded, as though he understood. 'Wait until he sees the baby,' he said. 'Something happens to you when you see your own flesh and blood for the first time. Everything changes.'

Helen was already hauling herself up. 'Little bugger's pressing on my bladder,' she said. 'Why don't you make some more tea?'

'There's some of that nice liquid soap you like by the sink . . .'

In the bathroom, she pulled down the toilet seat and sat there for a few minutes. Waiting for the flutter in her guts to settle, fighting the urge to let go and crumble. Tears came far too easily of late, had become her default setting, and she was sick of it.

When she went back into the kitchen her dad gave her the frozen muffins in a plastic bag, and she said she hoped that the woman across the road knew what a bloody good thing she was on to. He blushed, but looked pleased all the same.

'I'm not sure she's that interested, tell you the truth.'

'Course she is,' Helen said. 'Or she wouldn't let you park in her slot.'

'I suppose not.'

'I'm telling you.' She sat and stirred her tea, and watched him. Thinking about what she'd said, and loving him just a little bit more because he didn't get her stupid joke.

Snooker wasn't Easy's game any more than golf was. He thought pool was OK, though, simpler and faster, and he played a few frames with SnapZ and Mikey at the end of the hall, killing time while he waited for Wave to finish his business.

Mikey and SnapZ were the two Easy hung with most after Theo, but he didn't think either of them was likely to win *Mastermind*. SnapZ was into his music, fancied himself as some sort of drummer. He was always slapping out beats on tabletops, wired-up and yapping when, to Easy's mind, he ought to be keeping quiet.

'How can I concentrate on my shot, man?' Easy stood up from the table and spread his arms. 'You always twitching and clicking your fucking fingers like a mental case.'

SnapZ sniffed and stepped back, jammed his thumbs into the pockets of low-slung Levi's.

Mikey laughed, said 'mental case' and laughed again, his voice high with a slight lisp. He was the tallest of them, and most of the time his height disguised the weight he was carrying, but in the hot weather even a baggy T-shirt couldn't hide what Easy described as a 'pretty fair set of titties'. Easy and SnapZ liked to sneak up on him and cop a handful, and though Mikey was usually laughing as he lashed out, Easy didn't think he found it that funny.

Easy bent down to take his shot, missed a long pot and said, 'You put me off.'

Mikey and SnapZ both laughed.

The Cue Up snooker club sat between a travel agent's and a plumber's merchants on the main road behind Lewisham bus station. Twenty-four full-sized tables on the first floor, with a small lounge area on the second alongside offices and storerooms. There was a bar at one end near the stairs, dividing half a dozen pool tables from a selection of fruit machines and video shoot-'em-ups. Food and drink were theoretically available, though service was erratic and rarely came with a smile.

The place could get busy in the evenings, but was quiet enough on a Wednesday lunchtime. Lights were on above four of the tables. Aside from those few playing snooker or pool, there were only the cleaner, the hatchet-faced woman behind the bar, and the old man who hung around all day poncing cigarettes and eating toast with brown sauce, pumping whatever money he'd saved on food into the fruit machines.

Easy lost a tenner to SnapZ when he fouled the black, but won it back off Mikey, who played every shot way too hard, as if the silly fucker was breaking. All the time, moving around the table, Easy kept one eye on the stairs, looking to see if Wave was coming down.

He was halfway through a frame with SnapZ when he heard Wave's voice, low and fast-talking, like a ragga bass-line. He handed his cue to Mikey and told him to finish the game.

Wave appeared at the bottom of the stairs, talking to a white man in a tasty grey suit. He nodded when the man leaned in close to whisper something, shook his hand before the man jogged away down the stairs towards the exit. From a triangle or two above, Easy thought, watching the man go. Maybe higher. It was like he'd told Theo that time: plenty of the money up there going into white men's pockets.

Easy watched as Wave strolled across to the bar. He was joined by Asif, a huge Asian guy who Easy and his mates on the crew called As If. He had been knocking around with Wave for the last couple of months; had been hanging back a few steps while Wave and the white man were talking and saying their goodbyes.

Wave bought bottles of Stella for himself and his shadow and moved towards an empty table at the far end of the hall.

Easy gave it a few minutes, bought two more bottles, and followed, weaving his way through the grid of tables, casual and full of himself, bobbing his head like there was a tune going through it.

While As If was lining up a shot, Easy put a bottle down next to the one Wave had already set on the table. 'Got you another one in,' he said.

Wave nodded and watched As If miss a red. He walked to the table and missed one of his own.

'Who's winning?' Easy asked.

'Been two minutes, man,' Wave said. 'Nobody potted nothing.'

While Wave was at the table, As If stepped close and eyed Easy up and down. Easy was wearing red and white today, same plain cap as always and there was no way he was going to let As If pass comment. He looked at him like he could smell something and spread his arms wide. 'What?' As If said nothing. 'Look at *you*, head to toe in cheap shit. High & Mighty started doing a discount range, then?' As If shrugged and moved to take another shot.

They played on for ten minutes. Easy said, 'Bad luck, man' a couple of times and 'Shot' when Wave sank a red that was sitting over the pocket. He sucked in a breath when a pink rattled in the jaws.

'What d'you want?' Wave asked eventually.

'You know my bredren, T?' Wave waited. 'Doing lookout, running and all that right now.'

'Skinny sort with fluff on his chin?'

Easy nodded. 'He's about ready to move up, for definite.'

'You reckon.' Wave put down his beer, went back to the game.

'I swear.' Easy's eye was caught by the wooden triangle hanging from the end of the table. 'He's sound, man, you know? No foolishness in him. He works hard and he's sharp too, sharp as anything.'

'I'll get back to you.'

'Safe.' Easy bounced on the balls of his feet. 'Just saying, you know, he'll step up fast if he has to, no danger.'

'I *said*.'

'I can vouch for him, man.'

Wave looked back over his shoulder. 'So, put it in writing.'

Easy swallowed, tried to laugh it up. 'Are you high?'

Wave turned back to the shot. 'Put this testimony of yours down for me, so I can study it properly when I have some time. You thinking of promoting somebody, you do things properly. You get the *references*, check me?'

'No problem,' Easy said.

'And I get to wave it in your face if your skinny friend fucks up. Make you eat it.'

'Not going to happen, man.'

From the other end of the hall there was a shout from Mikey, laughter from SnapZ. Wave told Easy to go across and get his friends to keep the noise down. Just before he did as he was told, he caught a look from As If, a raise of the eyebrows he didn't like one bit. He'd give the Paki fucker a slap when he got half a chance.

Heading back towards the pool tables, thinking, thinking, thinking.

He was solid with Theo, no doubt about that, but he wasn't doing this just for him; not really. He was looking out for himself, too. He wanted people to know that he could see the big picture, that he could be relied on when it came to reading the people in the crew. Who could be trusted and who wasn't worth pissing on. He needed Wave to see *his* potential as someone who could oversee things a bit more. To think about moving *him* up.

Now he'd opened his mouth, got himself 'testimony' or whatever to write. *And I get to wave it in your face if your skinny friend fucks up . . .*

Things could *definitely* have gone better.

He started bawling Mikey and SnapZ out when he was only halfway across the hall.

NINE

Babies never stopped wanting stuff, Theo reckoned, except when they were asleep, which was never when you needed them to be. They cried, you fed them. They cried, you changed their dirty arses. They cried just to piss you off sometimes, that's how it seemed . . .

Then the clever little buggers looked up at you, or you smelled the tops of their heads, and it didn't matter so much.

Javine had gone out around seven. He'd only had the baby for three hours but he felt as if he'd already run a marathon. He'd tried to keep on top of things, tidying as he went along, getting everything straight so that Javine wouldn't come back to a mess. So that there wouldn't be a row. He'd been determined not to screw it up, had followed the instructions Javine had scribbled down for him at every stage.

Make sure milk is OK on back of your hand.

Use cotton balls and warm water – the wipes aggravate his eczema.

Nappies on the right way round this time, dickhead!!!

He'd felt wiped out before eight and he didn't know when Javine was coming back. He'd wanted to ask while she was getting ready, but thought he'd better not push it. He'd managed to nod off for a few minutes in front of the TV, with the baby happy enough in his bouncy chair, but that hadn't lasted very long.

Feeding him had been fun, as it went. Theo had enjoyed the snuffling and the slurping, the little fingers that clutched at the neck of his T-shirt. The getting the wind up part had been funny as well, if only to begin with. He'd laughed out loud at the little belch, said, 'Yeah, get it out, man,' then done some serious telling off when he'd seen the trail of milky sick down his favourite shirt.

Use a muslin square for winding.

The doorbell rang five minutes after he'd got the baby off.

Put him on his front and rub his back.

He needs his dragon and his mobile switched on.

He might need to hold your finger for a few minutes.

Theo jumped up and ran to the door, trying to get there before the bell went again, but the crying started as he reached for the latch.

Easy. Grinning, with beers rattling in a plastic bag. Theo turned away, leaving the door open.

When he came back into the living room five minutes later, the baby grumbling against his shoulder, Easy was settled on the sofa with a can open, watching *Men & Motors*. He nodded towards the TV. 'There's some rubbish on with strippers after this.' He looked up and watched Theo standing there, rubbing the baby's back, shushing him. 'This is ridiculous, man, you doing this shit.'

Theo shrugged. 'Javine never gets to go out.'

'What about a babysitter?'

'It's five quid an hour,' Theo said.

'You should be able to go out if you want to, man.' Easy sat back, shaking his head. 'That's *basic*. Check your bredren, do a bit of business if you need to.'

'Can't afford it.'

'You need more dosh coming in to start with,' Easy said. 'You need to find something else, you get me?'

'Maybe I should take up babysitting.'

The baby seemed happy enough against his chest, so Theo lowered himself down next to Easy, reached across to take a beer. Easy leaned over to rub the baby's arm.

'What's his name?'

Theo looked at him. 'You *know* what his name is, man.'

'I can't remember everything.'

'His name's Benjamin,' Theo said. 'Benjamin Steadman Shirley.' Benjamin after Javine's father and Steadman after his own. Shirley even though he and Javine were not married.

Easy nodded. 'He's nice, man.'

'Yeah.' Easy had said it like he was looking at the features on a new mobile phone or the picture on a plasma screen.

They watched TV for a while and talked about all sorts, then Easy started to nudge their conversation towards business. He made Theo laugh, moaning about one of the runners. 'It's taking him five minutes to get the money where it needs to be. It should be taking two, maximum. It's like he's got a wooden leg, man, I swear.' Then he told Theo about the meeting with Wave earlier in the week. How well it had gone. 'He thinks it's a good idea, you know, what we talked about.'

'Which is what?'

'You sliding up a little. What d'you think?'

'What did he say exactly?'

'What I said. If *I* think it's a good idea, *he* thinks it's a good idea. I told him you could be trusted, you work your arse off, all that.'

'Cheers, man.' Theo stroked his son's head, watched the strippers do a job on *Men & Motors*. 'How much more you reckon I'll be bringing in a week?'

Easy crushed his empty beer can and reached for another. 'More, that's all that matters, yeah? All this is *detail*, man. We just got to make it happen first, you get me?' He dug into his pocket, pulled out a piece of paper and showed Theo what he'd written about him – the testimony that Wave had demanded. While Theo read it, Easy sat there squirming as if it were a love letter.

Theo was sensitive to his friend's embarrassment and blew him a kiss. 'You're a sweet boy.'

'Fuck you.'

Theo decided not to bring up the fact that it was barely legible, or mention the spelling mistakes in every sentence, guessing that Wave wouldn't care too much anyway. He passed back the piece of paper. 'No, honest. I appreciate it, for real.'

'You better not let me down, man,' Easy said.

'You know I won't. You said it in there.'

'You got to prove yourself, you get me? Pass the test, yeah?'

Theo laughed. 'What's this? Secret oaths and shit? Initiation or whatever?'

'Just proving you can step up, that's all.'

'You going to flush my head down the bog, like at school?'

'We'll sort it out, man. It'll be a piece of piss. You want this, though, T? You up for this, man, yeah?'

Theo could see the excitement in Easy's face, hear it in his voice, and he was smart enough to figure out why. Close as they were, Theo guessed that there would be a price to pay later on. Maybe Easy would ask a favour or two down the road or want a small cut of whatever extra would be coming Theo's way. That was fine. Theo knew how it worked, friends or no friends, and this was only happening because Easy had put a good word in.

A small price was fine.

He sat there, thinking about how it would be to drive around in something that the kids looked at from the shadows by the garages. To have enough dosh to keep Javine happy and to flash around when he needed to. Enough for himself, and a bit to lay aside for Benjamin, and maybe for Angela too.

Something to piss away and to put away.

And Easy sat there too, looking at Theo and his baby and thinking about where to get the car on the night. What kind of gun to use.

The flat was empty when Paul got back and he was halfway through dialling Helen's mobile when he remembered that she was eating round at her sister's. He stuck a pizza in the oven and watched the news while he ate. He slid open the door on to what was laughably called a balcony, sat with his feet against the railing, and lit a cigarette. It was a warm night, and he could smell the mint that Helen was growing in a pot; the jasmine that was stubbornly refusing to climb up a small wooden trellis.

With Frank having let him down, it was a major relief that things looked like working out with Shepherd. Now he could relax a little, afford to spend a bit more time doing what he was officially being paid for. Not that getting in with Shepherd was going to stop him sniffing around elsewhere. There were plenty of businessmen looking to take on consultants; keen to do business with the likes of him.

Coppers with an itch or two to scratch.

One thought lit the fuse of another, fizzing and corrosive, and his mood changed in the time it took to grind out the cigarette.

To. Stub. The. Cunt. Out.

An itch or two . . .

He'd seen the arsehole who had been giving it to Helen a couple of times. Watched him. He'd looked up his home address and driven round there, sitting outside until the man had come out and climbed into his poxy Ford Fuckmobile. Paul had stared long and hard at that car. He'd thought about driving at him then and there, flattening the twat against the side of it, then pitching his carcass into the back seat, which, all things considered, would have been a very classy touch.

There had been a few darker moments than that, when he'd really gone into things. When he'd coldly considered the ways he might do it; the more thought-out ways. He'd reckoned he could probably get away with it, too, if he was careful, and that even if he didn't, there might be the odd copper who would happily look the other way.

He'd done nothing, of course. Let it fade just a little, and fester. And tortured Helen whenever the chance presented itself.

She came back a little after eleven, and he was watching the door. A couple of glasses of wine had tempered the anger that had flared up, sitting out there with the plant pots, but he could still feel it ticking in him.

'How was Jenny?'

Helen hadn't taken off her coat. 'She's good. Sends her love.'

'Does she hell.'

Her head dropped and she walked straight through to the bedroom. When she came out, she said, 'I'm tired. I'm really not up for this, Paul.'

He watched her trudging into the kitchen, pushing fingers through her hair, and heard himself say, 'Sorry.' Heard her saying that it was fine; that they could have it out tomorrow if he still wanted to, and he knew that he really didn't.

She sat down next to him and asked how his day had been. He told her a joke Gary Kelly had been telling everyone and she laughed, and as they sat there watching TV, the silence between them was easier than it had been in a while.

He thought about the morning when she'd told him about the baby, and how it had been afterwards. The way each of them had taken the piss out of the stupid grin the other one was wearing. He turned to her, wanting to remind her, but saw that she'd drifted off, her head back and her mouth open. He put a hand on her belly, leaving it there until his own eyes closed and it slipped down on to the sofa-cushion.

He woke a couple of hours later with the taste of wine and stale fags in his mouth, and gently shook her awake.

TEN

Helen grabbed him on his way to the bathroom. 'Pinch and a punch, first of the month!'

Paul smiled, but only momentarily. He had overslept and should have left for work ten minutes before.

'I've made you some tea,' Helen said. 'And your cereal's on the table, so don't panic.'

She had already been up an hour; had showered, dressed and cleared away the remains of the previous evening's takeaway. They'd had a curry delivered and stayed up late putting the world to rights. Paul had moaned about the job, the hours and the aggravation, and had asked Helen whether she thought he should take the inspector's exams in three months' time. He'd seemed equally happy to talk about moving and nurseries, and after a few drinks he'd dug his guitar out from the back of the wardrobe. He'd played 'Wonderwall' and 'Champagne Supernova', and when someone in the flat upstairs had banged on the ceiling, he'd shouted, 'How do you like it?'

Helen guessed that, despite the moaning, he was having a better time at work than had been the case in recent weeks. Maybe the job had been affecting his mood more than she'd thought. More than *she* was, even.

When Paul came into the living room and sat down, Helen brought his tea. She leaned against the table and they watched a few minutes of breakfast TV: a preview of the new football season, less than a fortnight away; travel updates; a decent-sounding long-term weather forecast.

'I'm going over to Katie and Graham's tonight,' Helen said. 'They asked if you were coming.' Paul looked up. 'Calm down, I'm kidding. I told them you were at your leaving do. Bet that's a relief, isn't it?'

Paul grinned, his mouth full of cereal. Helen knew that he would rate another evening with Graham somewhere between a seminar on community policing strategy and sticking red-hot needles in his eyes, and she couldn't blame him. She had only accepted the invitation herself because she'd known Paul would be out and didn't fancy a night in on her own. She wondered if that was the reason why Katie had invited her over in the first place. She'd mentioned that Paul was going out before her friend had asked her.

She walked into the kitchen. 'I'll probably be dead to the world by the time you get back.' She was not planning to stay out particularly late, but Katie lived up in Seven Sisters and it would take a while to drive back from that far north.

'I'm staying over at Gary's,' Paul shouted through.

'Oh, OK. I'll see you in the morning, then.'

'Afternoon more likely. Gary's missus is away and I think he's got a bit of a lads' Saturday planned.'

'I don't think I want to know.'

'I'll call you.'

'It's fine. Have fun.'

'You too.'

'Try not to enjoy yourself too much, though, Hopwood . . .'

Helen didn't hear Paul walk out into the hall to get his jacket; hadn't realised that he'd been saying goodbye. When she came out of the kitchen, she was surprised that he wasn't there, and she jumped when the door slammed shut.

For the last couple of days, Theo had been exchanging lookout duties with Ollie, a nice enough white kid with dreads and a convincing line in patois. He was working a corner on Lewisham High Street, near the clock-tower, watching for trouble while Ollie ran ten quid back to the estate and waiting for him to return with the rock. The street market that ran up to St Saviour's Church was busy, which was normally good for business, and it occupied a few more of the boys in blue, which was never a bad thing. The police station itself, one of the largest in the city, was right opposite him, and, while Theo waited, he stared across at the illuminated hoarding on the bus stop a few feet away. Two cheery-looking coppers – a fat bloke and a good-looking woman – talking into a radio, and a big, bold message printed underneath: VISIBLY SAFER.

A hundred yards away, in the doorway of an electrical shop, a teenager was staring at the televisions, even keener for Ollie to return than Theo was.

It would only take a few minutes. 'Quicker than fucking Argos,' Easy liked to tell his customers.

Theo kept one eye on his punter, though he wouldn't be going anywhere. He danced from foot to foot same as always, wringing his hands; cheeks hollowed out from sucking on the pipe more often than he remembered to eat. Six months ago, Theo might have felt sorry for him, but not any more. Now he just needed a few more sad sorts like this one passing his phone number round; queuing up to buy and boosting his commission.

He was still waiting to see the deal get done when the Audi pulled up on a side street opposite.

Easy got out and called him over. 'We need to get together later,' he said.

Theo glanced back over his shoulder, watching out for Ollie. 'Yeah, whatever.'

'We're on, you *get* me? Wave wants to do this tonight.'

'Shit, I thought it would be a while. You know?'

'It's tonight, man, so gee yourself up, yeah? T . . .?'

'I'm ready, man,' Theo said. 'No danger.'

Easy grinned and smacked his hand against the roof of the car. Not wanting his friend to see anything in his eyes that should not be there, Theo looked over his shoulder again, as though he were just on the lookout, still going about his business.

Suddenly, Easy spotted something pinned to a tree on the pavement opposite and crossed over. Theo followed; watched his friend study the photocopied flyer and take out his phone.

Theo looked at what was written: a phone number and description; a picture of a missing dog, staring up at the camera, its eyes whitened by the flash. He'd had a dog himself as a kid, a ratty-looking mongrel far less cute than this one.

'You lost a dog, yeah?' Easy said, looking at Theo as he spoke into the phone. 'Well, I think I've got it.' He nodded, said, 'Shut up, yeah? You can have it back for five grand, or I'll kill the fucker.' He listened then made a face; stabbed at the off button. 'They found it already.'

'Does that ever work?' Theo asked.

'Once, but the miserable bitch knocked me down to five hundred.' He shook his head in disgust. 'This is supposed to be a nation of animal lovers, man.'

'We going to have to listen to speeches later?'

'Yeah, usual deal I reckon,' Kelly said. 'Bob'll call us all wankers and moan about the crappy watch or engraved hip flask or whatever the hell we're presenting him with.'

'It's something to look forward to,' Paul said. He pushed his fork through an almost edible cottage pie and thought about heading home from Kelly's place the next morning earlier than he'd told Helen; doing something with their free Saturday. It would be nice to make a day of it, get out of London, maybe. They had driven to Brighton on a few occasions, got the train down from Victoria once, and always had a good time.

He felt the phone vibrate in his jacket pocket.

Then again, you had to beat the traffic to get a full day in, and chances were he'd be in no fit state to make an early start.

He brought the phone out and down onto his lap, clocked the display, then walked away from the table to take the call.

'Just checking to see how things are going,' Shepherd said.

'Things are fine.'

'We've not spoken for a day or two, so I wanted to make sure.'

Paul pushed out through the glass doors into the lobby; studied the posters on the noticeboards as he listened. Shepherd sounded agitated. He seemed keen to know that their arrangement still stood, that Paul had kept certain things to himself. Paul told him that he had nothing to worry about, but that it was difficult to talk. Said that he'd call the next day and fix up a time for another meeting.

Shepherd laughed. 'I worry, that's all,' he said. 'You understand.'

Paul wandered back into the canteen, thinking that the day he understood the likes of Kevin Shepherd would be the day to chuck it in and make his own retirement speech. He caught Kelly's eye and signalled, then walked across to the counter to get them both coffee.

A proper car park, multi-storey or whatever, was out of the question, Easy decided. Too many cameras. Too many everywhere, he reckoned, with him and everyone else being CCTV'd up the arse twenty-four hours a day. It was one of the first things they taught the new blood: how to pass the merchandise so nothing was ever seen, even if the whole damn thing was caught on camera. It was just a question of keeping your hood up, or angling your body in the right way and finding the blind spot. Got to be second nature after a while, like they were just taking the piss.

They caught the overground across to Catford, found a side street behind the disused greyhound stadium with no CCTV that any of them could see. Easy and SnapZ took one side of the street and Mikey the other.

They didn't have to wait more than ten minutes.

The kid came bouncing along with a sports bag, like he'd been at the gym or something. As soon as he'd popped the central locking on his car and moved around to drop his bag in the boot, SnapZ was in front of him asking the time. Mikey was behind with the knife and Easy did the talking.

'We just want the car keys, so no need to be silly, you check me?'

Shock quickly gave way to resignation on the kid's face and he passed over the keys.

'That's nice,' Easy said.

The kid shook his head. 'It's a fucking *Cavalier*, man. What's the point?'

'Shut your mouth, or I'll stick you,' Mikey said.

Easy grinned. 'Wallet would be good as well, and that shiny mobile, seeing as we're here.'

Once he had been given what he'd asked for, Easy walked slowly round to the passenger side, leaving SnapZ to drive. They'd take the car round to one of Wave's lock-ups, stick some new plates on it and sit tight until later. Until it was time to collect Wave, then pick up the star of the show.

SnapZ turned the key.

'Sweet and simple,' Easy said.

Mikey took the kid's sports bag out of the boot and tossed it onto the pavement before climbing into the back. The kid picked it up and swung it against a wall, swearing.

He was still swearing as the Cavalier lurched away.

Helen stopped off on the Old Kent Road, picked up a bottle of the red wine she knew Katie liked. For those few minutes while she was waiting to pay, she resented spending the money, pissed off suddenly at the idea that Katie was inviting her out of pity. She had a good mind to tell her just how much *she* pitied *her*; what with her having a freak for a boyfriend, and the same pathetic desire to be popular she'd had when they'd been at school.

By the time she got back into her car she felt calm again, and more than a little guilty. She decided that, desperate as she was to give birth, she would miss being able to blame the violent mood swings on her pregnancy.

It started to rain as she drove up through Borough; got heavier as she crossed London Bridge.

She was hoping that once they'd got dinner out of the way, Graham might disappear into the attic or wherever it was he went to torture small animals, so that she and Katie could sit and gossip. It would be even nicer if she could drink. Two days earlier, she'd been told that the baby's head had engaged and it would have been great to raise a glass of something. Being off the booze was definitely something she *wouldn't* miss about being up the duff. In fact, as far as she was concerned, they could stick a glass in her hand the second the cord was cut.

She pushed north towards Dalston and Hackney, wondering if putting wine down as part of your birth plan would be frowned upon. If the midwife would sneak off to call Social Services.

If she would be sharing that first bottle with Paul.

Looking around the room, Paul decided that he hated just about everyone there. Of course, a pint or two earlier he'd loved them almost as much, and there was every chance he'd do so again if he put away a few more. The beer took hold of him hard: turning him from soppy bugger to surly bastard as quickly as his capacity to string a sentence together diminished; as often as he had to push his way through to the toilets.

The retiring officer had made his speech and, other than receiving a matching barometer and wall clock as opposed to a watch or hip flask, it had all gone much as Gary Kelly had predicted. Paul had cheered and heckled as enthusiastically as anyone else. Now, watching the crowd of shiny suits mill around the drab little room, laughing too loudly and drinking their way through the hundred pounds that had been put behind the bar, he knew one thing.

Pissed as he was, he knew that he wanted more.

There was no way he was settling for this when his time came. He wanted out well before anybody booked a room above a pub and started the whip-round for some piece of shit from H. Samuel. He wanted to be long gone, and well set up.

He caught Gary Kelly's attention across the bar and rolled his eyes. Kelly was a decent copper, but it wasn't hard to imagine him standing where Bob Barker was, twenty years down the road. Being good at the job was nowhere near enough, not even for the ambitious ones. You needed drive, and you needed bottle, and that bit of you that didn't really care an awful lot.

And you needed to lie, like it was breathing.

Theo sat in the window of Chicken Cottage on the High Street like he'd been told, a carton of wings in front of him and a paper he hadn't opened. He looked at his watch. It was past midnight, the time Easy had told him to be ready, and he started to think that it wasn't happening. That Wave had changed his mind or that some business had come up.

Maybe it had never been going to happen in the first place.

Maybe just showing up and being ready to do it *was* the test and there was no more to it than that. He wondered if Easy and the rest were watching him from somewhere right now, laughing their arses off at him sitting in the window like an idiot. Bricking it.

He picked up a chicken wing, but it was cold, so he dropped it back into the box. Outside, the umbrellas were starting to come down as the shower eased off. It had been raining on and off most of the evening, but it was still a warm night and he hadn't brought his jacket, even though Javine had stood in the doorway thrusting it at him.

She'd given him a look then, standing there, that said, *I hope whatever you're doing is worth it.* Or maybe the look had just said, *Love you, see you later,* and everything else was in his mind.

He had no idea.

He felt like his head was all over the place: nodding it in time to the music from the speaker above his head, salsa or some such; rolling it around on his neck, trying to keep calm and think about what the next few hours were going to be like; pressing it against the cool of the window, imagining himself taking out his phone and calling.

Telling Easy that he was OK where he was. That he'd work harder and longer. That he didn't need no leg up.

He opened his eyes when he heard the horn and stared out through the steamed-up window at the headlights. He didn't recognise the car, and it took him a moment or two before he could see that it was Easy, grinning at him like an idiot from the back seat, with Mikey and SnapZ either side of him. He saw Wave sitting behind the wheel, gently reaching across to pat the empty passenger seat next to him, then saying something to the boys behind.

Something that made them all laugh.

Theo nodded and stood up, took a swig from his bottle of water. He grabbed a handful of serviettes on his way out, already starting to sweat.

The cold air slapped him as he and Kelly staggered out onto the street. He took a few deep breaths, puffed out his cheeks, blinked slowly.

'Right,' Kelly said. 'We going to find a club or what?'

Paul squinted at his watch. 'You kidding?'

Kelly nodded across the road. Blacked-out windows and a neon sign that barely threw out enough light to illuminate the word: MASSAGE.

'We could always pop over there. Relax a bit.'

'I'm ready for bed,' Paul said.

They stood in silence for half a minute, watching what traffic there was move past. There was a decent breeze blowing and Kelly struggled to light a cigarette. He stepped into a doorway, lifted his jacket to provide the necessary shelter and lit up.

'We going to find a cab then?' Paul asked.

'You'll be lucky.' They watched a few more cars go by. 'Might get a dodgy one up on the main road. Al Jazeera minicabs, whatever . . .'

Paul felt as though he might throw up. He closed his eyes for a few seconds, waited for it to pass. 'Shit . . .'

'We'll have a good time back at mine,' Kelly said.

Paul puckered up. 'You on the turn, mate?'

'In your dreams.'

'You sure Sue won't mind?'

'Told you, she's away,' Kelly said. 'We can sleep in, go over to my local caff for a fry up, whatever.'

Paul thought it sounded good. Better than watching Helen tiptoe around him at any rate. 'I said I'd call home,' he said.

'Yeah, better had.' Kelly tossed away his cigarette butt and started singing 'Under My Thumb' as Paul fished in his jacket for his mobile.

Paul mouthed 'fuck off' as he dialled, and waited. He got Helen's voicemail and left a message.

Kelly moved off along the pavement, his arms outstretched, still singing. Paul put his phone away and followed. He joined in with what words of the song he could remember, the pair of them slurring like Jagger on a very bad day as they walked towards the traffic lights.

Sport – using the word in its broadest sense – had come to Helen's rescue, with Graham adding a love of televised darts to his catalogue of freakishness and leaving the two women alone for most of the evening.

They'd sat in the new dining-room extension and reminisced: about former teachers and almost-forgotten classmates; giggling and bitching like the thirteen-year-olds they'd once been. They usually ended up talking about schooldays, and Helen always relished the memories of a time when responsibility was negligible and worries were limited to maths tests and make-up.

Tonight, it had seemed a very long way away.

It was when Katie was talking about opening a second bottle of wine that Helen had glanced at her watch and been horrified to see how late it was. It had been almost quarter to two by the time she'd finally got out of there, and it would take at least an hour to get back from Seven Sisters, even at that time of night.

Still a fair bit of traffic around as clubs and bars emptied out. Friday night/Saturday morning, there was no such thing as an easy run.

She heard her phone ring as she drove past the Stamford Hill Estate. The handset was in her bag, and with nowhere handy to pull over she let her voicemail take the call. It could be nobody else but Paul at that hour. The tones sounded to signal that the caller had left a message. She could guess at its contents: *'Just called to say goodnight. Hope Graham wasn't too much of a wanker.'*

The swell of affection she felt was quickly sucked back by an undertow of guilt, and as she slowed for the lights she thought about something Katie had said in one of the evening's less raucous moments: 'You always knew what you wanted back then. You had it all mapped out. Kids, husband, career, the lot. It was like you never had any doubt, and the rest of us always knew you'd get it all, because at the end of the day you were always a jammy cow.'

Helen started at the blare of a horn from the car behind her and realised that the lights had changed. She held up a hand in apology and pulled away, remembering her friend's expression as she'd spoken and the song that had been playing in the background. How she'd nearly got into the wine herself right about then.

She turned on the radio dropping down onto Stoke Newington High Street, wondering what time Paul would get back from Kelly's place, and how hungover he'd be. She was looking forward to telling him all about Graham and his darts fetish.

He would find that funny.

It's a dry night, but the road is still greasy from the shower a few hours before; slick as it's sucked under the headlights, and there's not too much traffic rattling across the cracks in a main drag that's probably the worst maintained in the city.

It's morning, of course, strictly speaking; the early hours. But to those few souls on their way home, or struggling out to work in the dark, or already about business of one sort or another, it feels very much like night; the middle of the bastard.

The dead of it . . .

Wave had been in no hurry, taking the drive north from Lewisham nice and slow, even stopping once they'd crossed London Bridge to get himself a burger and something to drink. Parking up like it was a family picnic. Wiping the ketchup from around his mouth while Theo sat next to him, cracking on with Easy, Mikey and SnapZ, and trying to control the shake in his left leg.

Just before he'd started the car again, Wave had reached across to unsnap the glove compartment and told Theo to reach inside.

It was a .38 revolver, short-barrelled and not too heavy; stainless, with red gaffer tape wrapped around the handle. Theo had weighed it in his hand like it was no big thing. Not the first time he'd held a gun, but the first time it had really felt like one.

Easy had let out a whoop from the back. 'Sitting nicely, T.'

SnapZ had slapped out a drum roll on the back of Theo's seat.

Wave had eased the Cavalier out into the traffic. Said, 'Now we're cooking with gas.'

They drove up through the City, past Liverpool Street Station, and hit Kingsland Road about two-fifteen. Wave cruised around, hanging a left just before the canal and taking the Cavalier around the block a couple of times.

'We doing this or what?' Mikey asked, poking his head between the front seats.

'When I'm ready,' Wave said.

Mikey adjusted his cap and sat back again, squeezing his bulk between Easy and SnapZ. 'Sounds good, man,' he said.

Theo breathed deep and slow. He laid the gun down on the seat between his legs, eased his hands across the material of his jeans without making a thing of it, but when he picked up the gun again, the gaffer was still warm and slippery against his palm.

It had started to rain again. Wave flicked on the wipers. The rubber had gone on one of the blades and Theo craned forward, trying to see through the electric-red smear of water and taillights.

'So, we all excited, Star Boy?' Wave said.

Theo nodded, and was jolted back in his seat as Wave suddenly put his foot down, racing across a junction, then slowing; eyes fixed on the road ahead, scanning the oncoming traffic.

More whooping from the back, the rumble of feet stamping against the rubber floor mats. Easy leaned forward. 'What you say, T?'

Wave reached behind the wheel and turned off the headlights.

'I think *Theodore* just shit his pants,' SnapZ said.

Theo blinked, saw that look of Javine's. Another slow breath, taking in the clean, remembered smell of Benjamin Steadman, the top of his head . . .

Easy leaned close to Theo's ear. 'Sweet and simple,' he said.

Theo nodded.

Easy reached across and patted Theo's arm, then further to stroke the muzzle of the pistol. The smile was a little too wide; something chilly in the whisper.

'You know the *etiquette* . . .'

PART TWO

STICK MEN

ELEVEN

The detective inspector was probably a bit more talkative than he usually was, in an effort to avoid awkward silences, and most of what he said was addressed to the tabletop or, when he leaned back in his chair, to the flaking tiles on the ceiling. Not too much eye contact made, but he certainly wasn't being blamed for it.

'You've probably been in my position yourself,' he said.

'I've dealt with people a damn sight worse off than me, if that's what you mean.'

'So, you know what it's like.'

'You have my sympathy.'

'I didn't mean that,' the detective said, reddening. 'Just . . . you know that it's tricky talking about the case with a relative.'

'We weren't married.'

'All the same . . . there are good reasons why we don't normally do this. You understand that we probably wouldn't be here at all unless you were on the Job.'

The detective's office, which he clearly shared with someone else, was on the third floor of Becke House, the headquarters of the Area

West Murder Squad. He'd made it clear that, as senior investigating officer, the DCI would have been there himself were he not busy at the press office preparing a statement. A story had been run in local papers reporting a fatal crash, but now all the details – the victim's name, the second car, the gunshots – were going to be released, in the hope that it might shake something loose. That someone might come forward with information.

'You asking for help already?'

The DI's face was answer enough. Only two days since the incident and the investigation had slammed good and hard into a brick wall. 'No point me bullshitting you,' he said. 'Some of these people are happy to shoot you if you look at them the wrong way. Talking to us isn't exactly a priority with them.'

'Yeah, I know how these things work.'

It was a bright Monday afternoon and getting uncomfortably warm in the office. The sun was hot against the arms of plastic chairs and on the sides of faces; streaming through the windows, onto magnolia walls and across cork-boards, long since bleached to a dirty, veined cream.

The DI made momentary eye contact, then looked down at his desk. 'When's the baby due?'

'I'm thirty-seven weeks gone, give or take,' Helen said. 'So any time now, really.'

The DI looked up again, nodded, and let his eyes drift back down to the file on his desk. He mumbled, 'Sorry.' He'd already said it a good many times.

'Sorry for my loss?' Helen asked. 'Or sorry because my baby's going to be born without a father?'

Two days since the incident . . .

Two days since Paul Hopwood had been struck and killed by a motor vehicle while standing at a bus stop on Kingsland Road in Hackney.

Helen could see the embarrassment on the DI's face and

regretted her sharpness. He'd been right to suggest that she knew what these situations were like, and when she'd talked about dealing with those worse off than herself, she was not just being glib. As a DC on a Child Protection Unit, Helen Weeks had interviewed those who had lost children or whose children had been abused by people they loved and trusted. Even so, she knew how hard it was to be the one asking the questions. Spooning out the tired homilies. She looked at the man sitting opposite her and knew how badly he wanted to get out of that office. He was mid-forties, dark and solidly built, with hair that was greying a little more on one side than the other. Though it was understandably nervous, the smile was warm enough, but she had a strong feeling that it was far from being a permanent fixture. That he wasn't someone you would want to make an enemy of.

'Do you know what you're having yet?' he asked. 'Boy or girl?'

She shook her head.

'Any names?'

'No.'

She'd forgotten *his* name almost as soon as he'd introduced himself. Just one syllable, she remembered that much. It had been happening a lot in the last few days. Information wouldn't stick. Ordinary words sounded nonsensical, and she would drift away in the middle of conversations.

Her brain was far too busy painting pictures: blood and broken glass on a pavement; herself and a toddler holding hands at a gravestone.

'I thought it was supposed to be an urban myth,' she said. 'This headlights thing.'

'I think it *was* . . .' His mobile phone rang. He picked it up and studied the screen, mouthing another 'sorry' before dropping the call and sliding the phone into his jacket pocket. 'I think it started in America, came over here on the Internet or something.'

Helen had first heard of it a few years before: a warning for people driving through certain areas of the city at night not to flash their headlights at cars that were driving without theirs. A hideously random way for gangs to select 'victims'; to pick the car into which the gang initiate would be required to shoot. It was a myth, probably, but a horribly plausible one with the way those areas were going. Now, they had a scenario in which at least one gang had apparently decided it was as good a way as any of testing the new blood.

'They seem to change these initiation rites whenever they get tired of them,' the DI said, 'or they're getting too easy. A year or two ago it was squirting ammonia into people's faces. That one was popular with young girls because they could keep it in their handbags.'

'This a north London gang, then?' Helen asked.

'Not necessarily. The car was stolen in Catford—' He stopped as the tones sounded from inside his jacket. His caller had left a message. 'Doing the shooting this side of the river might have been a territorial thing. Letting someone else know they were around.'

'If it's a turf war, you must know which gangs are involved.'

'There's nothing going on that we know of. I'm just saying that we can't take anything for granted.'

'You know the people to talk to, though?'

'We're liaising with the Drugs Task Force, obviously. They're trying to point us in the right direction, but there's nearly two hundred gangs in London and like I said—'

'They're not very talkative,' Helen said. 'I know.' She thought for a few seconds. 'What about forensics?'

'The Cavalier was burned out when we found it, so I don't think we'll find much there. The BMW is still being examined.'

'Where?'

The DI didn't hear or chose to ignore the question. 'We've got the preliminary report back, but we're still waiting on ballistics.' He looked at her. 'We're obviously doing this on the hurry-up, Helen.'

She nodded. Of course they were. Always the same when there was a fellow officer involved. But his pause told her there wasn't a great deal they were expecting to find; certainly nothing that they didn't already know. There had been no shortage of eyewitnesses: to the BMW flashing its headlights; to the shots being fired from the Cavalier; to the BMW veering up onto the pavement and smashing into the bus stop. They had times, number plates, a few vague descriptions.

Other than who was responsible, it was as good as open and shut.

'What about the others at the bus stop?' Helen asked.

'Well. DS Kelly, who I think you know, got off with a few cuts and bruises. The second man was much the same. Flying glass . . .'

'And the woman in the car?'

Were her eyes closed at the end? When she hit him? Did she put her arms up to protect herself or did she see Paul's face when he flew across her bonnet, when he shattered the windscreen and it shattered him?

'She's doing OK too, I think. Broken collarbone. Her face is pretty smashed up.'

'Can I have an address?'

'Sorry?'

'I'd like to see her.'

He sat back in his chair, looked genuinely confused. 'Why?'

She didn't have an easy answer. The sun on her face and neck was becoming unbearable. She rubbed at her belly through the material of her dress. 'What am I supposed to do? I feel like I'm . . . fading in and out, you know, and I don't just want to sit around wondering whether I'll get a chance to bury Paul before the baby comes. I need to have . . . something to do. It doesn't really matter what.'

He cleared his throat. 'Have you got someone staying with you?'

'Place is too bloody small. My dad and my sister are in and out, but I'm happier with a bit of space to be honest.'

'What about Paul's parents?'

'They're in a hotel. They're . . . happier there, I think.'

'Have you decided about the funeral?'

The words tumbled out of her before she could check herself. 'Yes, and I think we should definitely have one. It's probably best, don't you reckon? He's going to start stinking the place up otherwise.' The DI reddened again, but it was Helen's turn to apologise.

'Don't worry.'

'Like the mood swings weren't bad enough *before* all this.'

'I just meant have you thought about whether you want an official police ceremony?'

'Not really. Not yet.' She *had* thought about it. Had decided that, much as she would prefer something quiet, she should leave it up to Paul's parents. She guessed that, when the time came, they would probably go for the speeches and the flags and the pallbearers in white gloves.

When the time came.

The inquest into Paul's death had been opened and – in line with standard procedure – immediately adjourned. It would reconvene once the police investigation was complete. How long was a piece of string?

'We'll talk to the coroner and try to get the body released . . . get *Paul* released, as quickly as we can,' he said. 'Might be another couple of weeks, though.' There was a knock and a face appeared around the door. 'What is it, Dave?'

The man's eyes darted to Helen and then quickly back to the DI. 'Your briefing started five minutes ago . . .'

The DI nodded and the man closed the door. 'Sorry, I need to crack on.' Helen started to get up but he raised a hand, stood up himself and walked around the desk. 'I'll be at least fifteen minutes,' he said. 'Probably longer.' He glanced back at the blue book sitting in the middle of his desk. 'Obviously all the statements, the reports and so on are on the system, but you're probably the same as me. Keep a lot of stuff in your notebook?' Helen said nothing. 'It's not really worth me taking it with me,' he said. 'It'll probably just stay right there on the desk, and I know I don't have to tell you that you really shouldn't be looking at it while I'm gone.' He walked to the door.

'I understand,' Helen said.

She sat for a minute or two after the DI had left, feeling a little breathless, then walked into the corridor, where she knew there was a water cooler. She helped herself to three paper cups' worth. Then she went back into the DI's office and opened his notebook.

His name was written at the top of the first page. Helen thought that it suited him. She guessed that he could be spiky and hard to shake off.

She turned the perforated pages until she came to the one headed HOPWOOD: 2 AUGUST. The name was elaborately underlined and there were doodles in the corners of the page – houses and stars. She took a pen from her handbag, helped herself to a sheet of A4 from the desk, and started writing things down.

TWELVE

Another hundred, hundred and fifty pounds a week.

The chance to sit on his arse all day in front of the television.

A key.

A gun.

These, it seemed to Theo, were the things that'd he'd got from 'moving up'. The rewards that had been waiting for him that bit further up Easy's triangle.

And there had been something else, something a little harder to pin down and a lot scarier. He knew that others in the crew would call it 'respect', even though the word got chucked around like an empty fag packet sometimes, and he liked the looks, the little nods. No point pretending he didn't. From the ones where *he* was now, and from those still waiting for a chance of their own. He wondered if any of them had a clue how much he'd been shitting himself on the night. Was *still* shitting himself. He guessed that many of them did; thought he'd seen something knowing, something *shared* in a few of those looks.

The scariest thing of all was having something to live up to.

'You watching this shit, man?'

Theo shook his head.

Mikey squeezed in next to him on the torn, vinyl settee and picked up the remote. Theo stared at the screen, watched the channel change every few seconds: a woman in an empty house; people on running machines; cars, cowboys, poker; some idiot fishing.

The sound down low because they had to listen out for the door.

Having run through all the channels twice, Mikey settled on an episode of *Diagnosis Murder*. He sat back. 'That's the geezer out of *Chitty Chitty Bang Bang*, man. Fucker looks *old* . . .'

The flat to which Theo had been given a key was at the end of a landing on the third floor of the low-rise; the turd-brown block opposite the one where Theo's own flat and his mum's were. This was where Theo had spent the last couple of days, with Mikey or SnapZ or maybe another one of the boys, on stash and cash duty.

Aside from the plasma screen and a PS3, there wasn't much in the place. Some mismatched furniture in the front room. The basics in the kitchen: cutlery and a kettle; microwave; a few plates and mugs in the cupboard where the rocks were kept, wrapped in cling film and sealed in Tupperware containers.

The single bedroom contained almost nothing but the bed itself, with a sleeping bag laid out on the bare mattress, a pile of old newspapers and a lamp plugged in at the wall in one corner. The metal cash box was hidden underneath a loose board. It was Theo's job to see that the notes were transferred into the box after every transaction, ready for As If to collect on Wave's behalf at the end of every day.

'Stash and cash,' Easy had said. 'Got *responsibility* now, T.'

What Theo had was plenty of time to sit around and get better at Grand Theft Auto. To talk rubbishness with Mikey or whoever. To call Javine when he felt like it.

Too much time to think.

'Same guy was in *Mary Poppins*,' Mikey said. 'Must be minted, man.

What's he need to do this shit for?'

Nobody was supposed to die.

Two shots into the *back of the car*. That was the deal; nobody hurt and away, job done. Jesus, what was the stupid cow doing, panicking and yanking the wheel like that, like she'd been hit or something? Veering up onto the damned pavement into those people and causing all that grief.

Fuck. Fuck. Fuck.

'No big deal,' Easy had said, but he wasn't the one with the gun in his hand, was he?

Theo didn't know any more about the man at the bus stop than what little had been in the paper. A thirty-second report on *London Tonight*; footage of the BMW being towed away. He didn't know his name, if he was married, had kids, anything. But he knew he should still be alive, and that the Old Bill would be taking things a lot more seriously than they would have done otherwise because he wasn't.

The crew took it more seriously, too; took *Theo* more seriously. Those nods and looks, as if he'd moved a lot further than he'd intended. Like he'd taken a big step up from street boy to major player in the crew.

He was aware of Mikey getting to his feet, reaching for the pistol on the table in front of the sofa, saying, 'You deaf or what?'

He hadn't heard the door.

He picked up his own pistol – not the one he'd used three nights before, which had already been spirited away by Wave – and moved across to the front door. The knock sounded again, clanging against the metal reinforcement. He looked at the monitor on the wall, at the picture from the camera mounted above the door outside.

Ollie peered up at the camera, then leaned in close to the intercom. 'Come on, fuck's sake.' He held up a pair of twenty-pound notes. 'Punter wants two, man. Needs them quick, you get me?'

Theo stared at the picture. Ollie's dreads looked almost silvery in the grainy black-and-white image. The gun felt hot and heavy at the end of his arm.

'Fucking let him in, man,' Mikey said.

Theo slid back the bolts and opened the door to let Ollie crash into the room.

Helen put on one of Paul's old Queen albums while she cleaned. Turned it up loud and sang along. She vacuumed everywhere, moving the lighter bits of furniture to get underneath and using vinegar on all the mirrors and windows. She emptied the fridge and washed it out; wiped down all the walls and kitchen cabinets. She would have got down on her hands and knees to do the floor but she knew it would be like lying across a space-hopper.

She was sweating by the time she'd finished, and she sat in front of the television until it got dark. She felt the baby shift and roll in her belly, and tried to cry.

It wasn't as though she didn't know this was often the way it went – that the tears could be the last thing to come. She'd seen how it could hit plenty of people, seen the way that even the news itself had a different effect on one person from another. She'd seen them scream, or laugh, or hurl abuse. A lot of the time there was just silence, a shutter coming down . . . in front of others at any rate. That's how it had been with her: sitting up in bed and scrabbling for the light when the phone had rung at four-thirty on a Saturday morning.

Listening, and feeling a switch snick quietly off inside.

She knew that the tears had to come at some point, but wondered if cleaning what was already clean and scrubbing at surfaces until your hands were raw might be a grieving of sorts. Wondered why she'd spent so much of the last few months crying like a child but couldn't squeeze out a single tear when she wanted to so badly.

Like she'd just wasted them all.

Jenny had brought a saucepan of soup across the day before – she was a fabulous cook, on top of everything else – and once Helen had eaten and washed up, she sat down with the plastic bag she'd brought back with her from Becke House.

Paul's personal effects: the suit and shirt returned from the Forensic Science Service lab; shoes, socks, underwear; briefcase and umbrella; wallet, car keys and mobile phone. She laid everything out neatly on the table, folding the shirt to hide the bloodstains at the neck, and tried to make some decisions.

She would have the suit dry-cleaned and take it to the charity shop. She needed to sort out *all* of Paul's clothes as soon as possible. To choose something for him to wear whenever the time came.

His blue suit with a white shirt. Maybe his dress uniform if that was what other people wanted.

She would take the car keys and head over to Kennington the following morning.

Drive Paul's car back.

Think about selling it, maybe.

The mobile phone had turned itself off. She fetched the charger that was plugged in by Paul's side of the bed and powered up the handset. The last call had been the one made to her while she was driving back from Katie's, an hour or so before the crash.

The message she'd listened to twenty or thirty times since then.

'*It's me. Just heading back to Gary's place . . . trying to find a cab or a night bus or whatever.*' There is singing in the background, then some shouting. '*Shut up. Sorry . . . that's Kelly being a twat. See you tomorrow afternoon, OK?*' More shouting, then laughter from both of them. '*Actually, better make that evening . . .*'

She knew with certainty which face he'd been pulling when he'd said that.

She blinked and saw his face again, pallid and blank, floating above the white sheet in the mortuary's viewing suite. They'd combed his hair. His mum had reached up and run fingers through it; said that he always hated it looking too neat.

She noticed the envelope icon in the corner of the screen, checked and saw that there was one unread text message. She called it up.

A message from 'Frank' received the day before: *What about next week for Chinese? F.*

Paul's mother and father had talked about putting an announcement in the paper, but nobody had quite been able to decide which one. They'd made a few phone calls, asked people to pass on the message, and between them and Helen, the news had probably reached most of Paul's close friends. She'd already considered going through his address book, to try to reach anyone Paul might have lost touch with, or with whom she had no contact herself. This seemed as good a time to start as any.

She dialled the number.

'Paul?' A quiet voice, a London accent.

'Is this Frank?'

'Who's this?'

'Sorry . . . my name's Helen. I'm Paul's girlfriend.' There was a pause. Helen was about to speak again.

'I know who you are.'

Helen was a little taken aback, stumbling over the words more than she might have done anyway. 'Look, I'm sorry to bother . . . be bothering you, but I wanted to let you know that Paul died at the weekend.'

'Fuck off.'

It was a reflex: matter of fact but disturbing all the same; the power of his dismissal. 'I'm really sorry.' She waited, listening to him breathe for a few seconds, until she decided he wasn't going to say anything more. 'I saw that you'd left a message, so—'

'How did he pass away?'

'There was a car accident.'

'Where? What sort of accident?'

'I'd rather not—'

'Was Paul driving?'

'No, he was . . . hit.' She glanced across at Paul's things on the table.

There was a bloodstain on one of the shoes as well. 'OK, like I said, I saw the message. I just wanted to . . .'

'I'm sorry about the language before.'

'It's fine.'

'No. It's unforgivable.'

His tone had suddenly become almost melodramatic, and Helen wondered what she must sound like to him. Calm? *Cold*, even? 'Listen, I know it's Frank, but I don't have a second name.'

'Linnell,' he said.

'OK.'

He said it again. 'Emphasis on the second syllable.'

She leaned across to take a pen and paper from her bag. 'There isn't a date yet – you know, for the funeral – but if you let me have an address I can let you know the details when we've got them.' Again she waited, until she'd begun to think that he'd hung up; she heard a cough and a series of sniffs. 'So, if you could—'

'I'll call you,' he said.

The line went dead.

THIRTEEN

Driving from Kennington, she could smell Paul in the car; his cigarettes and sweat. He'd obviously been smoking a lot more than he'd let on, and she felt herself getting cross with him. There were empty cans in the footwell and Kit-Kat wrappers and scraps of paper. 'And your car's a bloody disgrace,' she said.

At the station, she'd been keen to get in and out quickly. She'd shown her ID at the front desk and hurried through to the car park with her head down. She'd almost been away and clear, had just closed the car door, when the custody sergeant came bustling out. She'd met him in the pub a few times and he'd always seemed nice enough.

Every station had one like him: tough as old boots and soft as shit.

'Helen, hang on . . .'

She wound down the car window.

'I just wanted to say how sorry we all are. Christ.' He rubbed at something on the roof of the car. 'Couldn't believe it.'

'Thanks.' She couldn't remember his name. Harry? Henry?

'Such a ridiculous way for it to . . . happen, you know?'

'Yeah.' Not that she could see how it would have been any less ridiculous to be knifed by a drunk or blown up on a tube train.

'Listen, the lads are organising a bit of a collection . . .'

She nodded; of course they were. Love and marriage, fish and chips, dead coppers and whip-rounds. She didn't quite know what she was expected to say, so she just said 'thanks' and started the car.

The sergeant watched her back out and turn round; waved as she eased out of the car park.

The Met had a number of garages on either side of the river. One was in Hammersmith, hidden behind blue metal gates on a side street off the Fulham Palace Road. Helen parked up and walked round to the main workshop. It was a warm morning and the doors were open. A number of people were working on vehicles outside – two written-off police Saabs and a Mercedes with its passenger door caved in – while inside, a group of three men stood around a table, examining an engine block as if they were trying to decipher the Dead Sea scrolls.

The place was like any other garage, though perhaps a little cleaner and without the girlie calendars. There were winches and pits, benches and racks of tools. Gas bottles and cutting equipment were arranged along one wall and next to the other were stairs at the top of which Helen guessed there would be offices and engineering labs with high-tech equipment for more delicate work.

She showed her ID to one of the men working on the Mercedes and gave the name of the crime scene manager she was looking for. He pointed to the group studying the engine and Helen walked across to a big man wearing blue overalls and a dirty white baseball cap.

She flashed the warrant card again. 'I'd like to see the silver BMW,' she said. 'The Hopwood case?'

Roger Deering was the CSM whose name she had copied from the DI's notebook, along with the address of the garage and several other bits and pieces. He led her across to where three vehicles were lined up with covers stretched across them. He pulled off the cover from the car in the middle. 'Here you go . . .'

Helen walked slowly around the BMW, aware that Deering was

watching her. The front of the car had crumpled, with the bonnet buckled. She stared. It was impossible to tell how much of the damage had been done by the wall which the car had eventually hit, and how much was down to Paul.

'Is there anything I can help you with?' Deering asked.

The windscreen had shattered and imploded. It bowed back into the car like glass webbing. There wasn't any blood.

'I'm about done on this one, to be honest,' he said. 'You might be better off talking to the collision investigator.'

In a fatal traffic accident where death was deemed to be suspicious, the CSM took the role that would otherwise have belonged to a scene-of-crime officer. Like many SOCOs, the crime scene manager was not a police officer and could not give evidence in court. He or she would be responsible for the forensic examination of the car: taking swabs, prints and paint samples and liaising with other scientific experts where necessary. Once that had been done, a collision investigator – usually a specially trained traffic officer – would step in to take charge of accident reconstruction. Then the vehicle would be stripped down so that brakes and steering could be properly analysed; so that the car's broken body could tell its story.

A post-mortem of sorts.

Helen walked around to the near-side rear door and opened it. The back seat was missing and the mats had been removed. There was still some glass on the floor from the window through which the shots had been fired.

'We dug one bullet out of the wheel arch and the other out of the far door.'

Helen was startled. She hadn't been aware of Deering moving up behind her. She turned to look at him.

'They're with ballistics,' he said. 'So we'll wait and see. Thirty-eights, if you ask me.'

'Not that they'll ever find the gun,' Helen said.

'Right, right.' He nodded and let out a strange laugh,

like a strangled cough.

She found herself leaning back against the car, retreating a little from the CSM's gaze. She felt almost as though he were studying her.

'Why don't we go and get some tea?' he said.

He led her upstairs and into a small office. The filing cabinets looked pre-war and the two computers were grey with grime. Helen sat in a stiff-backed armchair against the wall, while Deering went to get the tea. He was back quickly with two mugs and an open packet of digestives. She took one and he carried a second chair across.

'You're his girlfriend, aren't you?' he said. 'The bloke that was hit.'

She looked up at him, her mouth full of biscuit.

The nod towards her belly answered the unasked question. 'Somebody said that he had a partner who was expecting.'

She smiled at the word; it wasn't one she'd heard from anyone other than her grandmother. She could suddenly hear a gentle hint of the North-East in Deering's accent. 'Expecting' sounding like 'expectant'.

'Did you see what you came to see?' he asked.

'I just wanted to see the woman's car.' She shrugged like that was perfectly reasonable. He nodded as if he agreed that it was, but still she wondered what he was thinking. 'Did *you* find anything?'

'Nothing I wasn't expecting to find. The bullets, obviously. Some of Mrs Ruston's blood on the front seat.' He looked at her across the top of his mug. 'She was the driver.'

Helen nodded. Another name she'd taken from the notebook.

'I don't think the airbag deployed until the car hit the wall. She broke her nose at the . . . first impact.'

'When she hit Paul, you mean.'

'That's correct.'

Helen took a slurp of tea and Deering did likewise.

'I haven't written everything up yet,' he said. 'I prefer getting my hands dirty, if I'm honest.'

'Like most of us.'

'Right, right.'

They sat in silence for ten, fifteen seconds. Deering removed his cap and Helen saw that he was virtually bald on top. She was surprised, as there was plenty of hair at the sides and he couldn't have been more than forty. He finished his drink and said, 'This feels a bit weird.'

'Why?'

'It's like there's something you think I can tell you. You know, that'll help you feel better. Truth is, I don't even know how fast the car was going.'

'That's not why I came.'

'Like I said, you'd be better off talking to the collision investigator.'

'It's fine, honestly.'

She wasn't just trying to make him feel more comfortable. She understood what he was talking about, but there were things she really *didn't* feel a need to know.

She had not seen the post-mortem and had no plans to do so. She did not know if Paul had died instantly. She knew that he had gone by the time he reached hospital, had been dead for a while by the time she got the call. That was enough.

Suffering and struggle. Last words. That kind of knowledge could not help anybody, surely. Then again, she might develop a burning desire to know that sort of stuff later on. It didn't really feel as though she were doing *any* of the things she was supposed to, or at least not in the conventional order. She certainly couldn't explain why she'd wanted to see the car.

Why she wasn't at home, curled up and howling.

The phone rang, and though Deering ignored it for a few seconds colour rose in his face. He ran thumb and forefinger around the edge of his cap. 'I'd best be getting on,' he said. The DI had said much the same thing. It was becoming obvious that heavily pregnant widows were not the most relaxing of company.

'Me too.'

'Have you got a card or something?'

She handed one over and Deering walked her back downstairs. She pointed to the pair of mangled Saabs on her way out. 'What happened there, then?'

'Chasing some drugged-up teenager across most of Essex,' Deering said. 'The driver didn't get out of it. Young PC with a couple of kiddies.'

As Helen got back into Paul's car, she found herself wondering where they kept all the pallbearer's white gloves.

Easy arrived at the stash house announcing that he'd brought lunch with him. Theo opened the bag and pulled a face.

'Fuck you, Jamie Oliver,' Easy said. 'That's the quality gear, man, the shish, yeah? I wouldn't be bringing no doner kebab rubbish, would I? That stuff's just pig's lips and stomachs and shit.'

They left Mikey sprawled on the sofa and moved through to the kitchen to eat. Easy had on a red tracksuit and a couple of new chains; heavy ones that Theo liked the look of. He decided he might get himself one come the end of the week.

'Got to do it, man,' Easy said. 'Why else you working your arse off? I'll take you to see this guy I know, get you the best deal.'

When they'd finished eating, Theo gathered up the plates and paper, flicked on the kettle. Easy stayed at the table rolling himself a spliff.

'You positive Wave got rid of that gun?' Theo said.

Easy slid the Rizla across his tongue. 'What's this now?'

'What do you think?'

'Still the bus stop thing, yeah?'

'Fuck sake, you not seen the extra police walking about out there?' Easy shrugged and lit up. 'You think that's a coincidence?'

'You got to breathe easy, T. Stay collected.' Easy opened his mouth wide, let the pungent smoke drift out and up. 'Nobody asking any questions.'

Mikey shouted through from the other room: 'Any of that coming my way?'

Easy passed the joint to Theo, who took it gratefully and drew hard.

Anything that was going to relax him was a good idea. He'd not slept well for three nights, and with the tiredness on top of everything else he'd found himself fighting with Javine for no reason. Shouting at the baby, which he knew was mental, and which only led to more arguments. He was increasingly unnerved by crowds and loud noises. It was becoming hard to concentrate, to think about business.

'So, this gun, yeah?'

'Wave says it's gone. He found it, he lost it again. No more.'

They both knew that Wave had young cousins, twelve and thirteen, and the smart money was on him using them to hold onto firearms. It was a common enough ploy. Kids . . . *real* kids, were less likely to be picked up with guns, and wouldn't be looking at a mandatory five-year sentence if they were. The likes of Wave didn't get where they were without playing all the angles; operating smooth.

'I don't want some ten-year-old passing that thing round in exchange for sweeties,' Theo said. 'All I'm saying.'

Easy laughed, took back the spliff. 'It's gone, T, I said. You need to trust me on this, yeah?'

Theo stared at him. That was another thing that had changed since the drive up to Hackney and back. He remembered how Easy had been with him that night: the looks and the laughing from the back seat; the back and forwards with Wave and SnapZ, getting in little digs and putting him down. There'd been something . . . hard about him, and cruel. Theo had seen him like that with other people when he'd had to be; knew that Easy had a wicked temper. But not with him; not before.

He'd pulled him up on it as soon as they'd got back. Easy and the others had been high on the night, while Theo just waited for the adrenaline to stop rushing through him, like a white-knuckle ride he couldn't wait to get off.

Easy had laughed, said, 'It's just chit-chat, man. Just trying to keep you on your toes and fired up for it, you get me? You still my Star Boy, T.'

Now, Easy looked across the table at him through a curtain of smoke; that smile building slowly as the skunk did its job. 'Got something I need you for,' he said.

'What?'

'Little bit of fundraising. No big thing at all.'

Theo spread his arms. 'Got this to look out for now, man.'

'It's sorted.'

Theo took what was left of the spliff.

'Wave gets a nice cut of whatever I come out with so he's happy,' Easy said. 'SnapZ looks after the cash for a bit, and you come with me. Next week you buy yourself three of these nice sick chains, you get me?'

'What's the story?'

Now the killer smile really kicked in. 'This one is *very* sweet and *very* simple,' he said. He reached a hand out towards Theo's face. 'And all I need is a boy with that nice, *innocent* look you got.'

Theo moved back, pushing his chair onto two legs. Thinking that it was bullshit. That even if it wasn't, the look was all that he had left.

'I'll bell you with the whats and whens,' Easy said.

They turned at the urgent knocking and watched Mikey jump up and move towards the door. There was a muffled conversation via the intercom and a few seconds later SnapZ came charging into the kitchen, nodding and grinning, dropping the early edition of the *Standard* onto the table.

Theo saw the headline and felt the puke rise up.

SnapZ didn't bother taking off his headphones and the beat that leaked from them was like an angry insect buzzing around the kitchen. He drummed his forefingers on the paper then pointed them both at Theo. 'Now you're a *serious* playa, T,' he said. '*Big*-time gangsta, for real.' He took the remains of the joint from between Theo's lips, sucked on it and hissed out the smoke. He nodded towards the newspaper, his voice far louder than it needed to be. 'Now you're a cop-killer . . .'

FOURTEEN

Frank Linnell tried to get back for lunch as often as he could, enjoying the chance to relax for an hour or two in the middle of the day, and happy enough that Clive was keeping an eye on progress at the pub.

He had picked up the paper on the way home.

Sitting in the office downstairs, he had read the entire story through twice: the front-page splash and full report across three further pages inside; the sidebar with the Commissioner's response and an appeal for information; the editorial comment condemning the shocking waste of life and demanding that something be done about the city's drug gangs.

There had been a tear or two the night before, when Paul's girl-friend had called. Now he shed a few more and had a stiff drink before he read the story a third time. Got all that out of the way so he could start to think clearly.

Through the open door he saw his sister Laura drift down the stairs on her way to the kitchen. He shouted that he'd be through in a minute and went back to the paper.

There were just the two of them now, his mother having passed on eighteen months before in the basement he'd had converted into a granny flat. Just him and Laura, rattling around in the big house in Blackheath. But Frank was happy enough. He knew some of the stupid things that were said about his domestic set-up – behind his back, of course; always behind his back – but he was long past caring what other people thought, and the arrangements suited him nicely.

When she was on the way out, his mum had urged him to do up the basement flat and rent it out, but it wasn't as though he needed the money, and he didn't want strangers around the place. Didn't relish the intrusion. A Russian girl came in to clean when he wasn't there, and a woman named Betty spent each Monday in his kitchen knocking up enough food for the week, leaving the freezer stocked with pies and casseroles, pasta dishes and fruit crumbles.

It wasn't doing his weight any good, mind you.

He didn't *need* anyone else around; he was never short of company. There were always a few of the boys knocking about talking business and what have you; and there were times, weeks on end if there was something serious on, when Clive more or less lived there. Even when things were quiet, a drinking partner or someone to watch a TV programme with was only ever a phone call away.

Whatever anyone thought or said, it worked for him. And, as Frank was fond of telling Clive, or anyone else whose ear he was bending, he was 'far too old and ugly to change anything now'.

He turned on the CD player – a bit of Elgar that he liked – and stared at the front page: 'POLICE OFFICER NAMED AS VICTIM OF GANG SHOOTING. FLASHED HEADLIGHTS LEAD TO TRAGEDY'.

There was a picture of the bus stop where it had happened; the metal frame mangled and beads of glass piled like ice in the gutter. There was crime-scene tape and a yellow INCIDENT board at the side of the road. On the inside pages the events had been recreated in a series of simple drawings, like a cartoon strip: a stick man pointing a gun from the window of Car A; and the moment of impact rendered with a jagged line where the front of Car B met the legs of a second stick man on the pavement.

He understood now why the girlfriend had been so vague about the 'accident' when she'd called, poor cow. She'd sounded nice, he thought. Not that he'd expected Paul to be with anyone who *wasn't* nice.

He listened to the music for another few minutes; closed his eyes and thought about the best way to proceed. The means to sort things expeditiously. He thought about stick men on their knees, begging; and later twisted in damp ditches, with holes in their perfectly round heads.

Then he wandered through to the kitchen, fancying that he might defrost a lasagne if he had one left.

'Will they charge him with murder? When they catch him?'

'They'll *go* for murder; probably get manslaughter.'

'I'm still not sure I understand the difference.'

'But they won't catch him,' Helen said.

She'd met Jenny at a Pizza Express in Waterloo. Her sister had seemed keen to talk about the investigation, the nuts and bolts of things, thinking perhaps that, being work-related, it might be easier for Helen to deal with than other stuff.

'I'm sure they're trying their best,' Jenny said.

Helen studied the menu, decided on an American Hot with extra jalapeños and a soft egg. Thought about salmonella and decided the egg might not be such a good idea.

It *was* marginally easier to think about the investigation rather than which coffin she was going to choose for Paul. But there wasn't a great deal in it. With so little progress, there wasn't much to say anyway; and Jenny's limited grasp of police procedure tended to limit the conversation a little.

It struck Helen more than usual how little interest her sister had ever shown in her work. She sensed that Jenny found what she did distasteful somehow. As though sordid tales of abuse and dysfunction could only sully her own perfect family, the picture of them all that she carried around in her head.

'You doing OK?' Jenny asked.

Not that Helen was any stranger to denial herself, of course. She conjured the same smile she'd been producing like a heavily drugged white rabbit over the last few days. 'Not too bad.'

'How's the baby?'

'Definitely cooked, I reckon.' Helen patted her belly. 'It's been a godsend, actually. It's hard to dwell on things too much when you're being sick or needing to pee all the time.' The pat became a rub. 'Plus, I've got someone else to think about, you know?'

'This might not be the best time, but I wanted to ask if you'd thought any more about the birth-partner business.' Jenny was fiddling with her napkin. 'I mean, now it's obviously . . .'

'There've been other things to sort out, you know?'

'I know, but it could happen any time, Hel.'

'Spicy pizza might do it.'

'*Seriously*. I even thought you might . . . you know, with the shock.'

'There *were* a few twinges,' Helen said. She remembered the panic cutting through the numbness; sitting there in the early hours after the phone call, waiting for Jenny to come and take her to the mortuary. 'I'd have a good story to tell the baby, anyway.'

'You need to think about it,' Jenny said.

Helen promised that she would and signalled to the waiter that they were ready to order. 'I meant to say, do you think Tim would like to come round, see if he wants any of Paul's clothes?'

Jenny reached for the sparkling water.

'Have a look through before I chuck stuff out.' Jenny's husband was a little chunkier than Paul, but Helen guessed that there would be plenty of shirts and jackets to fit him.

'Right . . .'

It was obvious to Helen that Jenny was flustered and uncomfortable. 'Paul had some nice stuff, believe it or not,' she said. 'I know he was a scruffy bastard most of the time . . .' She trailed off, seeing the relief on her sister's face when the waiter arrived at the table.

They gave him their order, and Helen went back to explaining the difference between murder and manslaughter.

★

Frank ate at the kitchen table, while Laura leaned against the island unit, working her way slowly through a plate of crispbread and cheese. After a few minutes she asked him what the matter was and he walked to the office to fetch the paper.

He dropped it in front of her and stabbed at the headline. 'That's Paul,' he said. '*Paul.*'

She quickly scanned the front page. 'Oh Jesus, Frank, I'm sorry.'

He sat back down at the table, picked up his fork and watched her read. She was his half-sister to be precise, but it was a distinction that never concerned Frank. They'd been close for years, but now that she was no longer part of her own mother's life, and with nobody knowing if the father she and Frank shared were dead or alive, they had never been closer.

Laura was the only family Frank had, that he was ever *likely* to have, but she was enough. She was twenty-three, thirty years younger than he was, and . . . *delicate.* That was the word that always came into Frank's head if he thought about her for long enough. Beautiful, *obviously*, and far brighter than he was – must have got that from her mother, he supposed – but definitely someone who bruised a bit too easily.

Who needed looking after, whether she liked it or not.

When Laura raised her head from the paper, she was pale. She'd tied her long hair up this morning; held it there with what looked, to Frank, like chopsticks. 'That's terrible.' Her voice was high and light, accentless. 'I don't know what to say. It's . . . *evil.*' There were tears in her eyes, but she didn't try to wipe them away.

'Not evil,' Frank said. 'There's nothing you can do about evil.'

'There's nothing you can do about *this.*'

121

'We'll have to see.'

'You can't bring Paul back.'

Frank walked across to join her. He looked down at the newspaper again, at the simple black-and-white drawings. 'This can't stand,' he said. 'It *cannot* stand.'

'You should just think about things for a while,' she said.

'Paul was your friend too.'

'I know.'

'You do remember how I met him, don't you?'

She nodded. 'Please don't do anything stupid.'

He didn't know what he was going to do yet; not in specific terms. Of course, he'd call Clive - it always started with that – and they would put their heads together. They would formulate a business plan, same as always.

'Promise me,' Laura said.

Frank picked up the paper and tossed it into the bin. He pictured more unhappy stick men with their little round mouths wide open in surprise; zigzags through the straight lines of arms and legs, and red streaked across the squares of their tiny, black-and-white world.

He carried his plate across to the dishwasher, opened the door and leaned down.

Said, 'Don't worry.'

FIFTEEN

Aside from a few minutes polishing off the remains of the soup Jenny had made, Helen felt as if she had spent most of the evening so far on the phone. Jenny had called within seconds of her arriving home; then Katie had checked in. Paul's mother had wanted to know if she had heard any more about the body being released and her father had rung to remind her that there was a bed made up if ever she wanted it.

Grateful as she was that so many people were concerned for her well-being, she'd taken the phone off the hook. But she'd replaced it almost immediately, deciding that both Jenny and Katie were just hysterical enough to send the police round, imagining that she'd done something stupid.

And anyway, she'd dreamed about Paul calling.

She wasn't sure *when* she'd dreamed it, if she had been half awake or fully asleep at the time, but the sense-memory was powerful; the feeling of elation on picking up the phone and hearing his voice.

'Must be a million-to-one chance: someone at that bus stop with the same name as me. Nice to know that everyone was so cut up, mind you. How's the baby, by the way?'

She knew such thoughts were not unusual; the feeling that the person who had died would come waltzing through the door at any moment. It was somewhere between denial and prayer, Helen supposed, and she felt a sense of relief that at least *some* of the things she was feeling were normal.

Still no tears, though.

She had gone down to the car park and cleaned out Paul's car, loading everything from the footwells and the boot into two carrier bags. She had just walked back through the front door when the phone rang again. There was a deep breath before she snatched it up.

'Helen? It's Gary.'

She felt guilty that she hadn't spoken to Gary Kelly since it happened. She knew that it was stupid to attach blame to anyone except the toe-rag who'd fired the gun, but that hadn't stopped her; hadn't stopped the irrational thoughts crowding in.

If the silly cow in the car hadn't panicked.

If Paul had been sober enough to react quicker.

If they hadn't been going back to Gary's place.

She asked him how he was and he told her he was on the mend. That the leave he'd taken was compassionate rather than medical and that he'd be returning to work the following week. He asked how she was, then began crying before she'd had a chance to answer.

Everyone but me, Helen thought.

'It's my fault,' he said.

'It's not.'

'I asked him to stay . . . because I didn't want to go home on my own. I might have reacted faster if I hadn't been so pissed.'

'Paul was pissed too,' Helen said. 'It was pretty obvious when he called me. He sounded happy, Gary. OK?'

'He pushed me out of the way, did you know that?'

'Yeah, I know.' Helen had been told what a witness at the bus stop had said he'd seen. How the two men had been standing close together and how the one who had died had shoved his friend away a few

124

moments before the impact. Helen listened to Paul's friend sobbing and couldn't help wishing that it had happened the other way around.

Once Kelly had stopped crying, they talked for a few minutes about practical issues. She asked him if he wanted to say something at the funeral and he said that he'd be honoured. She told him about the collection that was being organised at the station and that she'd decided to give all of the proceeds to a police charity. Kelly told her that he'd get it sorted.

'Whatever you need,' he said. 'You've got all my numbers, right? Just call if you think of anything else. Doesn't matter what time.'

Helen said thanks. 'Actually, there is something. Does the name Frank Linnell mean anything to you?'

The phone conversation from the previous night had been nagging at her all day. She felt herself tensing up whenever she thought about it and couldn't understand why. She had no idea who Linnell was, nor how he had known Paul, but a friend and work colleague like Gary Kelly might.

She *did* know that in the weeks leading up to Paul's death, she had been neither.

'Why d'you want to know about Frank Linnell?'

Something in Kelly's voice bothered her, and the lie came easily. 'You know how a name comes into your head and you've no idea where you've heard it.'

'You're probably better off if he stays in your head,' Kelly said. 'Frank Linnell isn't really someone you want to get close to.'

'Now I *really* want to know.'

Though Kelly had never actively worked on any Organised Crime Unit, he knew enough to give Helen a potted history: the swathes of south-east London that Linnell's organisation controlled; the list of charges that never stuck; the methods used to secure contracts for his assorted building and development companies. 'Not the nicest individual in the world, you know?'

'OK, thanks . . .'

125

'You doing a bit of undercover work for Organised Crime, then?' He laughed. 'It's a bloody good cover.'

'What is?'

'The whole pregnancy thing. Certainly had me fooled.'

Helen laughed too, but it was an effort. 'It was just a name somebody mentioned, I think. Must have been Paul, I suppose. Although he's never had much to do with any of that stuff, has he?'

'Not as far as I know. But, to tell you the truth, last few months I've not had a clue what he's been up to.'

'Sorry?'

'He was just a bit . . . distracted, I think. What with the baby and everything.'

'What do you mean "been up to"?'

Kelly sounded reluctant, but Helen pushed until he told her about the amount of time Paul had spent away from the station. His vague explanations when confronted. What he had said about an old case that was causing him some grief. Though Kelly never said as much, Helen could hear in his voice that he hadn't believed a word of it.

'I'm sure you're right,' Helen said. 'He was probably distracted.'

'Paul wasn't someone who liked the world knowing his business,' Kelly said. 'Fair enough, I reckon. I think he had a bit more on his plate than the rest of us, that's all.'

There wasn't too much more after that, and when she'd hung up, Helen walked through to the bathroom. She showered, then sat down in the cubicle to shave her legs. She tried singing along with one of Paul's REM albums while she was getting ready for bed, but she couldn't make out many of the words. When the CD finished forty minutes later she was still sitting on the edge of the bed in a T-shirt and pyjama bottoms, wondering exactly what Paul had had on his plate.

And why any of it concerned Frank Linnell.

Frank was alone, watching TV in the kitchen, when Clive arrived; he hadn't seen Laura for several hours. He took Clive's jacket and led him down the long corridor that ran off the entrance hall. They walked past the gym that Frank had installed the year before, and out into the conservatory.

He enjoyed sitting out here in the evenings with a glass of wine and a book of crosswords. Or, if Laura was around, they would sit together and he would talk through his day; maybe ask her advice about some of the places he was doing up. She was good with that stuff, although she'd always told him there were other aspects of his business she'd prefer he kept to himself.

'Hard to believe,' Clive said. 'How things turn out.'

'You've got that right,' Frank said.

Frank had not told Clive about Paul's death when he'd first heard about it from Helen. He had thought it best to keep it as a private matter, and might well have continued to do so had it not been for the revelations in the newspaper. The *manner* of Paul's death had changed everything.

They stood side by side and stared out at the garden. There were lanterns every twenty feet or so along the path and in most of the flower beds, throwing orange light up into the trees. A thick string of smaller lights ran along the fence and around the edge of a huge shed in one corner.

'I was thinking about that afternoon when he came to the pub,' Clive said. 'When that kid came in, remember?'

'Course I do. Why?'

'No reason. You just think about the last time you saw someone, don't you? How they were and all that.'

Frank had thought a lot about that afternoon since he'd heard about Paul's death. They hadn't fallen out, not exactly, but Paul had gone away dissatisfied none the less. Frank knew that he'd been right to refuse him; but still, he wished things could have been different.

'So where are we with this?'

'I've been putting out feelers since you rang, and so has everyone

I've spoken to. I think we're getting there.'

'We got names?'

'Like the paper said, nobody even knows if it's a firm from north or south of the river.'

'Shouldn't be too difficult.'

Clive nodded his agreement. 'It's a process of elimination.'

'I need your full attention on this.'

'Don't worry, I know it's important.'

'The pubs aren't going anywhere,' Frank said. 'It's not the end of the world if we come in a day or two late on the refit.'

'All being well we can start bending a few ears tomorrow.'

'First thing,' Frank said.

They said nothing for maybe half a minute. The sound of voices on the television drifted down the corridor from the kitchen.

'You seen the foxes lately?' Clive asked.

Frank nodded. He had been watching keenly as a pair of foxes had moved into the garden, suspecting that they had built an earth beneath the shed. He told Clive it had got to the point where they were no longer bothered by the movement-activated lights that flooded the lawn whenever they trotted across it.

'I sat and watched them for about half an hour the other night,' he said. 'Cheeky sod came right up to there.' He pointed. 'Cocked his leg against one of those pots.'

'Nice,' Clive said, laughing.

Frank was thinking of that moment, a minute or so after the last fox had disappeared back into the bushes, when the lights would click off. When the garden returned, in a second, to near darkness. He pictured the young men in that car, driving around in the dark and waiting for some well-intentioned mug to flash their lights.

Like he'd said to Laura, it could not be allowed to stand.

'You need me to stay?' Clive asked.

Frank shook his head, said, 'I need you making more phone calls. Some of the people who know about this are barely out of bed yet.'

A few minutes after Clive had left, the floodlights came on in the garden. Frank stared out, but couldn't see anything. Sometimes there was nothing to see. Sometimes, it was just a spider crawling across one of the sensors. But Frank stayed and watched anyway.

Theo had hung around at the stash house later than normal, lingering in the bedroom once one of the Asian boys had arrived for the evening shift, and moving between there and the toilet for an hour or so until it was darker and a little quieter outside; until he'd stopped shaking and shitting.

He pulled up his hood and walked quickly down to the Dirty South on Lee High Road. The bar had been called the Rose of Lee before he'd moved down to Kent, a decent, small-scale music venue that had been tarted up while he was away. Some of the live bands weren't that great, but there was usually a DJ laying down some decent break-beats or grime and a few faces from the crew hanging around late, getting a last one in on their way home or kicking things off if they were making a night of it.

This was *their* place, though every so often some idiot from the Ghetto Boys or a few dickheads from the Kidbrooke estate would come in like they didn't know and try to start something. Always had to watch out for that.

Theo sat on one of the battered old sofas near the door, with Ollie and another of the runners, a fourteen-year-old girl named Gospel, who Ollie was desperate to fuck. Nobody said too much, staring up at the big screen or watching the pool table. After a couple of drinks they drifted back to Ollie's place and smoked for a while, until people began to nod off and Theo knew it was time to go home.

He walked back across the estate towards his flat.

When he passed the kids by the garage, one of them tilted up his chin, said, 'All right, T?' There were nods from the others. Theo nodded back and kept moving, hearing their murmurs behind him; hearing sirens somewhere in the distance and feeling like something was flopping around inside him, like meat being turned over on a butcher's counter.

'*Now you're a* serious *playa, T. Now you're a cop-killer.*'

Easy hadn't said too much after SnapZ had come in, brimming with the news and loving it. Theo could see that even *he* was a little rattled. He doubted that SnapZ and Mikey saw it, but Theo knew Easy well enough to see how he was trying to cover it up; to play the whole thing down. Kissing his teeth and checking his watch. Glancing across at the paper.

Fuck, if *Easy* was shaken . . .

Theo began climbing the stone stairwell up to the third floor, his steps echoing against the treads, the metal handrail cold beneath his palm.

'*Christ!*' On the landing, he nearly collided with someone coming down. They each took a step back. Theo stared and recognised the old man who lived two doors along from his mother. He unballed his fists and lowered his hood.

'Theodore! Scared the shit out of me.'

Theo mumbled an apology; saw that the old man was carrying his rubbish downstairs. The bags had looked like wings or something in the half light and had scared Theo every bit as much.

'You want me to take those down?'

The old man didn't need asking twice, telling Theo that he was a credit to his mother as he trudged back up the stairs.

Theo cursed under his breath as he went back down again. He hated going anywhere near the big metal bins at the bottom. He hated the smell and the noise of things scurrying about behind them. But the poor old bastard had looked as though he had rocks in his bin-bags.

Ten feet away from the bins, Theo stood and lobbed in the bags, then turned while the second one was still clattering and took the steps back upstairs two at a time. He waited outside the door to his flat, bunching the keys in his fist so that they would make no noise. He leaned against the door and listened. The baby's cries sounded hoarse through the plasterboard.

He couldn't face it.

He swapped one set of keys for another as he jogged down two floors and along. He knew that his mother and sister would both have gone to bed ages ago; that he would not have to talk to anyone. Would not have to pretend everything was fine and chat about this and that when he felt like he was still waking up from something.

Like the worst was yet to come.

He opened the door to his mum's place and walked in without switching on any lights. He dropped down onto the sofa, leaned his head back and closed his eyes.

Helen hadn't really slept at all. She had started to drift off once or twice, but she'd been aware that she hadn't turned off the light, that the phone was ringing again, and she'd never quite gone under. Eventually, she'd given up.

It was nearly three in the morning. She made herself tea and turned on the radio, listened to other insomniacs calling to trade insults with an angry presenter, while she made herself busy. She took the plastic bags she had filled with the contents of Paul's car and tipped everything out onto the carpet. She binned the empty cans, wrappers and fag packets and tried to sort out the rest.

Sunglasses, sat-nav, assorted tapes and CDs, map books and tools from the boot, handfuls of paper.

'*I think he had a bit more on his plate than the rest of us . . .*'

She carefully laid out all the paper on the table. Lined the pieces up neatly, then arranged them in groups: petrol and supermarket receipts; car park tickets; assorted scraps with scribbled names and phone numbers.

Then she remembered that the phone had rung while she was failing to get any sleep. She checked the machine.

'I hope I'm not disturbing you, I just wanted to say that it was good to meet you earlier.' A gentle hint of the North-East. 'Sorry . . . it's

Roger Deering here, by the way. Should have said. Anyway, I really just called to say that if there's anything you need . . . please feel free to give me a call. If things get on top of you or whatever. I know it can't be easy, so . . . even if you just fancy a natter.'

He left his number, told her she could ring any time, said, 'God bless.'

Helen wandered back to the table, thinking that her overall impression of the CSM had been about right, that he was a decent sort, but also aware that her ability to read people had taken as much of a battering as the rest of her. She'd had Deering down as nice enough, then a bit creepy, then nice again, all within five minutes of meeting him.

She finished her tea and stared down at the pieces of paper, nudging them into line where necessary, straightening them. Letting her eyes drift across them she thought about what Gary Kelly had said.

The stuff about Frank Linnell. The rest of it . . .

'*He was just a bit . . . distracted.*'

About Paul keeping himself to himself: not going to the office when he should have done; being secretive when it came to exactly what he *had* been doing. She felt oddly relieved that she hadn't been alone in being given the silent treatment.

In being lied to.

'. . . *Last few months I've not had a clue* what *he's been up to.*'

Yes, a distance had opened up between them since Paul had found out about the affair; since there had been any question about who the father of the baby might be. But, if she were being honest with herself, Helen had sensed that there was more going on than simple anger and sexual jealousy. Now, there was little point in being anything *other* than honest.

It seemed clear there were things Paul hadn't told her; not because he didn't feel like it, but because he couldn't.

On the radio, a woman was talking about global warming and the host suggested it might be a massive conspiracy theory. Helen wondered if she should get on the phone first thing tomorrow and call some of the numbers Paul had scribbled down.

'*Hi, this will probably sound strange, but my boyfriend's just been killed and I know there are other things I should be thinking about, but your number was on a scrap of paper on the floor of his car and . . . well, basically I'm a nosy bitch, so . . .*'

She noticed that two of the car park stubs were from the same place: an NCP on Brewer Street, in Soho. She moved the stubs together and tried to think why Paul would have been going into the West End.

A Friday afternoon, then the Friday evening one week later. A fortnight before his death.

She went to fetch her diary and checked out the dates; thought back and realised that the second Friday had been the night Paul had come home late with garlic on his breath. She remembered lying there pretending to be asleep and wondering if he was seeing someone else. Kidding herself that he'd been out with people from work.

Way back, when she was wet behind the ears, she'd been out drinking with some old soak from the Murder Squad with too many years on his clock. Several pints in, he'd started on about the realities, the *strangeness* of dealing with violent death.

Helen had never forgotten it.

'Thing is, we only get to know these people after their deaths; after the poor buggers have been shot or stabbed and what have you. We don't even know what they look like, not *really*. Not their expressions, not how they walked and talked, not how they *were*. Sometimes, we find out all sorts of shit, rooting around in the nooks and crannies. We get to know what they were really like, even when we're not looking for it. And sometimes, so do the people they've been living with.'

Helen picked up the pair of NCP tickets and carried them to the table by the front door. She laid them side by side again, ready for the morning. Then she turned off the radio and walked back into the bedroom.

Ten minutes later, lying in the dark, she said, 'What's your fucking game, Hopwood?'

SIXTEEN

The CCTV monitoring centre that covered most of the West End was based above the Trocadero, a shopping centre and entertainment complex running between Coventry Street and Shaftesbury Avenue. While people three floors below them pissed away their wages on shoot-'em-ups and 'I ♡ London' T-shirts, or further afield on any of the assorted pleasures that Oxford Street, Soho and Leicester Square had to offer, a private security company paid by Westminster Council watched, and recorded their movements for posterity.

Or sometimes, as evidence.

Once she'd visited the toilet, Helen showed her warrant card at the reception desk and filled out a form detailing the dates and locations for which she wanted to see footage. She'd been through the process before, knew that it would take fifteen minutes or so to set up. There were a couple of magazines to read while she waited; Kandinsky prints on the walls to look at if she fancied it.

It was a bright Thursday morning. She walked to the window, enjoying the sun on her face as she looked out across Piccadilly Circus, the treetops of Green Park just visible in the distance.

'DC Weeks?'

The woman who stepped from the lift and called out Helen's name was probably younger than she looked. Helen hoped, for the woman's sake and for the sake of everyone who knew her, that she wasn't as miserable. She heaved herself up from the sofa, clocked the woman's expression.

People's reactions to her pregnancy – the touching, the giving of unsolicited advice, the patronising comments – were often unwelcome. Nevertheless, Helen found it disconcerting to see someone so visibly unimpressed; to be looked at as if she were . . . showing off.

She smiled and tried not to judge. She came into contact every day with those who could not have children, or had lost them: unborn; as babies; and older – to drugs, abuse or violence. She knew there were plenty of people around for whom her swollen belly would be anything but beautiful.

'A bit more notice would have been nice.'

Mind you, this one was a sour-faced cow . . .

They travelled in silence to the top floor and Helen was shown into the viewing suite. The carpeted floor and wall tiles absorbed most of the sound and the woman raised her voice a notch or two, which wasn't pleasant: 'Say when and I'll run the first tape.'

They still called it 'tape', even though all the footage was now stored on a series of hard disks, with sufficient memory for many thousands of hours. This meant that most of it could be stored for months, and in some cases years, before it was erased.

Helen gave the nod and the woman began tapping at her keyboard.

There were three large screens, showing images from the three cameras nearest to the location that Helen had specified. One was positioned directly above the car park's entrance ramp and Helen knew that there would be footage of Paul driving in, just a few minutes before the scene they were now watching had been captured.

Friday, 11 July, 1.12 p.m.

She stared at the screen that gave the best view: from a camera on the opposite side of Brewer Street and twenty or so feet to the right as she looked. She knew she wouldn't have to wait very long. The exact time was printed on the ticket stub and Paul would almost certainly have come out onto the street a minute or so later.

She glanced down as she shifted position in the chair, and when she looked back, there he was. Stepping through a grey door to the side of the main entrance, stopping for a second to get his bearings, then walking to the pavement.

Helen felt a little dizzy. She looked around to see if there might be a water jug anywhere; buggered if she was going to ask for one.

'He looks like a dodgy so and so,' the woman said.

At 1.15 on 11 July it had been raining heavily. On the screen, water ran in dark lines down the grainy, black-and-white image. Helen could not make out the expression on Paul's face, but she watched him standing there in his blue suit, leaning into the weather, and couldn't find much reason to argue with the woman.

She had requested footage from a number of other CCTV points in the vicinity, so that she could follow Paul in whichever direction he walked from the car park; tracking him from camera to camera as he went. In the event, it wasn't necessary.

She watched the black cab draw up and Paul step towards it. She saw the door open and Paul exchanging a few words with the passenger in the back before getting in. The cab drove away fast. Flicking her eyes to the screen on the far right, Helen saw it from another angle, heading straight towards the camera, before passing it and going out of shot.

'That's fine,' she said. 'Run the next one.' She reached into her bag for a mint while the woman sorted out the second piece of footage. Pressed her hand to her chest and watched it tremble.

Hearing Paul's voice on her mobile phone had been difficult enough, but seeing him hit harder. It was something about the silence, and the quality of the image – broken down and streaked in shadow. Something about watching past lives as they bled into the present.

Now, she glanced at the woman, at her fingers moving easily across the keys. She was probably trying to decide what to have for lunch, where to go on holiday, whether to buy the shoes she'd been coveting for weeks.

Casually calling up a ghost on request.

'Here you go . . .'

Friday, 18 July, 7.33 p.m.

Paul walked out of the same grey door and waited; looked at his watch; walked up and down the narrow strip of pavement.

'Same bloke,' the woman said.

'Same.'

'He the one you're after?'

Helen watched him, standing in that stupid way of his, with one foot crossed over the other. Watched him tug the cuffs of his shirt down from his sleeve, check his reflection in a shop window, then turn as he heard the cab pull up. She saw it straight away.

'Must have a few quid, jumping in taxis right, left and centre.'

'Can you punch up the end of the first clip again,' Helen asked. 'Freeze-frame the taxi for me?'

When the two images were side by side on adjoining screens, and Helen had double-checked, she scribbled down the letters and numbers. The same number plate, the same taxi, on both occasions.

But no extra passenger the second time. Pre-ordered or sent.

'Got what you wanted?'

Helen dropped the pen and paper into her bag, zipped it up, and thought, Got something to do this afternoon . . .

There was an empty seat between Clive and the man at the end of the bar. Clive ordered a lemonade, nodded. 'And whatever *he* wants.'

When the man saw who was buying, he asked for tea . . . and a pint of lager.

'You want something to eat?' Clive asked.

'Toast with brown sauce.'

'It's on me. Have what you want.'

'That *is* what I want.'

Clive took his lemonade. 'Suit yourself.'

'It's got all the goodness you need, see. All the major food groups.'

'Come again?'

'Bread. Fruit. It's a fruit-based sauce.'

The woman behind the bar raised an eyebrow at Clive before she turned away, as though she'd heard these ramblings far too many times.

'Don't take too long, Jacky,' Clive said. 'We haven't got all day.'

Jacky Snooks had a proper name, of course, but it had got lost somewhere during twenty-five years as an all but permanent fixture in the Cue Up. Story was that he'd been a useful player in his time. There'd been talk about turning professional until someone he'd fleeced on the tables once too often had slipped a couple of balls into a bag and whacked him across the back of the head while he was lining up a long black.

Glasses had helped with the consequent eye problems, but they couldn't do too much about the tremor in his cueing arm. Now, he was the one being hustled, robbed by the fruit machines he spent all day feeding, and though he could probably still beat most of the club's customers left-handed, he had found easier ways to make a living. There weren't too many problems with his vision these days.

As soon as Clive had finished his lemonade, he was away. He didn't look back as he made for the stairs; he knew Jacky would be following. Outside, Clive walked briskly and Jacky stayed a good distance behind, keeping the big man in sight, trying to finish what was left of his toast and sauce as they walked away from the main shopping area towards Brookmill Park.

The car was parked on a side street. Frank got out when he saw Clive approaching, and the two of them stood side by side, waiting for the slight and shambling figure to come round the corner.

Jacky Snooks hurried the last few yards, then stuck out his hand. Said, 'Not as quick as I was, Mr Linnell.'

Frank turned to Clive. 'We got a serviette or something in the car?' He pulled a face. 'Looks like he's had his fingers up his arse.'

The Child Protection Unit from which Helen had taken leave was based in one small office at Streatham station. It was a small team, too: one DI, a couple of sergeants, four detective constables and two PCs.

Helen wasn't thrilled to see almost all of them there when she walked in.

The only unfamiliar face belonged to the woman at the workstation nearest the door, and Helen guessed that she must be her maternity cover. The woman stood up, hesitated as though she were unsure which to do first – offer congratulations or pass on condolences. Helen saved her the trouble by looking away and kept on walking, all the way across the office and into the open arms of DS Andrew Korn.

He held her close, rubbing her back; gently 'shushing' even though Helen was making no sound.

It was Helen, finally, who said, 'It's OK.'

Korn stepped away and looked at her. He was thickset and fresh-faced; a couple of years younger than she was. 'What the hell are you doing here?' he asked.

'Desperate to see you all,' she said. 'And, you know, trying to keep busy.'

Korn nodded his understanding and Helen felt a pang of guilt. It was only half a lie.

She realised that she'd spent much of the previous few days feeling guilty; that this was what grief had come to feel like for her. It felt like anger as well. And fear: shit-in-your-knickers terror.

Korn dragged out chairs. 'Well, it's good to see you.'

A look, a wave, a few words. One by one, Helen made the appropriate connection with each member of the team. Then, while her replacement fetched some tea, and despite Korn's insistence that there were other things she should be thinking about, she caught up with developments in her absence.

The Crown Prosecution Service was still dragging its feet over whether there was enough evidence to prosecute a father of three, seeing as only one of his children showed signs of abuse. A woman had recanted her story and was now refusing to give evidence against her boyfriend, claiming that her son's bruises were all self-inflicted. As were her own.

'You sure you've been missing this?' Korn asked.

It was the usual story of frustration and fuck-ups, and Helen was well used to it by now. They talked most about a case she had been working where the right result looked imminent. Clinging as usual to the victories; knowing that each one was hard fought and well worth the effort.

'I'd come back tomorrow,' Helen said, 'if I wasn't lugging this thing around.'

'Have you got any help?' Korn asked.

'I'm doing OK, Andy. Honest.'

Korn was distracted by a query from one of his PCs, and while he was looking through the notes, Helen slid across to an unused computer terminal and logged on.

'I've got loads of stuff needs typing up.'

Helen looked up and saw DS Diane Sealey grinning at her from above her own computer screen.

'That's good of you, Di.'

'You know, if you're desperate to do something.'

'I'm going to check a few emails and get out while I still can,' Helen said. 'Go and have a word with the guvnor, see about making this leave permanent.'

Sealey laughed.

As soon as she was into the Police National Computer, Helen reached into her bag for the piece of paper and typed in the number plate.

'We're all thinking about you,' Sealey said.

Helen nodded, said that she knew, and dropped her eyes back to the keyboard; to the results of the search. She leaned across the desk and grabbed a pen. There was plenty to write down.

★

Frank had planned on talking in the car, but it was too hot, and he tried to walk whenever he had the chance. Laura told him it was good for his heart.

'Nice to be outdoors for a change,' Jacky Snooks said.

Brookmill Park had been extensively redeveloped during construction of the Docklands Light Railway. There were ornamental gardens and a decent-sized nature reserve. The footpath that wound alongside the Ravensbourne River was part of a longer one running south from the Thames at Creekside all the way to the coast at Eastbourne.

They sat on a bench near one of the ponds, with Jacky perched between Frank and Clive. The water was thick at the edges with brown blanket-weed, and butterflies moved near the surface, dancing over the heads of moorhens and Canada geese.

'It's drugs, for definite.' Jacky slapped a hand down on his leg for emphasis. 'I've caught a conversation or two and I know exactly what those toe-rags are talking about.'

'Coke? Crack? What?' Clive asked.

'Doesn't make any difference,' Frank said.

He wasn't surprised – it usually came down to drugs in the end. But he had wanted to make sure. If the gang whose members frequented the Cue Up was the one he was after, he preferred to know what manner of animal he was up against. He knew that some of these crews were simple strong-arm merchants; postcode gangs, fighting over territory. Others were no more than oversized rap groups. There

141

were even a couple, just a couple, formed out of a sincere commitment to non-violence. Frank sensed he was looking for an altogether different type, one whose upper echelons had a highly developed and determined business ethic.

It didn't matter what they were selling. The simple fact that they *were* selling told him enough. Frank knew very well that businessmen could be a damn sight more dangerous than thugs.

'Let's have some names, Jacky.'

'They're just like nicknames, you know?'

'That's fine.'

Jacky took a few seconds, then reeled off half a dozen names while Clive scribbled them down. Frank pushed harder: demanded descriptions, times of any regular visits to the club, information as to where else these characters might spend any time; anything Jacky might have gathered about a hierarchy.

Jacky did his best.

'You noticed anything different, last couple of days?'

'I'm not with you, Mr Linnell.'

Clive leaned into him. 'Fucking *concentrate*, Jacky.'

'Changes in behaviour,' Frank said. 'You know? A different atmosphere, a different mood. You can smell it.' He couldn't say precisely how the change would manifest itself, but Frank knew that, among the gang responsible for Paul's death, things would now be a little different. A police officer was dead and they would surely be smart enough to know what the repercussions might be. Whoever was calling the shots could say 'business as usual' until he was blue in the face, but, for the foreseeable future, nothing would be quite as it had been.

Frank had been in a similar position himself, as had Clive. Both knew that marked men could never fully relax.

Jacky grunted and nodded again, like something had come back to him. 'Now you mention it, I *have* noticed one or two of them acting a bit funny. Yeah, thinking about it—'

'Don't just tell me what you think I want to hear.' Frank's anger was sudden, and alarming; even to Jacky, who had been on the receiving end of it before. He stood up, the volume dropping as he walked towards the water. 'Do *not* piss me about.'

Clive dropped a meaty hand onto Jacky's shoulder and said, 'Look, I'd prefer to get this over with, tell you the truth. I'd like to get back in the car and find somewhere to have a nice bit of lunch, a decent glass of wine, whatever. But if you carry on treating us like morons, I *will* march you into those trees over there and stick your head so far up your arse you'll think nothing's happened. Fair enough, Jacky?'

Frank sat down again, leaned back on the bench.

'Look, I don't know if this is what you're talking about,' Jacky said. 'But there haven't been so many of them knocking around.' He looked from Clive to Frank, checking to see how he was doing. 'There's usually a few of them in every day, playing pool, having a laugh, whatever. But not so much in the last couple of days.'

'What about before that?'

'Before?'

'You see anything going on a week or so ago? Get the impression there was anything being set up?'

Jacky thought, then told Frank about the meeting upstairs: the young black guy with the stupid hair and his big Asian mate; the white bloke in the smart suit.

Frank looked at Clive, who shrugged and made a note of it.

Back at the car, Frank watched Jacky Snooks hurry away with enough money in his pockets to keep him in tea and toast for six months. He was probably no more than forty, but looked closer to Frank's age than Clive's.

There were plenty of people like him in their world.

Frank studied the scrawny figure in his grubby jacket and Asda jeans and knew that, when it came down to it, there was not a great deal separating the two of them. Or hadn't been, back when paths were chosen; when futures were decided in violent moments or flashes of brilliance. There wasn't very much between him and the likes of Jacky Snooks. He'd been a little more desperate, that was all. A little less scared, maybe.

But not much.

Helen woke up and looked at the clock: 3.18 a.m. She reached down and felt the wetness between her legs.

She waited for the cab downstairs, swearing out loud at Paul and wondering if she should call Jenny, or her father. Sweating. Carrying her wash bag and a change of clothes in a near-to-bursting plastic bag.

At the hospital, she was told that everything was normal.

'It's just spotting,' the midwife said, 'and baby is fine. There's nothing to worry about. Baby isn't coming just yet. He's perfectly happy where he is, OK?'

'Go home,' the nurse told her, 'and put your feet up. Relax and let the baby's father wait on you until the time comes. Everything's fine.'

SEVENTEEN

Some days, Theo might have called in to his mum's place on his way out. He would have checked everything was OK with her and eaten a bacon sandwich if he wasn't still stuffed from twin dinners the night before. He would have walked Angela to the bus stop on those days, or all the way to school if the weather was nice.

He was still getting himself up and out of the flat good and early, but he hadn't been round to his mum's since the previous Friday. He'd taken to eating breakfast on his own at a greasy spoon. Studying the newspapers and letting shit slop round in his head, like how it would be for Benjamin to grow up without a father around.

How it would be to think about that in prison.

Twenty fags every morning from the newsagent two doors along. A pile of papers several inches thick and a look on the newsagent's face that was the highpoint of the day. The old man never said anything, just how much it all cost, but you could see he thought it was odd. Boys like Theo weren't supposed to read one newspaper, let alone half a dozen, and certainly not the big ones without the scratch-cards inside. He smiled when he took the money, like he thought it was a good thing. Like he *approved*. Or maybe he just enjoyed taking the money.

In the café, Theo bit into his sandwich and looked at the front pages first, same as he'd done every morning since it had happened.

The police were drafting in another fifty officers; stepping up the hunt for the 'headlights' killer.

The Commissioner was promising that the man responsible for the death of his officer would be found and was urging anyone who might be shielding him to step forward.

The killer was ruthless and cowardly. Someone who thought that guns earned respect. He was probably no more than a teenager, or even *younger*, according to experts on London's booming gangs and gun culture.

Theo didn't see Easy come in, but turned fast when he heard the voice at his shoulder.

'You want something else, T? A latte or some rubbish? Maybe a croissant or whatever, to go with your morning reading.'

'I'm OK,' Theo said.

Easy went to fetch himself tea and when he came back he grabbed a folded *Daily Star* from an adjacent table. He dropped it in front of Theo and jabbed at the bikini-clad model taking up most of the front page. '*That's* the way to start your day, man. Some of that good stuff get you up and at the punters out there, you get me?'

Theo started to gather up his papers.

Easy nodded and leaned forward. Lowered his voice, nice and serious. 'I know what's happening here, T, but you got no reason to be fretting about all this, I swear. You got a solid crew round you, man. Hundred per cent.'

'The police are fired up, though.'

Easy shook his head, not interested.

'Seriously, you should read this stuff.'

'*Fuck* the police.' Easy looked round, like he was searching for somewhere to spit. 'They don't even know where to start looking. The Five-O are nothing. For real, T.'

Theo nodded and laid the pile of papers to one side. Easy leaned back and grinned the grin.

Subject closed.

'Now, we still on for tonight?'

'On for what?'

'I still need that innocent face.'

'Shit.' The job Easy had been talking about a couple of days before. Theo had forgotten all about it. 'I've hardly seen Javine and the baby in days, man,' he said. 'I'm working my bollocks off, you know?'

He was working longer hours, that much was true. Spending as much time apart from the family as he could get away with. Carefully avoiding anyone who cared.

Easy wasn't having any of it. 'You got to be *doing* this stuff, man. Last thing you need right now is to sit about and let all this mess with you, you get me? Besides, kind of job we're doing tonight, that's the reason you shot into that bitch's car in the first place, isn't it?'

The reason . . .

It was money, Theo supposed. Or respect, like the bigger newspapers said. Although, thinking back to the moment he pulled the trigger, it felt like he'd done it mainly because Easy and the others had been shouting and taking the piss. He told Easy that it was a stupid question, because he didn't know *what* they were going to be doing.

'It'll be a laugh,' Easy said. 'I swear.' He stood up, taking the *Star* with him and promising to call Theo later with the details.

Theo finished his sandwich, then went outside to smoke. He took a paper with him and stood on the pavement, looking down at the picture of Paul Hopwood. The thirty-four-year-old. The expectant father. Kept looking until the soft worm of ash fell onto the paper and he had to shake it away.

More shit, slopping about.

The entire sequence of ideas and impulses took no more than a few seconds, but Helen enjoyed watching the different expressions pass across

Ray Jackson's face, trying to interpret them, as he eased the taxi off his front drive and turned onto the road.

The confusion at seeing a woman trying to flag him down outside his own front door. The momentary dilemma when he saw her shape. The 'sorry, love, nothing I can do' shrug as he made his decision and put his foot down, wanting to get a full English inside him before picking up any fares, least of all mad women.

The anger, then the resignation, when he saw the warrant card being waved. As he slammed on the anchors and pulled over.

Helen walked up to the window, waited until it was wound down. 'Turn the engine off please, Ray, and hop in the back. We can have a natter in there.'

It was a neat little side street in North Acton. Mid-twenties terracing; trees in blossom outside every other house, lined up as nicely as the satellite dishes. Jackson did as he was told and held the door open as Helen climbed into the cab. She thanked him and he said it was all right, but could they get a fucking shift on, because he had a living to make. She said that she'd try not to hold him up.

'You had a passenger in the back of your cab, a police officer, on Friday, the eighteenth of last month. And on the Friday before that.'

'Which one?' Jackson asked.

'Sorry?'

Jackson took a couple of seconds. 'Which Friday?'

'You're not listening, Ray. *Both.* An afternoon and then an evening.'

'You got any idea how many passengers I carry every week?'

'You picked him up outside the NCP on Brewer Street.'

'I'll take your word for it.'

'You don't have to. We've got both pick-ups on CCTV.'

'So? Did I break the speed limit somewhere?'

'I'd like to know where you took him,' Helen said. 'I'd like to know who the other passenger was. The man who was already in the cab when you made the pick-up on Brewer Street.'

Jackson was fifty-something and solid. If Helen did not already know

148

that he was someone comfortable with a certain degree of violence, it would have been clear enough when he turned to look at her.

'I don't have to talk to you. I've done nothing. So, you can get out of my cab now.'

'I'm not finished,' Helen said.

'Sorry, love, that's me done.' He turned to look out of the window. 'Shouldn't you be at home knitting bootees, anyway?'

Helen swallowed. 'The police officer I'm talking about was killed a week ago.' She let that sink in. 'So, you *do* have to talk to me, or at least you do if you don't want us all over you like shit on a blanket for the foreseeable future. Everybody's done *something*, Ray, and you more than most. So, it's probably easier if we get this over with now, wouldn't you say?'

It was all nonsense, of course. There was no reason why even those officers who *were* investigating Paul's death would be interested in a taxi ride he'd taken a fortnight earlier. Helen gambled on Jackson not knowing that, and she was right.

He swore for a while, gathering himself or editing information in his head before he began to spit it out. He told Helen about one particular client he drove sometimes; a respectable businessman for whom he worked on an exclusive basis, alongside his regular fares.

'Sounds like a decent whack,' Helen said. 'Cash in hand?' She smiled at the reaction. 'Don't worry, I'm not the taxman.'

Jackson nodded. 'A lot of the cabbies are doing the same thing these days,' he said. 'There's a demand. We're cheaper than a limo service and we don't get lost.'

'This businessman knows who's driving his cab, does he?' Helen waited, but Jackson wasn't coming up with an answer. 'See, if he knows all about Parkhurst and Belmarsh and the reasons why you were in there, and he's *still* happy for you to chauffeur him about, I've got to ask myself just how "respectable" he is. Can't see Alan Sugar taking you on, can you, Ray?'

'It was all a good while ago.'

'Where did you take them? Your boss and the police officer?'

Jackson said that he couldn't remember where he'd driven to on the Friday afternoon Helen was asking about, or whether the two passengers had left the cab together. The evening job was to a restaurant in Shoreditch; Italian place. He couldn't remember the name.

'Any idea what they talked about?'

'I wasn't invited.'

'What about in the cab?'

'I never listen.'

Helen doubted that very much, but she could see that she wasn't going to get a fat lot more. As she slipped her notebook back into her bag, she noticed the faded stain on the carpet at her feet.

'What's that, Ray?' Her tone made it clear enough that she knew the answer already.

Jackson smiled. 'I don't think this copper died in the back of my cab.'

Helen said nothing; thinking about the state of her sheets, the two hours she'd spent at the hospital in the middle of the night. She reached down to scratch at the stain with a fingernail.

'Some twat had a nosebleed,' Jackson said. 'Fair enough?'

'They can be nasty . . .'

He opened the door and stepped out, waited for Helen to do the same.

'My car's parked at the end of the road,' she said.

Jackson opened the door wider. 'Shouldn't take too long to walk there then.'

Ollie and Gospel had been working a corner near the Lee Bridge end of the shopping centre since lunchtime. Now, it was just starting to get dark and Ollie reckoned they'd done about two hundred pounds' worth of business in the last eight hours. Two hundred and thirty, as soon as Gospel got back with the three rocks their latest customer was waiting for.

Wave would have to be seriously happy with those sorts of figures.

Ollie looked across the road at the short white man in the doorway opposite. He was a bit older than the usual punter, and a bit less jittery. He was staring straight back at Ollie, like he was asking the question. Ollie held one hand up, fingers spread.

Give it five minutes . . .

It had been ten, maybe more, since Gospel had left for the stash house with the punter's money. She was one of the quickest, too; didn't waste time gassing while she was handing over the cash. Ollie was starting to wonder if there might be a problem when his mobile rang.

He recognised Gospel's number on the display. 'Where the fuck are you?'

The man's voice was very deep and very calm. 'Your girlfriend's a bit busy, you hear me? Now shut your hole and listen.'

Ollie listened as he was given instructions: told where to go, to get there as quickly as he could and to talk to nobody on his way. He was already moving, but in no particular direction, weaving up and down the same few feet of pavement, his mind racing, the sweat starting to prickle all over his body.

'This is a big mistake, man.' He almost dropped the phone when he heard Gospel scream.

'Don't make me do that again,' the man said.

Ollie looked across the road and saw that his punter had gone. When he stepped back from the kerb, the man was at his shoulder. Leaning in good and close, so that Ollie could feel what he had in his pocket.

'I think you should do as you're told.'

From Acton, Helen drove down to the Uxbridge Road, pulled into a side street, and picked up a bus into the centre of town. She did not want to spend an hour trying to park and enjoyed watching the world go by from the top deck, but she started to regret making the trip at all from the moment she arrived. It was a hot day and the streets were crowded. It took her fifteen minutes to walk from Marble Arch to John Lewis, and when she got there the smell in the perfume department made her feel as though she might throw up at any moment.

Once she started to feel a bit better, she pottered very slowly around the maternity departments of Lewis's and a few other big stores. She remembered that the cot they had bought six months before was still boxed up in the small bedroom, waiting to be assembled. That there was still painting to be done. She bought packs of baby-grows even though she already had more than enough, and a plastic plate, mug and cutlery set that would not be needed for at least six months.

She trudged from shop to shop, sweating until she could smell herself.

Helen was not the happiest of shoppers at the best of times, had always been a 'get in, buy it and get out' woman. Jenny had laughed about it, said it was unnatural that any woman did not enjoy browsing. That somehow the shopping genes had not been divvied up equally between them.

Today, she browsed for hours, stroking the clothes and picking up the tiny pairs of shoes. She just needed to think about the baby for a while. About *herself* and the baby.

By five o'clock, when she got back to Tulse Hill, she felt like she'd run a marathon. There was the usual slew of messages on the machine: her dad and Jennie; Roger Deering again; Paul's mum saying that she knew there had been no decision made about a date yet, but that she *really* wanted to talk about music for the service. Two other callers had not bothered to leave messages.

Helen lay down on the sofa, wondering who to call back first. When she woke up three hours later, the room was dark. She opened her eyes and her first thought was of Paul, going somewhere he shouldn't in the back of Ray Jackson's cab. She thought about blood on a carpet and blood on a pavement.

And she felt ashamed of herself.

It was a week, *less* than a week, and already he was starting to disappear; the Paul she *thought* she knew, at any rate. And this was not about memory playing tricks or perception being warped by grief. This was her own stupid fault. She'd become too curious for her own good.

For anyone's good.

Would it not be better if she stopped now, forgot everything she'd found out, everything she'd begun to suspect? After all, whatever she thought Paul might have been up to, she didn't *know*, not for sure. Did any of it matter anyway, now that he was dead?

It was not a difficult question. That was another way in which Helen differed from her sister. She could never bury her head in the sand.

She turned on the lights and drew the curtains; made herself a cup of tea and sat down to write a list.

- Cot assembly. Ask Dad. Painting?
- Music. Hymns? Something modern. REM, maybe.
- Talk to Frank Linnell and Kevin Shepherd?

She jumped at the buzzer. It took her half a minute to get to the intercom, by which time whoever had been downstairs at the front door had already gone.

Ollie had walked fast along Loampit Vale, with the man who had posed as a customer walking twenty feet behind him all the way. He had turned off where he'd been told, to find the Mercedes waiting near the entrance to Tesco's.

Gospel was sitting in the passenger seat with her knees drawn up to her chest. A large black man sat next to her, squeezed behind the wheel. Ollie was ushered into the back by the older man, and they pulled away, with Gospel screaming abuse as the car went round the block then eased into traffic on the main road.

They drove north for ten minutes or so.

Ollie had got to know his companions well enough by the time the Mercedes turned onto side streets just shy of the river. They parked behind a smart development of executive apartments at Deptford Creek and talked some more. The light on top of Canary Wharf winked at them from across the water, and the tip of the Gherkin poked through the smog away to their left. Through the car window, Ollie could see the derelict wooden pier crumbling into the water, and a drifting necklace of long-abandoned motorised torpedo boats that had been home to a series of squatters for many years. The dirty-green water was deep here; deeper than anywhere else in the river. The only stretch in which the big aircraft-carriers could turn – he'd seen that on television some time – and probably the safest if you wanted things to sink and stay hidden.

By now, the man in the back with Ollie had a gun laid across his knee, but the big man up front with Gospel was clearly the one running things.

'It's not complicated,' he said. 'We just need confirmation, really.'

Gospel spat into the big man's chest, then whipped her head around to Ollie. 'Don't say shit.' When she turned around again, the big man punched her hard in the face, then stared down at the spit on his shirt.

There was a second or two before the girl began to moan and splutter; before she cupped her hands to try and collect the blood.

'This won't take a minute,' the big man said to Ollie. 'But that's enough time to decide whether you're going to be stupid or not.' He reached into his pocket for a handkerchief, then demanded one from his colleague on the back seat. The older man passed his own forward. The big man handed one handkerchief to Gospel, and used the other to dab first at his shirt, then at the gobbets of blood that had dripped onto the seat.

He looked at Gospel and sighed. 'How old are you?'

'She's fourteen,' Ollie said. 'Please . . .'

'Fucking *shut* up,' Gospel shouted, moving her hands away from her face just long enough to get the words out.

'You should be at school,' the man said. 'The pair of you.' He leaned across as though he might stroke her hair, but instead grabbed a handful of it and smashed her head back into the side window.

Ollie shouted out in shock and banged his fists against the passenger seat. He felt the gun being jabbed into his side and when he leaned back again, still shouting, he realised that he was crying. 'Jesus . . .'

In the front, Gospel's eyes were wide. Her breathing was heavy and wet.

The big man turned round to look at Ollie. Said, 'She's fine.'

'Say nothing,' Gospel spluttered.

The man rolled his eyes then turned them on Ollie. 'If you weren't actually involved in the incident we're talking about, you've got nothing to worry about. That's a promise. We just need to know that we're on the right lines.'

Ollie was rocking back and forth, tearing at his dreads. It was hard to think straight when he was focusing so hard on not shitting himself, right there in the car.

'Was it your crew?'

It felt like the gun was going to break through his skin at any moment. Push right through the ribs.

The big man shifted around in his seat, grunting with the effort and draping one arm across the headrest. 'Don't make me swap seats with my friend back there,' he said. 'He's not as gentle with young girls as I am.'

The old man laughed and blew Gospel a kiss.

There was a little more blood after that, but not too much, and when all the information that was required had been given, Ollie and Gospel were told to get out of the car. To take the soiled handkerchiefs with them.

As Ollie reached for the door, the older man dragged him back. Said, 'You're *white*, for crying out loud, and you've got black man's hair. What's all *that* about then, you silly cunt?'

The older man moved into the front. As they drove away, he fastened his seat belt and took a last look at the two teenagers in the rear-view. He saw the boy sink to the floor; watched the girl start lashing out at him with fists and feet.

'World's gone mad, Clive, you ask me.'

'Tell me about it, Billy,' Clive said.

EIGHTEEN

'Where d'you get the suit?'

'Charity shop,' Easy said.

'It stinks, man.'

They were in a line of slow traffic moving across Vauxhall Bridge, heading for an address in Paddington. Easy was driving the Audi, with Theo in the passenger seat. Mikey sat in the back, flicking through a copy of *Loot*.

'I didn't have time to get it dry-cleaned, you get me?' Easy glanced over. 'It looks OK, that's the main thing. A smart suit and that nice, innocent face.'

Theo didn't own a suit as such, but he had a few decent jackets. Designer stuff, nicer than the ill-fitting, stinky shit he had on now at any rate. But he had not wanted to leave the flat in his best gear; to try to explain to Javine why he was getting dressed up. Easy said that it didn't matter, that he'd take care of everything. He'd picked up the suit earlier in the day and Theo had got changed in the car.

'I can't find this damn ad,' Mikey said.

'Keep going,' Easy said. 'It's the section at the back, after the caravans.

I've circled the ones we can do tonight.'

Mikey turned the pages, and read: '"Dark Desire. Curvy ebony princess". Curvy means fat, right?'

'Yeah,' Easy said. 'Probably got bigger tits than you.' Mikey stuck one finger up above the paper, waved it at the mirror. Easy shrugged and accelerated towards an amber light. 'Listen, long as the bitch has been getting plenty of business, I don't care *how* big she is.'

They pulled up twenty-five minutes later at the end of a road between St Mary's Hospital and the station. Theo checked the number of the flat and Easy ran through things one last time.

'Ten minutes should be about right,' he said. 'Just to make sure she's nice and relaxed.'

'He's the nervous one, innit?' Mikey said. He leaned forward and poked Theo in the shoulder. 'If it ever got into the bedroom, I reckon he'd be limp, man, like a dead worm.'

Theo got out of the car and walked to the door of the flat without looking back. The road was well lit and he wondered how many people would be able to see his face if they were staring out of their windows at that moment.

The woman who answered the bell was not as large as Mikey had predicted, but there was plenty of her. She was in her forties and darker skinned than Theo. Nigerian, he reckoned. Her make-up was serious and he thought her hair was probably a wig, but the smile looked genuine enough.

He could see how a man, one who hadn't come here to rob her, might find her sexy.

'I'm Carlton,' he said. 'I called earlier to make an appointment.' It was Easy who had made the call. He had picked the name too, and enjoyed telling Theo all about it.

The ground-floor flat was small: a living room with a galley kitchen off it and a doorway through to what Theo guessed were a bedroom and a bathroom. It was clean and modern. There was a row of African masks above a dark leather sofa. There were smooth stones in wooden bowls and a curtain of beads separating the living room from the rest of the place.

'You like a drink, lover? There's wine and beer, or Coke.'

'Can I have a beer?'

'Whatever you want.'

She handed Theo a warm bottle and held aside the curtain of beads. 'You want to come through?'

Theo sat down and raised his bottle. 'I'll finish this.'

'It's your time,' she said. 'Speaking of which . . .'

Easy had agreed to a hundred pounds on the phone. That would cover one hour and all the basics. Theo handed over the cash and watched as she put it into a small wooden trunk against the wall.

She handed him a laminated card. Said, 'In case you want any extras.'

Easy looked at the card as if he were studying a menu, while she played the part of the helpful waitress, asking if there was anything he wanted explaining. There were a couple of items he wasn't too clear about, but he was happy to stay in the dark.

'How old are you?' she asked.

Theo saw no reason to lie.

'I've got a boy about your age,' she said. 'And a girl two years younger. She's at school and he's going to university next year.'

'OK.'

'We're doing all right,' she said. 'Doing very nicely.' She grinned and cupped her breasts, jiggled them, her black bra visible through the sheer housecoat. 'Thanks to these.'

Theo had been inside the flat no more than five minutes. 'I need to go and get some cigarettes,' he said.

'I have some.' She took a packet from her handbag.

'No, I need Silk Cut. I'll nip across the road.'

She shrugged. 'Up to you. The clock's running though . . .'

Theo walked out into the narrow corridor and opened the front door. When he walked back into the living room fifteen seconds later,

Mikey and Easy were following him.

Both were wearing balaclavas and pointing handguns.

'Don't scream,' Theo said.

'Don't *fucking* scream.' Easy pushed past him, moved fast towards the woman, the gun pointed high, at her head. Held sideways.

She staggered back against the wall and dropped to the floor, her eyes wide.

'Where's the cash?'

Theo showed him, then stood back as Easy took the money from the trunk. 'There's about a grand here,' Easy said. 'Bet she's got plenty more, under the bed, somewhere.'

'There's nothing else,' the woman said.

'Shut her up.' Easy nodded to Mikey and pushed through the curtain of beads. Mikey dug out a thick roll of black gaffer tape from the plastic bag he was carrying and pulled the woman to her feet.

Theo saw the look on Mikey's face. 'Just tie her up,' he said.

He followed Easy into the bedroom, watched as he emptied out drawers and overturned the mattress. There were candles burning on the window ledge and a small metal bowl filled with condoms by the side of the bed.

'Why are we doing this?'

'You see that cash, man?'

'Why the likes of her?'

Easy smiled, only too happy to reveal his genius. 'Because the likes of her don't go crying to the police so much. Piece of piss.'

'It doesn't need three of us, man.'

'It never hurts to be careful, T.' Easy opened a drawer, casually emptied out underwear. 'A few of these bitches have maids and shit. Filipinos and Thais. Some of them know kung fu and all that.'

'You've got a *gun*,' Theo said.

Easy made a face like he didn't understand, and carried on trashing the room.

When they went back into the living room, Mikey was sitting next to the woman on the sofa. Her hands and feet had been bound together, and the thick black tape had been wound tight around her head and shoulders. A sliver of flesh was visible below her nose; left uncovered so that she could breathe. Her eyes had been left uncovered, too. Theo wondered if that was because Mikey had wanted to see her reaction.

Mikey waved Theo over and handed him his mobile. 'Get a picture,' he said. 'Show everyone.'

With a whoop, Easy crashed down onto the sofa on the other side of the woman and leaned in close to her.

'Come on, man,' Mikey said. 'Take a couple.'

Theo held up the phone and framed the picture.

'Give us a smile,' Mikey said. The woman moaned behind the tape. Easy thought that was funny and said so. Mikey put one arm round the woman, leered at the camera and placed a fat hand over each of her breasts. 'So smile with your eyes then,' he said.

Theo took the picture and tossed the phone back to Mikey.

The next one that Easy had circled was ten minutes away, in Bayswater. A dominatrix calling herself Vixen, who had been happy to take the money from a nervous young boy who needed a little discipline.

Fifteen minutes after opening her front door, she was tied to a chair in her bedroom, struggling to breathe through the mask of black tape.

Theo had watched Mikey work. He had seemed more agitated this time, as had Easy. They had been rougher; angry that there wasn't more money on the premises.

'Bitch not dominating anybody *now*,' Mikey said, when he'd finished.

'I thought there were plenty of freaky fucks who liked this weird stuff,' Easy said. 'Whips and dressing up like babies.'

'Maybe she's giving it away too cheap.' Mikey bent down and gently slapped the woman's face. It sounded dull and wet against the tape.

'We should go,' Theo said.

Mikey wandered off towards the kitchen like they had all the time in the world.

'Relax, T,' Easy said.

'I'm fine. Can't see the point in hanging around, that's all. What if she has another appointment?'

'We paid for an hour,' Easy said.

'There's nothing else here.'

Easy walked around the bedroom as though there were plenty for him to enjoy, picking up sex toys, pulling faces. 'Look at all this stuff. I don't even know what some of this shit *does*, man.' He picked up a black latex bondage mask and pulled it over his head.

'Come on, E, leave it.'

'This smells rank, man.' Easy walked back to the chair and leaned down close to the woman's face. Said, 'Snap.'

Mikey came back in from the kitchen carrying a small knife. He knelt down next to the chair and raised his hand.

'What's that for?' Theo asked.

'I'm helping her to breathe,' Mikey said. 'Listen to the poor bitch snorting and puffing.' He placed the tip of the knife against the tape. Said, 'You'd best open your mouth nice and wide if you don't want to get cut up.'

The woman howled behind the tape, but it came out like the whine of something electrical.

Theo took a step forwards, but Easy raised a hand, and Theo watched as Mikey cut a hole in the tape. Saw a red bead bloom, and dribble down the gaffer onto the woman's neck.

'Shit,' Theo said. 'You've cut her.'

'It's nothing.' Mikey got to his feet. 'She's fine. See?' He wiped a hand across his mouth and began to undo his jeans. 'That's perfect.'

The woman continued to howl, rocking on the chair.

'The hell you *doing*?' Theo shouted.

Mikey ignored him, and grinned at Easy. 'You should do it with that mask on,' he said.

Theo said, 'I'm going to the car,' and backed away towards the door. Easy shouted something at him but Theo couldn't hear above the noise in his head, above the woman's whine, as he walked quickly out of the flat and jogged down to the street.

Ten minutes later Easy and Mikey came out. Theo watched them in the mirror as they strolled along the pavement like they were taking the evening air. They were both grinning when they slid into the car.

Theo looked at them.

'We didn't *do* anything,' Easy said. He started the car. 'What do you think?'

Theo thought plenty, but he kept it to himself as they drove away. Easy and Mikey talked enough for all three of them; gabbling about the cash and the buzz of it, and the big fat spliffs they were going to enjoy when they got back to their ends.

After fifteen minutes or so, when they'd crossed the river, Theo said, 'Why d'you need to wear balaclavas anyway?'

Mikey leaned forward from the back. 'Stupid fucking question.'

'What's your point, man?' Easy asked.

'Just seems like, if it all goes tits up, only face anyone sees, anyone can describe, is mine.'

My innocent face . . .

'Can't be helped. Don't make no sense them knowing what we *all* look like.'

'*I* know what you look like,' Theo said.

The Audi slowed and stopped for lights. Theo manufactured a smile and lightened his tone; tried to make it clear he was joking. 'So maybe you should bear that fact in mind when we're splitting up the cash later on.' He turned to Mikey. 'You check me, blood?' Then he looked at Easy. Neither of them seemed to find it very funny.

NINETEEN

There was a late-night grocer's a few streets down and Helen always enjoyed the conversations with the grizzled Turkish owner and his wife. Tonight's had been more difficult, as she'd taken the opportunity to tell them about Paul. They had been lovely, asked if there was anything they could do to help, and Helen could see the man hesitate about charging her when she took out her purse to pay.

She headed slowly back up Tulse Hill, with bread, milk and several packets of cheese-and-onion crisps in a plastic bag. It was a warm night, but the wind was building. Traffic on its way to or from the South Circular roared by her in the dark as she walked.

Past the row of odd, thirties houses whose mock-Tudor beams and pebbledash always struck her as bizarre. Past blocks much like her own: Baldwin House, Saunders House, Hart House; four or five storeys in every conceivable shade of brown that had probably been desirable in their day. Past the entrance to Silwell Hall, a nineteenth-century mansion now home to St Martin's in the Field High School for Girls. The ornate pillars and domed roof had been there far longer than the school itself, but still it had easily outlasted both local fifties-built secondaries, including the one Ken Livingstone had attended.

Helen turned off the hill and dug into her bag for her keys. Thinking about schools: about the shortage of decent ones in areas where she could afford to buy; about maybe getting out of London before it became an issue. As she approached the main doors of her block, she saw a man step out of a car on the other side of the road and walk towards her. He was tall, with shoulder-length blond hair. Well dressed, but even so . . .

She saw him look at her and gripped her key a little tighter. It was the closest thing she had to a weapon. The man kept coming, and she felt stupidly grateful for the automatic security light that came on as she neared the door.

She took the last few steps as quickly as she could. Heard the man behind her, the change rattling in his pocket. She reached towards the lock and he moved up close to her, as if he were another resident waiting for her to open the door for them both.

'You're the girlfriend.'

'I'm sorry?'

'Soon as Ray described you, I figured it out. Who you were, and the fact that you were talking to him off your own bat.' He smiled. 'That you weren't there in any . . . official capacity.'

Helen looked. Figured out who *he* was.

Kevin Shepherd put his hands in his trouser pockets and took a step back. As though he wanted to get a good look at her.

'Did you want something?' she asked.

'See, Ray's not the sharpest knife in the drawer,' he said. 'Claps eyes on a warrant card and makes all sorts of presumptions. Well, most of us do, don't we? But I know all about what happened to Paul and it's pretty obvious that whoever's investigating it isn't looking at the likes of me.'

Helen waited. He clearly had plenty more to say for himself.

'Probably looking for someone a bit younger than me. A bit *blacker*. And even if your boyfriend hadn't just been unlucky, been in the wrong place at the wrong time . . . even if he'd been shot in the head, I don't think they'd be sending someone like you after whoever did it. No offence.'

Helen shrugged, like there was none taken.

'Certainly not on their own, at any rate.'

'So?'

'So, you're probably just trying to work out what Paul's doing knocking around with me. You're thinking the two of us wouldn't normally have much in common.'

'You going to tell me?'

'I'm telling you that it might be best to leave it.' There was a good deal of concern in his voice. It was how many threats were issued.

'Best for who?'

He nodded at her. 'Jesus, love, look at the state of you. You should be thinking about the future, about how you're going to cope. Trying to get hold of a nice, black maternity dress.' He shook his head, turned the concern up another notch. 'Why go around digging shit up? Asking questions you might not like the answers to?'

It was the same question Helen had asked herself. Now she was standing in front of the man who knew the answer. Who looked as though he was itching to tell her.

'Well, thanks for the warning.'

'Not a warning.'

'Whatever.' She stared hard at him. She wanted to go inside, but not before he'd been the one to turn and walk away. Suddenly the light went off. They'd been virtually motionless for two minutes and the lamp had timed out. 'Time to leave,' she said.

A few feet away from her in the darkness, Shepherd sighed, as though he'd been pushed into a corner. Given no choice but to reveal what he'd far rather have kept to himself.

'Look, if it helps, just tell yourself that he needed a bit more money coming in, what with a kid on the way. That he was doing it for you.'

'I don't believe you.'

'Come on, it's not like he's the first copper I've done business with. You telling me you've never known anybody find three kilos of coke and hand in two? Nobody who ever helped himself?'

Helen felt the sweat prickle and start to run. The key was warm and wet in her fist. 'Did you ever give money to Paul?'

'Never had the chance, unfortunately, but we discussed the terms. He'd've done all right out of it, I can promise you that. You wouldn't have gone short of baby clothes.'

'Fuck off!' she said.

'Language . . .'

She repeated it, and, after a few seconds, Shepherd did as he was told. His movement reactivated the security light, and Helen watched as he jogged back across the road to his car. Change jangling, digging for the remote. She heard him push the music up loud once he'd turned the ignition, and saw him look back at her, just before the light inside the car faded and he drove away.

Faster than he needed to.

Afterwards it took her a few seconds longer than normal to get inside. She stood at the door like a drunkard, the key tapping and scraping against the lock as she tried to steady the tremble in her hand.

Mikey had started thinking about a visit to Linzi's while he'd been busy with Easy and Theo, and now, walking home from her place, he wondered why doing that kind of stuff made him so horny.

Linzi wasn't a whore, not really. She only took money from a couple of the boys, her favourite ones, and she certainly wasn't like any of those skanky bitches they'd visited earlier. She was sweet and knew what he liked. She said he looked nice without any clothes on, that she liked something to get hold of, and she always told him good stories about the others afterwards, when the spliff came out. Funny shit about how SnapZ had a tiny dick, or the way As If had cried once after she'd wanked him off.

Priceless . . .

He stopped thinking about why he'd gone. Decided that it didn't matter, that at the end of the day he couldn't think of a better way to spend some of the cash he'd made that night. They'd divided it up back at Easy's, then spun down to the Dirty South for a few drinks: bright blue Hypnotics all round. He'd cruised the main bar for an hour, shown some of the crew the pictures on his phone and flashed a few big notes around.

Until he'd felt like walking across to Linzi's place all the more.

Now, he was hungry . . .

It was only five minutes back to the estate, but he didn't want to risk waking his mum by rattling around in the kitchen, and then getting screamed at. He decided to cut over onto the main road, pick up something from one of the kebab places that stayed open late.

He turned the corner and saw the old man walking towards him; saw him look up and then drop his eyes to the pavement. He knew that he scared people like this. He pulled up his hood and dropped a shoulder to put a little more meat into the swagger; to put the terrors into the old boy.

One last buzz before bed.

He walked past, pushing the shoulder close, letting the poor fool think he had something coming. With his hood forward he never saw the old man's reaction. Never saw him stop a few feet on and reach into the pocket of his coat.

Mikey only realised what was going on when he heard his name called and turned around. A second or two before the gun was raised and the old man shot him in the face.

While Mikey was still dropping hard, the old man was turning and walking quickly away. Hands in his pockets. Still muttering about how the world was going mad.

Javine smelled wonderful: cocoa-butter on her neck and something sweet and citrus in her hair. He pressed himself against her, hands roaming across her back and buttocks as she pushed her tongue into his mouth, but still he stayed soft beneath her fingers.

She moved her mouth away from his and whispered. 'Don't you want to?'

'I'm tired.'

'You don't seem tired.'

He untangled himself and rolled away. 'So how do I *seem*?'

There was an engine racing in the street below, voices raised.

'Like you want to fight.' She raised the pillow behind her. 'Like you're *happier* having a fight.'

'You're talking rubbish.'

'It's been nearly a week.'

He let out a long, slow breath. 'I'm working more, all right?'

'I know . . .'

'You not happy with the extra money?'

'Yeah, I'm happy.'

'So stop having a go.'

Javine didn't say anything else, and soon the silence between them threatened to drown out the noise from the street. Theo was relieved when she turned her head at the whimper from the next room, and threw back the duvet.

He'd left the Dirty South before the others, content to leave them there taking the praise and milking it. He thought he'd slipped in quietly enough, but Javine had turned over, called out his name in the dark as he'd been getting undressed and talked herself awake.

Asked him how his night had been.

He'd come away from Easy's with four hundred pounds, knowing that the three of them had made at least a grand and a half. Maybe he'd been right. Maybe Easy was taking a slice in return for the part he'd played in moving him up; for giving him the break. Maybe Easy didn't think he'd *earned* a proper cut. He didn't know what Mikey's share had been, hadn't wanted to talk about it with him there.

But he'd find out tomorrow. Ask Easy what was going on.

He lay there and tried to concentrate on the money; to make it about the cash and the things it could buy. It was easier to do that than think about how he'd made it, and what he'd done to be in that position.

'Besides, kind of job we're doing tonight, that's the reason you shot into that bitch's car in the first place, isn't it?'

Thinking back a week, it felt like being scared of heights and jumping because that was the easiest way to stop being afraid.

'Lift it up, man, lift that thing up high. Show her what you got.'

'What she gettin'?'

'Do it . . .'

He still thought they could come crashing in at any moment. Easy could talk about how solid the crew was all he damn well wanted. Theo still froze at every siren; felt the slam of every door like a hammer coming down.

Javine came back in and got into bed. Slid across and said, 'He's fine.'

'That's good . . .'

She lay her hand on his belly and her head on his chest, began to kiss it all the way down. Theo closed his eyes and willed himself to get hard. To forget the image of a knife and a ragged hole; of a bloody smear across shiny black gaffer tape.

He'd put out some leftover chicken on a paper plate; watched when, an hour earlier, the dog fox had come loping across the lawn. It had stopped a few feet away from the food and sat down, wary. Then it had walked around to the other side of the plate and waited another few minutes before finally tucking into the free meal.

Nothing wrong with being careful, Frank had thought.

Now the garden was dark again, save for the dim lights in the beds, and Frank sat with a crossword in his lap and a glass of wine at his side. He preferred the cryptic puzzles, liked to time himself, but this one had him beaten all ends up. He couldn't get his brain into gear.

Clive had called a short time before. Brought him up to speed on the pub refit and on a bolshie site manager who had been causing him grief on a housing development up west. And the business in Lewisham.

Clive was good at what he did and always used people who were equally adept. Everything was in hand.

He looked up from the paper when Laura walked in. She was wearing jeans and a T-shirt, and her hair looked wet, as though she'd recently stepped out of the shower.

'You missed the fox,' he said.

'I was watching from upstairs.' She walked across to the window and leaned against it. She looked at him, like she was waiting to be told something else, but after a few seconds he went back to the puzzle.

He glanced up again when he heard her crying. 'What's the matter?'

'What did you do?'

He took off his glasses. 'You know, so why are you asking? You don't want to hear the details, do you?' She always knew. There was nothing he could keep from her, never had been. He'd known this conversation would happen from the moment he'd shown her the newspaper story a few days before.

She lifted her arm and pressed the sleeve of the T-shirt against her face. 'Is that the end of it?'

He dropped the paper at his feet. 'Not even close.'

'It won't change what's happened, will it?'

'I know that.'

'It won't help Paul.'

'Maybe it's helping me,' Frank said. 'You know what I'm like about letting people down.' That set her off again. 'You're the *only* one who knows what I'm like.'

She nodded and moved towards him.

Behind her, the motion lights came on in the garden, but Frank didn't take his eyes from hers. She was walking over, and she was leaning down to kiss him on the cheek, and that was more important than anything.

The boys who hung around by the garages got to Mikey first. They'd heard the gunshot and knew the difference between that and a firework or a car backfiring. Most people on the estate did, of course, and there were already several police cars on their way, but the boys didn't know that.

They stood around the body, five of them, looking down. They took it in from all angles, as curious as any other ten- or eleven-year-old would be.

For two of them, it was the first one they'd seen up close.

Somebody said something about the chains, about how Mikey wasn't likely to miss them, and another boy started talking about where the wallet might be. But the boy they all listened to, the one marked out by Wave for better things down the line, told them to shut their stupid mouths and show the respect that was due.

Told them that was not the way things were done.

They heard the sirens then, and somebody shouting from the estate behind them. Before the last boy turned away, he nudged the toe of his trainer forward; dabbed it into the pool of blood that was still spreading behind Mikey's head and running towards the gutter.

'Sticky,' he said.

PART THREE

WOLVES AND LEOPARDS

TWENTY

'I know we're not supposed to like these places,' Deering said. 'I know it's trendy to slag them off because they're taking over the world or whatever. But I do like the coffee.' The funny, strangled laugh. 'I *really* like the coffee . . .'

He was odd, no question, but Helen had decided that he wasn't quite the weirdo she'd marked him down as after the phone messages. Maybe the whole 'God bless' thing was just a verbal tick. Even if it wasn't, it didn't look like he'd be trying to persuade her to let Jesus into her life any time soon.

Helen was drinking tea. 'I like the coffee too,' she said. 'But the baby isn't so keen. Starts jumping around like a lunatic.'

Deering had called that morning, after Helen had spent most of an unpleasant Friday and Saturday arguing with people: with Paul's mother, who refused even to talk about 'rock' music at his funeral; with Jenny, who told her that they wouldn't be needing any of Paul's old clothes, but thanks for the offer; with her old man, who had taken umbrage at suggestions she'd made when he was struggling to put the cot together. Deering had asked if she fancied a coffee, and the idea of talking to a virtual stranger about it all, of getting things off her chest, sounded like a good one.

There was plenty to offload.

He'd picked her up just after ten, then driven down to the Starbucks near Brixton tube station. The place wasn't busy and Helen had made for a table in the window, thinking that she could people-watch if the conversation flagged. A quick coffee had turned into brunch, with toasted paninis and chocolate brownies that Deering had insisted on paying for, and when Helen saw that it was almost midday, she realised that they'd talked for nearly two hours without a break.

That *she'd* talked.

'I think your reactions to other people get more extreme,' Deering said. 'After you lose somebody.' He twisted a button of the faded denim jacket he was wearing over a dark polo shirt.

Helen had been surprised at how much younger he appeared outside the workplace, even though he'd made no attempt to hide his premature baldness. She thought his accent was stronger too, and wondered if he subconsciously suppressed it when he was dealing with other technicians and police officers.

'You're more likely to feel elated at any scrap of good news. Or to lose it with somebody when they annoy you.'

Helen said that she knew what he meant, that this was exactly how she had been feeling, but that there hadn't been much in the way of elation. Certainly not over the previous few days.

She had managed to control herself during the confrontation with Paul's mother, telling herself that this woman, with whom she'd never really seen eye to eye, was every bit as destroyed as she was. Helen still did not know if Paul's mother knew about the affair, and she wasn't likely to ask. The row with her father had been no different to a hundred they'd had over the years. The old man did not like being told what to do. He'd passed that on to both of his daughters.

But it had got seriously nasty round at Jenny's.

Sitting through a pleasant Saturday afternoon lunch; Tim with one eye on the football and the kids playing nicely. If anything, they were a little *too* well behaved, and Helen guessed that they'd been briefed not to say or do anything that might upset Auntie Helen. There was certainly no mention of Uncle Paul.

In the kitchen later, Jenny had said that she'd spoken to Tim and that he already had too many clothes as it was; that their own trip to the charity shop was long overdue. Helen had flown off the handle and Jenny had walked calmly back into the living room and told the children to go and play upstairs. It hadn't ended well, and Helen had not spoken to her sister since.

Now she sighed, but she could still remember the urge to throw something at Jenny, to scatter some of that nice, expensive crockery across the granite worktop. 'I'm buggered if I'm going to be the one to try and smooth things over.'

'That's what I mean,' Deering said. 'Everything's . . . heightened.'

'I'm angry with Paul more than anyone.'

'I know.'

'*Really* furious.'

'Your emotions are all over the place.'

Helen nodded, thought, Still no tears, though, then said it.

'That's normal, too. By which I mean there's no such thing as behaving "normally" at a time like this. There's no . . . template for grief, you know?' He twisted the button again. 'I went pretty mad myself.'

'Oh. Who?'

'My wife.' Deering smiled. 'A brain tumour, eighteen months ago.'

Helen studied him. Suddenly the man's attention to her, his solicitude, seemed to make perfect sense. She opened her mouth, struggling for the right words, but Deering saved her the trouble.

'She always had a lot of headaches, was pole-axed by the bloody things two or three times a week.' He placed a hand flat against his head, just above the right ear. 'We just called them migraines, and

Sally wasn't one of those people who'd rush round to the doctor's at the drop of a hat. By the time I'd talked her into it, she only had a few months.'

'I'm sorry.'

'I should have been a bit more pushy.'

'Don't be silly.' She watched him shrug, and lean forward, and move the empty cups away from the centre of the table. Watched him drop a dirty spoon into each one and line them up, so that the handles were perfectly parallel. 'So, how were you? Afterwards.'

He blew air from between pursed lips, like he didn't know where to begin. 'I just needed to talk to people who knew her. *Anyone* who knew her. I wanted to hear things I didn't know. Stories, things people remembered. I think I wanted to stock up on all that stuff. Memories, even if they weren't my own, that . . . wouldn't run out.' He smiled. 'Stupid, I know. Like they'd ever run out.'

Helen told him that she'd been doing much the same thing. He waited, but she didn't elaborate.

'It's always nice to know you're not the only weirdo,' he said.

She didn't tell him that she'd been looking for something, getting to know the man she thought she knew well enough already and finding out far more than she'd bargained for. She didn't tell him *who* she'd been talking to, of course; about the conversations with Frank Linnell and Kevin Shepherd. And she didn't tell him who she was planning to talk to later that day. She thought he might think it was twisted, somehow.

It probably was.

When Helen started taking more than casual glances at her watch, Deering announced that he needed to be going as well. He told her that he'd pretty much finished his report, but that there were a couple of minor things he needed to iron out with the collision investigator.

'What things?'

'It's nothing. Just some procedural stuff.'

'Never my strong point,' Helen said.

'You know you can call me,' Deering said. 'If there's ever anything you want to talk about. I do understand. Well, now you *know* I do.'

'Thanks.'

'Even if you just need someone to shout at.'

'You'll be sorry,' Helen said.

Outside, on the street, she watched people walking past, drinking in the good weather on their way to join friends at barbecue parties and pubs. She watched them chat and laugh, and hated each and every one of them.

Like Deering had said. Heightened.

She imagined it as something rushing through her body and wondered if any of this unnatural chemistry would be passed into the child she was carrying. Fed through the cord like a drug, until he kicked his way out, red-faced and screaming his little head off.

Javine had taken Benjamin round to a friend's for the day, so Theo had the place to himself. It suited him. He didn't know if his mum and Angela were at home two flights down, but the way things were, he preferred his own company.

It was a hot day and he walked around the flat in shorts and a vest, working his way through the last of his skunk and most of the cold beer in the fridge.

He'd put on some music, had tried to sit and listen, flicked through a paper and an old magazine, but couldn't sit still for more than a few minutes. He turned up the volume so that he could hear it loud and clear as he moved from room to room.

> 'Wolves and Leopards,
> Are trying to kill the sheep and the
> shepherds.
> Too much watch and peep,
> It's time the wolves dem leave the sheep . . .'

Theo didn't know if Dennis Brown was alive or dead, but he loved his voice, the way it made him feel.

Once the ancient music system they'd had at home had given up the ghost, he'd replaced some of his father's old reggae albums with CDs. Handed them over to his dad at Christmas or on various birthdays, then inherited them all later on. He listened to one or another every now and then: Burning Spear, Toots and the Maytals, the *Rock Steady* and *Tighten Up* compilations; Marley, obviously.

It wasn't any big retro thing. There were plenty of grime DJs and rap outfits laying down the illest beats and he liked to get out of it, same as anyone else, and lose himself. But he found something in these old albums that he couldn't get from the imitation-American stuff so many of his mates were listening to. How big their guns were, how many bitches they'd smacked, all that rubbish.

It went *seriously* well with a spliff too. His dad had been right about that much.

He lay down on the bed, closed his eyes and thought about how stupid everything had got since Mikey had been killed.

There had been more police around than ever. The High Street was still thick with the vans and conspicuously armed foot patrols. There were staring contests on every street corner and, for a while, Theo had felt relieved that at least they weren't out there looking for him.

Not all of them, anyway.

He'd even spoken to a couple. Not that he'd had any choice about it – they were talking to everyone. He hadn't said much, just given a name and address and told them that he didn't know anything. Got that look back like they'd heard the same thing a hundred times already that day.

One of them, a woman, said, 'Don't you lot *want* this shit sorted out?'

Theo knew *enough*, course he did. Suspected, at any rate . . .

There were always gangs who went up against others for business reasons, who targeted crews like theirs because of the drugs, because there was money knocking around to be taken. More often than not, though, it was all about territory. About ends, and the borders between them.

Easy had been overstepping those boundaries, and Theo knew it because he'd been fool enough to tag along. Breaking into houses and robbing from whores. They'd been slipping, no question, going into other areas, and it wasn't like Easy hadn't known what he was doing. Most of the time the lines were clearly marked – a particular tag sprayed on a wall; a pair of old trainers strung across a telephone line – but even where there wasn't a sign, people knew. Which pubs to avoid, the streets you did not *want* to wander onto.

Easy thought he could go where he liked, though, stupid fucker. Thought he had some kind of special visa or whatever, and now he had started something serious.

Now it was coming back to bite them all, wicked and hard.

Theo hadn't seen too much of him over the last couple of days, but he could see his friend was rattled. He didn't know if the rest of the crew could tell, but he saw it. Wave had been keeping his head down as well. Probably getting major grief from those in the triangle above him, worried that people would start buying their rocks from a crew that wasn't being shot up.

'*Wolves and leopards are trying to kill the sheep and the shepherds . . .*'

He got up and went back into the kitchen, threw away his empty beer can and stared into the fridge, thinking about lunch.

Javine wouldn't be back for a while. She was happy to stay out and Theo was happy to let her. Things had been tricky the last couple of days, since Mikey. It was always the same when somebody died.

It wasn't like she said too much. She just looked at him. Held on to the baby and looked, like '*Now* will you think about it? Think about getting us out of this shit-hole?'

Theo closed the fridge.

How was he supposed to do that? It wasn't like he was exactly minted as it was, plus there was his mum and Angela to think about. There'd never been any sort of promise made about looking after them, no quiet moment with his dad towards the end, but there hadn't needed to be. It was just assumed.

The track faded out and was replaced by another: drum and bass intro, with the soft horns coming in underneath. He remembered his father singing along with these songs, his voice high and hoarse; the old man still convinced he could sell it like a lover-man, swaying on the spot.

Growing up, Theo had felt like a freak having his dad around, but now he was the same as the rest of them. Most of the boys in the crew, at any rate. Absent fathers. That's what the papers were always banging on about, and the white people in colleges who did reports and all that nonsense. That's what they reckoned caused the trouble. Why the likes of Easy and Mikey, and Theo himself, went off the rails. They'd been robbed of guidance, that was the jist of it; by men who'd walked away or been taken. By cancer or a bullet.

Walking into the living room, Theo found himself thinking about the dead copper's kid, the one who hadn't even been born yet. He wondered how he would handle things. The kid Theo had robbed.

He turned the music up louder and stood by the open window. It wasn't like he could see it happening any time soon, but if there was *ever* to be a chance, for Javine to get what she wanted for the three of them, he needed money. Plenty of it.

He needed to get out of the flat. To go down and walk right past those blue uniforms and through the lines of vans with bars on the front and blacked-out windows. To go to work.

Frank picked up his mobile to check he still had a signal. He didn't want to miss Clive's call. The replacement driver, one of Clive's boys, came into the beer garden, or what would be a beer garden when all the work was finished, and reached for his sunglasses.

'Do you need a drink or anything, Frank?'

'I'm fine.'

'Sure?'

Frank held his hand up against the glare. Said, 'A lemonade or something.'

The driver went back inside the pub and Frank went back to the Sunday papers, the gentle but welcome breeze nagging at their pages.

The rear of the pub was something of a sun-trap, and there'd be no umbrellas until someone bought the place, but he had eventually found some shade tight against the fence at one side. There was still some decking to be laid and some potted plants to come, but it was already a pleasant enough place to spend a Sunday morning, and Frank felt it was important to be there. To make sure the work on the pub was progressing as it should, while Clive was busy with more important business elsewhere.

There was still plenty of stuff in the papers about the gang problems, but it was more general now. Paul wasn't front-page news any longer. There was a cursory mention in a leader or two, but only in so far as his death was symptomatic of a wider problem; one that had been highlighted by the latest gang shooting, that of Michael Williamson, aged sixteen, in Lewisham two days before.

It was the conclusion Clive had said they'd come to. Made sense. Made their lives nice and easy.

He was turning to the sports pages of the *Mail* when the driver returned with his drink: a tall one, with ice and lemon. 'No lemon next time,' Frank said. He felt sorry for the bloke, sweating like a pig in a dark suit and tie, but appearances were important. No such thing in his line of work as a casual day. That didn't apply to Frank himself, of course, who was happily wearing swimming shorts, sandals and a shirt he'd been saving up for the hot weather. Hawaiian, he called it, but Laura had said it looked like someone had been sick on it. 'Do people throw up a lot in Hawaii?' she'd asked.

Frank read the report on the West Ham game. He didn't really follow them any more; it was just a reflex. There was a midweek fixture he might try to catch, and some golf for which he made a mental note to set the Sky Plus.

He took a drink, then looked at the front page of the *Sunday Mirror*: pictures mostly, and though he tried he couldn't really take in the story. It was hard to concentrate on much with all the noise from inside; hammering and drilling. He was glad to hear it, mind you. He was paying these buggers time and a half to work Sunday and was there to make sure nobody was sitting on their arse, drinking tea.

'Give them half a chance,' Clive had said. 'Fucking sugar they get through as well. I reckon they should build a price for sugar and chocolate biscuits into their quotes.'

He wondered if he would hear the phone over the racket and moved it a little closer. He didn't want to risk missing the call so he set it to vibrate as well, in the hope that if he didn't hear the ring, he might at least see the handset jumping about on the table.

Looking at the story in the paper again, it became clear that some ex-reality-TV slag was sleeping with some other loser's boyfriend. She posed in a bikini to show everyone what her new lover was getting. Frank knew that it was all about shifting copies, business being business, but it still made him sick.

The priorities . . .

He downed the rest of his lemonade and started searching for the crossword. Paul might not be front-page news any more, but it cheered Frank a little to think that he was busy making some on his friend's behalf.

TWENTY-ONE

SnapZ could not remember what he had been dreaming about.

It had drifted away from him as soon as he had opened his eyes, like the face of someone he loved waving from the back of a fast car. But he knew it had been *nice*, something that left him feeling warm and had him wriggling beneath the duvet, until the banging came again. The noise that had crashed into his dream and dragged him from it; each knock ringing through the flat like a gunshot.

He looked at the clock on his bedside table. It wasn't even lunchtime yet and the night before had been *seriously* heavy. Most of the crew out on the lash; partying hard for Mikey. His head was still fuzzy and he could taste the drink on his tongue, the bite of the weed at the back of his throat. Could still taste that girl who'd got on her knees in the car park behind the Dirty South.

'Bitch couldn't wait to go down south,' he told Easy afterwards. 'And she was *well* dirty.'

Whoever was outside knocked again, louder. SnapZ threw back the duvet, swung his feet to the floor, took a deep breath.

Fuck's sake, wasn't lying in on a Sunday morning – *any* morning, if he wanted – one of the best things about this business? Flexible hours. That was why he'd moved out, got his own place. Before, his mum would have had him out of bed well before this; dressed up ready for her Sunday; forcing fried eggs and shit on him and telling him not to waste the day.

More knocking. This was no knuckles, either; this was the side of a fist, hard and heavy like it was going to splinter the door or something. Someone hammering, for real.

SnapZ started to curse, raising his voice above the noise, then swallowed it. There was always a chance it was Wave. Or Easy, maybe.

He shouted that he'd be there in a minute, reached for his pants, then for the rest of his stuff, slung across a chair the night before. It wasn't like Easy was any higher than him, had any more sway in the crew, and he certainly didn't fear him, nothing like that. But SnapZ had seen him snuggled up in corners with Wave enough times. He knew that Easy was *keen*, that he might just move up through the ranks faster than most if he kept licking the right arses. And it never hurt to keep your options open. It was always best to piss as few people off as possible, and the wrong word could do it. The wrong look, the wrong toes stepped on, something shouted out when you were still half asleep.

Could get you a blade in the guts a week later, just when you thought it was all forgotten.

He climbed into his jeans, pulled on a vest as he walked into the living room. He grabbed the gun from beneath the sofa cushion and stepped to the door. Put his eye to the spy-hole.

'Fuck are you?'

He didn't recognise the large black man on the step, but the look was familiar. Hands deep in the pockets of his hoodie, shoulders hunched, lips tight in desperation. Nothing he didn't see a dozen times a day.

'I need a couple of rocks.'

'Can't help you.'

'You SnapZ or what?'

'Who gave you the name?'

'Ollie and Gospel said you could sort me out. Come on, man . . .'

'This ain't fucking KFC, you get me?'

'Ten each, they said.'

SnapZ waited. He'd need to have serious words with that white boy about sending punters to his door instead of going to the stash house like he was supposed to. Cut off the pasty-faced little fucker's dreadlocks and shove them up his arse.

'I'll give you fifteen. I'm in a hurry, man.'

Like any of them weren't. Like anyone ever said, 'No rush, I'll pop back some time next week and pick them up.'

'Show me.'

The man dug around in his pocket, produced a crumpled ball of notes and separated out three tens.

'Downstairs,' SnapZ said.

'Come on, just two, that's all.'

'Wait for me outside the betting shop.' Commission on twenty plus ten clear profit for himself was a decent kick-off to the day. It was time he started finding a few customers of his own anyway. They all did it, and Wave looked the other way as long as it wasn't too obvious and there was still plenty going into the cash box.

'How long?'

'Ten minutes.'

'Shit.'

'Up to you, man. I haven't even had a piss yet.'

SnapZ watched as the man backed slowly away from his door and moved towards the stairs. Yeah, worth getting out of bed for; and even better, some of that warm feeling from the dream started coming back, moving up, smooth inside his belly.

More good news: there was half an inch of spliff in the ashtray on the table. He reached for his lighter and fired up what was left, clicking his fingers as he walked into the bathroom.

It was no more than a few seconds before anyone spoke, but that was

long enough for both women to get a good look at each other. To form
an impression.

Helen saw a face that would probably have been beautiful were it
not for the stitches; for the bruising, yellow-green around the eyes,
fading to reveal the dark circles underneath, and something else that
took every ounce of softness from its features. When the woman
stepped, a little warily, around the door, Helen saw the sling support-
ing her left arm. The bandage looked more than a little grimy.

It was clear that the woman knew exactly who Helen was. Her eyes
widened and started to fill almost as soon as they moved up from
Helen's belly. But the expression changed when Helen introduced
herself formally. When the woman who had been using her front door
like a shield found out *what* she was.

'I probably should have called,' Helen said.

Sarah Ruston shrugged, as though she didn't know what to say, and
asked Helen inside. She backed away so that Helen had to close the
door behind herself, and she was reaching into her pocket for tissues
as she led the way into the living room.

It was a double-fronted Victorian house on the north side of
Clapham Common. It was a great location on a quiet, tree-lined street,
and once inside, the envy Helen had started to feel walking from the
car was ratcheted up another notch or two. There were original tiles in
the hall and framed prints on the walls; and she glimpsed an enormous
stainless-steel range in the kitchen. Even better than Jenny's. The
living room had stripped floors and a pair of deep, artfully battered-
looking leather sofas. There was more art in wooden frames, candles
in the empty fireplace, a plasma TV and sleek, black up-lighters in two
corners.

It was the kind of place she and Paul had talked about buying,
dreamed about buying.

When Helen sat down, she said what a nice house it was. Sitting
opposite her, Ruston smiled but said nothing. Just rubbed at the
leather of the empty seat next to her. Helen could hear music drifting

down from the kitchen, something folksy; and there was more music, louder, coming from upstairs.

'Two coppers living together. Was that easy?'

'Not always,' Helen said. She waited but again got no response. 'Listen, I just wanted—'

Ruston turned at the noise of footsteps on the stairs and stayed watching the door until a man walked in. He was around forty, maybe ten years older than Ruston herself; tall and carrying a little too much weight. She introduced him as Patrick. Husband or boyfriend? Helen didn't know which; there hadn't been that much detail in the detective's notebook. She did know that Ruston worked at Canary Wharf, in one of the big overseas banks.

She didn't need to ask if it paid well.

Patrick stepped across and shook her hand. Like his partner, he was wearing Sunday casuals – designer jeans and a T-shirt – though Ruston was wearing a thin black cardigan over hers. After Deering had dropped her back at the flat, Helen had changed into the baggiest summer dress she could find, not really sure why she was bothering to dress up. Now, she felt like an overdressed fat girl who'd arrived too early at a posh summer party.

'Helen's a police officer,' Ruston said.

Patrick's smile became a sigh. 'Jesus, haven't we done all this?' He nodded towards Ruston. 'She must have given a *dozen* bloody statements. It might be nice if she could have some time on her own to . . . get over it, you know?'

Helen stared at the floor. Patrick was wearing Chinese-style slippers and she could see that the tops of his feet were hairy.

'It was her husband who was killed at the bus stop.'

Helen looked up but didn't bother to correct her. She saw Patrick's face change again. Saw the cogs turning and watched him fight the urge to ask the obvious question: Why are you here?

Helen was grateful for his reserve, his awkwardness; almost as grateful as he clearly was when Ruston asked if he fancied putting some coffee on. He took the orders – one coffee, one tea – and was gone, the door shutting loudly enough behind him to make Ruston start a little.

'Like I said, I really should have phoned or something.'

'It's OK,' Ruston said. 'I understand.'

Helen nodded, thinking that it was good of her. Thinking that Sarah Ruston sounded almost as if she understood everything. 'When are you going back to work?'

'End of next week, maybe.'

'That's good.'

'I'll give it a few more days. The collarbone's pretty good, but I don't want people thinking Hallowe'en's come early.'

'You look fine.'

'Right.'

Helen watched Ruston run fingers through her shoulder-length hair. She probably dyed it every three or four weeks, but now the roots were coming through. Helen could hardly blame her for not caring too much after what she'd been through. Then she saw the half smile that told her this was a woman who was used to being told she looked a lot better than 'fine'.

'What about you?'

'I've been better.'

'When's the baby due?'

'A couple of weeks, officially, but you know they can never be sure about these things. You got kids?'

'Patrick's got a couple. From before . . .'

'Anyway.' Helen reddened as she patted her belly. 'He could be putting in an appearance any day, basically.'

'You know it's a boy?'

'It's a feeling.'

'Exciting.'

'Scary. *More* scary now, you know . . .' She turned away and found herself staring at the print above the fireplace. For want of anything else to say, she asked where it had come from, and Ruston explained that she and Patrick had picked it up on holiday in Thailand. 'I always wanted to go,' Helen said. 'Nearly went with an ex once, but . . .' She stopped, realising what she'd said. Wondering how such things worked.

How long was it before a 'dead boyfriend' became an 'ex-boyfriend'?

'Do you want to talk about the accident?' Ruston leaned towards her, using her good arm to push herself forward on the sofa. 'It's fine if you do. I've been talking about it a lot.' Before Helen could respond, the door opened and Patrick returned with the drinks. He handed them out, then made himself scarce again. When he had gone, Ruston smiled and lowered her voice conspiratorially. 'He's been doing his best to look after me,' she said. 'He's worried, you know? Well, you heard him before.'

'It must have been terrifying. In the car.'

Ruston nodded. She looked as though she were still terrified. 'It happened incredibly fast. I know everyone says that, but one minute this car was alongside me and then there were the shots. Next thing, I was in the ambulance.'

It was probably the way she remembered it, Helen thought. Not that she could blame the woman for being selective, bearing in mind who she was chatting to over coffee.

Then I was ploughing into this bus stop and I distinctly remember your boyfriend flying across my bonnet . . .

'I'm sorry,' Ruston said. It looked like she was close to tears again.

'What were you doing in Hackney?' Helen asked.

That seemed to hold the tears at bay. Ruston stared at Helen as though she were failing to get a joke. 'What's that got to do with anything?'

Helen was embarrassed. Faked a laugh. 'The copper in me, I suppose. Routine questions, all that.'

'Do you want to know if I'd been drinking as well?'

'I'm sorry. Please don't be—'

'I'd had one glass of wine and I was well under the limit. I know that for sure, because your lot took a blood sample in the hospital. Very nice of them.'

'It's standard procedure.'

'I was coming back from a friend's,' Ruston said.

Helen nodded, still embarrassed, asking herself the question that Ruston's partner had avoided. Why on earth was she sitting here making polite chit-chat with this woman? She thought about what Deering had said, how talking to those who had been involved with his dead wife had helped him. The same thing was certainly not working for Helen, yet she couldn't seem to stop herself. She couldn't have known what she would discover about Paul, the doubts and suspicions they would foster, but this particular conversation was never going to make her feel better, was it? Perhaps that was the point.

Was she punishing herself for what she'd done?

'Did you think you were going to hate me?'

Helen blinked. It was as though Ruston had known exactly what she had been thinking. 'I'd thought about it,' she said. 'I thought I *might*, but I knew that would be stupid. It was your car that hit Paul, but it wasn't your fault. It was the man who fired the gun who killed Paul.' Ruston nodded, like she was grateful. 'Did you get a good look at him?'

'I told you, it was so bloody quick. But I went through hundreds of pictures anyway. Mug-shots or whatever. They all started to look the same after a while.' Ruston's hand flew to her face. 'God, I don't mean that in a . . . racist way. I mean, I was so tired and full of painkillers. Christ, I'm *still* full of painkillers.'

Helen waved it away and they both managed to laugh. The sun was streaming in through the large windows at either end of the room, bouncing off the varnish on the floorboards. The music had been turned off in the kitchen and upstairs, and for a few seconds there was silence.

Helen drained her tea, said, 'He was pissed.'

'Who?'

'You said you were under the limit; well, Paul certainly wasn't. He'd been at some copper's retirement piss-up, on the beer all night. Maybe if he hadn't had so much to drink, he might have been able to get out of the way. I don't know.' She looked around for somewhere to put her empty cup. Eventually leaned down and placed it on the floor. 'Anyway . . .'

'Was he a good bloke?'

Helen thought about the affair. About Paul's face when he found out. About his face eight days ago, paler than the sheet, on the mortuary slab. 'Too good for me,' she said.

Ruston sucked in a long breath then and it exploded from her a second later as a sob. She struggled to bring her crying under control, staring at her feet and telling Helen how sorry she was; fighting to get the words out.

Helen reached into her bag for more tissues and passed across an unopened packet. Nodding like it was all right. Feeling a sudden twinge of resentment for this woman; for someone else who seemed a damn sight more upset about Paul than she did.

At the stash house, business had been slow since Theo had arrived, but it had been slow for the last few days. The police presence on the street was not enough, would *never* be enough, to stop it completely, but there were always a few dealers that little bit more cautious, a few customers who preferred to shop somewhere where there were more hoodies on the street than blue uniforms.

Theo was half watching MTV. Some rap star he'd never heard of showing off his purple-baize pool table, while a kid called Sugar Boy crashed around in the kitchen, making them both tea. A handgun sat on the low table in front of the sofa, next to Theo's mobile and the notebook in which he had to keep a record of cash in and merchandise out.

'In case the taxman needs to see the accounts,' Wave had said.

There was cursing from the kitchen, then, 'This milk smells seriously rank, man.'

'I'm fine, anyway,' Theo shouted.

He'd give it another half hour, then see what his mum was doing. He knew she'd want to see him, that she'd have cooked enough Sunday lunch for half the people on the estate. That an hour or so would perk her up, even though she'd be disappointed Javine and the baby weren't there and would give him a hard time about it.

On the way across from the flat, he'd walked past the spot where Mikey had been killed; past half a dozen bunches of dying flowers leaning against the wall or lying in the gutter. The ink had run on most of the notes, blurring the traditional messages from his family. The text-speak tributes from those who knew him less well.

'RIP Mikey. U woz the best. Gone but not 4-gotten.'

All that.

There had been a small ceremony on the Saturday, when the flowers had been laid. Theo hadn't left any himself. Flowers didn't seem right for someone who had done what Mikey had done to that whore. He had hugged Mikey's mum, though, right after he'd hugged his own, feeling like she was going to crack his ribs as she held on to him, her croaky voice whispering shit in his ear.

A few people had said things, youth workers and community leaders whatever they were, and Mikey's mum looked embarrassed when people started turning towards her. But she didn't make one of those speeches. You know, how Mikey had been such a good boy, how he wasn't involved in drugs or anything like that. Theo had known Mikey's mum for ever and she wasn't stupid. She wouldn't lie to herself or to anyone else; same as his own mum.

They'd be starting the mural on Monday, Easy said.

Theo didn't know who would be doing it, but they'd picked a piece of wall near to where Mikey grew up – same place he'd been shot, more or less – and they were going to spray-paint a nice picture as a tribute to him. Everyone in the crew would tag it when it was finished.

Let everyone know they were still tight.

Sugar Boy came through from the kitchen, put a mug down in front of Theo. Said, 'I found some powdered stuff in the cupboard.' There were white globules floating on top of the tea.

Theo said thanks and ran through channels on the television while he watched Sugar Boy play with the gun. The kid had been fondling it like it was one of his girlfriend's tits all morning, talking about how someone should be made to pay for Mikey. Looking at Theo like *he* was the one who should be thinking about doing it. Like he was the one with the big reputation because of, you know . . .

'Show them who we are, man,' Sugar Boy said. 'Teach these fuckers a lesson.'

Not that anyone knew which fuckers it was.

On the TV, an old bloke in a smart suit was talking about some business opportunity or other, and Theo thought that if he was going to put some proper money together, he could seriously do with one. That it was a shame he couldn't draw for shit. Not even a stick man.

He reckoned that, as growth industries went, painting murals for the likes of Mikey was a pretty good bet.

TWENTY-TWO

The bathroom in Sarah Ruston's flat was every bit as tasteful as the rest of the place: wood and chrome, frosted-glass bottles. Helen took it all in as she sat, the gleam and the sweet smell of it, and thought again about moving.

About *having* to move.

The flat in Tulse Hill was still full of Paul. It wasn't that she was trying to get away from him – after all, she had plenty to feel guilty about already – but she felt like she should do what they had been planning. Or at least what she had been planning for them.

If she stayed there, she knew that it would crush her, coming out of the walls for her in the night. She would not be strong enough to bring up a child. Her hands cradled her belly, fingers moving back and forth. 'We need to get out,' she said quietly. She glanced up and caught a glimpse of Paul turning away from the shaving mirror. 'Don't get arsey, Hopwood, you're coming too . . .'

She flushed and washed her hands, sniffing at the blocks of scented soap in a wooden bowl on the shelf. She watched herself in the mirror folding the towel, placing it carefully back on the heated rail. Christ, she couldn't wait to get back into jeans again. Not to be breathless and pissing every ten minutes. To get a different kind of look from people when she walked past.

She hated this. Hated being the dumpy cow in the stupid dress.

'Why couldn't you just have gone out and shagged somebody yourself? Evened things up. I couldn't really have blamed you.'

If she were being honest, Helen had no idea what Paul's plans had been. She hadn't been sure two weeks ago, and now it seemed as though Kevin Shepherd and Frank Linnell and God knows who else probably knew better than she did. She felt a small shudder pass through her, remembering the look on Shepherd's face outside the flat. And Linnell's voice on the phone.

'*I know who you are . . .*'

Now she knew who he was too, or *what* he was, but she still felt like she needed to see him. Suspicion could crush you just as easily as guilt and bad memories. She needed to know the truth.

She spat into the sink and rinsed it away before she left the bathroom.

Sarah Ruston was waiting at the front door as Helen came down the stairs, and Patrick came trotting down a few seconds later to join them. To usher Helen out. He had changed and looked as though he'd just stepped out of the shower.

'Thank you,' Helen said. It was clear from the look she received in return that Ruston had no more idea what she was being thanked for than Helen herself did. 'And thanks for the tea.' Added to the two large ones she'd had with Deering, she felt like she was drowning in the stuff.

'No problem,' Patrick said. 'I'm sorry about what I said before. Just . . . with what Sarah's been through, you know?'

'It's not exactly been a picnic for *her*,' Ruston said.

'Course not. I was . . .'

'It's fine,' Helen said.

Patrick nodded, struggling for something else to say. 'Are you actually investigating what happened yourself? I mean, is that allowed?'

'I'm not investigating anything.'

'Do you think they'll ever find the boys in that car?' Ruston asked.

'I wouldn't put money on it.'

'Have they got anywhere at all?'

'I haven't heard anything,' Helen said.

Ruston lowered her head and opened the front door. Helen said thanks again and moved quickly towards the street, desperate to get out before there was any more crying. Patrick took a step after her, holding up his hand like it was something that had just occurred to him, but unable to disguise the fact that he'd been burning to say it since Helen had arrived.

'If you *do* talk to the police who are . . . on the case, I wondered if you might be able to do us a favour.'

'I'll do my best.'

'It's the BMW. I just need to know if they've finished with it. I mean, I know it's written off, but it's been ten days now or something and until we get it back, we can't, you know, get the insurance sorted out.'

Eight days, Helen thought. Eight days since Paul was killed.

She said she'd see what she could do.

It had been easy to get inside and take the kid's gun off him. What kind of a name was SnapZ anyway?

As soon as he'd heard the lock turn, Clive had stepped from where he'd been waiting, out of sight of the spy-hole, and pushed the boy back through his front door. He'd done no more than straighten his arms, smashing huge fists into the boy's chest and sending him back down the narrow hallway, as though a few thousand volts had been passed through him.

The flat was at the end of a landing on the second floor. Billy had been keeping watch from the other end, and, once Clive was inside, he quickly joined him. They took the handgun from the pocket of the kid's leather jacket while he was still writhing on the carpet.

'The stuff isn't here, man. There's nothing here. *Jesus.*'

Clive and Billy lifted SnapZ up and dragged him through to the small living room. He collapsed onto the settee and looked up to see Billy's gun in his face. Watched as Clive crossed to the stereo, pressed PLAY, waited for the music to start, then turned up the volume.

'What's this racket?' Billy asked.

Clive shrugged. 'Might get noisy.'

'There's no money either, I swear,' SnapZ shouted. 'Just what's on me.'

'We're fine for money,' Clive said.

'Take it, man.' SnapZ reached round, his eyes fixed on the gun as he struggled to pull out his wallet.

Billy slapped it from his hand and pushed the muzzle of the gun into his forehead. 'You got trouble hearing?'

SnapZ winced and closed his eyes. Waiting for it.

Clive picked up the wallet and opened it. He took out the notes and pocketed them, then tossed the empty wallet back onto the floor. 'Looks like business is going pretty well,' he said. He shrugged when SnapZ said nothing and sat down on the chair opposite. 'We just need a few words. A bit of information. The odd address. OK?'

'I just knock the stuff out,' SnapZ said. He was pressing himself into the back of the settee, as far away from Billy's gun as possible. 'I don't know nothing about what goes on higher up. Names and all that.'

'We've got names,' Clive said. 'It's just confirmation, really. Kind of like double checking.'

He asked his questions and SnapZ gave the answers like he was sucking in his last breaths; the fear rising in him, *off* him, as he realised what it was they were talking about.

His part in it . . .

Clive said thank you and stood up. He walked across, leaned down and drove his fist into SnapZ's face. 'That's for talking to me how you did earlier. Our conversation through the door.'

Billy watched the boy trying to stop the blood and laughed. 'Fucking KFC . . .'

'Take him through there.' Clive nodded towards the bedroom.

Billy hauled SnapZ from the settee and pushed him across the room, blood still leaking from his shattered nose onto the dirty green carpet. After a couple of uncertain steps, SnapZ veered right suddenly and threw himself into the bathroom, desperately trying to lock the door behind him. Billy shook his head. Clive walked calmly across the room, lowered his shoulder and eased aside the door.

Said, 'No point.'

Billy stepped past him and leaned down to drag the boy out, then smacked him across the ear with the gun when he started screaming. For a few seconds there was only a low moan, and the bass-line from the next room, like a racing heartbeat.

Clive picked up the gun from the table. 'Too young to be playing with one of these,' Clive said. 'Too young to be a man when someone takes it away from you.'

Billy pushed SnapZ into the bedroom, then down onto the unmade bed. SnapZ pulled up his legs and buried his face in his knees, smearing blood across his jeans.

'Lie down,' Billy said. 'And turn over.'

'What you going to do, man?'

Billy hit him with the gun again. 'Don't be so disgusting.'

Clive stood in the middle of the living room and looked around. The place was a shit-hole, the worst he'd seen. He didn't understand why these people didn't use the money they were making to try and better themselves. Why they didn't do something about how they lived.

He didn't give a toss how they made their money; he wasn't judging. How could he? As it went, he liked a smoke himself at the end of the day to even himself out a little, but he still thought it was shameful that they didn't make more of an effort. That they wasted what they'd made on gold rings and training shoes.

Looking like rap stars and living like fucking tramps.

'Are we going to get this done, mate, or what?'

Clive turned when Billy shouted. Saw him through the open bedroom door, standing over the bed. The kid face down.

'It's just that I've got a Sunday roast waiting indoors.'

Clive nodded. He picked up the remote to turn down the music and flicked open his phone.

Theo's mum always drank a glass of wine with her Sunday lunch. She always got sentimental and talked about how Sunday had been his father's favourite day. How he used to say that it was a day for families. And after lunch, there was always cards.

They played gin rummy, and today Angela was thrilled with how many times she managed to beat her big brother, punching the air as she laid the winning cards down round after round. Theo usually let her win a few hands, but today she needed no help. He couldn't focus for more than a few seconds; found himself drifting away. Angela and his mother grew short with him, as time and again he sat there doing nothing when it was his turn.

Afterwards, he sat smoking while his mum cleared away, and Angela bounded over, still beaming. 'Champion!' she sang.

'You were lucky, man. You got all the cards.'

'Pure skill.'

She sat at his feet, facing him; her thumbs flying across the buttons of her DS, murmuring to herself as she fired at monsters, collected treasure, whatever game it was. He looked down at the top of her head. His mum had done something different with her hair that Theo had never seen before; braided it in some new way.

'How's school?' he asked.

'OK.'

'Only OK?'

She glanced up from her game. 'It's great.' She dropped her eyes back to the screen, screwing up her mouth in concentration as she focused on the action. After a few seconds she looked up again and let out a long sigh, like she'd just been distracted from vital scientific research. '*What?*'

'It's fine . . .'

She lowered the game. 'I'm about to get killed by aliens anyway,' she said.

He wouldn't have *wanted* his sister to be miserable at school, but there was still that notion of getting away, of them *all* getting away; now becoming a fantasy into which he was escaping more and more. It would be that much more of a non-starter if it meant dragging Angela away from somewhere she was happy. Of unsettling her again.

It wasn't her fault that he'd got himself into this mess. Wasn't anybody's fault but his own, didn't matter what the papers or anyone else said.

'Be good if you could come to school with me,' Angela said. 'You're clever, so you could do all the things that are too hard.'

'Sounds OK.' He nodded like he was thinking about it, said, 'We've got a problem, though.'

'What?' Dead serious.

'I think people might suss me. I'm big for a ten-year-old, man.'

She shrugged, like it was a minor detail. 'You're clever, so you can work that out.'

'Right . . .'

'I'll still do games and art and dinner-time, and you can do everything else, OK?'

Yeah, he was a regular genius. Clever enough to be wondering whether *his* mother would have anything to say when it was his turn; while the crew sent their serious text messages and Angela laid flowers on the pavement. Clever enough to be messing up everything with

Javine and neglecting his baby son while his friends got shot down on the street.

He leaned across to stub out his cigarette, listening to the tinny melody from Angela's game playing over and over.

Were they ever his friends?

He thought about Ransford and Kenny. The football boys back in Chatham. Thought about them without feeling the tightness in his chest that came on whenever he went down to see the boys on the estate, out to earn his living.

They were more than friends; they always said that. Bredren. More than family even, that's what being in the crew means, but Theo never believed that shit for one minute, no matter how many times he touched fists and did the 'look how serious we are' nodding thing. Not Mikey or SnapZ; not really. Certainly not Wave. Easy was the closest, the *oldest* at any rate, but things were strange with him now. Had been ever since they'd climbed into that Cavalier.

Clever enough to have killed someone to earn himself a promotion.

Angela smacked him on the knee to get his attention. 'You all right, Theo?'

He looked across to see his mother standing in the doorway, running a tea-towel across a plate. Watching him, with something in her eyes that made his chest tighter than ever.

Another smack. '*Theo*?'

He turned back to his sister and lied.

'Billy all set then, is he?' Frank asked.

Clive looked into the bedroom. Billy was ready, but he couldn't say the same about the kid on the bed. He'd been thrashing about and shouting until Billy had indicated, rather forcefully, that he should keep quiet and stay still. Clive had heard the voice of a terrified child and seen the dark stain on the sheets beneath him. The kid had been well cocky before; on the other side of his front door with a gun near by. But that stuff usually fell away quickly enough near the end.

'Yeah, he's keen to crack on,' Clive said. 'Got roast beef waiting for him at home.'

'Sounds good,' Frank said. 'I've sent one of the builders out to pick me up a sandwich.'

'How's it coming?'

'They seem to be grafting hard enough, but I'm not sure if that's just because I'm here. That bloke doing the cornicing and stuff knows what he's doing, though. Looks lovely.'

'Want me to come over, so you can get home?'

'Meet me at the house later,' Frank said. 'We can see where we are.'

It was only the slightest shift in tone, but Clive understood well enough that they weren't talking about the pub renovation any more. This was the way they always did it; *had* to do it. Frank wasn't stupid and knew how everything worked. High-tech monitoring systems, intercepts and all that. If anything was ever produced, transcripts or whatever, there was no way it would stand up in court. The only people doing well out of that sort of nonsense would be Frank and his brief.

It was second nature now, and it helped that they knew each other so well, that they had developed a shorthand.

'I'll call before I come,' Clive said.

'Fine. Just so we can sort out the rest of the schedule.'

Clive took a pride in how he went about things; same as he did with any job he was doing for Frank. He was businesslike and never took this kind of work lightly. At the end of a day like this there'd always be a stiff drink or two taken, didn't matter how long you'd been doing it. Maybe a smoke, too, if it had been more than just the one job.

'I'd best leave you to get on then,' Frank said. That same little shift in the voice, like a cloud going over for a second. 'OK?'

Clive closed his phone, crossed to the stereo and turned up the volume again. By the time he reached the bedroom the kid had started shouting again, and Clive had to sit down on his back to keep him from coming right off the bed. 'Easy,' he said, reaching for the pillow and pressing it across the back of the kid's head. He leaned all his weight into it and gave Billy the nod.

Billy stepped across, light on his feet, and picked his spot.

There was a muffled thud and a scorch mark, not much bigger than the burn from a discarded fag-end; black and ragged at its edge. Clive had seen something like this a few times in films, American gangster stuff, and for some reason there were always a few feathers flying about afterwards. In slow-motion sometimes, like snow in a globe. The men who'd done the job always looked blank and strolled out of the room, while some kind of music came in, and the feathers floated down like they'd been shooting fucking chickens or something.

He'd never seen anything like that in real life; it was always just this. They probably did it that way for a nice effect. Or maybe, Clive thought, he simply never dealt with anyone who had feather pillows.

TWENTY-THREE

Helen helped her father clear away the lunch things, then dried while he washed up. When she and her sister were younger, they had enjoyed being part of a small production line while their mother put her feet up, with Jenny putting the dishes away and the three of them telling bad jokes or singing along with the radio. Today, Helen and her father went about their tasks in relative silence.

Her father had got a large steak and kidney pie in from Marks and Spencer and opened a can of beer. He'd talked her through his previous day's activities – the circling in the *Radio Times* of TV shows to be watched later, the lunchtime pint with the bloke two doors up, and the cup of coffee with the nice lady over the road – while Helen nodded and cleared her plate, the breakfast-time vomiting session having left her ravenous as usual.

'And how was your Sunday?' he'd asked.

She'd said something suitably non-committal, not keen to answer the questions that were sure to follow if she mentioned the lunch with Roger Deering and the afternoon she'd spent at Sarah Ruston's. She told him that she'd had a quiet evening in.

Watching her father finish his lunch, she'd taken her cue to apologise for the argument they'd had two days earlier, when he'd been putting the cot together. It hadn't been her fault, but that had never really mattered where her dad was concerned. He was a sulker, same as Jenny.

He'd looked across the table at her, reddening. 'Don't be so silly, love. It's me who should be saying sorry. I felt rotten all day yesterday.'

'Oh . . .'

'Miserable old bugger, I am.'

This was a first. She knew how badly he wanted to protect her, and she felt a twinge of sympathy for a man whose big hands did not fit easily into kid gloves.

Helen had caught on pretty quickly to the fact that her condition was something of a 'get out of jail free' card. With anything from an argument in the Post Office to a spot of mild shoplifting, pregnancy gave you a certain amount of leeway. After all, it wasn't a good idea to argue with a pregnant woman, to let the poor thing get over-emotional, to stir up those unstable hormones. Throw in a recent bereavement and it was becoming obvious that you could get away with murder. Being up the duff *and* widowed meant never having to say you were sorry.

She said it again anyway – sorry that her father had been feeling rotten – while making a mental note to start being a damn sight nastier to people.

'I *was* right about that cot, though,' he said.

Once the washing-up was done, her father turned away from the sink, drying his hands on a tea-towel. 'You've still not had a good cry, have you, love?'

Helen laughed and rubbed at the last plate. 'Are you kidding? I was blubbing at *Midsomer Murders* last night.'

'You know what I mean.'

'Drop of a bloody hat . . .'

'For Paul,' he said. 'You've not cried for Paul.'

207

Helen put down the plate as her father stepped across to her and she began to cry again, but for all the wrong reasons. He shushed her and rubbed her back, and she pressed her face into his shoulder, smelling his aftershave and moving her cheek against the soft material of his shirt.

'Told you,' she sobbed. 'Drop of a bloody hat.'

When she'd pulled away and put the plates into the cupboard, they talked about the funeral. There was still no news on the date, but Helen guessed that it wouldn't be too long before the body was released. She told him that Paul's mother was still being awkward. Helen did not want any flowers, being all for donations to a police charity instead, but Caroline Hopwood was as traditional on that score as she was when it came to the choice of music.

'It's understandable.'

'Is it? I'm carrying her bloody grandchild.'

'I'm sure she'll come round.'

'I don't know how much I care, to be honest,' Helen said. 'I'm just not up to fighting about it.'

'Do you want me to have a word?' her father asked.

Helen remembered the awkwardness at the party for Paul's thirtieth, the stilted conversation on the single occasion that her father had met Paul's parents. She remembered the jokes that she and Paul had made about it afterwards. 'I'll sort things out,' she said. 'Thanks.'

Her father nodded and opened the fridge. Brought out a trifle that he'd picked up along with the pie.

Helen smiled. 'Pushing the boat out,' she said.

'I was going to ask if I could help carry Paul,' her father said. He cleared his throat. 'Carry the coffin. You've probably got his mates doing it, members of his family, I suppose . . .'

'It'll be coppers,' Helen said. 'An honour guard, in dress uniform. Paul's mum wants the full ceremonial bit. Twenty-six-gun salutes, trumpets, the whole thing.'

Her father nodded, impressed.

'I'm kidding.'

'It's not a problem, really. Just thought I'd volunteer.'

'You'll probably need to carry *me*.'

'I don't know if I'm up to that,' he said.

She stood close and watched as her father dished up a large portion of trifle. 'I should probably be getting back,' she said. 'Why don't you take that over to your girlfriend? Mind you, you'll need to watch your waistline if you want to get anywhere with her.'

'Who says I haven't?'

She punched him on the shoulder, looked around for her bag.

'Call me when you get home,' he said. 'Or later. Doesn't matter.'

Helen nodded. 'If I'm in any fit state. *Midsomer Murders* is on UK Gold every bloody night . . .'

Helen's car was parked more or less opposite her father's front door. Crossing the road, she froze at the squeal of tyres and watched a black Jeep accelerate away from the kerb fifty yards to her right. As it passed her she could see that there were two men inside staring straight ahead, and she wondered if she'd seen a similar car, maybe the *same* car, outside her own block a couple of days before.

She was telling herself that she was being ridiculous, that there were a lot of black Jeeps around, when her mobile rang. It was Martin Bescott, Paul's DI at Kennington.

'We've got some more of Paul's stuff,' he said.

'Oh? I thought I took it all.'

There was a pause. 'We found a second locker. Paul's . . . replacement wasn't too keen on taking his old one, so . . .'

Helen said she understood. Coppers were more superstitious than most.

'Had to force the bloody thing open in the end.'

'Can't you just give it to charity?' she asked. 'Save me, you know . . .'

'Well, yeah, there are some old trainers, a few other bits of kit. But

I thought you'd probably want the laptop.'

Now it was Helen's turn to pause.

'Helen?'

'I'll pop over and get it,' she said.

★

Theo had spent most of the morning at the stash house, stuck there talking shit with Sugar Boy, who had been sent over by Wave when SnapZ had failed to show up. Theo had been hoping that the first day of a new week would be a good one. That the money might start coming in a bit faster and that he might start feeling less jumpy, a bit less like someone waiting for something bad to happen.

He'd been well out of luck on both counts, and as soon as it was anything like lunchtime, he'd jogged back over to the flat to share a sandwich with Javine.

He'd barely sat down when Easy showed up, his fat, ugly pit-bull straining at the leash on Theo's doorstep. He'd bought the thing as soon as Wave had got one; laid out seventy-five pounds to some Essex wide boy knocking them out round the back of the Dirty South and managed somehow to get the stupidest beast on the estate. Wave said that someone must have kicked the thing in the head when it was a puppy. Easy seemed to like that. Thought that he and his sick-in-the-head dog belonged together or something.

Javine started mouthing off as soon as she heard the yapping. She couldn't stand the dog and didn't want it anywhere near her or the baby. Theo tried to pull the door behind him when she started losing it shouting that she didn't want any dumb animals in her house, didn't matter if they had four legs or two.

Easy shrugged. 'Let's walk,' he said.

They strolled around the estate first; Easy enjoying the attention from the kids by the garages, the dirty looks from a few of the older women – the mothers and sisters – as he watched his dog do its business in the scrubby square of grass, parading around what passed for a playground before they cut out onto Lewisham High Street.

It was seventy-something degrees and rising. Easy wore a silk shirt, open over a vest, rust-coloured, like his combats and trainers. Theo had picked out low-slung jeans and a Marley T-shirt, the Timberlands he'd bought after the break-ins he'd done with Easy three weeks before.

With the bit of cash he hadn't put away.

'How's tricks, Star Boy?'

Theo told Easy that tricks were OK, that he hadn't seen too much of him the last few days. Not since Mikey.

'Been busy, T.'

Theo nodded back in the direction of the stash house, where he'd left Sugar Boy holding the fort. 'Things are pretty slow.'

'Exactly. Got to whip up new business where you can, you get me?'

'So where you been whipping it up?'

'Here and there, man.'

'Anywhere you shouldn't?'

'Meaning?'

'When we went robbing, when we turned them whores over. Maybe that was stepping on someone's toes, all I'm saying.'

Easy threw a hard look Theo's way, almost knocked over a girl wheeling a pushchair. She swore at him and he ignored her. 'Whose toes? Fuck you talking about, man?'

'Doesn't matter whose. Anywhere that's not here is somebody else's.'

'You always been a worrier, T.'

'Yeah, maybe.'

'Ever since we was kids, man.'

A uniformed copper and two community police support officers – plastic plods – came sauntering towards them. The copper got a good eyeful of Easy and Theo, while the CPSOs seemed rather more concerned about the pit-bull.

Easy gave them all a grin, yanked the dog away. They turned the corner onto Lee Bridge. 'All these extra pigs gonna be trotting off soon,' he said. 'Things can get back to normal, yeah?'

'You reckon?'

'This is the Wild West, man. You can see it on their faces, they don't fancy it.'

They stopped a few yards further on when Wave's Mercedes drew alongside and stopped on yellow lines. As If was behind the wheel and calmly signalled the car behind to come round when its driver sounded his horn. Theo watched as Easy strolled across and leaned down to talk to Wave through the window. They talked for a few minutes and Theo saw Wave's eyes flash across to him; saw him nod and laugh at something Easy had said. Theo nodded back. He knew they were talking about him and tried not to think about it.

Could have been anything. The clothes he was wearing, whatever.

When Wave had driven away they carried on walking. Easy said he was still planning on giving As If a good slap when the chance presented itself, then he talked about the various hassles he was getting from assorted women. He had a fair few on the go, so he claimed, and there were at least two children knocking around somewhere.

'Like to keep my options open,' he said. 'Get some *variety*, you know what I'm saying? Never been one to settle.' They walked on. 'I tell you, man,' he laughed, 'that woman of yours is a serious handful.'

'Yeah.'

'*Serious . . .*'

Theo smiled and stepped carefully to avoid a brown smear on the pavement. Thought, Yeah and she's *my* handful.

They talked rubbish for a few minutes, Easy pouring scorn on some local DJ he'd heard on the community radio station and bragging about how he'd put the fear of God into some loser who'd cut up his Audi on Shooters Hill. Theo did his best to look relaxed. He was still thinking about those three uniforms around the corner; the look on the face of that copper as he made eye contact. He struggled to listen to Easy's ramblings above the whine in his brain as it raced and his imagination fought to escape from dark corners.

'T? You listening, man?'

'Nothing worth hearing, man.'

'I'm hungry. You hungry?'

They stopped at the McDonald's just inside the Lewisham Centre. 'I need a piss as well,' Easy said. 'Two birds with one stone, man. Sweet and simple.' He handed the leash to Theo, asked him to look after the dog while he went inside to get them both McFlurries.

Theo waited while Easy went about his business, trying to control the dog as it lunged at passers-by, fighting the temptation to let the mutt run free, see how it handled a busy main road.

Easy came out and handed Theo his ice-cream. 'Before,' he said. 'All that stuff about stepping on toes. You think it was my fault Mikey got killed?'

'I never said that.'

'Felt like that was what you was saying.'

'It's fucked up, that's all,' Theo said. 'Shouldn't be happening.'

Easy shrugged. He ate fast, and when he was finished he lobbed the plastic container towards a litter bin. He turned to Theo, spread out his arms, the dog chasing its tail at his ankles. 'This is the way it is, man. You get me? It's *supposed* to be like this.'

'What? Feeling shit scared?'

Easy narrowed his eyes, wrapped the dog's leash around his wrist, yanked the animal close. 'Who's scared?'

Theo stared at the traffic.

'You finishing that?'

Theo handed over his untouched McFlurry, then closed his eyes and tried to remember the taste of barley wine on a windy balcony, enjoying the sun on his face for half a minute while he waited for Easy to finish.

She and Paul had never lived in each other's pockets. They had kept their own space, *given* it to each other, and been happy enough with that. They'd seen their own friends and never felt the need to report every conversation, to ask the other who they had been talking to whenever the phone was put down. They had rarely been compelled to co-ordinate diaries and each had held a separate bank account; an independence that had been easy, though it had later become enforced, especially by Paul, in the aftermath of Helen's affair.

She told herself these things in an effort to explain away the existence of the computer she had collected from Kennington on the way home. To play down its presence, sleek and grey on the table in front of her. To make herself feel a little less apprehensive as she fired it up.

She'd opened all the windows in the flat, but it still felt muggy; *close*, her father would have said. She was sweating in baggy shorts and one of Paul's old T-shirts. A cold glass of wine, or better still a beer, would have been more than welcome.

Bescott had been waiting for her in the car park.

He had taken her into his office and handed over the laptop wrapped inside a plastic bag. He'd seemed friendly enough but, as always, it was hard to decide how much of that was down to her condition. Her . . . circumstances. There'd been something in his face, though, like he was trying too hard, and Helen couldn't help wondering if he, and others above him, harboured the same suspicions about Paul's activities that she did. How long would it be before an earnest-looking sort from the Directorate of Professional Standards came knocking?

The Rubberheelers.

The screen on the Mac turned blue as the system booted up.

How hard would the DPS pursue an investigation if the officer in question was dead? Was there a danger that she herself would be implicated? She knew how these people worked and how they might presume that, as Paul's partner, her own integrity had been compromised.

She clicked on the icon above Paul's name and told herself she was being ridiculous. Worst-case scenario, they'd probably want to go through Paul's stuff and take a look at whatever was on this computer.

Poke around for dirt.

Same as she was.

The desktop appeared and Helen felt like the breath had been punched out of her: a grainy picture of herself and Paul, grinning at the camera in a Greek taverna three summers before. Paul's hair had been cut really short and his face was red. Her tits were almost coming out of a bikini top she should never have worn.

'You tosser,' Helen whispered, stabbing at the keyboard. 'Make me feel even worse, why don't you?'

She opened Paul's 'Home' folder and looked around. All the default system files were where they should be. There was nothing at all in 'Pictures' or 'Movies', and the 'Documents' folder contained only the expected user data.

The Mac had barely been used, or at least not been used for very much.

They'd shared the IBM at home, switched between users on the same system. Paul's desktop had always been littered with random documents and clippings, assorted folders bulging with downloaded songs and mildly offensive video clips courtesy of Gary Kelly and other mates at work. She'd been the one with nicely organised folders with names like 'utility bills', 'baby' and 'council tax'.

On the laptop, it was easy enough to spot the folder she was looking for. It contained a single document, labelled 'Victoria'. Helen double clicked to open the file and was asked to enter a password.

She stared at the empty box on the screen for a minute, at the blinking cursor inside, then entered Paul's surname and date of birth. Like most people, he'd used his birthdate as the PIN for his bank account.

No good.

She tried his mother's name, married and maiden. His father's. Then she tried her own name, asking herself as she typed why it wasn't the first thing she'd thought of.

The password you have entered is incorrect.

How tricky could it be, for God's sake? Paul wasn't . . . *had not been* any kind of a whizz when it came to this stuff.

Victoria . . .

Maybe he *had* got his own back, after all. Christ, could this be about something as simple as a bit on the side? A bit of posh too, by the sound of her. It was a painful thought, but perhaps less painful than the alternative.

There was still Kevin Shepherd to explain away, though. And Frank Linnell.

She began to type quickly, shouting at herself any time she mistyped and when she accidentally hit the CAPS LOCK; trying out words as they popped into her head and jabbing at the ENTER key. Anything that might mean something to Paul: the name of his best friend at school; the dog he had when he was a kid; Queens Park Rangers; *The Great Escape*; Freddie fucking Mercury . . .

The password you . . .

She slammed down the lid as hard as she dared and sat there until she got her breath back. Until the sweat had begun to cool on her neck and shoulders.

She remembered that Jenny's husband Tim was good with computers, how he'd bored the arse off them any number of times talking about networks and firewalls. She thought about asking him to help, then quickly thought better of it. She knew that Jenny would have a field day as soon as she found out, would interrogate her endlessly. Maybe she could ask Tim to do it on the sly and keep it to himself. A blow-job might do the trick; she knew he'd always had a thing for her.

Jesus, where the hell had *that* come from?

The baby kicked, good and hard. She felt dizzy suddenly, lightheaded. She went into the kitchen and drank half a bottle of water.

Once she felt steadier, she took the laptop to the bedroom, wrapped it inside the plastic bag and stashed it away at the bottom of the wardrobe, behind Paul's guitar. She felt herself redden even as she was doing it, but knew that whatever was on the hard disk needed to be hidden.

216

She thought that Frank Linnell might have the answers, but it wasn't going to be easy finding him. There was no way she could ask anyone to help without needing to explain why, and it wasn't feasible to stroll into her office and sit down at the computer. Tracing a number plate, as she'd done with Ray Jackson, was a simple enough business, but any usage of the PNC would involving logging on and entering her password. The session would be a matter of record.

Christ, if she just had the name of one of Linnell's businesses, it might be as simple as picking up the Yellow Pages.

Back in the living room, she glanced across at the rest of Paul's stuff, still sitting where she'd left it on the table: his diary, tapes and CDs, the mapbook from the car, his sat-nav unit.

'Come on, Hopwood, admit it. That's bloody genius . . .'

Maybe not, but it was a decent idea, and even though it might take a while, it wasn't like she had much else to do.

Maybe this time the technology would be on her side.

TWENTY-FOUR

They'd found SnapZ first thing that morning.

There were police all over the estate again; shouts and sirens, its dawn chorus. A blanket of blue, vehicles clogging up the side streets, and yellow tape flapping around the entrance to the block where SnapZ had lived. The rumours started flying pretty fast, and by mid-morning anyone with ears knew what had happened.

A crew-boy down. *Another* one.

According to some mouth almighty, who had heard it from a gobby copper, a girlfriend had phoned the police the day before, when she had been unable to get SnapZ on his mobile for twenty-four hours. The report had been dutifully logged and forgotten. Twenty-four hours before that, a woman had called to complain about a distur-bance in a neighbouring flat; about how it wasn't the first time the toe-rag living two doors along had ruined her Sunday by blasting out his music and slamming doors. That had received even less attention, reports of excessive noise or anything approaching a domestic coming somewhere below dropping litter and dogs fouling the pavements when it came to the Lee Marsh estate.

Easy had been spot on. They just didn't fancy it.

It wasn't until some sharp-eyed desk sergeant put the two reports together and noticed the one name they had in common that anyone got off their arse. An hour later they were smashing in SnapZ's door. Then, before they had a chance to take off their stab vests, those officers who had been happily returning to desk jobs or foot patrol in Greenwich and Blackheath were racing west, pale and pissed off, back to SE13.

Theo stood watching from just behind a crowd of fifteen or twenty that was as near to the action as it could get. Most of them probably didn't know that they'd already taken SnapZ away; were still waiting in the hope of getting a glimpse of the drama.

It was an odd mix: shopkeepers; a family or two who lived on the estate; and a few bemused souls who looked like tourists and must have taken a seriously wrong turn. One or two of the crew were hanging around as well, to pay their respects or maybe just to gain some comfort from being close to the others. Theo had seen Gospel and Sugar Boy loitering, had exchanged those all-purpose nods before letting his eyes drop.

Near to where he was standing, a small boy stood with his father, slurping at an ice-cream and craning his head to get a good look at whatever was happening. Theo's guts were jumping. He'd called in at the café early on and now he felt like he might chuck his bacon sandwich up at any time.

After another ten minutes or so, a pair of bored-looking uniforms ushered the crowd further back and some of them started to drift away. Theo knew that people would already be preparing their speeches. There were a few local news teams there as it was and he knew that the bigger ones would be arriving later on. National TV and stuff, probably.

As the father and son walked past him, Theo caught the small boy's eye, the shrug and the look on his sticky face.

Nothing to see.

Others, going back to whatever they'd been doing, shared a different expression.

Nothing they hadn't seen before.

Theo hoped his own face wasn't giving too much away. That it gave no hint as to what was going on inside his head; *raging* in there. He hadn't got a clue why, and even less who, but he knew now that all this had nothing to do with Easy and his . . . excursions. Knew that it was not about territory.

There were thirty, maybe more in the street crew, with plenty of others further up, in the triangles above, for those who knew where to look.

Mikey dead, and now SnapZ. It was more than a coincidence.

As far as the media were concerned, the explanation would be simple. They would be marked down as casualties in a vicious gang war or a dispute about ends. They would probably be seen as victims of something bigger, too: symptoms of alienated this and disenfranchised that, the product of a messed-up ethnic underclass or some such.

But Theo knew they also had something more specific in common, something they shared with only Theo himself and two others. The night ten days before when that police officer had been killed. When *he* had killed that police officer.

Mikey and SnapZ had both been sitting on the back seat.

Theo turned away and all but collided with Gospel. She kept her head down, ran a hand through her locks. 'Out of order, man,' she said.

Theo felt his breakfast starting to move.

Gospel moved away like she was in a hurry. 'Out of fucking order.'

'Yeah,' Theo said.

Helen had to admit that some of these small-time toe-rags were pretty bloody clever.

Before she'd taken her maternity leave, she'd heard about a spate of car thefts in which kids would break into cars with sat-nav systems, hit the HOME button and be directed to a house which they would promptly burgle, safe in the knowledge that the homeowner was somewhere else. Finding out that his car had just been nicked.

The gadget could, of course, be put to more noble use; not that what she was doing felt particularly noble.

Paul had known his way around most of south-west and central London, so he had only really used the sat-nav for getting home if he found himself north of the river or needed to drive to another city. Helen knew that the 'recent destinations' were listed in the order they'd been programmed into the unit, and hoped there wouldn't be too many to work through. She recognised a couple and discounted them. Then, remembering what Gary Kelly had told her about where Frank Linnell operated, she started looking for addresses in the south-east of the city.

The first two were a waste of time: Linnell was obviously not based at Catford police station, and the terraced house in Brockley turned out to belong to a retired couple whose daughter had been a witness in a murder case Paul had investigated a few months earlier.

The old woman had remembered him. 'Nice man,' she'd said. 'Polite.'

Helen had started out early, and just after ten-thirty she turned into a side street by Charlton Park and stopped near a pub a mile or so south of the Thames. She saw a black Range Rover parked alongside and a skip out front and remembered that Kelly had also spoken about Linnell being in property development.

Third time lucky.

As she walked from the car, a man in paint-spattered overalls came out of the pub and emptied the contents of a heavy-looking plastic bucket into the skip.

'Is the boss in?' Helen asked. Her warrant card stayed in her bag. The man grunted – could have been 'yes', could have been 'no' – and went back inside.

She found herself some shade and waited.

Five minutes later, the door opened again and a well-built black man appeared. He sized her up, then asked what she wanted to drink. Helen was a little taken aback, but tried not to show it. 'Just some water would be fine.' The man held open the door for her.

He walked her through the pub, where half a dozen men were painting, hammering and drilling. She heard two of them talking in an East European language. Polish was her best guess. There were so many Poles working in the UK as plumbers and builders that their government had recently issued an official request, asking if they could have a few back.

Frank Linnell was sitting in the garden. He stood up when she walked onto the patio, said, 'Helen, is it?'

He was fifty-odd, but looked fit enough in blue gym shorts and a white polo shirt. There was no grey to speak of in hair that was curly at the neck and greased back with something. The face was . . . softer than Helen had expected.

She sat down opposite him at a small, slatted table and said thank you when the big man laid her drink down.

'Just shout if you want another one,' he said.

'Nice out here, isn't it?' Linnell said. 'Be bloody gorgeous in a day or two. Tell you the truth, I'm not even sure I want to sell the place.'

Fresh turf had been laid between where they were sitting and a new fence thirty or so feet away, and one side of the patio was filled with rows of hanging baskets and potted plants, their tubs still wrapped in polythene.

'Stick a couple of swings or a slide over there on the grass, be smashing.'

Helen took a long drink and a deep breath. Looked across at a man who, if a fraction of what she'd heard was true, was on the wish list of half the city's senior detectives, and who carried on speaking as if they'd known one another for years.

'Can't be too long now.' He pointed at Helen's belly. 'Looks about done in there, I reckon.'

'Try not to make any loud noises,' she said.

'Going back to work straight away? Or . . .'

'Not straight away.'

'Most advantageous arrangement for the kiddie, if you ask me.'

'We'll see.'

'And what about today?' Linnell took a sip of his own drink. It looked like Coke, but there was no way of knowing if there was anything else in it. 'You working today?'

'I just came to talk about Paul,' Helen said.

Linnell smiled. 'I'd like that.'

For the second time in as many minutes, Helen had been put firmly on the back foot. She told herself that Linnell, and those who worked for him, were probably well practised at doing it; urged herself to relax and stay focused. The baby was kicking up a storm and she quietly shifted position to make herself more comfortable. She moved a hand across to her belly beneath the table, and started to rub gently. 'How did you know Paul?' she asked.

'We met six years ago,' Linnell said. He began to play with a gold chain around his neck, drawing the links back and forth between his fingers as he spoke. 'He was part of the team on a case I was close to. The *murder* of someone I was close to. Afterwards . . . all the way through, matter of fact, Paul was terrific. One or two of his colleagues were not quite as . . . sympathetic, if you know what I mean. When you've got a reputation, some people can only see things one way. Paul always treated me the same as he'd treat anyone else who was a victim.'

'And after that?'

'We stayed in touch.'

'That's it?'

'We became friends, I suppose.' He shrugged, like it was all very simple. 'We were *friends*.'

'Did you see him often?'

'Every month or two, give or take. We were both very busy. Well, you know . . .'

'So you had lunch, went to the cinema, what?'

'We had lunch, we talked about this and that, went to the pub. I took him to the Oval once to see a day's cricket.' He laughed. 'We got thoroughly pissed on.'

Helen was nodding, as though there were nothing out of the ordinary in what Linnell was telling her, but her insides were churning and it was nothing to do with the baby playing football with her kidneys. She needed to get up a head of steam, to ask the more awkward questions that she'd been rehearsing since the previous night. She saw the warmth in Linnell's face as he spoke about Paul and wondered if there might really be no more to it than the friendship he seemed to treasure so much. It crossed her mind that he might be gay, might have been in love with Paul. She glanced down and saw that he wasn't wearing a wedding ring.

Maybe Paul had known that Linnell had a thing for him and was using it to his advantage somehow.

'You want anything to eat?' Linnell asked.

Helen gave a small shake of the head, said, 'Did you ever talk about the Job?' It was clear from the look that passed across Linnell's face that he knew what she meant. *His* job, if you could call it that, as well as Paul's.

'First few times we met up, I suppose, just making conversation really, but not after that. It was kind of an unwritten rule. We didn't want that kind of thing getting in the way.'

Helen noticed he was still fingering his chain. Thought, Getting in the way of *what*? 'So he never asked you about any work associates? Never asked about anything you were doing?'

'Like I said, it would have got in the way. Made things awkward.' He swirled the melting ice around in his glass. 'Do your friends always talk to you about abused kids?'

On the back foot again. Linnell was making it clear that he knew plenty about her, and what she did. He might have dug around; she didn't doubt that he knew other coppers who would have been happy to do his digging for him and pass on the information. Or he might simply have heard it from Paul during one of their cosy chats. Sitting at the cricket, maybe.

Either way, it made Helen feel as though she wanted a long, hot shower. 'When was the last time you saw him?' she asked.

He thought about it. 'About two weeks ago. Something like that. He came here, matter of fact.'

'I know,' Helen said. Just to make it clear *she* had done some digging, too.

'He brought me over some lunch.' Linnell enjoyed the memory, but the smile slipped off his face fairly quickly. 'I wish we'd parted on better terms, tell you the truth.'

'What?'

He looked a little uncomfortable, wrapping the chain around a finger now, but then he shrugged, as though deciding there was no harm in telling her. As though he'd worked out that she probably wouldn't be too surprised. 'What I said before, about not talking about work? Well, we did, the last couple of times we got together. Paul had asked me to help him out, to pass on a few names. People I thought he could . . . talk to.'

Helen swallowed.

'I told him I couldn't help,' Linnell said. 'Well, that I didn't want to. It wouldn't have been right for all sorts of reasons.'

'What kind of people?'

'People in my line of work. Businessmen. People you might also have come across in your line of work.'

'Like Kevin Shepherd?'

'Who?' He looked like he'd never heard the name before.

Helen's tongue felt thick and heavy in her mouth. 'Why did Paul want you to do that?'

'Come on, love.'

'Have a guess.'

'What, same as you have, you mean?'

Helen reached down for her handbag, drew it closer to her, feeling

225

like she might need to be out of the chair and away at any moment.

Linnell turned away from her and stared out across the small garden. 'Things turning out how they did, I wish I'd helped him. You go over those things when you lose someone, don't you? You replay moments. I'm sure you've been doing the same thing.'

'I doubt we've been doing the same thing.'

'Stupid really.' Linnell cleared his throat. 'I'd've been happy to lend him some money if that's all it was. He only had to ask, you know?'

'You should never borrow money off friends,' Helen said. She emphasised the last word. Still not convinced there hadn't been a more formal arrangement.

'Was he in any kind of trouble, money-wise?'

There was no way Helen was going to answer. She would not give him any of herself, of herself and Paul. There was no way she was going to tell him the trouble Paul had been in was something he'd kept strictly to himself. She felt anger building in her, like a desire to piss or puke; at Paul, Christ yes, but also at herself for being stupid. As though she could ever come away from this feeling any other way.

At Linnell especially, right at that moment, seeing that he meant it. How much he cared. Seeing that tears had welled up in his eyes the second before he had turned away.

The big man stepped out onto the patio and told Linnell he was needed inside. Someone had drilled through a cable.

Linnell put a hand over Helen's when he stood up. 'Stay and finish your drink, love,' he said.

Theo sat in the stash house, not because he was expecting to do a roaring trade, not with the streets crawling with the Met, but because it felt like the safest place to be.

Ever since Mikey, he'd been wondering whether he should start carrying a gun all the time. Easy and Wave did, liked to show them off like bling whenever possible. Most of the others *said* they did, patting their pockets like they had their dicks in there, but Theo had never bothered. He had always thought that carrying a gun made you a target, fair game. Easy said that was stupid; that as a member of the street crew he was a target anyway, and that people would presume he was carrying whether he was or not.

Easy talked sense every now and again. A gun might have been a better investment than those Timberlands.

Even if Theo couldn't quite bring himself to get one for personal use, there was always a gun to hand in the stash house, which was why it was as good a place as any to sit and think. To hide. He knew how to use it, knew that he could have it in his hand by the time anyone had managed to get through the reinforced steel door.

'Like Fort Knox,' Easy had said. 'Only time you're in trouble, some fucker comes knocking with a JCB.'

Mikey and SnapZ had both been there in Hackney that night and now both were dead. But was Theo being stupid? Maybe Mikey had paid for what he did to that hooker. Maybe SnapZ had been doing business of his own that nobody knew about. His mind worked through the possibilities but was unable to come up with any explanation for what was happening that didn't sound ridiculous.

Maybe it was coppers?

He'd killed one of their own, after all, and he knew how that kind of thing went down. He'd seen a film once, an Eastwood movie before he went serious and got old, where cops were taking the law into their own hands and killing drug dealers and rapists and all that. What if they knew who had been in that car; had known all along and decided that five bullets were a lot less trouble than five warrants? A good way to cut down on paperwork . . .

Theo heard shouting outside the door and froze, his eyes seeking out the gun on the table in front of him.

He waited. Just kids, enjoying all the excitement.

He needed to call Javine, let her know where he was and what was happening. He opened his phone and dialled the number, trying to relax so she wouldn't hear anything in his voice.

It wasn't easy.

On the way across from the estate he'd passed the place where they were doing the mural for Mikey. Like always, they'd gone to town, made him look like some kind of angel. Golden-skinned with shiny white teeth.

Theo had stared at the painted bricks and thought about SnapZ and the rest of them. He couldn't help wondering if they were going to need a bigger wall.

Feet up in front of the box – in dressing gown and pyjama bottoms, with tea and a rapidly diminishing packet of Jaffa Cakes – was going some small way to easing the memory of the meeting with Frank Linnell.

The feeling of being handled.

It wasn't like she'd expected to come away with too many answers, or any answers at all, but she hadn't banked on walking out of that pub with even more questions.

At work, cases often turned out to be far more complex than they'd first appeared: the horrified relative who turned out to be the abuser, who it was subsequently revealed had been abused himself. There was always something else going on. Most of her colleagues dreaded such cases; were worn down by the long hours and the paperwork, by the *weight* of all that pain.

But Helen thrived on it.

Some people opened a can of worms and fought to get the lid back on double quick, but Helen had always been more inclined to thrust her hands in good and deep. To let the slimy, twisted things curl around her fingers until she developed a feel for them.

She *enjoyed* trouble, wasn't really happy unless she'd got a few problems to sort out, that was what Paul had said. The messier the better.

'Yeah, right, Hopwood. Pretty ironic, considering . . .'

She changed the channel and stuffed another Jaffa Cake into her mouth; turned up the sound and swung her feet to the floor when she saw what was happening.

A reporter talking straight to camera, a spray-painted wall behind her. She was young, black and suitably earnest; trying to ignore the group of young boys doing their best to get into shot. 'This was another gang shooting,' she said. The second murder in only a few days that had shocked this tightly knit community. Police in Lewisham were now working flat out to get to the bottom of the killings, but it looked very much like they had a gang war on their hands. Two of the boys leaned into frame as the reporter handed back to the studio. Shouted at the camera and struck poses.

Helen remembered what the DI had said when she'd sat in his office that first Monday morning after the crash. Paul had died in north London, but the car had been stolen in the south. Perhaps the gang responsible were involved in a turf war, so had deliberately carried out the shooting on rival territory. It had just been a question of *which* gangs, the DI had said, which wasn't so easy to work out when there were so many of them. When none of them were queuing up to help out the police.

Now, they might have made it a little more obvious.

It was certainly a decent enough place to start looking. She had a hospital appointment first thing, but bugger all else after that. No reason not to give it a go.

Get those fat fingers in a little deeper.

TWENTY-FIVE

The woman who came in every Monday, the sainted Betty, sorted out most of Frank's meals for the week, but he enjoyed making his own breakfast. He relished the thinking time. Listening to media poofs and politicians talking out of their arses on Radio Four, while he made himself a pot of tea, cooked and mentally ran through the day ahead. Sometimes Laura would be around early, and they'd enjoy the time together, but there was no sign of her this morning.

That was OK; he had a lot to think about.

He chopped a tomato to stir into his scrambled eggs and thought what a nice girl Helen Weeks was. That said, he hadn't really expected her not to be. Why would Paul have been with any other sort?

Paul had never said too much about her, and Frank hadn't pushed, but he'd sensed there'd been some trouble around the previous Christmas. It was hard to tell whether it came from him or her, and it probably made no difference either way. But you didn't need to be Einstein to work out it would have been around the time when she got herself up the stick.

Not for the first time, Frank was thankful to be well out of all that carry on. Happy enough to remember a few special people from his past, and to pay for a bunk-up every now and again. It was the easiest way to avoid grief.

Last winter, Frank had told Paul he was there for him if there was a problem – if he needed to talk, night or day – and had left it at that.

He pushed his tomato from the chopping board into the pan and added some more butter. That was the secret of perfect scrambled egg, plenty of good, salted butter.

Paul had been right to play his cards close to his chest, though, Frank could see that. She was bright and suspicious, this one; on top of which she wasn't afraid to dig. It probably made her a bloody good copper. Matter of fact, he was grateful she didn't work for Serious and Organised. Soon as he thought it, Frank wished he'd said as much to her the day before. He had a feeling she'd have found it funny.

He poured the eggs on to his toast, carried the plate across to the table, added plenty of black pepper.

The previous Christmas, he'd given Paul a silver hip flask, and Paul had given him a Bruckner CD he'd been banging on about. The Vienna Philharmonic playing the Seventh. It was the same one he fetched out and played into the early hours, the night Helen had called to tell him that Paul had been killed.

Laura had come down half asleep and asked him what was wrong, but he'd sent her back to bed.

When he'd eaten, Frank loaded the dishwasher, then walked through to his office to give Clive a call. He wanted to move matters forward. He'd always been one for getting a job done as quickly as possible and pushing on to the next thing. Hot irons and all that . . .

Besides which, he never liked to give anyone the chance to work out he was coming for them.

Detective Inspector Spiky Bugger called just as Helen was leaving the hospital. He said he was sorry that she hadn't been told very much; apologised that she'd been left out of the loop. She said she understood, knew that it was probably because there hadn't been much to tell her, and he didn't argue.

He seemed keen to keep it short, just wanting to let her know that they were following up a few fresh lines of enquiry. He promised to try to keep her better informed. She told him she'd be grateful, and insisted she was fine when he asked how she was.

Half an hour later, walking down from the multi-storey above the Lewisham Centre, Helen had a pretty good idea what those 'fresh lines of enquiry' were. Having seen the news the night before, and several more reports on TV first thing, she knew that many of the DI's team, if not the man himself, would be walking the same streets as she was at that very moment. She half expected to bump into him, queuing for a parking ticket, and wondered how the conversation would go if she did.

'Small world . . .'

'What are you doing here?'

'Just out for a walk. Exercise is good for the baby.'

'In *Lewisham*?'

'It's very underrated.'

Helen knew that few people would *over*rate Lewisham, based on a cursory stroll around its main shopping area at any rate. Granted, anywhere that had seen two fatal shootings in less than a week was hardly likely to feel like Hampstead or Highgate Village, but even so. The place felt like somewhere people would visit only if they had to; only if the life they endured behind their own four walls was close to intolerable. Somewhere to get in and out of quickly. There was a leisure centre, a decent-looking park and a library, and Helen knew that if she had the time to look, she'd find a variety of smaller communities untouched by the tension and the violence. But around the DLR and bus stations, outside the pubs and shopfronts, the noise, the *industry*, only seemed to heighten the edgy atmosphere.

The heart of the place felt clogged and close to giving up.

Helen walked along the High Street. The usual chains: Boots, Argos, the compulsory Starbucks. There seemed to be an inordinate number of places to eat – McDonald's, KFC, Jenny's Burgers, Nando's, Chicken Cottage – interspersed with pound shops and low-end grocers'. She could picture the look of horror on Jenny's face.

'What, no M and S? And *how* far is the nearest Waitrose?'

Within an hour, Helen had spoken to a dozen or more people, found locations where it was not unnatural to fall into conversation: waiting for a cashpoint, at a bus stop, in the queue in a small baker's. Not produced her warrant card. She'd decided that the conversations would be more illuminating without it, and she did not want to risk being seen by any of the officers who were investigating the murders officially.

People had plenty to say; had opinions that they were more than keen to pass on. Deeply felt, dismissive or, to Helen's mind, plain ridiculous.

'Life's not worth tuppence round here right now, that's the truth.'

'No more than some of these little bastards deserve.'

'So where d'you think all these guns are coming from? Ask yourself that. Who supplies them? The government, that's who. They *want* us to kill each other.'

Helen walked away from the main street, across Lee Bridge and into the quieter areas behind the station. Over towards the estates: the Lee Marsh, the Kidbrooke, the Downton and the Orchard. There were plenty of youngsters hanging around, enjoying the sunshine. And more than enough men in uniform eager to pass the time of day with them.

At an intersection, where two police vans were parked, she saw a smallish crowd gathered in front of a mural. People were taking photographs, and a camera crew had set up and was doing vox pops. There was rap music coming from a portable beat box on the pavement.

She read the dedication: 'Michael Williamson. 1992-2008.'

A column of graffiti ran down one side: a list of signatures, tags sprayed against a white background designed to look like a scroll. A roll of honour. Helen stared at the multicoloured tangle of swirls and symbols on the brickwork. She couldn't decipher most of the names, but made out a few.

Wave. With three wavy blue lines underneath, like the sea.

Sugar Boy.

Easy. With 'S & S' in a circle beside the name; the letters drawn as hissing snakes.

On the far side of the street, near the entrance to the Lee Marsh, Helen saw a cluster of boys lurking by a low block of garages. She wandered across, aware of the looks being exchanged when they saw that she was coming. There were six or seven and she doubted any of them was yet a teenager. Pointless to speculate as to whether they'd be in school if it were not the summer holidays, or to presume for one second that they were too young to be tied up with one of the local crews. Not for the first time, Helen wondered why CP units such as her own didn't spend much more time trying to protect children *before* the damage was done.

She nodded back towards the wall, to the man with the camera and his colleague sticking a microphone into the faces of passers-by. 'They're talking about a gang war,' she said.

All except two of the kids began to drift away, seemingly unconcerned, joking with one another as they went, but keen to put distance between themselves and the conversation. Of the pair who were left, it was immediately clear that the shorter boy was the more talkative; but that was not saying a great deal.

'Talking about all sorts,' he said. 'They don't know nothing.'

'What do you think?'

The sullen expression on the boy's face changed. It was only for a second, but in that moment Helen could tell he was pleased to have been asked his opinion. The boy wore jeans and a baggy basketball shirt, and his hair had been cut very short. When he turned slightly, Helen could see that some kind of pattern had been shaved into the back. 'If it's a war, the other crew won't know what's hit them, man.'

'Who's the other crew?'

The boy shrugged, glanced at his friend. The other boy was gangly and unco-ordinated, as awkward as a baby giraffe. He kicked at the ground and spun slowly round on one leg; took a couple of steps away; turned and ambled back.

'Are you in that crew?' Helen nodded back towards the mural.

'Maybe,' the chatty boy said. He stuck his thumbs into the pockets of his jeans and spread his short legs. He was at least a foot shorter than Helen.

'You know the people on that list? Wave and Sugar Boy?'

'Everyone knows Wave.'

'Is he the leader?'

The boy shrugged again. His friend sucked his teeth, looked like he was ready to be on his way.

'If it's not a war, who do you think killed Michael and . . . the other boy?' Helen had heard the second boy's name on the news, but it had slipped her mind.

'Mikey and SnapZ,' the boy said.

'Why were Mikey and SnapZ killed? What do *you* think?'

The boy cocked his head, like he was mulling it over. Helen gave him the time, looked from one boy to the other; at the attitude and bum-fluff. She had no idea what either of them might be capable of, but still felt like she might be able to buy information from them with sweets and fizzy drinks.

'Disrespected someone, maybe,' the kid said.

'Who?'

'Doesn't matter. That's enough, you get me?'

'I think so.'

'You got to have a rep and you got to keep it, yeah? You got to be the buff man and that means stepping up to anyone who don't behave the way they should. I'm telling you, man, anyone try to boy me they better be ready to pay.'

Helen nodded to show she understood.

'Everyone knows that. Mikey, SnapZ, *everyone* . . .'

'How does someone join the crew?' Helen asked, like it had just popped into her head. 'Is there like an initiation kind of thing?'

The boy tilted up his chin. 'You some sort of undercover copper?'

Helen felt herself blush, felt it deepen as the taller boy stepped forward and looked her up and down; as she saw something that should not have been there in his eyes. She had no doubt that these boys were already sexually active, that they had ceased to be children in all the ways that mattered.

The taller boy sent a thin string of spit from between his teeth. Said, 'You fat or just pregnant, man?'

It took Helen ten minutes to walk the relatively short distance back to the High Street. Walking was becoming increasingly difficult, as was driving, with her seat pushed right back away from her belly and her feet struggling to reach the pedals. That morning, at her final ante-natal appointment, the doctor had smiled and told her that everything was fine. All the boxes had been ticked. 'Just sit around all day and spoil yourself,' he'd said. 'Get ready for the big day. It'll soon be over.'

So what the hell was she doing trudging around Lewisham, sweating and feeling stupid? Wasting her time. Feeling further out of her depth than she could ever remember.

She thought about how those boys had made her feel. She'd been in more dangerous situations, after all. She'd been physically threatened by a predatory paedophile in an interview room and had stared him down, yet now two children had unnerved her to the point where she could still feel the tremor in her legs.

For once, the urge to turn on her heel had been stronger than the urge to lash out.

Helen knew that having a child changed you in fundamental ways; she'd seen it in Jenny. She knew that it made you less confrontational and less inclined to take any sort of risk. Paul had asked her once during a particularly nasty argument if she really thought she'd be able to hack it when she went back. If she honestly thought she could handle the Job; *her* Job especially.

She'd laughed it off back then, but she wasn't finding the suggestion particularly funny any more.

Back at the shopping centre, she decided to call into the supermarket and pick up a few things for dinner. Struggling out through the doors, she collided with a baby-buggy and dropped one of her carrier bags. As she watched the young mother walk away without a backward glance, a teenage boy stepped out of the newsagent's next door and walked across.

'You OK?'

Helen delved into the bag and was annoyed to see that two of her six eggs were smashed. 'Just about,' she said.

The boy took the egg box, carried the mess across to a bin a few yards away, then walked back. 'That was out of order.'

'It's not like she couldn't *see* me,' Helen said.

He waited until she was steady, with a bag in each hand, then nodded and walked away. She thanked him, but he was already lighting a cigarette, hurrying to get across the road before the signal changed. Helen shouted after him and the boy stopped on the far side, pointing at himself to be sure it was him she was calling out to.

By the time Helen had caught up with him she was out of breath. 'You couldn't give me a hand with these to the car, could you?'

They walked back across the road in silence, and around the corner of the shopping centre, moving through the crowds towards the car park entrance.

'You live round here?' Helen asked.

'Over there.' The boy nodded towards the estates.

'I've not exactly had a great day. So, you know, this is . . .'

Another boy came striding towards them, slowed as he got close and grinned at the boy with the shopping bags. 'You're a *seriously* dark horse, T,' he said. He nodded towards Helen. 'Got yourself a nice lickle MILF tucked away.' He winked and pointed at Helen's belly. 'That one of yours, is it?'

The boy carrying her bags stepped around, shaking his head, and the other boy moved on, laughing, along the pavement. 'Sorry.'

Helen shrugged. 'What's a MILF?'

'You don't want to know.'

'Like I said, the day can't get much worse.'

'Mummy I'd Like to Fuck,' the boy said. He glanced across as Helen moved to avoid a man with a large dog. 'Sorry.'

Helen was parked on the first floor of the car park, and the boy waited for her on the stairs, stopping every two or three steps to let her catch up. 'There's a lift, you know,' he said.

Helen leaned against the wall for a second. The narrow stairwell smelled of urine and burgers. 'If I can't make one flight of stairs I might as well just curl up and die,' she said. After she had validated her ticket at the pay station, the two of them walked towards her car. 'It's not a nice place to be at the moment, is it?'

The boy looked around.

'Not the car park,' Helen said. The boy smiled. 'Round here generally.'

'Pretty sweet if you're a florist,' he said. 'Or if you're in the mural-painting business.'

'What's *your* business?'

'Don't have one.' He looked at his training shoes. 'Just try and pick up a bit of cash where I can.'

'Did you know either of the boys who were killed?'

'Both of them.'

'Sorry.'

'They weren't friends, exactly. Not *proper* friends.'

'Still. Must be scary.'

He shrugged.

'Think it'll carry on?'

'I reckon.'

'This is me,' Helen said. 'Thanks.' She unlocked the car and the boy lifted her bags into the boot. The sound of cars screeching around the tight corners bounced off the walls on either side of them. She opened the door. 'Probably a good time to take a holiday, if you ask me.'

The boy finished lighting another cigarette and shook his head, narrowing his eyes as the smoke drifted back into his face. 'Can't see me getting on me toes any time soon,' he said.

'Well, keep your head down at least, eh?'

'Yeah.' He took a drag. 'You got a name for it?'

Helen was confused for a moment, then he pointed and she realised that he was talking about the baby. 'No. Not yet.' She and Paul had tossed names around for a while until he'd found out about the affair. Then the subject was quietly dropped. Now that she had nobody to consult, it was something to which she'd given remarkably little thought. She smiled. 'Maybe I should name him after you,' she said. 'You hear about women doing that, don't you? Naming their kids after the midwife, or the taxi driver who rushes them to the hospital. Be as good a name as any, probably.'

The boy grinned and shook his head. 'Seriously bad idea,' he said.

'Oh well . . .'

Helen got into the car and yanked at the seat belt. Aware of the boy watching as she reversed out of the tight space. She raised her hand to him as he stood aside to let her drive away.

TWENTY-SIX

It had become a thing now.

There'd been no let up since SnapZ's death, and there seemed to be cameras on every corner. Hordes of journalists from the big papers as well as the red tops; standing around in those jackets with elbow patches, pointing their recorders at anyone in a hooded top, nodding like hungry dogs and getting hard-ons. All mad keen to get some scoop; to get a bit of that lovely danger on their front pages.

And there was no shortage of people willing to give it to them. Kids who'd never so much as nicked a bag of crisps talking like they were proper gangsters, turning on the talk and walking away with a tenner for their trouble. 'Make sure you spell my name right, man, you get me?'

Even some of those in the crew were getting in on it.

Theo had seen a bunch of them, Sugar Boy and a few of the others, framed at the end of a dark alleyway at the edge of the estate, turning it on for *London Tonight*. Some of them were wearing bandannas pulled down over their faces, dark glasses, all that. One idiot was posing with a gun. It might have been his; might have been a replica the TV people gave him. All of them striking their best hard-man poses and gobbing off.

'You ain't part of a crew, you got nothing, man.'

'Closer than family.'

'When one of your bredren is shot, you all feel it, you get me? You feel it *here*.' The fist against the chest, and the nodding.

Theo had wanted to charge across and slap their stupid faces and tell them to shut their mouths. Take the cameraman's gear and shove it up his arse; smack his fist to his own chest and tell them all that what *he* felt in there was the same thing that made you stammer and shit your pants. Made it hard to breathe when you were wide awake and staring down at your son in the middle of the night.

He'd been at the stash house since just after eight, had taken to leaving the flat earlier and earlier. Getting his paper and fags, and waiting outside the door for the café to open.

They'd walked in and shot SnapZ in his own place.

Theo had never felt particularly safe at home anyway: people had been knifed in his block often enough. But this was different. Trouble was, what was he supposed to say to Javine? It was tricky to suggest that she should take Benjamin out for the day, *stay* out until he got back, just in case, you know, someone came knocking with a gun in their hand while he was hiding out like a pussy on the other side of the estate.

Sugar Boy came in around ten-thirty. They talked for a few minutes about what was happening, and Sugar Boy showed Theo the cash he'd made talking shit to reporters. Theo turned on the TV, tried to lose himself in it.

He'd suggested that Javine should pop down and spend a bit more time with his mum, but that hadn't gone down well. Nothing had been going down too well over the last week or two, if he was honest.

'Try spending a bit more time with her your own self. And your son too, come to that.'

'I have to work.'

She didn't need to say any more. It was there in the way she hoisted

241

up the baby and held him there, rubbing his back while she stared across his shoulder at Theo. Right: out working and being a buff man like your little friend Easy. Like Mikey. Like whoever put a bullet in his stupid head. A buff man, a *proper* buff man might think about really taking care of his woman and his son; might think about getting a job where a gun wasn't a tool of the trade.

But she didn't know that he'd killed anyone. That someone, for whatever reason, had set about making those responsible pay with their lives. That he couldn't think straight or make a decision and hadn't slept or shat properly for a fortnight.

'We'll knock on your mum's door a bit later,' Javine had said eventually. 'Pop in for ten minutes, OK?'

She didn't know that he felt like a sheep, bleating for its life, with a wolf outside the door.

There was still concern in Helen's mind that anyone investigating Paul might also be interested in her, so when she'd stumbled half asleep to the phone at eight-fifteen and heard an officious-sounding police officer introducing himself, she'd feared the worse.

The panic had subsided when the officer had explained that he was calling to finalise the arrangements for the forwarding of Paul's pension; to talk through bank details, set up standing orders and so on.

That had heralded a different sort of panic altogether.

Although the funeral arrangements were theoretically in hand, somewhere between Paul's mother and the Police Federation, Helen knew there was still a raft of administrative duties that would have to be dealt with at some point: the closing of accounts; life insurance; HP payments. The will itself, which she and Paul had made out one afternoon using one of those DIY kits from WH Smith, was fairly straightforward, as far as she could remember, with each of them the sole beneficiary of the other. None of it could be taken care of properly until the inquest had returned a verdict and a death certificate was issued; but even so, she preferred not to think about any of it, at least not until after the baby was born. Her father had volunteered to help out with that side of things, and for once she'd been delighted to take him up on his offer.

On the phone, the officer from Financial Liaison Services had been gently efficient and sensitive to her situation as he'd talked her through the process. It was the worst part of his job, he'd told her. When it was over she'd thanked him, then rushed to the bathroom to throw up.

Now, after a few pieces of toast and a shower, she walked across to the desk, to the deep drawer that was as close as she and Paul had come to any sort of filing system. She flicked past files that contained mortgage details, car documents and mobile phone bills, and drew out the clip folder that held Paul's bank statements.

She turned on the radio and carried the folder across to the sofa.

Maybe she should try to deal with all the other stuff, too. A distraction – a nice, dull, *safe* one – would have been welcome. She would surely have been better off spending her days talking to building societies and insurance companies, wallowing in the sympathy of call-centre workers, than behaving as she had. Dashing around like a mad bitch and digging up enough dirt to bury Paul three times over.

On the radio, a woman was talking about how she'd coped with a severely disabled son. The presenter said she was amazing. Helen got up and retuned to Radio One.

Paul had held current and savings accounts with HSBC; did most transactions over the phone or online. Helen took out a sheaf of statements going back six months and flicked through them. It was odd that such a dry and ordered series of names and numbers could be so telling, could provide an instant snapshot of a person.

Payments made to Virgin, HMV and Game; the local Indian restaurant; the branch of Woodhouse in Covent Garden that sold the easy-iron shirts he was fond of wearing with jeans. Direct debits to Sky and Orange. A small standing order paid to a charity for deaf children ever since Paul's niece had been diagnosed a few years before.

She found the payment for the watch he had bought for her birthday two months earlier. He'd said that he'd hung on to the receipt in case she wanted to change it, but she'd told him it was fine. She'd meant to pop in and check the price the next time she was passing the jeweller's, but had forgotten. She saw now that it had cost thirty quid less than he'd told her it did.

'You sodding cheapskate, Hopwood.'

There were plenty of payments that she did not recognise: card transactions that she could check with the bank if she wanted to, but none for any large amount; and besides, it was payments *into* the accounts that she needed to look hardest at.

Salary, a few cheques from Helen herself, the tiny dividends on some shares he'd been given by his mother. Nothing that looked significant. If he had received payments from the likes of Shepherd and Linnell, they must have been made into another account.

There was no sense of relief as Helen clipped the statements back into the folder. She knew that there was something she was not meant to find. And whatever else Paul had been, he had not been stupid.

She was the one who couldn't keep secrets.

Helen walked into the bedroom to get dressed, pulled out a T-shirt and wondered if what she'd been looking for might be tucked away at the back of the wardrobe, behind Paul's guitar. With limited technical ability that was about as frustrating as a dead-end could get. She'd run into brick walls plenty of times at work, of course, but there was usually somebody on the team who had the expertise to find a way around them.

This time she was on her own.

In the next room, a DJ they had both always hated droned on about some gig he'd attended, confident as ever that his own C-list social life was of more interest to listeners than any music he might play.

A memory: Paul, snarling at the radio as he fetched milk from the fridge, '*Pointless, fat bastard.*'

You could try to find a way around a brick wall, or you could just stand and stare at the bloody thing. If all else failed, you could just keep throwing yourself at it, because the pain felt good.

Felt better.

It was just a look. No more than a glance up from his cue as he leaned across the table, and something like a smirk passing across his face, but it was enough to bring up the hairs on Theo's neck, to tell him something bad had happened.

Something else.

They had gone into the Cue Up for a bit of lunch: a sausage sandwich and something to drink; a frame or two of pool and an hour away from the stash house and the heat of the afternoon. Easy was in a good mood. He had suggested twenty quid a frame, but Theo had seen Javine's face again, heard that tone in her voice, and agreed on a tenner for best of three.

The place was no busier than usual. The same faces talking low across the snooker tables or hanging around near the bar. The same old guy muttering over his tea and toast and boring the arse off the woman behind the counter.

Easy won the first frame and was well ahead in the second; would probably have walked it anyway, even if Theo's mind had been on the game.

'Can't pot shit today,' Theo said.

'Outclassed, Star Boy, simple as that.'

'You're right.'

Easy had on a new chain, thick as rope. It swung against his cue when he leaned down to take a shot. 'You're not concentrating, man.' He smacked in a stripe. 'Not for days.'

'There's a lot going on.'

'Maybe.'

Theo nodded towards the window, the street outside. 'You got a problem with your eyes, man?'

Easy grinned, shrugged. 'That's when you need to focus most, you get me. Other people taking their eye off the ball, dodging the Five-O, grieving, all that. That's *exactly* when you need to be sharp. *Someone* got to keep this crew slick.'

'Wave not doing that?'

Another stripe went down. 'Wave doing what he does.'

Theo hadn't seen a great deal of Wave since it had all kicked off. Hadn't seen too many of the crew hanging out in threes and fours like they usually did. It was all down to Mikey and SnapZ, he knew that; but still, there were faces he'd not spotted on the usual corners for two or three days, maybe more.

'As If keeping his head down, is he?'

'If he knows what's good for him,' Easy said.

'Hanging out with Wave?'

'Hanging out of his arse, more like.'

'Not seen Ollie around for a bit either,' Theo said.

Then that look up, like a punch, and a dreadful certainty that began to take hold as Theo waited for Easy to turn away and leaned a hand down on the edge of the table to steady himself.

He thought back to a Saturday night, two days after Mikey had been killed, when the crew had gathered in the Dirty South. To drink and smoke themselves stupid. To regroup.

He had listened to a band playing in the back room, then wandered back to join the crew when he'd had enough. Easy had been loud and full of himself, moving from one member of the crew to the next; geeing them up like a football coach trying to talk a losing team back into it at half time.

Ollie had been nursing a bottle at a table in the corner, and Theo remembered Wave and Gospel deep in conversation a few feet away on a sofa near the door. He'd noticed the cuts and bruises on Gospel's face as she'd leaned in close to whisper; seen Wave put fingers on the back of her neck as she talked, clearly already getting a piece of what Ollie wanted.

Theo had seen the look on Wave's face when Gospel had finished talking, and the look on Ollie's when he saw Wave turning to stare him out. He saw it all again as he thought back, and heard Dennis Brown's voice, high above the ragged, remembered thump of the band in the back room. Words from the song he'd been listening to a few days before.

> 'Wolves and Leopards,
> Are trying to kill the sheep and the
> shepherds.
> Too much informers,
> Too much tale-bearers . . .'

He knew, when Easy looked up from the pool table, that he wouldn't be seeing Ollie again. He could only hope, for the kid's sake, that Easy hadn't been the one to get hold of him. He knew about his friend's capacity for violence. As If had a foot on Easy at least, but Theo knew who his money would be on if it ever came down to it.

Easy left a ball rattling in the jaws, cursed and stood up. 'You're on, T.'

Theo's mind was racing. If Wave knew that Ollie had been talking to somebody out of turn, perhaps he also knew who that person was. Perhaps he was already taking steps to stop what was happening. Maybe Easy would be dispatched to deal with that situation too . . .

'T . . .'

Theo leaned down and swiped the black ball into a pocket with his hand.

'Fuck you doing, man?' Easy said.

Theo put down a ten-pound note and said, 'I'm going home.'

Helen had wandered down to the Turkish grocer's as soon as the lunchtime news had finished. The owner's wife had given her some freshly made baklava stuffed with pistachios. Helen had bought some bread and cheese too, and had taken the lot into the small park opposite to eat.

When she got home there were three messages on the machine. The first two were hang-ups. There had been a few in the last week or so, and on each occasion the caller had withheld their number had waited ten or fifteen seconds before putting down the phone. As if he'd been content not to speak, or too afraid to say anything.

Helen felt fairly sure the caller was a man. And that it was not a wrong number.

The third message was from a woman, a civilian administrative assistant at the Area West Murder Squad.

The senior investigating officer was apparently satisfied with the way the investigation had been proceeding. He had conferred with the coroner, who was happy to authorise burial and issue a temporary death certificate. In light of this, the SIO would himself be happy to release Sergeant Hopwood's body the next day.

Happy.

TWENTY-SEVEN

The pub wasn't far from being ready, and Clive said that he was sorting out things in SE3, so Frank went in early to the office he rented behind Christ's College School and spent the morning catching up with several of his other business interests.

There was a pile of planning-permission documents to go through and searches on three new commercial properties he was in the process of purchasing. He agreed weekend rates with a new Polish contractor and organised 'gifts' for two different councillors, whose goodwill would come in handy for a new development he was contemplating in Battersea. He made a few calls and arranged for several cases of decent wine and 'his and hers' watches to be delivered.

It was all part of the game. Legitimate expenditure. His accountant would write off those purchases as 'corporate hospitality' when the time came to do the books.

Then he drove out to see Laura's mother. He was alone in the car, driving himself for a change. He didn't want to give any of his employees, not even Clive, access to this aspect of his private life.

She lived in a maisonette, which Frank had bought for her a few years before in the nicer part of Eltham. He'd given her a little car too, just something she could run around in; but Frank got the impression that she didn't leave the house much these days. Though the business was up and running by then, Frank had started visiting as often as he could once he'd found out that he had a sister, and he always came away feeling like he'd done a good thing.

She was thrilled to see him, same as usual. She told him how grateful she was that he'd come to see her, how grateful she was for *everything*, and her eyes were brimming before he was even inside. He could smell the drink on her as she pulled him into an embrace.

They talked about Laura, as always, while Frank drank orange juice and she opened another bottle of wine. She asked him about his business and he told her about the pub. She said it sounded wonderful, that she used to enjoy an evening out, when pubs weren't full of loud music and people watching football.

'Laura would sit outside, good as gold. We'd bring her out a bottle of Coke and some crisps.'

'My mum did that with me,' Frank said.

'There you go then.'

'He liked a drink, didn't he?'

As soon as 'he' was mentioned, the tone of the conversation shifted. Frank's old man had walked out on him and his mum, then done exactly the same thing many years later, when Laura was about the age that Frank had been. Laura's mother would often produce a picture of a thin-faced man who looked horribly like Frank. Then she would invariably say, 'You're more of a dad to her than that useless twat ever was.'

Frank had been looking for his old man for years, handing over good money to private detectives and getting nowhere. He still lived in hope that one day he'd catch up with him.

Show the useless twat *exactly* how he'd turned out . . .

'He liked a drink, but the drink didn't like him.' There were not too many happy memories for either of them where Frank's father was concerned, and the voice of the man's second ex-wife was laced with booze and bitterness as she spoke. 'Amazing when you think about it, that you and Laura both turned out so well.'

'Down to you and my mother,' Frank said.

'Genes are powerful things, though.' She poured herself another glass. 'You ever worried about what you might have inherited from him?'

'Never thought about it.'

'That why you never had your own kids, Frank?'

'No . . .'

'It's not too late, you know.'

Frank shook his head. 'I don't believe all that.'

'*Never* too late.'

'It's up to you how you turn out. There's never any excuse. It's never anyone else's fault if you mess it up.'

'You didn't mess it up, though, love. You've done so well for your-self.'

'Right. And nobody can take credit for that but me.'

Half the glass of wine had already gone, and another gulp took care of the rest. 'You'd make a good dad, Frank.'

Frank stood up and walked across to the mirror above the gas fire. He straightened the chain around his neck and sorted out his hair while she talked about how his father would get sometimes when he'd had a few too many; about how he couldn't keep his hands to him-self . . . or his fists. Somewhere beneath the disgust, though, Frank could hear the sadness in her voice. His old man had been a good-looking sod, there was no getting away from that, and Frank knew that there hadn't been anyone important in this woman's life since he'd walked out.

He guessed that, deep down, she still felt something other than contempt for the miserable bastard who had so royally fucked her over.

'Why did you ever shack up with him in the first place?' he asked.

She pressed the empty glass against her cheek. 'Rotten taste in blokes, simple as that.'

'Same as Laura,' Frank said.

An hour later, heading home, he thought about driving into Lewisham. It was only another ten minutes on from his place, after all.

A couple of miles and a world away.

Thinking about Laura had led, naturally, to thinking about Paul, and Frank thought it might be interesting to drive around the streets where some of those responsible for his death still lived, for the time being. Get a feel for the people who had dreamed it up. For the stick men . . .

Besides which, there might be more than a few people looking to get out of the area quickly, things being what they were. Property-wise, there might be some bargains to be had.

Jenny picked Helen up just after six. As they pulled onto the main road, Helen looked back, thinking that she'd noticed a black Jeep four or five cars behind them. Jenny asked her what she was looking at and, unable to see the car any more, Helen gave up. It was difficult to crane her neck round, and for all she knew it could have been any four-by-four.

She felt scared and stupid and told herself to calm down. Tried to enjoy the view, lit up and laid out to one side of them as they drove south to Crystal Palace: the Eye, St Paul's, Canary Wharf.

Jenny had booked a table in a gastropub she had seen reviewed in *Time Out*. Wooden floors, weird paintings and something jazzy from the speakers. It was earlier than Helen preferred to eat dinner, and she guessed that she'd be raiding the fridge again before bedtime, but she knew that Jenny had to get home to sort out her kids, that Tim was not great at looking after them, or himself.

'It'll look like a war zone by the time I get back,' Jenny said.

Helen ordered grilled squid followed by lamb chops while her sister went for pâté and a chicken Caesar salad. They shared a bottle of sparkling water and talked easily enough.

The argument they'd had the previous weekend had not been forgotten, and Helen had been expecting the atmosphere to be a little tense, so she was amazed when Jenny apologised. Helen was usually the one who made the first move, unwilling to live with the guilt that her sister was so good at generating after any disagreement.

'Don't be silly,' Helen said. If anything, being on the receiving end of an apology only increased the guilt. It was as though she had a bottomless reservoir of it.

'I've been feeling terrible about it.'

'Don't worry.'

Jenny took Helen's hand and squeezed, and it was done and dusted. This was how it had always been between them. Cat and dog, or best mates.

'It's fine, honestly,' Helen said. 'I was just all over the place.'

'It's understandable—'

'I *am* all over the place.'

Jenny nodded. 'Of course you are.'

On the way from Tulse Hill, Helen had told her that Paul's body was being released to the undertaker's, that the funeral would be in a few days. They'd talked about whether Jenny should bring the kids and eventually decided against it. They'd all be travelling over to Paul's parents' place in Reading for the ceremony and a few drinks afterwards, and they discussed whether Helen should stay over; how much more she might alienate Paul's mother if she decided to travel back.

'We'll all help,' Jenny said.

When she'd mentioned her state of mind, Helen had not been thinking about the funeral. For a second or two, she came close to telling her sister everything – Linnell, Shepherd, the stuff she thought was on the laptop – but decided against it. She felt a need to tell *someone*, but knew that she would be more comfortable talking to Katie or even Roger Deering – someone with no axe to grind – than she would ever be talking to Jenny or her dad. There was no logic to it, she accepted that. *She* could think whatever she liked about Paul, could decide that he'd done despicable things behind her back, but she couldn't bear the thought that anyone else might judge him.

In the end, Helen decided to go down a road that was well known to her sister. 'It's Adam Perrin,' she said.

Jenny put down her water. 'You're not inviting *him*, are you?'

Helen laughed, though it had crossed her mind that he might turn up. It would be easy enough for him to get the details, after all. 'I think he might have been calling.'

They'd met on a residential course, a little over a year before. He was there with several other firearms officers and had seemed the least obnoxious as they had laughed and talked too loudly in the hotel lounge. Helen had been drinking rather a lot around that time, putting it down to stress at work, but she certainly wasn't looking to get involved with anyone. She'd enjoyed the chat, the flirting. He was well built, with short blond hair. Different from Paul . . .

'You *think*?'

'Calling and not saying anything.'

Jenny looked as confused as Helen felt. She didn't know why the man she'd had the affair with had come into her mind. Why she'd been imagining their phone conversation, the stinging comments that she'd hoarded up, waiting for a chance to deliver them:

'Sniffing round widows. That's very classy, even for you.'

'Don't be stupid, Helen.'

'You should at least have waited until I'd buried him.'

'Is that what you think about me?'

'I don't think about you at all.'

'I only slept with you, you know?'

'I don't really remember.'

'I didn't kill anyone. And you put plenty into it.'

'Yeah, well, I was drinking then . . .'

It felt good to lash out, even if it was only in her imagination.

The waitress arrived. They sat back in their chairs and let her lay down the plates. Jenny waited a minute, got stuck into her starter, then said, 'You should see him again.'

'*What?*'

The place wasn't busy, with only a few other tables taken, but the sound carried easily and both of them turned down their volume.

'I don't mean straight away, for Christ's sake.'

'Oh, *good.*'

'Later, maybe.' Helen had lowered her head, was shaking it, and Jenny waited for her to stop. 'You felt something for Adam. You know you did.'

'It was a fling. It was stupid.'

'It happened because you knew something was wrong between you and Paul.'

'*I* was the one who messed things up, OK?'

Jenny said nothing, just looked embarrassed, aware of the people behind her.

'You were just thrilled about it because you never really liked Paul in the first place.'

'I never liked seeing you settle for something,' Jenny said.

'Bollocks.' Over Jenny's shoulder, a woman at the corner table was craning her neck. Helen looked right at her until the woman turned back to her dinner, then spoke again in a whisper: 'That's bollocks, Jen . . .'

The tension that Helen had feared was crackling across the table. Eye contact was impossible, and when Jenny reached across to pour more water, they both stared hard at the glass.

'You never really said about the baby.'

'It's Paul's,' Helen said.

'You never said, that's all.'

'It's Paul's.'

The main course arrived, and they spoke about their father after that, about Jenny's kids, but the conversation was half hearted and sporadic. Helen's lamb was perfect, and she was hungrier than she thought she'd be, but still she couldn't finish.

It was late, and Theo was at home watching a DVD with Javine when Easy called round with cans of lager and some weed. Javine grudgingly took a joint off Easy and told him to keep the noise down, but said nothing else and sat there glued to the screen, refusing to be driven off to bed. Easy made a comment or two about the movie and rolled his eyes, until eventually Theo took the contrasting hints from both of them and told Easy they should take their beers outside.

They shared a joint and stared down over the wall that ran along the edge of the walkway. There were two girls riding bikes around in the dark, and a young couple on the tyre-swings in the centre, swaying slowly, next to each other. He couldn't see them, but Theo knew that the kids would be standing around on the far side of the garages near the street. They'd be winding each other up and staring hard at any car that drove past, making sure everyone knew that they didn't give a shit.

Theo thought they were like baby rats.

'What was all that with the pool yesterday?' Easy asked.

'I wasn't in the mood, that's all.'

'Let me know next time you're not in the mood. The cash comes in handy.'

Three floors below them, the boy on the swing shouted something to the girls on the bikes. One of them shouted back and rode away into the shadows; into the cut-through that led to the neighbouring estate.

'You thought much about Mikey and SnapZ?' Theo asked.

'Thought, Thank fuck it wasn't me!'

'What happened, I mean.'

'Everyone knows what happened, T.'

'Thought about *why*, though?'

Easy sighed out smoke. 'This that territory nonsense again, man?

Whose toes I been stepping on, all that?'

'No . . .' It was a warm night and Theo was wearing a vest. He glanced down at the thin material stretched against his chest; watched it shift as his heart thumped underneath.

'Been talking to Wave,' Easy said.

The material began to move a little faster.

'You remember the triangle thing?'

'Yeah.'

'Things need to change a bit, yeah? With what's been happening. Some different people going into the house and a few new faces coming in at the bottom. Working the corners and running and all that, you get me?'

Theo nodded. Job opportunities for a few of the baby rats.

'It's a chance for you to move up, man.'

'*You* moving up, then?'

Easy slurped at his beer. 'You move up same time as I do, Star Boy. The two of us get to watch over things together. It's a cushy number, T, I swear. Keep an eye on how it's all going and pass it on to Wave. You'd be like my – what is it? – my lieutenant or something.'

'Let me think about it, man.'

'Nothing to think about.'

'I'll see.'

'What?' He nodded back towards Theo's front door. 'You want to talk it through with your *girlfriend*?'

Theo said nothing.

Easy stepped closer to him, the mocking edge to his voice replaced by something darker. 'You better *really* think about this, you get me? This is fast track we're talking about now.'

Theo was already thinking. About the extra money, and the fact that things could hardly get any worse. About how much his last move up had cost him.

'What you said before: "Thank fuck it wasn't you . . ."'

Easy shrugged. 'What?'

'We were all in that car, man.'

'So?'

'Mikey and SnapZ. And Wave. You and me.'

The remains of Easy's joint went sailing over the wall and down. He was breathing heavily. Theo watched the slow shake of the head, the attempt to find an expression of shock or disbelief. But he could tell he was suggesting something that had already occurred to Easy himself. 'You've fucking lost it, Star Boy.'

'It's not a coincidence, all I'm saying.'

'You had a bang on the head or something? That bitch been chucking pans at you, man?'

'We should talk to Wave, maybe.'

'That stuff I wrote about you . . .'

'Be careful, that's all.'

Easy smacked a hand against the wall as he spoke, the anger building. 'All that crap, that testimonial or whatever . . .'

'I'm shitting it, Eez, don't mind telling you, yeah?'

Easy was in Theo's face then; pushing his beer can against Theo's neck and spraying him with spit. 'You can shit yourself all you want, yeah, but don't talk your pussy-arsed rubbishness to me. I don't want to hear it, and I don't want to see you thinking it. And I don't want to see you open your mouth with this any more. You get me?'

Theo nodded.

Easy pushed himself back, and stared for a few seconds, then hurled his can fast and hard at Theo's chest. He was already walking away as the beer flew everywhere and the can bounced and spun on the floor.

The shouting had brought Javine and one or two others to their front doors, but Theo didn't look up. Just watched the can frothing on the concrete walkway, and the beer running like piss and dripping down onto the grass below.

Paul and Adam Perrin had been laid out in the coffin together, both in their best dress uniforms, head to toe, like children sleeping in the same bed. They weren't bothering with a lid, for some reason, and as soon as the first clump of earth hit their faces, they sat bolt upright together, their timing perfect, like a double-act, spitting out dirt and laughing.

'It's fine,' Paul said, looking up at Helen. 'Not a problem, I promise.'

'What about going with *both* our names?' Adam asked. 'What about Adam-Paul?'

'Paul-Adam sounds a lot better,' Paul said, and the two of them were suddenly fighting. It was played for laughs, though, and they flapped their hands at each other, like a pair of old women swinging handbags, getting sillier by the minute until the vicar had to shout at them from the graveside; letting them know in no uncertain terms that they were upsetting the mourners and that he really needed to get on.

Helen woke up.

The pillow felt sopping and spongy, and the baby was kicking and kicking. Like he'd had enough, *heard* enough; was ready to come out and make her feel better.

TWENTY-EIGHT

Wave knocked on the door of the stash house, yanked at his dog's chain and ordered him to sit. He waited, then leaned close to the door to shout; told Sugar Boy that if he'd been asleep he was going to get woken up with a good kicking.

'No sofas and PS2s when you're back on the corner, you get me?'

It was Friday and Wave was keen to go about his business. To get what he'd come for and call in at all the other places he collected from. Pass on the takings to the usual faces and pocket his commission; get himself papered up good and proper for the weekend.

No need to queue at the ATM, and he didn't need a PIN.

He dug out his key and opened the door, pulling back the dog to let him know who should cross the threshold first. He raised his voice as he stepped inside, slammed the door shut, letting Sugar Boy know for sure that the Wave was about to come crashing down on him.

Sugar Boy was sitting on a wooden chair next to the sofa. Wave took a step towards him, the pit-bull straining in front, but stopped when he saw the two men move out: one from the bathroom; one from the bedroom at the back.

Each man had a gun. Both had been fitted with silencers.

Sugar Boy started to cry.

Wave dropped the dog's lead and reached towards his pocket, but the smallest shake of the head from the bigger of the two men was enough to tell him he was being seriously stupid. He raised his arms, said, 'Just take all the cash. I'll show you where.'

The older man turned and shot Sugar Boy, then turned back quickly and shot the dog.

Wave cried out and dropped down, scrabbling across to throw his arms around the dog. He pressed his face to the animal's neck and squeezed, only dimly aware of the fact that Sugar Boy was still alive; of the moans coming from the other side of the room. He opened an eye in time to see the older man step across the low table to finish off Sugar Boy with one in the top of the head.

'Right, now then,' the big man said.

Wave pushed himself up to his knees and took a deep breath. He tried to speak but it came out as babble. There was blood in his hair and smeared across the side of his face.

'You can tell us about the money if you like, but it won't help.'

'I'm getting paid anyway,' the older man said.

'This is about Paul Hopwood.'

'The fuck's he?' Wave spluttered.

'He *was* a police officer, waiting for a bus.'

Wave raised himself a little higher, spread his arms; getting it. 'This the Hackney business, yeah? Shooting at that car.'

'The Hackney business,' the big man said.

Wave looked relieved. His shoulders dropped and he managed something like a smile. He ran hands through his hair. They came away bloody. 'This is a serious fuck-up then,' he said. 'Lines of communication and all that. That was a *complicated* business.'

'Pretty simple from where that copper was standing.'

'There's stuff you need to know.'

'So, tell me . . .'

261

Clive listened while the man on his knees reeled off the facts that he hoped might save his life; while he tried to stay calm and pass on his information. Clive was certainly interested, putting together what he was being told with something that Jacky Snooks had said.

Piecing it all together, ready to tell Frank.

When Wave had run out of steam, Clive asked if there was anything else he thought might be important. Wave said that he'd told him everything he knew and was trying to stand up when Clive shot him twice in the chest.

Clive and Billy exchanged looks, each letting the other know that they had done well. Then they dropped the guns into the canvas tool-bag that Billy had brought with him.

'You want to look around?' Clive asked. 'See if you can find this money he was on about?'

'What do you think?'

'Up to you.'

Billy said that he wasn't too bothered, so they started to tidy up.

By the time Helen had got back the night before, there had been a message from Jenny, saying that she hadn't meant to upset her; that she was sorry if she'd said the wrong thing. There had also been a message from Roger Deering, asking how she was doing. And another hang-up which may or may not have been Adam Perrin.

Listening, she had thought about whoever had rung her bell and walked away. Her run-in with Kevin Shepherd. About the black Jeep she had begun to look for every time she left the house.

She called Jenny in the morning and left a message to say that everything was fine. She didn't bother calling Deering back. The dream had left her oddly positive and she'd woken feeling good about having things to do; things that *had* to be done. While they might be unpleasant, they would not involve chasing her own fat arse, hating herself for what she was doing and growing to hate the man she would have to bury in a few days' time.

She called Paul's mother and they talked through the arrangements. It was the warmest conversation they'd had in a while. Helen realised that not knowing when and how she would be able to say goodbye to her son had made Caroline Hopwood unusually awkward and unable to deal with people. She could only hope that, now things were finally being organised, there might be a similar return to normality in herself, too.

There needed to be, if this baby was going to have a mother worthy of the name.

They sorted out the music and the flowers, and Helen was assured that the vicar conducting the service would make a good job of it. He was someone they'd known a long time, Paul's mother told her, and he had officiated at Paul's sister's wedding.

'So he knows the family . . .'

Caroline had been as super-efficient as ever, and had already drawn up a contact list. Helen was asked to call any friends with whom Paul's family had had little contact. This was more or less the same group of people she had told about his death almost a fortnight earlier. She phoned Gary Kelly and Martin Bescott, other colleagues, and some of the lads Paul played cards with every now and then. She tried to keep each conversation short and sweet, and was grateful when she got the chance merely to leave a message.

One call was always going to be harder than the rest, but it was one Helen had promised to make. She knew instinctively that he would be there, invited or not, even though his name had certainly not been on the list Paul's mother had made.

'Helen . . .?'

'Oh . . . yes.'

'Your number came up on the phone,' Linnell said. 'How are you?'

'I'm fine. I was just calling to let you know about the funeral.'

'That's good of you. I was starting to wonder.'

'They've only just, you know, released Paul's body.' Helen was pacing around her living room as she spoke. She could hear music in the background. The volume dropped suddenly and she heard Linnell clear his throat.

'I've got a pen,' he said.

She gave him the time and venue for the ceremony itself. She didn't say anything about what they might be doing afterwards and was grateful he didn't ask.

'What about flowers?' Linnell asked.

'You don't have to.' Helen had already foreseen the scenario of Paul's mother browsing among the wreaths, asking who had sent each one and how they were connected to Paul. 'In fact, I'd prefer it if you didn't.'

'A donation, then?'

'I need to make lots of other calls, so—'

'Have you picked out a headstone?'

'Sorry?'

'I'm sure you'd want Paul to have something special. He *deserves* something special, and I know they can cost an arm and a leg.'

'We'll find something.' Helen felt hot. She sat back against the arm of the sofa. 'I won't be using cardboard and a marker pen, if that's what you're worried about.'

'Sorry, I didn't mean anything,' Linnell said. 'I'd like to make a contribution, that's all.'

Helen struggled for something to say; listened to Linnell breathe for a few seconds before she hung up.

Christ, it was sick. Almost funny.

They would probably club together for the stone – Helen, Paul's mother, his sister maybe – and whatever came from Helen's side would be money that was now hers alone but had been earned by both her and Paul.

So when Linnell had suggested making a contribution, Helen could only think that, in all probability, he already had.

Theo felt the flutter start when he let himself in and smelled it.

He was shaking by the time he'd closed the door behind him and seen the stains on the carpet. Three big ones – two near the table and one on the far side of the room next to the single wooden chair – just starting to dry but still glistening against the worn and dirty material. There was a trail of smears and spots snaking away into the bedroom, and Theo stood still for a minute or two, afraid to follow it.

They'd got into the stash house.

The place he'd felt safest.

Had they come there looking for him?

The night before, after the business with Easy, he and Javine had spent the next hour screaming at each other. She'd heard enough of what Easy had been saying and let Theo know *exactly* how stupid he would be to follow in the footsteps of his worthless friend. She'd stood in the doorway, her face and neck all tight and creased up with it as she leaned towards him and spat her anger out.

Theo had shouted right back: telling her that he hadn't agreed to do anything; that he was only thinking about how they could do with the extra money; that she had no fucking idea what was going on in his head. He'd carried on shouting even after she'd gone to comfort the baby. He'd shouted because he hadn't liked her telling him what to do and because he'd been boyed out on that walkway by Easy; made to feel like he could- n't make a big man's decisions.

Not that it was likely to matter now, whichever way he might have jumped. It was tickling his nose, the smell in the room: metal and sweat, and something . . . *burned*, like the streets on Bonfire Night.

He walked slowly into the bedroom, knowing what Javine's reaction was likely to be if he found Easy in there. Not sure who he *wanted* to find . . .

There was much more blood on the floorboards and a small pool by the headboard, where some had dripped from the bare mattress. Theo stood at the end of the bed and looked at the bodies: Wave's tossed across Sugar Boy's. Bare flesh where a shirt had ridden up and an arm stretched out across a face. He knew they had been after Wave; that Sugar Boy had just been unlucky.

He felt weightless suddenly, and wasted.

He wanted to lie down where he was and wait for them to come back. To slip between the cracks in the floorboards like the blood. He wanted to run until the soles of his Timberlands were gone and the skin on his feet was worn through and raw.

Now he really had a big man's decisions to make, because he saw exactly what there was to be afraid of. Theo guessed that when the trigger was being pulled, the killers had felt less for the boys they were shooting than they had for Wave's bloated, ugly dog; flat out at the end of the bed, like he was watching over them.

He'd spent a lot of money installing a top-of-the-range Bose system in his study. Sub-woofers, direct reflection speakers, the lot. It wasn't exactly like being in a concert hall, but when Frank cranked the levels right up, he had to admit it was pretty incredible.

He sat with his eyes closed, listening to the Bruckner fill the room: the strings cutting right through him, the horns almost loud enough to make the windows shake and the timpani bouncing off the walls when it really kicked off towards the end of the third movement.

He'd read the CD notes from start to finish, same as he always did, hungry to put everything into context. Apparently, Wagner, who was his big inspiration, had died while Bruckner was writing the Seventh. Frank thought he could hear a lot of regret, real sadness, in some of the recurring tunes, the themes, or whatever they were called. On top of that, von Karajan had croaked just a couple of months after conducting this very recording, which, as far as Frank was concerned, made it even more poignant. The sleeve notes said that Hitler had been very fond of it by all accounts, that he thought it was almost as good as Beethoven's Ninth. But that couldn't be helped.

Strange, Frank reckoned, to think that someone like that could have appreciated something so beautiful.

When he opened his eyes, he saw that Laura had come downstairs and was standing in the doorway. He knew it wasn't really her kind of thing; asked if he'd disturbed her. She said it was fine and that she quite liked it, but Frank turned down the volume anyway.

He told her about Paul's funeral, that he'd been talking to Helen again.

'You'll be there, won't you?' he asked. 'You *should* be there.'

'Of course I'll be there.'

'I'll buy you a new dress.'

'Does it have to be black?'

'Well, there's something of a fashion for blues and browns at funerals these days,' Frank said. 'Even light colours sometimes. But I think traditional is best. Most respectful.'

'Whatever you think.'

'You know she's having a baby, don't you? Paul's girlfriend.'

'You never said.'

'Any time now. You should see the size of her.'

'That's nice,' Laura said. She walked further into the room and sat back against the window ledge. 'It's terrible, though. The circumstances, I mean.'

Frank nodded. 'But she'll always have a part of Paul with her. That's a bonus. Something living and breathing.'

'It'll help her.'

'That's important. I *know*.'

They listened to the music for half a minute.

'Is this the one Paul gave you?'

Frank nodded.

'Tell me about it.'

So Frank took the liner notes from the jewel case and read them aloud to her, explaining, when the music was drawing to an end, that this was the really sad part, the bit that was sometimes called the 'tragic sonata'.

It was getting dark outside. When the CD had finished, Frank asked Laura if she'd like to listen to something else, but she said that was enough classical music for one day. Told him she was going back upstairs to listen to something a bit more cheerful.

'Some horrendous noise with too many drums and no bloody tune?' Frank asked.

She laughed and said she'd do her best to find something *really* annoying.

Frank followed her out and watched her walk upstairs, then carried on towards the kitchen to organise some dinner for himself.

TWENTY-NINE

The copper at Helen's door on Saturday morning was definitely not there to talk about pension arrangements. But thankfully he was not a Rubberheeler, either. The man who introduced himself as DCI Jeff Moody handed across his identification, and Helen recognised the distinctive logo. The big cat leaping across a stylised globe was supposed to represent a fierce determination coupled with an international outlook, but the design was also revealed to have cost £160,000 of public money, and the subsequent fallout had hardly been the best bit of early publicity for the newly formed Serious Organised Crime Agency.

Helen invited Moody inside, joking about the badge as she showed him into the living room and asked if he wanted tea. He told her that water would be fine. That as far as the logo row went, the Olympics had rather got them off the hook, their multicoloured squiggle having cost almost four times as much and being even less popular.

'It gives people fits too,' Helen said.

'Well, *we* have been known to do that . . .'

Helen laughed as she brought in his water and kept up the small talk, but all the time her mind was racing, trying to work out what a senior officer at SOCA might want with her; fighting not to let her face show she had anything to be afraid of.

Moody was fifty or so, tall and skinny, with glasses and a decent head of greying hair. He wore a nice suit and tie and Helen guessed that most people would have him down as an accountant; an architect, if they were being generous. He sat on the sofa and Helen took a seat at the table, instinctively unwilling to let him look down on her. She guessed that he knew exactly what she was doing.

He cleared his throat and took a file from his briefcase. 'You've been busy, Helen. Especially considering your situation.'

Helen's mind was still jumping around. At least he hadn't said 'condition'. She said something about needing the exercise.

'*Very* busy . . .' He flicked through the pages of his file, glanced up. 'You know broadly what SOCA does, yes?'

Helen said she knew as much as anyone who wasn't involved but had read the literature. The so-called British FBI, an amalgamation of the old National Crime Squad, National Criminal Intelligence Service and parts of the Inland Revenue, Customs and Immigration. A couple of years on, and some people were already saying that this supposedly holy alliance had proved to be something of an unholy mess.

'Not hard to see why there might have been teething problems,' she said.

Moody smiled. 'Right. Coppers and taxmen isn't necessarily a marriage made in heaven. Not to mention the ones who get to wear those special rubber gloves.' He was trying his best to be likeable, and Helen thought he was making a decent job of it.

It looked as though he finally had his papers in order. 'So . . .'

'Do you need any more water?'

He said he was fine. 'You should know we've been tracking your movements since you ran a check on Ray Jackson's vehicle registration.'

Kevin Shepherd's tame cabbie. Helen did not know what to say.

'Jackson's someone of interest to us, for reasons I'm sure you can work out, so any enquiry related to him is flagged up on our system straight away.'

'That's handy,' Helen said.

'Since then, we know you've had meetings of one sort or another with Kevin Shepherd and Frank Linnell. Well, you've been doing all sorts of things, but they're the ones we think are most significant.'

'"Significant" how, exactly?'

Moody waved a hand, like he was saving her the trouble; as though there were a very quick and simple way for them to proceed. 'We know *why*, Helen.'

She could do little more than nod.

'We know you were following in Paul's footsteps.'

'Not at first . . .'

'Do you mind telling me how you came up with Ray Jackson's name?'

Helen took a few seconds, then told Moody about the parking tickets. She described her visit to the CCTV monitoring centre and told him that she'd seen Paul taking the same taxi on two separate occasions. How that got her interested. She felt like she was confessing to being a suspicious, distrustful bitch, and she was breathing heavily by the time she'd finished.

Moody stood and offered her his glass of water. She shook her head and he sat down again. 'It can't have been easy from that point on.'

'Not very, no.'

'Mixed emotions . . .'

'That's putting it mildly.'

'Look, I can imagine what you must have been feeling, going through, on top of . . . everything else. Well, I wouldn't have a bloody clue, in point of fact, but I can guess.' He laid the papers to one side. 'I'm sorry that had to happen.'

'Sorry?'

'But you can leave it now, OK?'

Helen waited. One hand was flat on top of the table, but the other was balled into a fist by her side.

'SOCA recruits from all across the service, OK? And most of that doesn't make the press releases.'

'Listen, you're starting to do my head in—'

'You can relax, Helen, is what I'm saying. Everything's fine. Paul was working for *us* . . .'

Leaning out from the end of the walkway, Theo could look across the corner of the estate to the neighbouring block and see the comings and goings. He'd stood there the day before as well and watched for hours: the arrival of the police vehicles, half a dozen at least; the men and women setting up the tapes and tents and spreading out onto the adjacent streets; the body bags taken out and loaded into the mortuary van.

The dog had come out in a black bin-liner.

As soon as he'd got out of the stash house, he'd called Easy, told him to ring back straight away. Then he'd called again, worried that Easy might take his time after the argument they'd had, and told him exactly why he needed to talk to him. Afraid that Javine would be at home, he'd called the police from the street, given them the address, then gone back to his flat and spent half an hour in the shower, trying to scrub away the stink.

There didn't seem to be much going on now, but Theo couldn't tear himself away. He wondered when Sugar Boy's mum and dad had got the call. Wondered what that stuff was that coppers smeared under their noses before they went in, and if you could buy it in Boots.

He checked his phone again, even though he knew he had a perfectly good signal.

He was still waiting for Easy to ring him back.

'Paul's job was to target fellow officers,' Moody said. 'To secure evidence that might convict any officer who was passing information to organised-crime figures. Individuals, gangs, whatever.'

'How long?' Helen asked. She had moved over to the armchair and was looking through some paperwork that Moody had considered suitable for her to see. There were photocopies of reports and surveillance logs, details of meetings. Most of the names and locations had been blacked out.

'A little over a year. It was going pretty well.'

'Who knew about it?'

'For obvious reasons, it was all done very discreetly,' Moody said. 'As far as anyone Paul worked with, the details of the operation were only passed on to DCI level and above. Martin Bescott didn't know, none of Paul's close colleagues. It was as much about compromising fellow officers as risking the integrity of the operation.'

'And that included me.'

Moody nodded. 'He couldn't have told you anything anyway. It wouldn't have mattered what you did for a living.'

Helen passed back the sheaf of papers and stood up. 'It's what I did for a living that made me suspect him, though.'

'An instinct maybe,' Moody said. 'You don't need to blame yourself on that score.'

She walked into the kitchen and leaned against the worktop. After a few moments she reached into the sink for a cloth and ran it back and forth across the surface. She was thinking through moments with Paul that suddenly took on new significance; replaying conversations in her head. She could hear Moody shuffling more papers in the sitting room and clearing his throat.

She walked back in and sat down again. 'So Paul was working on Kevin Shepherd?'

'Shepherd is a target Paul had been making decent headway with before the accident. You met him, so you know the kind of person we're talking about there.'

'He's an arsehole.'

'Correct, and he's an arsehole we suspect has made payments to a number of officers on various units.'

'What about Frank Linnell?'

Moody took off his glasses and leaned back. 'We're not too sure about that one. He's not someone we have an active interest in. Plenty of our colleagues *do*, of course . . .'

'So what was Paul playing at?'

'What did Linnell say?'

'Don't you know?'

He smiled. 'You were being observed, Helen, that's all. Nobody's bugging your phone.'

'He said they were friends.'

'Maybe it's as simple as that, then.' Moody's smile widened. 'I used to play tennis with a pretty well-known forger.'

Helen was still not convinced. 'He also said something about not giving Paul some names; not being willing to help him out.'

'I'll look into it,' Moody said. 'If it'll put your mind at rest.'

Helen could tell he meant it, and that it was something he was willing to do for no other reason than that. She told him she'd be grateful, and that she would be happy to do some more detective work herself, but that she was going to be a bit . . . tied up over the next week or so.

Moody thanked her for the water and said that he ought to be making a move. 'Is there anything else you found out through doing all this that you think might be useful? Did Shepherd say anything, or . . .?'

'The computer,' Helen said. She told him about the laptop that Bescott had turned up, that she'd hidden away.

'Thank Christ for that,' Moody said. 'We'd sort of lost track of it after what happened to Paul.'

'Operation Victoria, that the one?'

'Did you . . .?'

'I couldn't open the file,' Helen said.

Moody seemed happy enough. 'It's my daughter's name actually,' he said. 'It's a bit random really. Like naming hurricanes.'

Helen stood up and asked if he'd like to take the laptop with him. He shook his head. 'I'm on my way to catch the Eurostar.'

'Nice,' Helen said.

'Conference. Chief inspectors and above.'

Helen pulled a face. 'Sorry.'

Moody reached for his jacket. 'I'll arrange for a car to come and pick it up,' he said. He moved towards the door. 'There's a lot of hard work on that thing. *Paul's* hard work.' He looked a little embarrassed. 'I wouldn't want to leave the bloody thing on the train.'

Theo snatched up his phone when he saw who was calling, moved quickly into the bedroom and shut the door behind him.

'You did the right thing, belling me first,' Easy said.

'Where you been at, man?' Javine was watching TV in the next room and Theo was doing his best not to shout, but it was a struggle. He was relieved that Easy had called back but angry that it had taken so long. He felt like something inside him had been twisted. 'I walked in there and found them. Jesus, *both* of them.'

'I know it hurts, man. I feel it too.'

'I *found* them.'

'Breathe easy, Star Boy.'

'Wave and Sugar Boy all shot up, and that fucking dog.'

'Yeah, that was cold.'

'Where you *been*?'

'Things have got to be dealt with, T.' Theo could hear traffic and music. It sounded as though Easy was driving. 'Shit like this happens and there's arrangements to be made. Restructuring or whatever.'

Theo pressed the phone between his chin and his shoulder and tried to light a cigarette. He dropped the lighter.

'You listening, T?'

'It's like I said the other night.' Theo bent down for the lighter, managed finally to get some smoke into his lungs. 'It's all about what we did in that car, that copper who died.'

'I'm not talking about this now.'

'You see it now though, right? You *understand* now?'

'Yeah, you're the smart one, T. Top of the class.'

Easy had said it as though Theo had just got the right answer on a TV quiz show. Like it didn't matter. 'You really need to listen,' Theo said. 'There's just you and me left now, you get me?'

For a few seconds there was just the noise of an engine, and drum and bass from Easy's car stereo, or somebody else's. Then Easy said, 'No, *you* need to do the listening, T. You need to shut up and get your-self settled, smoke a couple and stop giving yourself a fucking heart attack. We straight?'

Theo grunted. He knew there was no point arguing.

'I'll check you tonight.'

'Where?'

'Dirty South. Later on, OK? We'll get it all sorted.'

Theo listened as the music was turned up, a second before the line went dead.

THIRTY

Nice and slow, up and down . . .

Saturday afternoon was not the cleverest time to be trudging around the supermarket, Helen knew that, but she'd needed to get out. She'd tried to sit there after Moody had left and take in everything he'd told her, all that it had meant, but it was way too much to process. Too much, sitting there, with Paul's things all around her. With the smell of him still in the flat and a voice, hers or his, letting her know just how stupid she'd been.

How she'd betrayed him . . . again. How she'd pissed on his memory.

Sainsbury's was packed, as she'd known it would be, but still she felt more comfortable negotiating the crowded aisles. The implications of what she had learned were sinking in that little bit easier while she had something else to think about; as she occupied herself with slowly filling her trolley.

Nice and slow, up and down each aisle in turn. Why had she automatically assumed he'd been bent, or screwing somebody else? Why the hell did nappies take up so much room?

The hubbub was a welcome distraction, and the voice that announced bargains over the Tannoy, or ushered staff to particular counters and checkouts, was less harsh than the one in her own head. Besides which, a supermarket run was well overdue. Her dad's muffins had long gone and she was reluctant to drop hints to Jenny about how great her soup had been, so she was all but living on toast and biscuits at home.

God, she needed more biscuits. She should probably get the ones Paul liked, the plain chocolate ones, because he'd been an honest, hard-working copper and she was an evil minded whore.

People were nice too, walking around and getting on with things; normal men and women who didn't know her, and each small encounter lifted her spirits. A smile from an old man as they both moved their trolleys the same way to avoid a collision. The offers of help as she bent to pick up bottles of water or reached for something on a high shelf.

'Here we go.'

'There you are.'

'Steady on, love, don't want to be having it in here.'

And some odd looks as well, of course. And the sly nudges as other shoppers tried not to stare at the heavily pregnant nutter, moving at a snail's pace and mumbling to herself.

'You're right, Hopwood, I'm a nasty piece of work, but you always knew that.'

Cheese, semi-skimmed milk, natural yoghurt . . .

'So come back and haunt me, then. Why not? Rattle your fucking handcuffs at me in the dark.'

Bleach, toothpaste, toilet roll . . .

'What was I supposed to think, for crying out loud? Maybe if you'd *been* here.'

Then she saw the little boy: running up the aisle towards her, side-stepping a trolley in his haste to get to his mum; waving the packet of cereal he wanted so badly. The same sort . . .

She saw it and froze. Heard the cereal rattle as the boy ran past, and as Paul poured it into his bowl. Then everything started to slip away.

She was already falling forward as she felt it rise like boiling milk; as she heaved it up. Her foot felt for the brake on the trolley's wheel and missed. She was hot as hell. She told her hands to let go, but they weren't listening. Her head was swimming with the people who had stopped to watch, the colours they were wearing, as the trolley took her with it; pulling her down to her knees at the same time as the wail began to escape, and the first fat sob felt like a kick in the chest as she hit the floor.

A woman, the boy's mother, asked if she was all right. Helen tried to speak, but then the woman hurried away to fetch someone, and when Helen glanced up again all she could see was the little boy staring at her. He started to cry right back at her while she watched a security guard come marching round the corner. He leaned down behind her and put his arms through hers; asked if she wanted a hand back to her feet. But she was crying so hard that she couldn't answer, so he stood up again. He told her to take as long as she liked.

Helen could hear him telling other shoppers that the lady was all right. Then he said something into his walkie-talkie, and, in the gap between sobs, as she sucked in breaths like a baby, she heard it squawk back at him.

The security guard had refused to let Helen drive, putting her into a cab, taking her keys, and promising to drive her car home for her when he'd finished his shift. He was the second person in a few days whose name she'd asked and who she'd told that she might name the baby after him. He'd told her his name was Stuart and had looked a lot more taken with the idea than the boy she'd met in Lewisham.

She was thinking about the boy, about the look on his face while she'd been driving out of that car park as she watched the taxi pull away and walked the few yards to her front door. She had the key to the main entrance in her hand when she heard a voice behind her.

'Helen?'

She turned, half expecting to see Adam Perrin, and was relieved to see a balding, middle-aged man who raised his hands in mock-surrender and looked nothing but concerned. He'd obviously recognised the tension on her face.

'Sorry,' she said. She felt wrung out anyway, and remembered how scared she'd been when Kevin Shepherd had come looming out of the dark at her; had as good as threatened her on the same spot.

'How are you feeling?' the man asked.

She guessed he was one of her neighbours. She and Paul had often talked about getting to know them better, perhaps throwing a party for the whole block, but they had never quite got round to it.

'I'll be better in a couple of weeks. As soon as I've got rid of *this*.'

The man smiled. 'That's good. Only, you know, we were wondering how you were doing.'

'I'm fine. Thank you.'

'The funeral's the day after tomorrow, isn't it?'

'Sorry?' She noticed that he was carrying a small recorder. 'Who's "we"?'

'Just the local.' He stuck out a hand, which Helen ignored.

'And locals sell to nationals. I know how that stuff works.'

'It's obviously a big story for us. A *local* tragedy.'

Helen turned back to the door and fumbled to get her key in the right position. She heard the reporter step closer.

'It would be good to let people know how you were really feeling,' he said. 'What you've been going through. What you think it might be like having the baby after—'

She turned round quickly and saw another man getting out of a car parked where the taxi had been. She saw him adjust a camera and raise it up. Watched the flash start to fire.

'Come on, Helen, just a few words . . .'

She pushed past him and moved as fast as she could towards the photographer. 'Get back in that car,' she said. 'Do it *now*.'

The reporter was behind her, still asking questions, but she kept on walking; enjoying the look on the photographer's face as he finally stopped taking pictures and stepped quickly back.

'Sod off before I take that camera and stick it up your arse.'

There was no DJ playing at the Dirty South that night. A sign that had been taped to the door read: *Tonight's performance has been postponed as a mark of respect to the families of Michael Williamson, James Dosunmo, Errol Anderson and André Betts.*

Mikey, SnapZ, Wave and Sugar Boy.

Somebody had scribbled 'live 4 ever' just above the words promising that those tickets already purchased would be valid for the rearranged date.

The bar was a little quieter than usual too, for a Saturday. There was no music over the speakers and the sound on the big-screen TV had been turned down. The bar staff were being kept busy enough, though, and there were plenty of coins lined up around the edges of the pool table.

Theo stood at the bar waiting for his Southern Comfort and Coke. Looking around, he could see most of the crew gathered near the arch through to the back room, several of them already playing pool and the others huddled in small groups. There was no sign of Easy.

When he'd got his drink, Theo wandered across and spoke to a few of the boys. Most seemed pleased to see him and talked easily enough about this and that, though several of the younger ones were edgy, their eyes everywhere but on him as they spoke. Though he'd been prepared for it, nobody asked him about what he'd found over at the stash house.

He was relieved that Easy had not spread the word around.

If it had been common knowledge on the estate, it would only be a matter of time before someone would want to go through it all with him in an interview room, and Theo didn't fancy that. The police were stretched now, for sure, but he knew they hadn't stopped looking for whoever was in that car the night the copper died. Even if some-one else had already beaten them to the punch.

But the police were not Theo's biggest worry any more. He was pretty sure now that the trigger-men were not carrying warrant cards.

He watched as Easy finally walked in and the atmosphere at the back of the room changed. Easy was smiling, moving casually around the bar, like he was passing out good news. Theo saw him approach each small group and talk for a minute or two before moving on to the next. There was plenty of fist-kissing going on and nodding dogs.

When a thickset white bloke tried to push past without asking, Easy stared him out and stood his ground. The man said something Theo couldn't make out and walked the long way round. Easy turned back to the crew like nothing had happened, giving Theo a nod too, through a gap in the crowd, just to let him know that he'd clocked him.

Theo moved across and tried to talk to Gospel, who was playing pool with one of the Asian boys. He told her she should try to leave as many balls as possible over pockets, and asked if she'd seen anything of Ollie. She looked past him and shrugged; said it wasn't her job to keep track of everybody. When she finally returned his look, Theo pointed to the blue-green bruising beneath both eyes and the cut across the bridge of her nose.

'Who d'you fall out with?' he asked.

'Someone who didn't mind his business,' she said.

From then on, she pretended to be concentrating on the game, and when the boy she was playing missed, she hurried around to the other side of the table to take her shot. She fluked one and the boy told her she was a jammy bitch.

Theo walked across to a table near the big screen and waited for Easy. He glanced over and saw him talking to As If, who had been stand-ing on his own, looking lost. Easy's mouth was doing most of the work.

After a few minutes Theo saw their knuckles touch and guessed that the two of them had sorted things out in a very different way to the one Easy had been threatening.

Theo turned away and caught Gospel staring. Her eyes dropped quickly down to the table when she saw him looking.

'Still seeming tensed up, Star Boy . . .'

Theo raised his head as Easy kicked back the chair opposite. He had a Hypnotic in each hand.

'Got a twenty's worth of skunk in my pocket as well,' Easy said. 'Sort us both out for the night, no danger.'

Theo took his drink and sipped it . . . watched Gospel leave the pool table and disappear into the toilets.

Easy caught him looking and grinned. 'Javine would rip your head off, man.'

'Yeah, well, Ollie's out the frame now, isn't he?' Theo looked for some reaction, but saw none. 'Got everything organised, then?' he asked.

Easy shook his head, like he didn't follow.

Theo raised his glass and gestured towards the cluster of crew members against the back wall. 'Things moving on, yeah? Sweet and simple.'

'More or less.'

It was obvious to Theo that Easy had spent the last couple of days talking to the people in the higher triangles, the ones deciding who went where and who did what. Who plugged the gaps. He'd always been a good talker, better than Wave even, and he looked comfortable enough stepping up into a dead man's shoes.

'You're saying I'm not upset about Wave and Sugar Boy, right? Any of them? Trying to make out like I'm not bleeding.'

'I never said that, man.' Theo knew that Easy had not liked Wave a whole lot, but that he'd felt it good and deep for SnapZ and Mikey, had showed it as much as anyone else. He'd seen him looking like he'd had the breath kicked out of him, saying nothing and close to tears in this very room, the night after they'd found Mikey. 'Just that you've shrugged it off so fast, yeah? Like all you're thinking about is the next thing.'

Easy leaned forward. 'Listen, T. You think if David Beckham was hit by a bus, the chairman and fucking shareholders or whatever would cancel the next Man United game?'

'He doesn't play for them any more.'

'I don't care. It's just an example, man.'

'Nobody got hit by a bus.'

'I said it's a fucking *example*. Christ . . .'

'There weren't any *accidents*,' Theo said. 'None of it is random, you see what I'm saying?'

'Right. We were all sitting in that car, I get it. The night you got moved up, which happened because I stuck my neck out for you, yeah, which you forgot pretty quick, seems to me.'

'You *know*, but it's like it means nothing.'

'So what are *you* going to do, T? If you're next on the list? You got a nice sharp scheme?'

'No . . .'

Easy raised his hands like that was that. Point proved. He leaned back on the chair, turned his head to tell a girl walking past how nicely she was moving. When the chair dropped forward again there was something else in his eyes.

'Thing of it is, anyone comes looking for me, whatever fucking car I was in, they better be up to the task.' He dabbed at his pocket with one finger. 'I've got plenty for them to think about, you get me?'

'Wave probably thought the same thing,' Theo said.

Easy seemed to get bored pretty fast after that and got up without a word to talk to a couple of the younger lads. Theo stayed where he was, thinking that it was a long time since they'd talked about nothing; since they'd just pissed around and enjoyed themselves. He remembered how much Easy had made him laugh, hitting golf balls at that old man, stuff like that.

Suddenly Easy was at the table again, telling him to get up, that they were leaving. Theo did as he was told without thinking, at least not about anything other than the skunk Easy had on him, and followed him across the bar and out onto the street.

He saw Easy produce the knife when they got outside. Saw the people smoking at the wooden tables on the pavement scatter, then realised that they were ten yards behind the big white bloke who had fronted Easy out earlier on.

'Fuck you doing, man? This is mental . . .'

Easy started moving faster, only a few feet behind the man now. Theo stopped, shouted, telling Easy that he was an idiot, and watched as the big man looked round and saw what was coming before cutting hard right into the alleyway that snaked around to the back doors of the bar. Easy screamed something and sprinted after him, waving the blade around at the same time that Theo turned and bolted. As he put his head down and ran, tearing off in the opposite direction until he was streets away.

THIRTY-ONE

When she'd called him to pass on the details of the funeral, Helen had arranged to meet up with Gary Kelly. He couldn't make up his mind which piece to read at the service and she'd promised to help him decide. He'd kindly offered to come and pick her up. 'I know what it's like,' he said. 'My wife couldn't squeeze into our Astra at four months.'

They had a cup of tea at the flat and then drove down to a café behind Brixton tube station. It looked like an original fifties place, but neither had any idea how authentic any of it was. They both went for mugs of tea and fry ups.

'Do you need a lift tomorrow?' Kelly asked. 'I wasn't sure where the cars would be leaving from.'

'It's fine,' Helen said. 'I'm staying at my dad's tonight and we'll drive up together in the morning.'

'Well, anything I can do, you know you've only to ask.'

'You're doing plenty.'

'This is really hard,' Kelly said. He spread out pieces of paper in front of him on the table and pointed at one. 'You know how much Paul loved his music, right?' He read out a poem that someone called

Charlie Daniels had written when his friend Ronnie Van Zandt had died. 'He was the lead singer of Lynyrd Skynyrd,' Kelly explained. 'Died in a plane crash, so . . . both terrible accidents, you know? I thought it might be appropriate.'

Helen thought it wasn't bad, told Kelly it was nice, but that she wasn't sure Paul could ever be described as a 'proud bird'.

Kelly nodded and pushed it to one side. He showed her something he'd found on the Internet, a poem by Charlotte Brontë that Helen thought was thankfully unsentimental, and a simple Gaelic blessing, which he told her had been read at his father's funeral. 'That one's got a music angle as well,' he said. 'John Lydon used it in a song, so . . .'

'Oh, OK.'

'So, which do you think?'

Helen hadn't really been concentrating as she should have been. She hadn't checked about confidentiality with Jeff Moody, but now that the operation had come to an end with Paul's death, she assumed there wouldn't be any problem. It wasn't as though she were planning to put an announcement in the *Police Review*. She was trying hard to keep the smile off her face but clearly not succeeding.

'What?'

'That stuff you told me about Paul keeping things to himself, remember? Not being sure what he was up to or whatever?' She told Kelly about the visit from Moody, about the operation Paul had needed to keep so secret. Describing it out loud for the first time, she could hear the enthusiasm in her own voice; the pride in what Paul had been doing. It was something she had grown almost unfamiliar with.

The Irishman looked shell-shocked. 'Cagey bastard,' he said, finally. A grin spread slowly across his face, too. 'There I was thinking he was knocking off some WPC.'

'Trust me, I'd've known about *that*.'

'Yeah, Sue's the same,' Kelly said. 'I've only got to think about it.'

Helen nodded.

'So . . . how long?'

'A year and a bit. Moody said it had been going very well. He was obviously good at being sneaky.'

'Certainly had me fooled.' Kelly shook his head, dabbing at what was left on his plate with a fried slice. 'Christ, it makes sense now. No wonder we didn't see much of him in the office. CID must have seemed seriously bloody humdrum. Dangerous game as well, I should imagine. Some of these bastards can be well nasty if you get too close.'

Helen wiped grease from her fingers. 'Yeah, well, he never took the easy option. Wouldn't have ended up with me if he had.'

'He did well on that score,' Kelly said. 'Don't you worry.'

They swapped stories for a few minutes, and Helen told him how hard it had been finding the time to make all the arrangements. Kelly went quiet after a while, pushing aside his plate and staring down at the printed eulogies.

'Did you ever think he might be bent, Gary?'

Kelly looked up at her and nodded. 'For about five minutes.'

That made Helen feel better.

'You did too, right?' he asked.

She told him about tracking down Linnell and Shepherd, and the secret file on the laptop that she couldn't access. Explained how screwed-up and stupid she'd felt, without going into detail about what had happened at the supermarket the day before.

'Look, it's done and dusted now, all right? You've got to think about the baby and the future. You're shot of it all now.'

'Well, I will be when I've got rid of that computer.' She smiled. 'Bloody thing's stashed away like some secret pile of porno mags.' That reminded her of something. 'Listen, I'd like you to have Paul's guitar. I know you're as mad about music as he was, so . . .'

Kelly nodded slowly. 'That's grand, Helen. I'd like that.'

'Maybe you should do a song tomorrow.'

'He'd never forgive me,' Kelly said.

'Talking of which . . .'

They went back to the pieces of paper, determined to make a decision. She asked him to read the Brontë poem again and concentrated hard this time. It was oddly life-affirming, which she knew some people might find odd, considering the circumstances, but she liked the idea. It seemed appropriate, considering how close she was to bringing a new life into the world.

When Kelly had finished, Helen asked for the sheet of paper and read again the lines that had touched her most:

> What though Death at times steps
> in
> And calls our Best away?
> What though sorrow seems to win,
> O'er hope, a heavy sway?

'Let's go with this one,' she said, passing back the poem.

Kelly seemed pleased. 'Good call,' he said. 'He was our "Best", after all, right?'

Helen wasn't going to argue.

The pub looked good, he reckoned. Better than good: *classy*. The scaffolding and the skip had gone, the windows had been cleaned to let in some light, and Frank reckoned he was just about ready to look at potential buyers for the place.

He walked around the empty room, his footsteps echoing off the polished wooden floor. He ran a hand along the length of the bar and stared up at the light-fittings and the new mouldings on the ceiling. They'd made a fine job of it, no question; ensured he'd get the price he was looking for. He might even pop back for a jar when the place was up and running.

They'd put stained-glass panels above that window shattered by the brick on the day Paul had visited. It was a nice detail. He walked across to where the two of them had eaten their lunch on a trestle table; bits of shell and vinegar running all over the plastic.

'It's just a favour,' Paul had said, and he'd mentioned something stupid about honour. It wouldn't have made any difference in the end, given what had happened, but he still wished they'd parted on better terms; that Paul had thought better of him. It left a nasty taste.

Hindsight gave everyone twenty–twenty vision, Frank knew that, but still, he wished he'd done more *then*, when it would have been easy. That he didn't have to make up for it as he was now, after the event. It would have cost him a damn sight less, that was for sure.

And hadn't he promised himself all those years before that he would never let it happen again?

There was a driver waiting outside, and Frank was about ready for the off when he noticed brown streaks bleeding through the gloss around the door. He looked closer, then marched through to the other bar to check the woodwork in there. The cheeky beggars hadn't bothered with a second coat, and there was even a bristle or two trapped in the paint.

He called the contractor and let him know what he thought. 'I'm not having it,' he said. 'That's all there is to it.'

In heavily accented English, the contractor tried to explain that his team had already moved on to another job. Frank told him that he didn't give a toss, that unless someone was round there with a brush in his hand within the hour, the only thing he'd be contracting would be seriously unpleasant.

He couldn't bear things not being right. Controlling, obsessive, it wasn't important what you called it; to Frank's mind, it came down to *caring*, plain and simple. Didn't matter what it was, only an amateur was content to leave a job unfinished.

Helen ran the bath good and hot. Lowering herself in slowly, she decided that a few of those wall rails and handles would have come in handy; some of that stuff they advertised in the middle of the afternoon, when the old and infirm were supposed to be watching TV. A walk-in bath even. She remembered laughing when Paul had seen the ad one day and asked how they worked. Why all the water didn't run out when you opened the door.

She was glad she'd decided to spend the night at home and have her dad pick her up first thing instead. He'd sounded disappointed when she'd called to tell him, but she knew she'd be far more relaxed on her own. As relaxed as she was likely to get, anyway.

'Whatever makes you happy,' her dad had said, meaning 'less miserable'.

She'd brought the radio in from the bedroom and settled back for a long soak. Her belly rose out of the water and she flicked tiny waves across it with her fingers, watching little streams running down from her distended belly-button. She talked softly to the baby for a few minutes, rubbing a soapy hand across the part where she thought the head was, and when her breasts started to leak a little, she wiped away the creamy trails with a flannel.

She knew that things would start to get a lot better, if she could just get through tomorrow . . .

At her mother's funeral, she and Jenny had been able to get through it together. She knew that this one would be very different. Yes, Jenny would be there, and a few close friends, and she knew that Paul's family would find it every bit as hard as she did. But they would have each other to lean on, to share in the pain and the numbness. Helen knew that in all the ways that really mattered, she would be spending the day alone.

Just her, and the unborn child to whom she would have to explain it all one day.

Christ, she hoped it was nothing like her mum's funeral. Paul's mother would probably take great pride in laying on a decent event afterwards, but curling sandwiches and relatives whose names nobody could remember seemed almost unavoidable. Unless they did things differently on occasions like this one; after deaths like Paul's. When nobody in their right mind would laugh at an inappropriate moment, or smile wistfully at memories of a long innings.

She couldn't even rely on booze to help her through it all, as she and Jenny had done at their mum's.

She rubbed her belly again. Said, 'Your fault.'

On the radio they started to play an old Oasis track that she'd loved when she was a student; an off-your-face, party anthem. She leaned forward to turn it up, then stopped when she heard a noise. Like something being dropped out on the landing between the flats or a door closing.

She turned off the radio and listened.

Perhaps the noise had come from upstairs. Jesus, had she forgotten to close the door properly when she'd come in? Maybe someone had just gone out next door.

There was no mistaking the next noise: a drawer closing; the one above the living-room cupboard. She knew that rasp, like a sharp intake of breath as it caught on the runner.

Like her *own* . . .

She strained to hear above the drumming in her chest and the lapping of the water around her, which suddenly seemed deafening. She listened as the door to the bedroom was opened. The steps were light, but she heard the boards give as someone approached the bed.

There was nowhere to run. She had to protect herself.

Moving as gently and silently as she could, Helen inched herself along the bath until she had enough room to manoeuvre. She leaned down on the edge, one hand on either side to distribute the weight evenly, and began to haul herself out.

Carefully, little by little . . .

It seemed obvious that whoever had entered the flat had no idea she was there, and she wanted to keep it that way. At least until she could get to the bathroom door and lock it. She was halfway out when her hand slipped and she crashed back into the bath, crying out as her head cracked against the edge, and sending torrents of water up the walls and onto the floor.

The pain in her head was forgotten in a second as she fought to get herself upright, to control the rapidly mounting tide of panic. She knew that whoever was in her bedroom must have heard her and would know now that they were not alone.

She listened.

For a few long seconds there was silence, but then she heard the footsteps again, coming out of the bedroom, no more than ten feet away. She heard the intruder move slowly down the hall and stop outside the bathroom door. She stared at the handle, cold suddenly and shivering; knowing that she could not reach the door before whoever was outside had opened it.

The decision made itself: she reached towards the end of the bath as she began to shout, her hand closing around a glass candle-holder. 'Fuck off! Just get the fuck out of here *now*.' She hurled the glass bowl at the door, closing her eyes for a second as it shattered, then grabbing frantically at anything else she could reach; anything that had weight. Shampoo and conditioner bottles, a wooden back-scrubber, the soap-dish, the soap itself; screaming as she threw them one by one against the door. 'I swear I'll kill you. You come in here and I'll *kill* you . . .'

She felt the rush come up through her as she moved, knowing that she was ready to do it. Her teeth dug into her bottom lip until she could taste blood, and when there was nothing left to throw she began to kick and thrash, her voice cracking with fury as she beat her hands against the water. 'Fuck off. Just fuck off and leave us alone . . .'

For a minute, perhaps two, there was silence. The remaining water began to settle around her. She was about to make a lunge for the lock when she heard a voice outside the door, still close to it.

'Helen? Is everything all right?'

A familiar intonation; a trace of Geordie.

Deering.

THIRTY-TWO

While Helen got changed, Deering waited outside the bedroom door, explaining what he'd seen when he'd arrived outside the block five minutes before:

'I was just about to ring the bell when this bloke comes tearing out.'

'What did he look like?'

'No idea,' Deering said. 'He was wearing a hoodie and he kept his head down. Average height, I suppose, but I couldn't tell you much beyond that. The door almost smacked me in the bloody face when he came crashing through it.'

Helen had put on tracksuit bottoms and a T-shirt and was about to get her dressing gown from the back of the door when she felt the shaking start in her legs. She sat on the bed and waited for it to stop.

'There didn't seem much point letting the door slam shut again, you know, so I just sneaked in before it closed. When I got upstairs, your door was wide open and I heard you screaming.'

Whoever had been in her flat could have got into the block the same way, Helen supposed, she'd done it often enough herself, but that didn't explain how he'd got through the flat's front door. She knew very well she had shut it properly. She started to think about anyone who might have had a set of keys. Jenny, and there had been a few workmen over the years. Perhaps Paul had given someone a set?

'Helen?'

'Sorry.' She looked up at the bedroom door. 'I'm OK. I'll be out in a minute.'

'I'll go and make some tea . . .'

By the time Deering brought it through from the kitchen, Helen was on the sofa in the living room; her legs were up and her knees pulled close to her chest. She wrapped her dressing gown a bit tighter around herself and watched as Deering cast a semi-professional eye around the place. It didn't take him long to reach the same conclusion as she had.

'Who else had keys?'

She gave him a few names but was finding it difficult to think straight.

'You should make a list when you're feeling up to it,' he said.

She nodded towards the bathroom door. 'I made a hell of a mess in there.'

'You got rid of him.'

'There's glass everywhere.'

'I'll sort it out.' He started to get up but stopped when Helen waved away the idea. He saw her jump slightly and watched an odd smile spread across her face. 'Are you all right?'

Helen had slipped her hands inside the dressing gown and was pressing them tight to her belly. 'The baby's got hiccoughs,' she said. The smile grew wider, and there were tears in her eyes. 'I was worried after what happened. When I slipped.' She dug out a tissue from her dressing-gown pocket, then twitched again and laughed.

'I'm not surprised,' Deering said. 'Poor little bugger's had a bit of a shock.

I'd have a damn sight more than bloody hiccoughs.' He stared at her. 'What?'

'Nothing, it's fine,' Helen said, remembering what she'd shouted when she'd been trying to get rid of the man outside the door. When she'd felt ready to kill him. Remembering that she'd said 'us'.

Leave us alone.

Deering pointed. 'You've cut your lip.'

Helen licked at it, then dabbed her mouth with the tissue.

Deering sipped at his tea and looked around again. 'Can you tell if anything's been taken?'

'Doesn't look like it, but he didn't really have much of a chance.'

'That's something, I suppose.'

'There's not a lot to take: TV, DVD player, I suppose. It's not like there's a secret stash of jewels.' Helen had spoken to enough victims of burglary over the years, and once they'd got over the shock, most of them talked about feeling vulnerable and violated. She wondered if that was what might be waiting for her down the line, or if it would simply fail to register, when measured against the bottomless reserves of grief and guilt. 'It's hard to feel particularly lucky at the moment, though.'

Deering nodded. 'You've not had the best few weeks, have you?'

Helen laughed, though it quickly became a shiver and she pulled the dressing gown tighter.

'I don't want to teach my grandmother to suck eggs and all that, but you should really call the police.'

'I know.' She was not exactly relishing the prospect. In all likelihood she would be treated with due respect and sensitivity, but a couple of cack-handed probationers was always a distinct possibility.

'They'll come quickly at any rate,' Deering said. 'If you explain your circumstances.'

'I wouldn't bank on it. I think there's a gig at the Academy tonight.'

'Do you want me to do it?'

Helen thanked him, but said she could manage. She got up and made the call, making sure they knew she was Job.

'At least let me wait with you,' Deering said when she'd hung up. 'Help you clean up a bit afterwards.'

'There's really no need.'

'It's fine, honestly,' he said. 'I wanted to talk to you anyway.'

'Right . . . sorry,' Helen said, suddenly realising that she hadn't even asked Deering why he'd come to see her in the first place.

Easy loved his burgers and his chicken, same as the rest of them, but that was all most of those boys ever ate. It was usually a time thing – being able to grab something on the run and get back to business – but even when it was about nothing else but the eating, they'd still settle for shit. Wearing four figures' worth of chains and spending less than a fiver on your dinner, it didn't make sense.

You couldn't eat chains or a flashy watch.

Sometimes, he liked to spend whatever it cost and get something decent; something that didn't come quick; with champagne if he was minted, or maybe a glass of wine where they poured a bit out first for you to taste. It was important to do that, to look like it was something you were used to.

Unless there was some girl he was trying to bone or something to celebrate, he preferred eating on his own, too. It wasn't like he didn't want to be *seen*, but he loved the food and didn't want any distractions. Chit-chat and whatever was fine over KFC, but he wanted to enjoy what he was eating and he couldn't relax with rubbishness flying at him across the table. He'd always been impressed with people who could do that, sit there and eat with nobody but themselves. He thought they must be pretty special; comfortable with what they were doing, you know?

He'd driven over to Brockley, to a French place he'd seen in the paper; a bistro or whatever. It wasn't as posh as some of the places he'd tried up west, but the food was out of this world. He'd had snails, and beef in pastry, and some fantastic pudding with meringues floating around in thin custard. Waiters in some of the other places took one look and acted like a turd had been walked across the carpet, but the woman bringing his food tonight had been nice, even if she was about as French as he was, and he'd left a big tip, same as always.

Walking back to the car, he wondered about calling in at the Dirty South for a drink. See what the atmosphere was like; if things had settled.

He came around the corner and saw some fucker at his Audi, working at the window with a screwdriver, like he didn't care.

'Fuck you think you're doing?' Easy moved fast, ready to do some damage, and the man at the car stepped back. 'You're fucking dead, man. Stupid fucker.' He was almost on him when the man produced the gun and suddenly Easy was the one who felt stupid.

'Get in the car,' the man said.

Easy heard footsteps behind him and another voice, which said, 'Do as you're told.'

He got behind the wheel, while the big man who had come from nowhere climbed into the passenger seat beside him. Told him it was a nice evening for a drive. The first man got into the back and Easy winced when he felt the muzzle of the gun poking into the soft flesh behind his ear.

He remembered what he'd said to Theo about being ready for this, but he could feel the beef rising up and the taste of that wine, and in the end, the only thing he could do was what he was told.

Sweet and simple.

'I've put all this in my report, obviously,' Deering said. 'But I wanted to tell you in person, too. Because I know you.'

'"All" what?' Helen asked.

'Remember when we met up last week and I said there were a couple of things I was still trying to clear up.'

'Just procedural, you said.'

'I didn't want to tell you anything until I was sure.'

Helen reached for her tea, but it was nearly cold. The baby had settled down. She told Deering to continue.

He cleared his throat and set down his tea. He seemed, to Helen, like someone who had carefully thought through what he was going to say and how he was going to say it. She felt another small shiver as she wondered why that would be.

'The first thing was the glass.'

'Which glass?'

'The glass from the window in the BMW,' Deering said. 'You saw it when you came to the garage.'

Helen nodded, remembering the back of the car, the mats removed. The pieces of glass beneath the seats and in the rear footwell, glittering against the dark metal.

'Plenty in the car, but *none* on the road. I checked.'

'I'm not with you. Wouldn't all the glass have been inside the car anyway? It would fall inwards, surely.'

'The vast majority of it, certainly, but you'd still expect a few fragments to have fallen onto the road. I read the initial report and double-checked. I spoke to the first officer on the scene, and to the collision investigator after he'd been back. There was no glass.'

'Maybe it was scattered by passing cars or a street-cleaner had been past.'

'Possibly.'

'Maybe the traffic officer wasn't very thorough.'

Deering cocked his head, acknowledging that possibility too, but he seemed eager to press on. 'Maybe, but the collision investigator *certainly* was, which was why I was also worried about the speed.'

'What's that got to do with anything?'

'He took all the necessary measurements, checked for skid patterns and so on, and was able to calculate exactly how fast each car was going when the incident occurred. The answer, oddly, was not very.'

'So?'

'Twenty miles an hour, *tops*, when the BMW was supposedly trying to get away, at a time of night when there was very little other traffic on the roads.'

'It *was* raining pretty heavily.'

Deering shook his head. 'In fact, the only time the BMW got up to anything like a decent speed was after the shots were fired, when it veered towards the bus stop.'

Now Helen was utterly confused. 'What's funny about that? Wouldn't you speed up if somebody was shooting at you?'

'Yeah, well, that's the thing,' Deering said.

The effect of what he'd said, or his expression as he spoke, must have been clear for him to see on Helen's face. He looked concerned suddenly, and lifted his mug. 'Let me get you another one of these.'

Helen shook her head, eager to hear it.

'OK . . . Well, I told you we'd dug two bullets out. One from the wheel arch and one from the bottom of the off-side rear door, right? Thirty-eights, like we thought.'

Helen nodded.

'But they weren't in the right place.'

'What's the *right* place?'

'The Cavalier isn't that high off the ground. I mean it might have made sense if the BMW was one of those low, sporty models, or if they'd been firing from a higher car, a big four-by-four or something, but the angles are all wrong.'

'The angles of the shots?'

'Right. Look, they were shooting like this.' He leaned forward and stretched out an arm towards her, two fingers shaping themselves into the muzzle of a gun. He saw Helen's face and dropped his arm, embarrassed. 'Hang on, look at these.' He hurried to fetch a briefcase that he'd left by the door and produced a series of computer printouts. 'They've got a software program that can map the trajectory of the bullets based on the relative heights of each vehicle.' He passed the sheets across and pointed. 'You can trace the path that each bullet took. See?

Neither point of impact is where it should have been.'

Helen studied the sheets, trying to take in what he was saying. 'Wouldn't the bullets have changed their trajectory anyway, once they hit the glass?' It was the best she could come up with. 'That might explain why they ended up where they did.'

'The first bullet, possibly,' Deering said, as though he'd been through this already. 'But there wouldn't have been any glass for the second bullet to pass through. It's nothing to do with the glass. It's all about where the shots were fired from. And *when* they were fired.'

Helen stared at the sheets while Deering got up and walked behind the sofa.

He pointed down. 'Like this . . .'

Helen looked up and stared at Roger Deering, and the panic she'd felt in the bathroom just a short time before seemed like a distant memory. It was replaced by something deeper and more desperate; a terrible notion that she could feel strengthening its grip on her by the second.

'You said "when".' Her voice was a whisper.

'The shots were fired earlier,' Deering said. 'I don't know when exactly, but certainly before the accident. They were fired by someone standing outside the car while it was stationary.'

'You're telling me the whole thing was staged? What happened . . .'

He held up his hands. 'I'm not telling you anything. Just what I found out, that's all.'

'It wasn't an accident.'

Deering looked uncomfortable, as though they'd passed beyond the limits of his expertise. 'Not the sort of accident we thought it was, no.'

'You're saying that all this was done to cover up something else. That Paul was . . . targeted.'

'I'm not saying that.' He looked even more uncomfortable. 'I *can't* say that. There were other people at that bus stop, Helen.'

But she knew something that he didn't. She knew about Operation Victoria.

'It's fine,' she said. 'Thank you.'

She knew that Paul had been killed deliberately.

Helen jumped when the doorbell rang, and Deering saw the movement. 'That wasn't the baby, right?'

She got up from the sofa without a word and walked slowly towards the door.

Deering followed and put a hand on her arm. 'Listen, I'd like to come tomorrow. If that's all right.'

She said yes without really taking in the question.

'So, what are you going to do tonight? Once they've finished?'

Helen turned. She wasn't thinking straight, had been moving like a sleepwalker, but she knew one thing for certain. She didn't want to spend the night alone in the flat. 'I want to go to my dad's,' she said.

Deering nodded and told her he'd drive her over later. He rubbed her arm. 'You'd better let them in.'

THIRTY-THREE

As it was, she wanted it over with as quickly as possible, and she never wanted it to end.

The last bit was the worst, as she had always known it would be. Those few seconds when the coffin slid out of sight. The goodbye moment. When words tumbled and bumped around her head: the things she'd never said and the things she *needed* to say, now, after everything she had thought and felt in the weeks since Paul had died. But when it came to it as the short velvet curtains closed, with music not quite drowning out the mechanism's hum or the sobs from the people close to her, there was only one thing she really wanted to say to him: 'Sorry . . .'

Her dad had been brilliant; not that she'd expected anything else. He'd said it wasn't a problem when she'd woken him in the early hours to let him know that she'd changed her mind about coming over. In the morning, he'd cooked her breakfast and told her she looked fine, and had stayed close from the moment they'd arrived at Paul's parents' place.

Helen hadn't told him about the break-in.

'Doesn't seem right,' he'd said when they'd set off. 'Gorgeous weather on a day like this.'

'It was nice for Mum's too, remember?'

'I think it only rains at funerals in films.'

It wouldn't have mattered anyway, Helen thought, as Paul was being cremated. She remembered Paul and Adam fighting in a grave – and wondered why she'd dreamed about a burial.

No one would have guessed that she and Paul's mother had ever exchanged a cross word. The embrace when Helen arrived was warm and strong, and though Helen wasn't quite sure what it meant, Caroline Hopwood said that her son 'would have been proud'. While everyone stood around in her living room, she moved among them with a bottle and some glasses, keen to ensure that each person had a drink, or was at least offered one. Most took a small brandy, and Helen heard one of Paul's aunties talk about needing a 'stiffener', which seemed an unfortunate choice of word, considering. She told her dad and he laughed.

'She's bearing up,' he said, watching Paul's mother drift from group to group. It was his phrase of the day, though some variation or other on how kind the weather was being ran it a close second.

Paul's dad and sister were equally welcoming, even if they weren't holding up quite as well, with less to keep them busy. Paul's father was ten years older than his wife and never said much. When Helen went into the kitchen to see if she could lend a hand, he shook his bald head slowly and pulled her close, and only let go when someone said that the cars had arrived.

'I can't bloody do this,' he said. He looked as though he wanted to lie down and never get up again.

It was a ten-minute drive out to the crematorium. Sun streamed into the big Daimler, bringing the smell out of the cracked leather seats. Sitting there with her father and Paul's parents, Helen watched the reactions of pedestrians as the cortège drifted by. She remembered being on the way to her mother's funeral and seeing people stop and lower their heads; watching a man raise his hat. Perhaps they just didn't do that any more, she thought. Maybe one more person's passing meant less now that everyone was used to seeing so much death and destruction on live TV. She mentioned it to her father, and he leaned across to watch with her.

'Maybe people have just got no manners any more,' he said.

There were a lot of police already gathered outside the chapel. Helen saw cigarettes being stamped out as the car approached. Gary Kelly and Martin Bescott were standing with many of Paul's other colleagues from Kennington CID. She saw Jeff Moody with what she guessed was a small group of SOCA officers, and there were plenty there in uniform, as part of the official police presence.

She was helped from the car by the driver and spoke to several people. She said something about how lovely the grounds looked, but she was drifting, as though none of it were quite real.

In the doorway to the chapel, the area commander introduced himself, and told her that Paul had been a fine officer who had been doing great work. Helen thanked him. For a moment, she wondered if he knew about Operation Victoria, but guessed that he was saying what he usually did on such occasions; that he'd probably never heard of Paul Hopwood until he received the memo. She turned to look at the hearse as they started to unload the coffin, and was aware of the area commander taking a piece of paper from his top pocket, sneaking a last glimpse at the speech he would be giving in a few minutes.

The pall-bearers stepped forward, each in immaculate dress uniform, and were briefed in low tones by the funeral director. Helen thought they looked beautiful, and nervous. As they took the coffin's weight on their shoulders, she glanced across at Paul's mother and watched pride and grief struggling for control of her expression.

A Metropolitan Police flag had been draped across the coffin and now Paul's dress cap was laid on the lid, behind the simple wreath of white flowers that Helen had chosen. She was aware of eyes on her and wondered what her own expression was. She felt blank and heavy. Like she was falling.

She leaned into her father as the pall-bearers started to move. They came slowly; not quite a slow march, but in step, staring straight ahead. The look on the face of the officer nearest her was like a punch to her heart, its dutiful determination. So she let her eyes drop and looked instead at the highly polished boots as the coffin was carried past her; at the sharp creases in their dress trousers and the small stones that were kicked aside with each step.

Paul's father put a hand in the small of his wife's back and they moved into line behind the pall-bearers.

'You ready, love?' her father asked.

Heartburn had kicked in half an hour after breakfast. It was just starting to ease. Her tights were itchy and she'd need the toilet soon. When she sucked in a breath she could taste cut grass and wax, and she hoped that her legs wouldn't give out before she had a chance to sit down.

'Don't let me down, Helen.'

'Only the once, Hopwood. It won't happen again.'

She put her arm through her father's and followed the coffin.

After the service, Helen spoke briefly to Roger Deering and Martin Bescott, introducing them to each another. Bescott said that Paul would be greatly missed by the team, and Helen thanked them both for coming. She had several reasons to be grateful to Deering, even if he was a little too touchy-feely. She thought Bescott seemed nice enough, and wondered why Paul had so rarely had anything good to say about him.

Together with Paul's mum and dad she joined those moving along the line of wreaths laid out in front of the flower bed that skirted the building. After a few minutes she stopped leaning down to read the cards and let others move past her. She stepped back and stared up at the elaborate golden dome above the chapel, an afternoon sky behind that was perfectly blue in all directions.

The weather *had* been every bit as kind as her father had said.

Looking to her left, she saw Frank Linnell at the end of the line. He'd probably sent flowers anyway, she thought, and was checking to see that they were suitably impressive. He saw her and raised a hand, and she turned away quickly in case he decided to come over.

To look suitably gutted and tell her what a beautiful service it had been. To pass her a fistful of notes when nobody was looking. 'Just a little something for the stone, love. My gift . . .'

Walking towards the cars, she heard footsteps catching up with her.

'Helen?'

She turned, expecting to see Linnell, and saw Detective Inspector Spiky Bugger, clutching his order of service. 'DI . . .' She struggled to remember the name, only for a second, but long enough for him to spot it, to look at his shoes. 'Thorne.'

'Tom.'

'It's nice of you to come,' she said.

He looked uncomfortable in his suit, with his neck bulging slightly above a collar that was clearly too tight. 'I just wanted you to know that we've seen the crime scene manager's full report.' He lowered his voice. 'That we'll be making an arrest tomorrow.'

'Right.' Unless something she didn't know about had happened, she had a good idea who they would be arresting. 'I'd like to be there.'

The look said that he'd been expecting that reaction. 'I'll see what I can arrange,' he said.

She told him she was grateful. 'What about the people in the car?'

'Well, we know we're looking in the right place.'

'A gang war.'

'Not exactly. We traced the owner of the stolen Cavalier when he tried to make an insurance claim. He didn't want to tell us very much.'

'Surprise.'

'But we persuaded him to come down and take a look at the bodies of the boys who were shot.'

Helen nodded. She knew that police officers could be more persuasive than usual when it came to catching someone who'd killed one of their own.

'He identified two of them as being in the group that had nicked his car. So, as I said, we're in the right place.'

'But . . .?'

'It's not a gang war. Or if it is, it's pretty one-sided. So, we don't know who's shooting these kids, but we're fairly sure they're . . . the right kids.' He shrugged. 'Anyway, this isn't really the time. I just wanted to let you know we're getting there . . . and to say "sorry".' He flicked the order of service against his fingers. 'And . . . good luck.'

'Do you have kids?' Helen asked.

'One on the way,' Thorne said. 'Not anything as far gone as yours, but . . . on the way.'

'Well, best of luck to you, too.'

He was already turning to go, smiling at Helen's father who was passing him in the other direction, on his way to the car.

'Who was that?'

'Friend of Paul's,' Helen said.

Her father held the car door open and she slid in next to Paul's parents. Last one in, her father sat opposite, moving his jacket quickly out of the way so that the undertaker could close the door. He leaned across and patted Helen on the leg, asked how she was bearing up.

They were back at the house by four. Paul's father opened the living-room doors on to the patio while Caroline and a few of her friends laid out the food. The sandwiches were on platters from M & S. There was cold chicken and pasta salad, cakes and mixed berries.

'No sausages on sticks,' her father said.

Helen sat on a sofa out of the sunlight and talked to Gary Kelly, who perched on the arm, trying to juggle a paper plate and cup. She told him how good his reading had been.

'I fluffed one of the lines,' he said.

'Nobody noticed.'

'I just wanted it to be perfect.'

She reminded him about Paul's guitar and told him to come round and pick it up whenever he wanted.

'We were singing that night,' he said. 'The Rolling Stones at the top of our voices. The woman at the bus stop told us to shut up.'

'That was usually my reaction when Paul started singing,' Helen said. She watched Kelly wander back to the table to refill his glass. He looked as though he wouldn't be straying too far from the drinks, and she couldn't blame him.

She wasn't alone for long. There were perhaps thirty people in the house, and she couldn't count too many who didn't come across at least once to ask if there was anything she needed. If there was anything they could do. She usually just asked for more water or another sandwich.

Jenny and Tim came over after an hour or so to let her know that they were leaving. There was a babysitter to sort out. Helen told her sister how attentive everyone had been, and how wearing it was becoming.

'People are just being nice,' Jenny said.

'I suppose.'

Jenny leaned down to kiss her. 'You'd be pissed off if everyone ignored you.'

'It's weird, though,' Helen said. Not a single one of them mentions . . . *you know what.*' She pointed melodramatically at the bulge beneath her dress. 'I don't believe they haven't noticed. I know black's supposed to be slimming, but that's bloody ridiculous.'

Once her sister had gone, Helen sat returning smiles until her face started to hurt, then wandered out onto the patio. She found Paul's father sitting on a low wall, smoking. He looked as though he didn't want anyone to see him.

'Paul used to do that,' she said. 'He'd sneak out on the balcony. Like

I didn't know.'

Paul's father took a long drag. 'You women always know.' And another. 'We can't get away with anything.'

'Right.'

'He was a sly little sod, mind you, even when he was a kid.' He smiled sadly through the smoke, remembering. 'You never knew what he was up to.'

The old man didn't seem to want to say too much more after that, so Helen walked around the garden for twenty minutes, until her legs began to ache and she had to go back inside to use the toilet. Afterwards she sat near the door, thanking people as they began to leave. She was able to tune out after a while, to pull the right faces while she thought about what Deering had told her, and what Thorne had said outside the chapel.

She knew now that the break-in the previous night had been no ordinary burglary, and it was a fair bet that the boys who had been in that Cavalier when Paul was killed had not been acting alone. Now, somebody was killing them. Perhaps the person who had hired them wanted to make sure they could never tell anyone.

'God bless, love.'

'Thank you.'

She wondered if those investigating Paul's death were starting to put the pieces together themselves. Or if she knew more than they did.

'We'll be thinking of you.'

'I know you will. Thank you.'

After conferring with her father, she let Paul's mother know that she was about ready to head back. It was never going to be an easy get-away.

'We just presumed you'd want to stay.'

'I know you've got a houseful already.'

'It's fine, honestly. We've made up beds for you and your dad.'

'I should really get back,' Helen said. 'I think I need to be close to home, you know?'

'This is your home too, Helen.'

'All the same . . .'

At the door, Caroline Hopwood hugged her and said that she wanted to do everything she could to help in bringing up her grandchild. It would be lovely if it was a boy, she said. She didn't have a grandson. Helen promised to let her know as soon as there was any news and, when her father drove them away, she waved from the car window, all the way to the first corner.

★

It was gone nine o'clock by the time they reached Tulse Hill, and although it was still light and sunny outside, the flat seemed cold. Helen was exhausted, but she hadn't known quite how badly until she'd waved her father goodbye and all but fallen through the front door. She made herself tea and got out of her dress and tights. She sat on the balcony in her dressing gown and tried to let things settle.

'Sly, even when you were a kid then, Hopwood?'

She wondered how long it would be until she stopped talking to him. If it would happen before she could no longer see his face clearly.

Inside, she took the order of service from her bag and smoothed out the crease in the card. It ran through the picture of him on the back. In the end, the music chosen by Paul's mother had been nice, but Helen was still angry with herself for not standing up to her a bit more.

Worried it had looked like she didn't care.

She searched through Paul's old Queen albums until she found the track she wanted. 'Who Wants to Live Forever?' was still playing on repeat fifteen minutes later, when she slipped into bed.

She lay there as it grew dark, listening to the music and wishing that she could tell Paul about the day. That they could laugh about it. Wishing that it had still been like that between them before he'd died. Wanting to curl up, and to smash things, and to hurt whoever had left her feeling like this. Whoever had scooped the hole out in the middle of her. She lay there, and the kicks inside were like little screams.

She was due to have her baby in two days.

THIRTY-FOUR

'I thought it was nice,' Laura said.

'They're usually . . . *nice*, though, aren't they?' Frank had carried a tray of breakfast things through to the conservatory. It was a gorgeous morning and he enjoyed looking out at the garden while he ate and flicked through a couple of the papers. '"Nice" is so bloody . . . *safe*, though,' he said. 'Don't you reckon?'

'People like to feel safe when they've just lost someone. How else would you want them to feel?'

'Just for once I'd like to see a funeral that says something about the person who's died, you know? That tells you a bit about what they were really like.'

'I thought what that police officer said was really moving, and the readings . . .'

'Yeah, *nice*, I know.' Frank shook his head. 'That copper was probably saying the same thing he says at every one of these. Don't get me wrong, I'm not suggesting people should be dancing around and telling jokes or anything like that, but there should be a bit more . . . celebration or whatever. And a bit less God poking

His nose in wouldn't hurt, either.'

Laura smiled. 'I like all that, too.'

'Paul didn't have a religious bone in his body, and his girlfriend doesn't strike me as a God-botherer either, so what's the point?' He took a bite of toast and sat back in his chair. 'Paul would have hated all that. He'd've sat there taking the piss out of the vicar or trying not to fall asleep.'

'I think somebody got out of the wrong side of bed.'

'Yeah, I didn't have a great night.' He stared past her, out across the back lawn. The garden looked good, though he needed to tell the lazy sod that did it to take a bit more care with the edging. 'I'll seriously miss him, that's all. Need all the friends I've got, my time of life.'

'You're not old, Frank.'

'Feels like it sometimes.'

'Course you'll miss him,' Laura said. 'I'll miss him, too.'

'It would have been great if yesterday had been *about* him a bit more, that's all I'm saying. His personality, you know?' He flicked crumbs from his shirt onto the plate. 'Maybe I'm just getting awkward as I get older.'

She came and sat down next to him. 'Maybe you've been to too many funerals.'

The Clapham branch of the Workz was probably much the same as all the other high-end gyms and health clubs across the city: chrome, steel and smoked glass; extra-fluffy towels and chi-chi toiletries; a hefty annual membership fee which was a decent incentive to go twice a week for a few months, until you realised that life was too short to waste time on a rowing machine.

Helen sat in the corner of the salad 'n' smoothie bar, flicking through a brochure while she waited. She'd been on the phone since before seven, organising things, and it felt good to have mapped out her day already. This would be a nice way to kick it off.

She watched Sarah Ruston come down the stairs from the women's changing room; watched her toss a bag onto a chair and walk across to the bar to order something. Her hair was tied back, damp, and she wore a sleek, black tracksuit with red piping. The face seemed much improved, even from a distance, though her arm was still in a sling.

Looking pretty good, though, all things considered.

Ruston turned, sucking at the straw in her drink, and saw Helen stand and wave. Her eyes widened, and after a few seconds she picked up her bag and walked across. 'What are you . . .?' She looked at her watch. 'I've not got very long, I'm afraid. I'm supposed to be meeting Patrick.'

'That's OK,' Helen said. 'I've only got a couple of minutes myself.'

Ruston sat down on the edge of a chair. Her eyes stayed low and she noticed the brochure on the table. 'Thinking of joining?'

'Well, it *would* be nice to get back in shape once I've got rid of *this*.' Helen smiled. 'But at six hundred quid a year, I think I'll just try and do a bit more walking. Maybe go mad and buy a workout video.'

'Yeah, it is a bit steep,' Ruston said. 'I wouldn't bother, but membership comes with the job. They've got one of these places near the office, and we get to use all of them, so . . .'

'So, why not?'

'Why not?'

'You're a bit bloody keen, though, aren't you?' Helen nodded at the sling.

Ruston tried to smile and lifted her arm. 'Actually, I took it off when I was working out, and I only did an hour on the treadmill. Probably get rid of it for good next week.'

'Even so.'

Ruston sipped at her juice.

'I always think it's weird,' Helen said. 'Coming to places like this, sweating like a pig and trying to keep your body beautiful, when you're filling it full of shit the rest of the time.' She looked for a reaction. 'What is it? Crack? Coke as well, I should imagine.'

'Sorry?'

'I mean you wouldn't step straight off the treadmill and walk into a pie shop, would you? Doesn't make any sense.' A female employee in a tight white coat walked close to the table. Ruston looked up hopefully, but Helen paid the woman no attention. 'Slumming it a bit, though, I would have thought, going all the way across to Lewisham to buy the stuff. Isn't there some nice city boy in an Armani suit who could have sorted you out?'

The blood had left Ruston's face fast, the all-but-faded bruises a little paler suddenly.

'You must have owed them plenty,' Helen said. 'I mean, you've got to have one hell of a hold over someone to make them do what you did. Something like that. Or maybe you were so off your Botoxed face that you didn't even think about it . . .'

Ruston cried for almost a minute. She pressed the heels of her hands against her eyes and kept her head down; there wasn't too much noise. Helen watched, and loved it.

'I don't need to hear a sob story,' she said, when Ruston finally looked up. 'You know, before you start wasting your breath. I think, considering where I was yesterday, I might be the wrong person to try that out on, don't you?'

She'd let them get all the details later, in an interview room, but Helen could hazard a decent guess. A City high-flyer with a high-maintenance lifestyle and a very expensive habit. Credit cards long maxed out and debts piling up, until the supplier you're into for serious money comes up with a novel way to pay off what he's owed. The lovely house around the corner was probably mortgaged up to the hilt, unless the older, richer other half was taking care of it.

At that point Helen wondered how much Patrick knew.

'I didn't have any choice,' Ruston said.

Helen could have flown across the table at her then, told her that the choice between settling a bill or killing someone might normally cause a person to stop and think a bit. She could have punched every word of it into her.

314

'They threatened to hurt my family.'

'What do you think you did to *mine*?'

Now, Ruston was fighting to get it out over the sobs; clawing at the arm of her chair and shaking her head; wiping away the snot with a sleeve. 'I didn't know anyone was going to be killed. They didn't tell me anything. They just showed me *where* . . . what speed to drive at . . . I didn't know who . . . the . . .'

'Who the *target* was?' Ruston opened her mouth, but all that came out was a cracked whine, like a nail on a blackboard. 'You drive a car at someone, it tends to do a lot of damage.'

'I'm sorry . . .'

'You will be.'

Helen stood up and moved around the table when she saw Patrick come breezing across the atrium towards them. She leaned down and took a firm grip on Ruston's damaged shoulder; said it nice and calmly, so Ruston would know she meant every word. 'I wish you'd broken your neck.'

If Patrick was at all thrown at seeing her, he didn't show it. He jerked a thumb back towards the entrance. 'What's all the excitement? There are two police cars outside.'

'Sarah might be tied up for a while,' Helen said. She could see two officers in the reception area, brandishing warrant cards at the woman behind the desk. A couple more were on their way in, pushing through the glass doors. She'd thank them on her way out.

She stopped in front of Patrick before she left. 'Just to let you know. I couldn't give a fuck about your BMW.'

Theo carried his plate across to a table in the corner, then went back for a couple of tabloids that had been read and left sitting on the counter. It would kill half an hour, maybe. He guessed that this was what it was like to lose your job, except that there hadn't been any notice, and getting laid off didn't usually involve wondering when you were going to get a bullet in your head.

Everything had fallen apart since they'd found the bodies in the stash house. The police had gutted the place and the sniffer dogs had gone crazy. Now it was just one more empty flat in the block. All the business had ground to a halt, with punters buying elsewhere and everyone in the crew standing around on corners wondering what was going to happen; when someone was going to tell them what to do next.

A few days before, Easy seemed to have got things sorted – smoothing everything over and reorganising the stock and the selling. But Theo hadn't seen him since Saturday night. Nobody had. Truth of it, he was getting sick of the others asking what Easy was doing and where he was.

Theo had called him plenty of times, but Easy's mobile was switched off or the battery had died.

Or whatever.

There was still stuff about the murders on the front pages, but nothing he hadn't seen before. Seemed like they were just rehashing old stories to keep up sales, while they were waiting with bated breath for the next one. Like they knew it was coming. He thought about how Easy had gone mental outside the bar; how he'd nearly given them another body to get all worked up about.

Theo had gone back down to the Dirty South on the Sunday morning and checked around the back for blood. He'd found nothing, was relieved that Easy seemed to have been happy enough waving his blade around and scaring the shit out of the bloke. He'd watched all the news reports as well, just in case, and seen no mention of anything, which was good. Not that a stabbing was going to be a mega-story, not any more, but all the same.

All he could do now was sit on his arse and keep safe, keep everyone around him safe, until someone told him what to do next.

He turned the pages slowly as he ate, one eye on the door like it always was, feeling the weight of the gun he'd taken from the stash house in his pocket. The one that Sugar Boy hadn't been quick enough to get to.

He stopped chewing, stopped *breathing* for a few seconds, when he saw the picture. And the headline above it: DISTRESS OF COP'S PREGNANT WIDOW.

Her face was tight and her mouth was open like she was shouting, but he knew it was the woman he'd spoken to a week or so before. He'd been surprised at the weight when he'd lifted her up. The woman with the blue Fiesta, the broken eggs.

Theo read the story, but he wasn't really taking it in. He'd helped her and she'd thanked him for it. Christ, she'd even said something in that car park, some joke about naming her baby . . .

He remembered the noise as the BMW hit. *Felt* it. The metal and the glass and the low thump as they drove away and he tried to look back through the rain.

'*Be as good a name as any, probably.*'

He stared down at the picture and let his breakfast go cold. The headline said 'distress', but it didn't seem that way to him.

She looked like she wanted to kill someone.

THIRTY-FIVE

Helen looked up at the CCTV cameras on each corner of the roof as she waited at the front door. She'd seen others at the gates where she'd turned off the road and wondered if he'd been watching her as she'd driven up. Not a surprise really, that a man like this was careful. He had plenty to protect, and there were probably a good few who'd be happy to see him lose it all.

But then, he'd have a few of his own too; people who could warn him of any threat, or gather information when others were struggling. A network. And his own methods for getting people to make some noise when an official investigation had its nose pressed against a wall of silence.

It made no sense, the idea that whoever was behind Paul's death was also responsible for the shootings. If you were trying to cover your arse, why set up something that would necessitate getting rid of a whole gang afterwards? So, with whoever had used the boys in that car to do his dirty work out of the picture, it wasn't a big leap.

There weren't exactly many other contenders.

Helen had called Jeff Moody early, after several conversations with the Murder Squad to sort out her appointment at the Workz. When she'd mentioned Frank Linnell, he'd assured her that he was still making enquiries, checking into the precise nature of Linnell's relationship with Paul.

'I think I might be able to find a bit more out myself,' she'd said.

'Not sure that's too clever.'

'I gave up being clever weeks ago,' Helen said.

This time there wasn't a problem asking for Linnell's address.

The hallway felt like the lobby of an exclusive hotel, with an expanse of veined, brown marble and an over-the-top chandelier. There were oil paintings on the walls and a wide stairway curving upwards to three, maybe four, more storeys. A good few million, Helen reckoned.

Linnell showed her through to a kitchen that made Jenny's feel like her own. She sat at the table and watched him make tea. She was surprised that there didn't seem to be any live-in staff around, that there didn't seem to be anyone else in the house.

'You look amazingly well this morning,' he said. 'Considering the kind of night you probably had. I didn't get a lot of sleep myself, to be honest. It's hard, isn't it, to just crack on like nothing's happened?'

'I suppose.' Helen stared at his back as he poured milk and stirred. He was doing it again, talking as though his relationship with Paul meant as much as hers did.

'Got no choice ultimately, though, have we?' He carried the mugs over, asked if she wanted biscuits. He said the woman who did his cooking made the most amazing cakes, if she fancied some.

Helen had eaten already, and been sick twice.

'You did well yesterday,' he said. 'Showed a lot of strength, if you don't mind me saying. More than most of us did, anyway. There was a tear or two shed, I can tell you that.'

Helen took a scalding sip of tea, enjoying the burn. She didn't want to make small talk about the funeral, didn't really want to talk about anything she didn't have to. She wanted to get into it. 'You've heard about these shootings in Lewisham?'

He nodded, wrapping hands around his mug. 'Can't get away from it, it's all over the news.'

'Four murders in nearly two weeks,' she said.

'Twelve days.'

'I'll take your word for it.'

'Something needs to be done,' Linnell said. 'Not just by you lot. By people higher up . . . Sort the mess out.' He shook his head. 'I don't want to sound callous, but it makes me feel a bit sick, you know what I mean? You bury someone like Paul, while there's people walking around doing *that*, like life's not worth the price of a takeaway. Makes you want to throw your hands up . . .'

He looked as though he meant it. Maybe the likes of Frank Linnell could do that, she thought; could dissociate their own actions from those of others, however terrible they were. Or maybe he'd been fronting it out in situations like this since before she was born.

'They were the boys in the car,' she said. 'The ones that were shot. They were in that Cavalier when Paul was killed.'

Linnell didn't put quite as much effort into looking shocked. 'Hardly *boys*.'

'The youngest was fourteen.'

He shrugged. 'Don't you think you give up the right to any sympathy when you make your living the way they did? When you start carrying guns?'

'Do you?'

'Look, you'll understand if I'm not heartbroken. You *should* understand, at any rate.'

'Should I?'

'Wasn't there even a bit of you that was happy when you found out?'

Helen couldn't hold his stare and her eyes drifted across to the dresser in the corner. There were a dozen or more photographs in brightly coloured frames on the top: a black-and-white shot of an old woman with a baby; a more recent picture of a different woman standing with a young girl; Linnell himself posing with various men in suits. And several photos of a young woman. She was exceptionally beautiful, with long brown hair, huge eyes and a smile that suggested she didn't quite accept the fact. Helen knew very little about Linnell's private life and wondered if she might be his daughter.

Linnell turned and followed her gaze. 'I've got a couple of Paul somewhere, if you'd like to see them.'

'No, thanks.'

They both turned away from the pictures.

'Look, I know why you're so pissed off,' he said.

'Do you?' Do you have the slightest idea? Helen thought. Do you understand for one second that whatever the boys in that car did, whatever they were part of, they did not deserve what you doled out to them in return? Do you seriously believe that what you've been doing is justified or, in some self-serving, fucked-up way, *honourable*?

'You can't stand the thought that Paul chose to spend any time with the likes of me.'

Helen swallowed. 'What Paul did was his business.'

'I'm not saying I can blame you for that.'

'I'm not here to talk about Paul.'

'I take it you've found out what he was doing.' He waited, but Helen said nothing. 'Which means you're also deeply pissed off about the fact that he told me and didn't tell you.'

'Why do you think that was?' She had been determined to remain calm, but she was raising her voice. 'He told you because you were part of the operation. He was hoping you'd be useful to him, that's all.'

'If that's what you choose to believe, fine. But if you listen, it'll make you feel a lot better.'

'I don't need *you* to make me feel better.'

'I was the only person he could confide in,' Linnell said. 'Think about it. Who am *I* going to tell? Believe what you like, but I don't pay a single copper for anything, and if what Paul was up to caused problems for some of my competitors who do, then so much the better. Yeah, he came to me right at the end for a bit of a leg-up – which, believe me, I wish I'd given him – but that was as far as it went.' He was fingering his gold chain again now, wrapping it around his finger. 'I think he needed to tell someone, you know? I think it was doing his head in a bit. And it couldn't really be anyone else.'

There was some relief, a welcome dose of understanding, but the feeling evaporated quickly and left a bad taste. Helen couldn't stomach the idea that what Linnell was telling her was supposed to be some kind of comfort, any more than she could bear the thought that he might get away with taking revenge on the boys in that car.

But there was not a great deal she could do about it.

'So, you know nothing about these shootings, then?'

'Other than what you've just told me, you mean?'

'And what you've seen on the news, of course.'

He downed what was left of his tea and smiled. 'I really don't know what you expect me to tell you, Helen.'

When she pushed back her chair, Linnell stood up and reached out a hand as if to help. She ignored it. He watched her stand and start to walk out, tutting quietly, as though he were disappointed in her, thought she was being ill-mannered. He asked her if she was sure about that cake, said that he'd be happy to wrap a piece that she could take with her.

He opened the fridge, but Helen kept on walking.

Theo had heard it in his mother's voice when she'd called, and he could see it on her face when he let himself in. When she got up from the sofa and moved across to hug him.

'You had a drink?'

'Had a *few* drinks.'

'What's the matter?'

'Why does anything have to be the matter?'

'It's not Sunday,' Theo said.

They sat down at the front-room table. She didn't offer him anything or ask if he'd already had something to eat. She took off her glasses and rubbed her eyes.

'Is Angela OK?'

She looked at him as if it were a ludicrous question. 'Angela's at school.'

'You were getting me worried, that's all.' He smiled, but he was feeling like he might not want to for much longer.

'*You're* worried?' There was a flash of anger in his mother's eyes, rare and fierce.

'What?'

'You been worried for how long? The couple of minutes since you came through that door?' The drink made her accent thicker; put the lilt and the stretch into the words. 'You want to know what it's like to worry *all the time*?'

Theo kissed his teeth and looked away, thinking that she had no idea.

'To worry so you can't sleep? So much worry for one of your children that you have no time to think about the other?'

'Come on, Mum . . .'

'Come on, *nothing*.' She shook her head slowly and stood up. 'I don't want to fight with you, Theodore.' She walked across and picked up her handbag from the sofa. 'I didn't mean to get angry with you.'

'It's fine.'

'Shouldn't have opened that bottle.'

'Once in a while isn't going to hurt.'

She carried her handbag back to the table and sat down. 'I think you worry more if you have your kids late, like we did. You think that you won't be around for them as long, you know?'

'I know.'

'Course, turned out we were right in your father's case.'

Theo wondered for a second if he'd been so caught up with everything that he'd forgotten an important date: his father's birthday or the anniversary of his death. But both were months away.

'He always told me you were too clever,' she said. 'He'd sit over there and say that you had all the brains, that you obviously got them from his side of the family.'

'Yeah, he said that to me, too.'

She smiled, then the sigh cut through it. 'Too clever to get tied up with anything stupid, he said. To get into any trouble.' She paused and fiddled with the catch on her bag. 'Nobody had a better heart or worked harder than he did,' she said, 'but I tell you, he couldn't see *shit* sometimes.' She paused and looked at Theo.

Theo looked at the table. He could not remember the last time he'd heard her say anything like that about his father.

'I can, though,' she said. 'Mind you, you'd have to be blind not to see what's going on round here. Or stupid. You know I'm neither of those things, don't you?'

'Course I do—'

She raised a finger to silence him. 'So . . .' She opened her bag and pulled out a small, blue, plastic book. She pushed it across the table.

Theo opened it. 'What's this?' It was obvious enough, though: the building society's logo on the front; the list of payments on every page.

'You could go,' she said. 'You, Javine and Benjamin.' She pointed to the book in his hands. 'It's not much, a little under nineteen hundred pounds, but it's enough to get somewhere. Enough to look after yourselves until you find something.'

Theo offered the book back to her. 'I think you should stick to drinking on Sundays, yeah?'

She didn't even look at it.

He flicked through the pages; the payments had been made every fortnight without fail. His mouth was dry and his fingers felt sweaty against the plastic. He still had the gun in his pocket. 'We could *all* go,' he said.

Hannah Shirley shook her head.

'Why not?' He leaned across the table. 'Like we did last time.'

'I don't *want* to go,' she said. 'I've got lots of friends here and Angela has her own friends now, too. It's not like when we moved away last time. I don't want to unsettle her.'

Theo remembered what she'd said a few minutes earlier: his mother had lavished all her worry on him and he knew that his sister deserved a little of it. 'You can't afford to give me this,' he said.

She pulled a mock-offended face. 'I'm not a useless old woman, you know? I'm fifty-one years old. I still get your father's money from London Transport and until your sister finishes school, I can get myself a little part-time job. I'd *like* to do that, maybe work in a shop or something. It would be good to get out of this house a bit more, tell you the truth. I'm good with people, you know?'

'I know you are.'

'And *you*,' she pointed, 'need to be looking after your own family a little bit more.' She sat back in her chair and stared at him for a few seconds, then she threw up her arms, as though it had all been a bit of nonsense; a nice hypothetical discussion. 'Anyway, I'm just talking.' She smiled and reached a hand across to one of Theo's. 'It's just the drink talking.'

Theo nodded. 'OK.'

'Right. I'll go and make us some tea . . .'

When she'd gone to the kitchen, he looked through the savings book that his mother had left on the table. Some of the amounts were almost ridiculously small, a couple of pounds, but they had gone in every fortnight and the list of payments was many pages long.

Theo felt the tears bubble up and burst. As he wiped them away, he looked up to see his mother watching from the kitchen doorway.

'Don't you be afraid of doing *that*, either,' she said. 'Your father never did; he was one of *those* sorts of men. Even when he was ill, I had to do all the crying for the both of us.' She leaned against the door frame. 'Only time I remember him doing it was when England beat the West Indies . . .'

Laura came down a few minutes after Helen had left and sat on the bottom stair. 'I heard you arguing,' she said.

'Not really.' Frank paced slowly around the hallway. 'She just got a bit worked up, that's all. You can hardly blame her for being upset.'

'I don't know how she does it,' Laura said. 'How she walks about and sees people and gets on with things. I think I'd just want to crawl into a corner.'

'Yeah, she's certainly tough. She's going to have to be, mind you.'

Then he asked Laura what he should do. If he should help Helen out by passing on what he knew. He didn't tell her *how* he knew, for obvious reasons, but even as he was asking the question, he knew he was probably kidding himself. Laura was always able to read him, to know what he'd done or was thinking of doing; but even so, he kept the whys and wherefores to himself. It was just something he'd found out and he wanted to know if she thought he should let Paul's girlfriend know about it. Simple as that.

'You want to do this because you feel guilty?'

He'd been right: kidding himself. 'Don't be daft. It's just that, bearing in mind what it is, this feels like the proper way to go about things. It feels . . . appropriate, you know?'

Laura sat, chewing a nail and Frank went to fetch himself a Diet Coke from the kitchen. When he got back, she was standing on the first-floor landing, on her way upstairs again.

She leaned over the banister. 'Yes,' she said. 'It's the right thing to do.'

There was a bright red '5' flashing on Helen's answering machine when she got back to the flat.

Jenny, her father and Roger Deering had all called to see how she was, each one telling her to phone back if there was anything she needed.

Gary Kelly had wanted to arrange a time to call round and collect Paul's guitar.

The fifth caller had not identified himself.

She played the message through a second time, trying to identify a voice she recognised but couldn't place; then a third time, as soon as she'd fetched a pen and paper to take down the relevant information.

The address, the name of the man she would be meeting, what she would need to see.

She knew that the place would be open late, but there was no way she could summon the energy to go out again tonight. She already felt as drained as she would be after the shittiest week at work. She decided to try to get a good night's sleep and go in the morning.

With tomorrow being her due date, Helen knew what Jenny and her father would have to say about it, and that they might well be right. She'd used it as an excuse with Paul's mother, but she knew it would probably be more sensible to stay close to home.

She played the message through again, but still couldn't identify the voice. If the baby *did* decide to be punctual, it wasn't like there was any shortage of hospitals. And it hadn't taken her long to get to Lewisham last time.

THIRTY-SIX

Helen arrived at the club no more than half an hour after it had opened, but the man she'd been instructed to look for was already there, and exactly where she'd been told he would be. He was sitting at the bar hunched over a mug of tea and a plate of toast, and when Helen got close, she saw that he was studying the form in the racing pages of the *Sun*, circling his selections in blue biro between mouthfuls.

There didn't appear to be anyone else in the place.

Jacky Snooks wasn't pleased at being interrupted, but when Helen showed him a warrant card and told him what she wanted to talk about, his demeanour changed. He seemed surprised. Interested.

'How d'you find out about that, then?'

'Doesn't matter.'

Snooks shrugged as though it probably didn't. He tore a chunk from a slice of toast and gestured with what was left. 'That real? Or have you got a cushion shoved up there as a disguise, like?' He hissed out a laugh, showing a mouthful of soggy toast and dodgy teeth.

'Not a cushion,' Helen said. She nodded towards the snooker

tables stretching away behind them in the half light, still hidden beneath patched, silver covers. 'And I really don't fancy squeezing this thing out lying on one of those, so if we can speed this up.'

Snooks popped the rest of the slice into his mouth and wiped his hands on the legs of his trousers. 'A twenty tends to hurry things along,' he said.

Once the cash was tucked into his shirt pocket, he told her that one of the local crews hung about at the club, or used to, until a couple of weeks ago. He hadn't seen too many of them since then.

'Any names?' Helen asked.

'Just those bloody silly nicknames they all have.'

'I'm listening.'

He mentioned a few names that Helen recognised from the mural she'd seen the last time she was in Lewisham. The roll of honour. It confirmed what the anonymous caller had said, and she started to feel the excitement building; shortening her breath.

And she knew there was more.

'Tell me about the man in the suit,' Helen said. 'The one you saw them talking to.'

Snooks was starting to cast longing glances back towards his newspaper. 'I saw a bloke in a suit. End of story, really.'

'I'll have that twenty quid back, then.'

Snooks sighed, turned on his chair and pointed to the stairs. 'Coming down there, they were, like they'd had some kind of meeting upstairs. This is going back five or six weeks, something like that. Wave . . . the one with the stupid hair, who acted like he was in charge, and his Paki minder. And this white bloke in the suit, looked like an estate agent or something. All very pally, shaking hands and that, and there was a few of the others standing around, looking like they didn't know what was going on.'

Helen didn't bother asking for a description. The man who'd left the message on her machine had said she could do better than that.

'Who else did you tell about this?'

'I don't know, a few people. I can't remember.'

Even if Helen hadn't known he was lying, it would have been obvious from his face, the apprehension in it. 'Come on, I didn't find out by magic, did I?'

Snooks looked uncomfortable, as though he'd already said more than his twenty pounds' worth.

Helen didn't suppose that it would matter much. She waved away her own question and told him he could go back to his racing once he'd pointed her in the direction of the manager.

'Why didn't you just take it?'

'We don't need it.'

'Course we don't. We can just borrow some from the bank, right? We can just use some of our savings, all that money we've got stashed away. Yeah, no problem.'

Theo knew, as soon as he'd opened his mouth, that it had been a mistake. Javine had seized on it like a pit-bull, and had been giving him grief ever since, like he'd blown some big chance.

'She was just *saying* all that stuff, man,' Theo said. 'About getting a job, about it being fine and all that. You didn't see her face, though.'

'It's what parents are supposed to do. They make sacrifices, yeah?'

Theo shook his head. 'Yeah, when you're a kid, when you can't look after yourself. After that, it's up to you. *You're* supposed to take care of *them*.'

They were in the living room. Benjamin was lying on his back in the corner, under a brightly coloured baby gym, squealing and flapping his arms at the little mirror that dangled above him. Theo sat on the sofa while Javine moved in and out from the kitchen, where she was getting a feed ready.

'It's just a shame, you know?' she said. She stood in the doorway, shaking a bottle. 'When something's on a plate like that and you miss out. It's not like it happens all the time.'

It was OK when she was shouting – he could shout back – but he couldn't stand it when she used that sad voice. Like she didn't want to make a fuss, but she was just disappointed. Like it wasn't his fault he'd let them down.

'It might have been a chance for us to go, that's all.'

If he regretted telling her that his mum had offered him the money, he could have kicked himself for telling her why. He'd felt guilty even *thinking* about getting away somewhere, about leaving his mum and Angela behind, and it was even worse now that his mum had brought it out into the open. It was like she could tell it had been on his mind. Was it really what she wanted or was she offering to help because she realised that he couldn't cut it? That he needed saving, like a little boy?

Even now, thinking that it would be the wrong thing to do, he felt selfish.

Maybe they would be all right without him. It wasn't like they had ever been able to rely on him for anything. But how would *he* handle it? Not being on the spot if he ever *was* needed. Not seeing Angela growing up, or being there to look after her when boys just like him came sniffing around.

'You're a good son,' Javine said.

'Who has to go crying to his mother for cash.'

'She *offered* it.'

'It's her life savings.'

'I know you're thinking about your mother, T . . .'

She didn't have to say any more. But what about me? What about Benjamin?

Theo watched her turn and go back into the kitchen, heard the fridge door close, and the microwave hum as she heated up the bottle. 'We don't need that money,' he said.

He looked across at Benjamin, kicking his legs and staring up at his image in the little plastic mirror. If he got away with his life, wherever he might end up, Theo knew that all he really wanted was for his son to be able to look at himself and feel OK about it.

The manager of the Cue Up was a balding blob called Adkins. He had a fat backside and wore a tie with a short-sleeved shirt, which always struck Helen as faintly ludicrous. She wasn't certain what he'd been up to at the computer in his small, cluttered office, but he wasn't in the brightest of moods when he opened the door.

Once again, the warrant card seemed to do the trick, although Adkins barely glanced at it before leading Helen across to a cluster of grimy-looking monitors below the single window.

It looked very much like he'd been told to expect her.

The security set-up looked comprehensive enough, with feeds from a camera at the entrance to the club, several in the bar and playing areas and others on stairwells and outside the toilets. The arrangements for reviewing the tapes, however, were somewhat less efficient than those at the CCTV monitoring centre, where Helen had watched Paul getting into Ray Jackson's cab two weeks earlier.

'Might take a while,' Adkins said.

'How long?'

'Don't hold your breath.'

It was stifling in the office, and while Adkins was searching through the footage, Helen walked across to a small water-cooler in the corner and helped herself to the drink her host had shown no inclination to offer. She felt the sweat prickling across her back and belly, and even after three cups her mouth felt dry and she was finding it hard to swallow.

The baby was moving. Several times every few minutes, she felt her stomach shift; a deep lurch, low down, that she had not felt before, and which snatched her breath for a few seconds each time. She could not be sure if it was her body anticipating the imminent natural trauma, or the nerves . . . the fear at what she might be about to see.

What someone had decided she *ought* to see.

'Here you go.' Adkins walked back to the computer and dropped into his chair. 'Help yourself . . . Second one from the left.'

Helen moved over and leaned down to get a better view, putting herself in line with the window to reduce the glare on the monitor. It was a small screen, just eight or nine inches, housed in a battered steel box. The picture was frozen: a fuzzy, black-and-white image of a corridor; the dark line of a handrail in the bottom left-hand corner.

'I've paused it,' Adkins said. 'Just press PLAY.'

Helen hit the button and watched. Nothing happened for half a minute, save for the time-code changing, second by second, in the bottom right-hand corner. The only sound was a low hiss. She turned and asked where the volume controls were.

'No audio on that system,' Adkins said. 'Too bloody expensive.'

When Helen turned back, she saw two figures moving quickly towards the camera with a third a few feet behind. The two men at the front were deep in conversation, nodding, gesturing with their hands.

Wave and the man in the suit.

Just before they reached the camera and began to distort, they turned right and moved out of shot, heading down the stairs. The third figure, a well-built Asian youth, followed. Helen rewound the tape until the moment before Wave and the man in the suit disappeared. Then she froze the picture and sat there in front of it, equally still.

Stared at a face she recognised, whose smile she had returned; a face that she had seen care-worn and folded into sympathy just two days before.

Adkins heard the gasp as she sucked in a breath. 'You all right, love? You're not . . .?'

'I need this tape,' she said.

'Fine. I'll make a copy.'

'I want it now.'

While Adkins was still hauling himself upright, Helen ejected the tape from the VCR. He shouted something after her as she walked out, but she didn't hear it. Didn't care. Down two flights and out onto the street, wanting to run but watching her step; the cassette clutched so tightly that she felt as though her fingers might push through the plastic casing.

Remembering something Ray Jackson had said, sitting in the back of his taxi. Something she should have realised was significant.

A sleek blue Mercedes was idling at the kerb opposite the entrance. Jacky Snooks was bending down, talking to the man in the back seat. When Snooks stood up and stepped to one side, Helen saw Frank Linnell. She stopped a few feet away, desperate to get to her own car, but knowing there would have to be an exchange of some sort. That Linnell had been waiting for it. Glancing into the front, she recognised the driver as the man who had let her into Linnell's pub and brought her a drink. Now she remembered his voice, too, and finally knew who had left the anonymous message on her answering machine.

'Helen . . .?'

She saw the expression on Linnell's face and began to understand why.

Linnell leaned out of the window and nodded towards the tape in Helen's hand. 'Anyone you recognise?'

'Never seen him before in my life,' Helen said.

Frank stared out of the back window as Clive drove him home, following the 380 bus route that ran all the way from the High Street to Belmarsh Prison. Once they were through the traffic the Mercedes would be cruising up Lewisham Hill, turning east towards Wat Tyler Road and Blackheath. Down the other side and across a vast expanse of green with detached houses around its edge; huge three- or four-storey places that had not been converted into flats. For now, though, the view was limited: doorways crowded with bin-bags and names on signs that he could barely pronounce. He'd hung around in these streets as a younger man, done business in them thirty-odd years before, but now he scarcely recognised them.

'It's like Eastern Europe,' he said to Clive. 'It's vexatious to the spirit.'

He didn't know if it was down to immigrants, or to drugs, or to guns being passed around like football cards. He didn't have any answers. There was always the odd mental case, even back then, but Christ . . . When you could get sliced up for looking the wrong way at somebody's shoes, Frank knew something had to be done, and maybe the likes of him were better placed to do it than the police or politicians.

Frank couldn't say if Helen had been lying to him or not. It didn't really matter as things stood. He knew he'd done the right thing, giving this one to her. This was something she could do for Paul, and it might make her feel a little better after everything she'd suspected him of. She also was in the perfect position to get it organised. Even if she didn't know the individual in question, she had the contacts to find out who he was. Frank would probably be able to get the name himself, eventually, but he knew that passing it over to Helen was the more satisfactory option. He'd been thinking about the best way to handle it ever since Clive had told him what had been said in that stash house; since he'd put that together with what Jacky Snooks had told them.

It was frustrating in the short term, maybe, letting the law handle things, but this way would pay dividends down the line. A copper always suffered more inside. Whoever he was, he'd pay for what he'd done to Paul a hundred times over, and every day.

Payback could be an instant pleasure, Frank had decided, but sometimes it was better to invest in a little of it.

He wondered if Helen Weeks might send some of her colleagues after *him*, when she'd had her baby and things had settled down a bit. He felt safe enough, had kept the proper distance from everything, but he guessed there might be a little aggravation coming his way later on. She clearly knew about his business with the stick men. That much was obvious from the third degree she'd given him a couple of days before. Making suggestions and asking if he knew anything, as though he was just going to hold his hands up and cough to it, right there in his kitchen.

Silly . . .

He liked her well enough, and had been civil to her for Paul's sake, but neither of them were daft, were they?

Up the duff or on their holidays, it didn't matter; the likes of Helen Weeks were never off duty. That was why he and Paul had never talked business; at least not until the very end. It had made sense to both of them. Every proper friendship had parameters, after all.

Frank stared out at the shops and the youngsters doing nothing outside them and wondered who he was trying to kid. If it was all sorted out and the muck was hosed away overnight, he knew that something else would be along soon enough to replace it. Something even worse, probably. That kind of gap in the market didn't stay unfilled for long.

Same went for the stick men. Once all that was done with, another group of them would say, 'Thank you very much', and move in sharpish to take up the slack.

There would be someone sitting at Paul's desk too, by now. And how long until the girlfriend found someone to help bring up his kid?

'Got much on for the rest of the day?' Clive asked.

Frank turned from the window and sat back. 'Up to my eyeballs.'

Life moved on.

PART FOUR

LIGHTS OUT

THIRTY-SEVEN

'How long overdue are you?'

'A week and a half,' Helen said. 'They're inducing me if nothing's happened by the weekend.'

'I suppose we should crack on, then.'

Jeff Moody was sitting opposite her on the sofa, as he had been the first time he'd visited the flat. He was wearing what seemed to be the same blue suit, though Helen guessed he probably had several of them. He certainly wasn't the type to waste time shopping, especially not recently. He'd been busy.

'How's he being?' Helen asked. She couldn't bring herself to say his name.

'Fronting it out,' Moody said. 'It's not going to be straightforward.'

Helen nodded. Things rarely were, though she was usually the one handing out the explanations to the frustrated relatives of victims. She'd felt frustration too, of course, but it was only now that she really understood how trivial hers were by comparison. She would always have the opportunity to move on to another case. Victims, and those close to them had only one life.

Moody opened his briefcase and passed across a photograph. Helen looked down at the bunch of keys in the picture; the faded leather fob she'd seen a thousand times. 'We found those in Kelly's house,' Moody said. 'It's obviously how he got in here.'

'Hard to explain away, I would have thought.'

'He claims Paul gave them to him, in case you both got locked out.'

Helen shook her head. 'That's Paul's set. I've checked, and they're not in the bag I got back after the crash. He must have taken them.'

'I think . . . he might have taken them from Paul's body,' Moody said, 'at the bus stop, while they were waiting for the ambulance to arrive. The witness says he was down on the floor next to Paul. It would have been easy enough.'

Helen swallowed, handed back the photograph. 'Not going to be easy to prove, though.'

'Like everything else.'

'We've got the CCTV tape. We've got him talking to Wave.' Moody nodded. 'What about Sarah Ruston?' Helen asked.

'She's co-operating.'

'In return for a reduced sentence?'

Moody shrugged; they both knew the way things worked. 'She's identified Errol Anderson, a.k.a. Wave, as one of the men who gave her the instructions, who fired the shots into her car the day before, ran through all the times and speeds and so on. She claims there were two of them, but she can't give us a positive ID on the second one. It might have been one of the other boys who were shot, but she can't be sure. He kept his hoodie up the whole time.'

'But we've still got a direct connection to the gang.'

'We've got film of Kelly talking to one of them. We have no way of ascertaining what was said.'

'It's one hell of a coincidence, though, don't you think?'

'Yes . . .'

'He happens to be talking to a gang who then arrange the crash that kills one of his colleagues. A close personal friend who just happens to be investigating bent coppers.'

'It's not me that needs convincing, Helen.'

She took a deep breath, told Moody she was sorry. He reddened and waved her apology away. 'How does *he* explain it? The meeting at the snooker club?' Helen asked.

'Well, against his solicitor's advice, he's being quite chatty.'

Helen remembered the fake concern on Kelly's face as they sat and talked about which reading he should give at the funeral. 'I bet he is.'

'He claims *he* was doing undercover work. Some anonymous tip-off or other.'

'On whose authority?'

'Off his own bat. Says he knows he was taking a risk, not following the proper procedure and all that. Happy to admit he's a bit of a glory-hunter.'

'Better than being a murderer, right?'

'Right . . .'

'So how's it looking? Overall.'

Moody leaned back, puffed out his cheeks. 'The problem is that it's such a weird one, and the CPS haven't got a clue how to handle it. They had a hard enough time working out what to charge Ruston with.'

In the end, they'd opted for manslaughter. Helen had slammed down the phone when Tom Thorne had called to give her the news.

'Like I said, it's not going to be straightforward.'

'He's going away, though?' Helen said. 'You told me he would.'

'Look, it's all circumstantial, but if we're lucky, the weight of that evidence might well be enough. The keys, the video, what have you. Motive's going to be a problem, though.'

'What was on the computer?'

'As far as anything that might be relevant, not a lot. Certainly no mention of Gary Kelly or anything that might implicate him.'

'He needed Paul out of the way before that happened.'

Moody nodded. 'He couldn't be sure that it hadn't happened already, though, which was why he wanted the laptop, why he broke into your flat. He wasn't banking on finding you at home.'

'I'd told him I was staying at my father's that night,' Helen said.

'What we need to know is why Kelly thought Paul was a danger to him in the first place. How he found out about the operation.'

Helen had barely left the flat for a week. She had sat, and eaten and slept, and thought about exactly what Gary Kelly had done, why he had arranged it as he had.

'That's what'll help us nail him,' Moody said.

It had to look random, like the worst case of someone being in the wrong place at the wrong time. The nature of Operation Victoria meant that even an 'accident' might have seemed suspicious. Paul could not just forget to turn the gas off or fall down a flight of stairs. And any sort of contract hit was clearly out of the question.

Once Kelly had decided what to do and how to do it, he must have been patting himself on the back for days.

The crash not only got Paul out of the way, but completely eliminated Kelly himself from the merest hint of suspicion. He was almost killed himself, after all, with a witness at the bus stop helpfully validating the fact. Helen had been thinking about that, too. The man at the bus stop had talked about Paul pushing Kelly out of the way as the car veered towards them, but he could have misinterpreted what he'd seen. Witnesses did that routinely, and in far less stressful situations.

It was nice to think that Paul's last actions, however misplaced, had been heroic; but when Helen closed her eyes she saw Kelly as the one doing the pushing; ensuring that Paul was hit while he got himself clear. Staggering away with a few nice cuts and bruises, weeping for his mate, dropping to the floor to take Paul's keys as he lay dying.

'Helen?'

'I think I know how Kelly found out,' she said.

'Go on.'

'Kevin Shepherd. He was in Shepherd's pocket.'

Helen told him about her conversation with Ray Jackson in the back of his taxi. The comment whose significance she'd missed. It had been no more than a slight misunderstanding or at least that was what she'd thought at the time:

'You had a passenger in the back of your cab, a police officer, on Friday . . .'

'Which one?'

'Sorry?'

'Which Friday?'

She remembered that Jackson had been flustered for a second or two. He had covered up his slip, and she hadn't seen it. 'When he asked, "Which one?" he initially meant which copper, not which day.'

'Shepherd pays a *lot* of coppers,' Moody said. 'That's why Paul was looking at him in the first place.'

Helen shook her head. She was certain. 'Shepherd told Kelly about Paul. That's what you need to be working on.'

Moody thought about it. 'It makes sense, from a timing point of view at least. Shepherd was the only target Paul was working on when he was killed.'

'There's your motive,' Helen said.

'I hope you're right. Then *all* we have to do is convince the CPS. They might still decide the best we can hope for is conspiracy to commit.'

'As long as he goes down, Jeff.'

Moody's briefcase was open on his knees. He leaned across it. 'Look, if there's any chance at all of putting Kelly away for what happened to Paul, they will.' He shut his case, cleared his throat. 'But I know he did it, which means, apart from anything else, that he's seriously bent. If all else fails, *I* will put him away for that. OK?'

Helen didn't answer, so he asked her again. She could see that Moody meant it, and knew that she could hope for no more. She thanked him and he promised to call as soon as there was any news. Then he made her promise to do the same.

'What about Frank Linnell?'

'Well, it's not my area, obviously, but we've passed your information on and those investigating the shootings in Lewisham will certainly be looking at him. The way people like Frank Linnell operate, though, I don't think that'll be easy either.'

Helen agreed, but it wasn't what she had meant. 'I was talking about Linnell and Paul. You said you'd try and find out.'

'Yes, right.' He looked uncomfortable, as though he had news that was not so much bad as embarrassing. 'We're as certain as we can be that there was never any illegal business arrangement between them, so all I've got is a little history.'

'Linnell told me that,' Helen said. 'Some case that Paul was working on.'

'Linnell's half-sister, Laura,' Moody said. 'She was murdered by a boyfriend six years ago and Paul was one of the DCs. Looks like they stayed in touch afterwards.'

Helen remembered the photographs in Linnell's kitchen. Not a daughter, then. 'How was she killed?'

'Stabbed. The jealous sort, apparently.'

'How long did he get?'

'Well, that's the thing. He was stabbed to death himself while on remand in Wandsworth. Two days before he was due in court.'

'Somebody saved the taxpayer some money.' It was clear from Helen's face who she thought that 'somebody' might have been.

Moody's smile was suitably grim. 'Well, I spoke to the original SIO and that's what he reckons, anyway. Never came close to proving it, of course . . .'

Helen was still seeing the young girl's face; and Linnell's face, when he was looking at the pictures. She didn't find it hard to believe that the shootings in Lewisham weren't the first time Frank Linnell had meted out his own form of justice.

'So, as far it goes with . . . Linnell and Paul.' Moody was gathering together his things. 'Just friends. No more to it than that.' Seeing the look on Helen's face, he opened his mouth to say something else, but she stopped him.

'You once played tennis with some bloke who was a forger. Yes, I *know*.'

Moody held up his hands, as though his point was made.

'How many people did this forger kill, though?'

THIRTY-EIGHT

She slept for most of the afternoon after Moody had left, and spent the rest of it stretched out in front of the television, looking for distraction but for the most part failing to find it. For perhaps ten minutes at a time something would engage her and briefly take her mind somewhere a little less dark.

She took in bits of a programme about stand-up comics at the Edinburgh Festival, and remembered how she and Paul had talked about going. They would occasionally go down to the Hobgoblin in Brixton and had always enjoyed it, and they'd both said how great it would be to get some time off and spend a week up at the Fringe, seeing a few of their favourite comedians. They could do the castle, too, Paul said, and all the other touristy stuff. He reckoned he had Scottish blood in him somewhere and had been determined to find out if there was a Hopwood tartan.

'You're as Scottish as I am, you silly bugger . . .'

Watching the programme, Helen decided that she *would* go, as soon as she got the chance. For a very stupid second or two she even thought about going to the Hobgoblin that night; calling Jenny up, seeing if she fancied it. She could do with a laugh, and the comedians would certainly have enjoyed taking the piss out of her waddling off to the toilets every twenty minutes.

It was a terrible idea, of course. She'd had plenty of those recently.

Barring that, and the time spent idly competing with the contestants on *Countdown*, she lay there like a zombie. It was strange, she thought, how that phrase was used to describe people who were somehow out of it; miles away, unfocused. Strange, because in those horror films Paul had made her sit through, zombies were anything but unfocused. They had only one impulse as they crashed around and smeared bloody hands down people's windows; one fixed idea, terrible and all-consuming. Now, something equally brutal was occupying her own thoughts while she lay there and let the sound and the pictures wash over her.

She thought about Gary Kelly, and how she might get to him.

How she could talk her way into the interview room, or the remand cell, with her warrant card and some cock-and-bull story or other. She worked out in great detail what she would say to him before she did what she'd come to do, and what damage she could safely inflict without endangering her baby.

Ask him to read that poem again, maybe.

See how many other expressions he could do.

It was sour, stupid stuff that made Helen hate herself, and made her hate Kelly even more for what he was turning her into. She drifted in and out of sleep, wincing at the voices and the absurdly cheerful music, but unable to raise herself up to turn it off.

It was just gone six when the phone rang. She would remember the time later because she'd been dimly aware of the theme to the six o'clock news, the noise of the phone cutting through it.

It was a DCI from the Murder Squad. Spiky Bugger's boss, by the sound of it. 'Helen, we took a call. Can you hear this OK?'

She heard a number of clicks, then the faintest hiss before the voice of a police operator came on the line. After five seconds of silence the operator urged the caller to speak; asked again about the nature of the call. The caller's voice was muffled at first as he said something to the operator. Then, more distinctly, he said that he wanted to leave a message. The operator told him to go ahead.

'This is for the woman whose old man was killed at that bus stop, yeah?'

There was a pause. The operator said she was still listening.

'The pregnant one.' Another few seconds of silence, then some mumbling as though he were talking to himself. Finally he spoke clearly again. 'I was the one who shot into the car, OK? I'm sorry for what happened . . . it wasn't supposed to. Won't make no difference to you, probably, but it wasn't.' He sniffed, cleared his throat. 'That's it, that's the thing. I'm getting on me toes, yeah . . . so, I just wanted to let you know before I go.' More hiss and clicking; a hum that might have been the noise of distant traffic. 'I'm sorry . . .'

There were a few more seconds of ambient noise and one long breath before the call ended.

Poor as the quality of the recording had been over the phone, Helen recognised the voice as well as something it had said. Remembered the boy's face as she'd listened and the conversation as he'd lifted her bags into the car.

'*Probably a good time to take a holiday, if you ask me.*'

'*Can't see me getting on me toes any time soon.*'

She'd told him to keep his head down . . .

'Helen?'

'I know him. It's a kid I met in Lewisham.'

'Sorry? You *know* him?'

'I just bumped into him.'

'Where?'

'Just . . . on the street. Jesus . . .'

'Is there anything you can tell us that might help? Anything he said? A description?'

Nothing that wouldn't sound ridiculous. *He carried my shopping. He seemed nice enough. He asked about my baby.* 'Not really,' Helen said. 'We only spoke for a minute.'

'Well, if you think of anything . . .'

She put down the receiver, walked across to the sofa and turned the sound back up on the TV. Something about mortgage rates. A fatal house fire. Too much salt in processed food.

He was calling to say sorry, that it was his fault. So he couldn't have been in on it. For the first time, she wondered how many in that car *had* been?

How many of the dead boys?

'*Won't make no difference to you, probably . . .*'

He hadn't known.

It wouldn't be dark for another couple of hours, but she decided to get an early night. She'd thought she and Roger Deering had made a decent job of clearing up the bathroom after the break-in, but stepping back from the sink, a small piece of glass had gone into the sole of her foot. Slipped into the soft part.

Sitting on the edge of the bath, picking at the glass with tweezers, Helen looked up and saw herself in the mirror. Her dressing gown had fallen open. Her breasts were swollen and sagging, the veins livid beneath the skin. The waistband of her tracksuit bottoms was folded down on itself, pressed flat by her belly. Her ankles looked thick.

She wrapped the piece of glass inside the bloody tissue and tossed it into the toilet; ran a hand down a pale, hairy shin.

A mummy *nobody* would like to fuck.

And thinking it, wondering if her sister knew what a MILF was, Helen remembered the conversation between the boy and one of his mates as they'd been walking towards the car park. The boy's embarrassment as his friend had postured and pointed and made his dirty suggestions.

'*You're a* seriously *dark horse . . .*'

She remembered what the other boy had called him.

It wasn't much to go on. Next to useless, probably. Certainly not enough to go bothering DI Spiky Bugger or his boss at nine o'clock at night.

Helen winced as she put weight onto the foot, but she'd walked it off by the time she'd reached the bedroom and started to get dressed.

THIRTY-NINE

Friday was a bad night to try to get anywhere quickly. The traffic had started to build on the hill down into Brixton and was almost solid on Coldharbour Lane from the Ritzy to Loughborough Junction. Helen banged her hands against the wheel in frustration. Time was not on her side, or that of the boy who had made the call.

Linnell had found the others easily enough, after all.

She knew now that the boys in the Cavalier that night had been killed in revenge for Paul's murder, when all they had done – *unwittingly*, some of them – was provide a smokescreen for it. Kelly's plan had worked out better than he ever could have hoped. Those who were ignorant of the set-up had been his victims every bit as much as Paul had been, and the boy who had held the gun, who *thought* he had fired the shots, might well be the last one left.

The traffic was just as bad towards Camberwell, so she turned south, deciding to go the back way instead.

He had been used, Helen decided; that was all. But Frank Linnell would not know that. And even if she were to let him know, she wasn't sure he'd be inclined to care.

She was still thinking about Linnell as the traffic eased through East Dulwich, and about the girl in those photographs.

Linnell's murdered sister.

Helen wondered if the girl had been the reason why Paul's relationship with Linnell had survived for so long. Paul had been deeply affected by a few cases in the time she'd known him, and it was easy to see, just from the pictures, why he would have found it hard to let go of this one. Why he might have wanted to stay close, even when there was nothing left to investigate.

Had he fallen a little in love with a murdered girl? In some ways, that was easier to accept than the alternative. To think, he'd called some of *her* friends wankers . . .

'She was pretty, Hopwood, I'll give you that.'

She got lucky with a few green lights and it wasn't quite a quarter to ten when she turned onto Lewisham Way. She parked on a double yellow, a hundred yards or so from where the Lee Marsh and Orchard estates backed onto each other, and stuck a MET POLICE card on the dashboard. She might get a brick through the window, but at least she wouldn't be clamped.

Across the road there was a small parade of shops: a newsagent's, a bookmaker's and an electrical-repair shop. Three boys were passing a joint around outside a Threshers, and she could hear a car being revved up on a street somewhere behind them.

There were two more estates, the Downton and the Kidbrooke, a few streets further up, but this was where the boy had pointed to when she'd asked him where he lived. She had not given much thought to how she might find him and now, looking at the various blocks, she wondered where on earth she was going to begin. There were probably a hundred and fifty flats in each block. God alone knew how many people.

Helen walked into the open space at the centre of the Orchard Estate, across a square of browned grass with spray-painted benches dotted along each side. She stood for half a minute and tried to get a sense of the geography. It was a warm enough night, but there was a decent breeze moaning around the walls and she wished she'd brought a thicker jacket. She looked up at each three-storey block, a doorway to lifts at either end and concrete stairwells up to the first level. There was music thumping from somewhere high to her left, but it faded as she crossed to the far corner and moved through the walkway that connected the Orchard to the Lee Marsh next door.

The central area was identical, save for a rudimentary children's play area, and there was music from two, no three, sides. Words she couldn't make out above the drum and bass. She could feel its frantic, insistent rhythm in the metal of the children's slide when she leaned against it.

There was a row of garages set back from the road on one side, and she recognised the group of kids she'd spoken to when she'd been there the first time. The day she'd met the boy.

Four of them, moving around slowly in shadows that were almost gone.

She kept walking towards them, feeling her heart thump, the dryness in her mouth. At work, she'd been in worse places on risk-assessment visits, but she had never been this scared; this aware of the fear, at any rate. She'd had back-up then, obviously, but she knew it was more than that.

Now there were two hearts thumping inside her.

The short one she'd spoken to before was playing on his mobile phone and barely looked up when she approached. Two others had their heads together. The tallest one – the baby giraffe – whistled when he saw her and the four of them huddled a little closer.

Helen stopped a few feet away from them and waited a second or two. Said, 'Am I pregnant or just fat? Remember?'

The baby giraffe took a step towards her and thrust his thumbs into the waistband of his jeans. Showed her another few inches of his Calvin Kleins.

'I'm looking for T,' Helen said.

'Yeah?'

The short one glanced up from his phone for just a second. Helen tried not to show any excitement at the fact that they obviously knew who she was talking about.

'I need to speak to him.'

The baby giraffe grinned. 'So, bell him. I'll lend you a phone if you like.'

'I don't have his number.'

Another look from the short boy. Clearly they took it in turns to be the sulky, dangerous one.

'Listen, I really need to see him. It's urgent.'

For a few seconds, nobody spoke. It seemed as though the conversation had already been forgotten and the boys were happy just standing there, listening to the music. Then the taller one looked at her again.

'What's so *urgent?*'

She'd known straight away that the warrant card would be the wrong way to go. Just as instinctively, she knew that she should work with what she'd got. She put her hands on her belly and pulled a face. 'What do you *think?*'

There was laughter and shoulder-bumping. 'You don't even know where he lives?' The jeans were pushed down even lower. 'Just a quickie, yeah?'

'Nothing quick about *this*,' Helen said. 'He had his fun, so now I'm going to make him face up to his responsibilities.'

The baby giraffe finally stopped laughing and gestured casually towards the block on the far side of the square. 'T's up there, man. Third floor somewhere.'

The short boy looked up. 'Fuck you doing?'

'You seen T's girlfriend, man? There's going to be some *serious* sparks flying when this one comes knocking.'

'Not your business, you get me?'

'Going to be majorly hilarious . . .'

Helen turned while they were still arguing and walked towards the block, aware by the time she got near the lift that they had slowly followed her into the square.

The lift was noisy and smelled like she expected. Its walls were scratched but shiny, as though they'd been recently cleaned. Higher up, the wind was that much sharper against her face, a small slap, as she stepped onto the third-floor walkway and moved towards the first door.

The first of thirty or more.

She knocked but got no reply; moved on to the next door and got the same result, although she could hear that there were people inside. The third door opened a few inches, then was slammed shut without a word as soon as she'd asked the question. The old man in the next flat along listened carefully, then asked if she was from Social Services.

She was breathless, and four doors into it.

Maybe she should have made that call. They might not have found the right place as quickly, but a decent-sized squad of officers would have swarmed through the estate quick enough when they had; brought him out a damn sight faster than she could.

Helen stared helplessly along the walkway as she got her breath back. She was just wondering if she should simply stand there and shout, when she was beaten to it.

'Hey, T! Best get out here, man . . .'

She looked over the wall and saw three of the boys from the garages down below her.

The baby giraffe put his hands to his mouth and shouted again. 'You've got a *world* of pain waiting out here, T.' He shared a laugh with the others and yelled again, his voice rising above the drum and bass and echoing around the square. 'Hey, T. Come and meet the family!'

Helen waited. Fifteen seconds later, she heard a door opening and saw the boy step out onto the walkway fifty yards ahead of her. She watched him lean over and shout back, telling the boys below to shut up. He must have caught the movement as she started to walk towards him, because he turned suddenly and stared at her.

She kept walking, watching as he looked away for a few seconds, then slowly turned to face her. The boys were still shouting. A couple of other doors had opened and people had put their heads out to see what was happening.

'I need to talk to you,' Helen said.

'What's your name?'

He had backed into his flat and Helen had followed, turned off a narrow corridor into a living room. She found him standing by the window. There was a television on in the far corner and she could smell dope. A few seconds later a young girl carrying a baby pushed past her and moved across to join the boy.

Helen asked again.

'Theo,' the boy said.

'Who's this?' the girl asked.

Helen walked over and turned off the television. She could see cardboard boxes piled up behind the sofa, plastic bags stuffed with CDs and computer games. The couple watched her and said nothing, but as soon as Helen tried to speak, the girl began shouting: 'The fuck you think you're doing coming in here?' The boy put a hand on her arm but she shook it away. 'I'll tear your fucking head off . . .'

'You need to be quiet.'

'I swear—'

'My name's Helen Weeks.' She dug into her bag for her warrant card. 'I'm a police officer.' The girl didn't bother looking; shrugged like it made no difference. The boy studied his feet. 'My partner was killed a few weeks ago. He was standing at a bus stop . . .'

The girl looked at her now and hoisted the baby a little higher. He seemed happy enough, nuzzling at her neck. The girl nodded and spoke quietly. 'I saw that on the news.'

Helen stared at the boy but he refused to raise his head. 'Theo?'

He angled his body towards the girl. 'You should go. Get the baby down or something.'

'I'm going nowhere.'

'I can't do this if you're here.'

'That was those boys in the car, right?' The girl looked at Helen. 'The shooting?'

'Yes, but it's complicated.'

The girl sniffed and looked as though she was trying hard not to cry. She turned back to the boy. 'What did you do?' She punched his arm with her free hand and started to shout again. 'You and your *friend*, what did you do?'

'He didn't do anything,' Helen said. 'Theo, you need to listen. You weren't responsible.'

He looked at her properly for the first time. 'You got the message, yeah? I was the one who fired the shots.'

'There weren't any shots.'

He shook his head slowly. 'I don't know what you're doing here. What this is *for*. It's not like I could feel any worse, yeah?'

'There were blanks in that gun,' Helen said. 'The woman in the car drove at the bus stop on purpose.'

The girl leaned into the boy, suddenly scared. The baby was reaching across, grabbing at his father's shoulder. 'What's going on, T?'

'Remember when you fired into that car?'

'Yeah, I remember.'

'The back window was open, right?' The boy nodded. 'So why was there glass all over the back of the car? The shots had already been fired, and the woman in that car was in on the whole thing. It was meant to look like an accident, OK? Like it was random.' The boy was still, and staring, ignoring the hand of his baby, which was now slapping at his shoulder. 'Somebody wanted my partner killed.' Helen felt a twinge, like ligaments stretching low down, and sucked in a breath. 'Wanted . . .

Paul killed.'

The room seemed very hot all of a sudden. The front door had been left open and the music from outside was carried in on a breeze that felt like the blast from a hairdryer.

The boy moved quickly, lurching across the room, pushing himself off the far wall and returning to the window. When he turned, his hands were shaking and it looked like he was fighting hard to control his temper. 'Who else knew?' he asked. 'In the car, I mean.'

'I don't know. Errol Anderson, for sure.'

'He's dead.'

'I know,' Helen said.

'They're *all* dead.'

Now the girl looked terrified. 'T . . .?'

'You're going away somewhere,' Helen said. 'You said in the message that—' Helen stopped when she felt it and took a step back. Her hands moved down to her thighs, wiped at the wetness on them, and she watched as the drips hit the carpet.

'You OK?' the boy asked.

The girl stepped towards Helen. 'Her waters have gone.' She thrust the baby at the boy and walked quickly out of the room; came back a few seconds later with a roll of kitchen towel. 'The bathroom's through there,' she said.

Helen took the towel and tore off half a dozen sheets. 'Have you got a taxi number?'

'Yeah, if you can wait,' Theo said. 'They don't exactly break their necks to get here. *Shit . . .*'

'Can you drive?' Helen asked.

FORTY

It had been a trickle rather than a gush, which meant there was no great urgency. Helen felt unexpectedly calm, knowing it could be another twenty-four hours yet, perhaps more.

The risk of infection was probably a greater worry than imminent labour, and even though the advice in these circumstances was to get to hospital as soon as possible, she was happier trying to stick as close as possible to her birth plan. Lewisham University Hospital was no more than ten minutes' drive from the Lee Marsh Estate, but Helen asked Theo to take her home instead, confident that she would have plenty of time to collect her bag, turn round and get to King's College Hospital in Camberwell.

It took Theo a few minutes to get used to the controls of Helen's Fiesta but, even allowing for the strangeness of the situation, he seemed twitchy and ill at ease. He checked his mirrors every few seconds, and kept looking at his hands clamped around the wheel.

'Do you drive much?' Helen asked.

'Not for a while,' Theo said.

The traffic had eased in the previous hour and they moved fairly easily through New Cross before turning south.

'Somebody wanted him killed, you said. Paul . . .'

Helen had her window open, had been leaning close to it, taking in breaths of warm air. She turned to look at Theo and nodded.

'Who was it?'

'It doesn't matter.'

'You got him, though?'

'I think so.'

'What about the woman in the BMW? Why on earth would she agree to, you know . . .?'

'She's got a drug habit. Owed somebody a lot of money.'

'Wave?'

'Looks like it,' Helen said.

Theo's hands tightened around the wheel and he looked away into his wing mirror. 'Still down to me on one level, then. Maybe I sold her some stuff.'

Crossing Peckham Rye Common, Helen felt a contraction take hold. She clenched against it, but only remembered to look at her watch after the first few seconds. 'Fuck . . .'

Theo looked across. 'What?'

She shook her head and waited for it to end; let out the breath and sat back, panting. 'Twenty-five seconds, give or take,' she said. 'We're fine.'

'Sure?'

She nodded, but watched the needle of the speedometer creep a little higher. 'You said you weren't close to the other boys,' she said. 'When I saw you before. The ones who were shot.'

'Some more than others, I s'pose.'

'That the way it is in a crew? Just people you work with?'

Theo thought about it, leaned on the horn when a motorbike swerved a little close. 'Depends what happens. I bet you don't get on with every copper you meet.'

'That's true . . .'

'It's whether you do it for the money, or if it's a . . . lifestyle, whatever.'

'I talked to someone who really believed that the government was sending in the guns,' Helen said. 'That they were happy with what was going on.'

Theo shook his head. 'People talk rubbishness. So why's the government having them . . . amnesty things for knives?'

'People need to see them doing *something*.'

'Nobody cares anyway. They still using blades like pens or something.'

'You carry one?'

'Sometimes.' He steered the car left at Herne Hill station and accelerated along the east side of Brockwell Park. Said, 'I've got a gun on me right now.'

Helen was surprised to find herself nodding – as though he'd simply made some comment about the weather – and leaning back towards the open window.

'You know who killed them? Wave and the others?'

'I've got a fair idea.'

'Is it a secret?'

Helen searched for the words. 'It was . . . a friend of Paul's.'

'I could do with a few friends like that,' Theo said.

When they reached the flat, Helen told him that she'd be no more than a few minutes. She got upstairs as quickly as she could and went straight to the toilet, that particular need having been *distinctly* urgent since she'd climbed into the car.

She threw a couple more things into her overnight bag, then called Jenny and told her to come to the hospital.

'Was it a trickle or a gush?' Jenny asked.

Helen told her how predictable she was. 'There's plenty of time.'

'Have you ordered a cab?'

'It's waiting outside,' Helen said.

They had barely driven away from the block when she felt the wave of another contraction moving across her; a powerful tightening through her stomach and hips. She clenched against it, grunting with the effort, and Theo pulled in hard to the kerb.

'That one was half a minute,' Helen said, when it had stopped.

'Is that good or bad?'

'Was it fifteen minutes since the last one, do you think, or less?' Theo held up his hands. 'Let's just get there,' she said.

Theo put his foot down.

Helen wasn't even close to panicking, but it crossed her mind that blues and twos might have come in handy; that she could always flag down a passing squad car if one happened by and get an escort.

Theo was pushing the Fiesta as hard as he could, gunning it when he had the chance and weaving through gaps in the traffic when he didn't. They were flashed by a speed camera on Denmark Hill and Theo slammed his hands against the wheel.

'I'll live with it,' Helen said.

When she asked him, he told her a little about Javine and the baby; about his mother and sister, who lived two floors below him. She asked about his father and he told her he had died. She didn't sense any invitation to dig further.

'So where were you planning on going?' she asked.

'Javine's got a mate in Cornwall,' Theo said. 'She's been down to check it out a couple of times. Sounds OK, and we can stay there until we find somewhere.' He glanced across with something close to a smile. 'Don't think there's a *massive* black population, but you know . . .' He jumped a zebra crossing with a pedestrian halfway across and Helen told him it was fine.

'Maybe you shouldn't go anywhere,' she said.

'Yeah, well, that makes sense, everything being so great at home and all that.'

'Come on, you must know you're in danger. You saw what happened to the boys in that car.'

'You said you know who did it, though.'

361

'But I'm not sure we'll ever prove it.'

'All the more reason to get on my toes, no?'

'He's the sort of person who'd spend the time finding you,' Helen said. She waited until he looked across; made sure he could see she was serious. 'I think you should go to the police.'

'Yeah, right, whatever.'

'You didn't do anything.'

'I was in that car,' Theo said. 'I had a *gun*. You know the business I'm in, yeah?'

'They're not interested in the drugs.'

'I think they'd be interested in possession of a firearm with intent, though. That's not nothing, is it?'

'Look, you're the only witness who was in the car. If you give evidence, there's every chance they'll drop it. I'll write a full report, do everything I can. *Here!*' She pointed at the entrance to the hospital car park.

'You're worried about me being in danger, yeah?' He turned to her as they slowed. 'I give evidence, I'll be running from a whole different set of people. It doesn't end with Wave. You see what I'm saying?'

As they turned into the car park, Theo said, 'Actually, I'm not sure they're all dead, the others in the car. There's someone missing.' He drove as quickly as he could over the speed bumps, Helen holding tight to her belly across each one. 'His name's Ezra Dennison.'

'I'll mention it.'

'Easy. He's sixteen, yeah?'

'I'll make sure the right people know,' Helen said.

Theo parked as close as possible to the maternity wing and went round to help Helen out. They walked a few paces, then stopped at the automatic doors. Helen told him that she would be fine from then on; that there was no need for him to come in and that her sister would be meeting her. He asked if she wanted him to drop off the car back at her flat.

'Streatham police station isn't too far away,' Helen said.

'Yeah.' He poked at the ground with the toe of his trainer. 'You had your say on that one.'

'Really, you should do it. You'll all be safer.'

'Maybe.' He backed away towards the car.

'Just tell them exactly what happened.'

Theo opened the car door. 'What I did and what I *thought* I did. You know? Not sure the difference really matters.'

'Just *tell* them,' she said. 'We can sort it all out in a couple of days.'

'You should go in.'

'Please. And get rid of the gun on the way . . .' Helen turned and walked through the doors, catching the eye of a woman on her way out who had clearly overheard and looked away fast. She heard the car drive away as she dropped her bag at the desk.

FORTY-ONE

Theo called Javine as soon as he'd left the hospital. He told her that everything was OK, that he'd be back as soon as he could, and that he'd try to explain everything. He'd expected an earful, but she'd been calm; just said that they wanted him home.

He was heading south, without paying too much attention to any particular route, just wanting to drive around for a while. He wasn't going anywhere near Streatham, though, he knew that much. It felt like a massive weight had been lifted and the last thing he wanted to do was march straight back into the shit. He knew that copper's girl-friend thought it was for the best, that he'd be better off in the long run and all that, but she wasn't where he was. She had no idea.

She could say all she liked, but he knew how it was. He went walk-ing into a cop shop, saying, 'I'm that gang-banger you've been looking for,' there wouldn't be no open arms.

And like he'd told her, there might be a few people from triangles he never even knew about, wanting to talk to him afterwards.

Better off him and Javine taking their chances.

He reckoned Helen Weeks was OK, though. For a minute or two, he wondered how she'd react if he borrowed the car for a while, used it to get Javine and Benjamin away. They didn't have too much stuff, could probably do the whole thing in one trip, and he wasn't sure his dad's old Mazda would make it halfway to Cornwall.

Then he realised that if she found out the car wasn't where it was supposed to be, she'd presume that he'd nicked it. She was probably stressed enough as it was, and she'd be bringing a kid home on top of everything else. He decided it wasn't worth the aggravation, that he could probably get a good deal on a hire car. It wasn't like they needed anything fancy.

And he didn't like the idea of Helen thinking badly of him.

Money wouldn't be too much of a problem anyway, not for the next few months at least, while they got themselves sorted. He'd meant what he said when he told Javine they didn't *need* his mum's money; even if he didn't want to tell her why.

There'd been a grand, or just short of it under that loose board in the stash house. He'd grabbed the cash box, shaking like a fucking leaf, and shoved it into a plastic bag with the hundred or so rocks from the kitchen cupboards before legging it out of there.

A few months at least, if they were careful.

He knew what Easy would have said: '*Sweet and simple, Star Boy . . .*'

Driving good and slow along Norwood Road, Theo wondered if his friend had been taken for a mug that night, too. Easy had nicked the Cavalier, Theo knew that much, but had he been involved in putting the whole thing together? Had he known exactly what he was doing when he pressed to get Theo moved up?

When he as good as placed that gun in his hand?

Theo still hoped he might have the chance to ask him one day.

He pulled up at the lights, thinking that he'd talk to Javine about getting out of her friend's place as soon as they could. They'd be sharing one small bedroom with the baby and they'd probably have enough for a smallish deposit on something. It was a tourist place, so he guessed there might be a few jobs going, stuff in hotels or whatever. Javine could ask her friend to get hold of a local paper and check it out before they got there.

He turned on the radio and flicked through the stations. He stopped and turned it up when he heard a reggae track fading out, but he didn't know the song. He was vaguely aware of a car drawing along-side, though he didn't see the window moving down.

Looking at the lights as they began to change.

The gun was already coming up when Theo glanced across at the man in the car, and the DJ was saying who the song was by. Someone his father might have sung along with once. But there was only time for the merest glimpse of his father's face, of Javine's and Benjamin's.

Not even enough time to cry out, in that second or two before the dark.

When he'd had the sound system installed in the office, Frank had made sure he could hear music from almost anywhere in the house. There were wall speakers mounted in the bathroom and sitting room, and out in the conservatory, of course, where he spent most of his evenings these days.

He'd fancied something light and summery; sat listening to a Vivaldi concerto, with a glass of wine and an upmarket property mag-azine on the table in front of him. He was watching and waiting for the lights. He hadn't seen the foxes for a while, and had left out ever more food over the last few nights, in the hope of enticing them back.

'Yours isn't the only garden they go to, you know,' Laura said. 'They're not pets.'

'I bet nobody feeds the buggers as well as I do, though. There's half a leg of lamb sitting out there.'

'Maybe they're vegetarians.'

They watched for another quarter of an hour, until Frank told her he was almost ready to call it a night. She walked across and sat next to him, began flicking idly through the magazine, pointing out the properties she thought were nice.

'You don't think I let you down, do you?' Frank asked.

'How many glasses of wine have you had?'

'Do you?'

She reached for his hand. 'Don't be silly.'

'What about afterwards? What I got organised in Wandsworth.'

'Well, you can't expect me to love it, but I know you only did it because you care.' Her voice dropped. 'I know you've got your own way of doing things.'

'I'll have to settle for that,' Frank said.

The music started to build again, after a long slow passage. The solo violin was jagged and stuttering, almost impossibly high.

'You didn't let down Paul, either.'

Frank could see that Laura was uncomfortable, that it was hard for her to talk about these things, but he knew that ultimately she would forgive him anything. She was the only one who would. It was there in her eyes, and in her arms as she leaned across and laid her head on his chest, absolving him.

Frank was alone, asleep in the chair, when the lights came on an hour or so later and a well-fed ginger tom came creeping from the bushes on the far edge of the lawn. Watchful for a minute or so, low to the ground, then hurrying across the lawn towards its meal.

FORTY-TWO

Just short of nine hours into it, they said it was almost over.

'Come on, love, nearly there . . .'

Then again, they had been saying that for a while.

Jenny was doing her best to be supportive, telling Helen to breathe and keeping cool in the face of the subsequent abuse, her face contorting as if she were feeling it herself when the contractions hit. Each one was a searing wave that began in Helen's side and swept across her; rock hard and paralysing by the time it reached the middle and squeezed her like a lemon for a minute or so. Her throat was hurting almost as much as the rest of her by the time the pain had ebbed again.

She'd started on gas and air once the labour was established, floated away for a while, but had started screaming for an epidural after four hours, when she was still only three centimetres dilated. Shouting at the midwives and the walls, and at her stubborn fucking cervix. After what had seemed like another hour, a young anaesthetist had come in looking flustered and reeling off the risks: the one-in-twenty chance of her blood pressure dropping; the one-in-a-thousand chance of rupturing the membrane around the spinal cord; the *extremely* slim chance . . .

She'd told him, in no uncertain terms, that she didn't care.

After five minutes of painful jabbing he'd shaken his head. 'Can't get the bloody thing in.'

Jenny had grinned at him across the bed. 'I bet that's what the father said.'

The father . . .

Just a stupid joke, Helen knew that, and it had been terrible to see the look on her sister's face when she'd realised what she'd said.

'I only meant . . .'

Helen had wanted to tell her that it was all right, but another contraction had forced all the breath out of her. Held her rigid as they all went back to work.

'Too late anyway,' one of the midwives said. 'Pretty much fully dilated now, darling.'

There were two of them, working together in a well-practised nice cop/nasty cop routine. One was telling Helen to imagine her cervix opening like a flower, while her partner just urged her to 'get her head down' and 'work harder'. She was the one who took control when they got down to the blood and guts. 'Concentrate, Helen. Push this baby out. *Do* it.'

She hated the agony, didn't believe for a single second any of that new-age, holistic rubbish. It was not something she'd 'earned' for forty-two weeks, and it was not 'part of the experience'. Each time, she felt as though the next contraction might kill her; but still, when it came, she pushed with all the strength she had left. The mixture of emotions was enough to take at least some of the feeling away, to lessen the agony just a little, while she drove the muscles in her abdomen until they sang.

She tensed as she felt the next one coming.

Jenny squeezed her hand.

She pushed . . .

She knew that she would have to live with the guilt and the painful memories. Those things had found a home, had lodged inside her.

Like a shard of glass slipping into the soft part of a foot.

She pushed and screamed, inside and out.

'Here he comes. Last one now.'

She would deal with those things.

She would beat them down as best she could, for both of their sakes. For the baby that she knew – *prayed* – was Paul's.

She felt strong suddenly, and focused. Energised. She was the fierce, still centre of the turning world.

'Just one more good one, love . . .'

Her bowels opened, and it felt like her belly would split like a watermelon any second. She wanted to claw it open to fight the burning in her stomach, and pelvis and back. It felt as though she were being turned inside out.

But she kept pushing.

She'd known worse pain.

ACKNOWLEDGEMENTS

As always, there are a great many people without whom I would have remained in the dark . . .

Thanks are due once again to Tony Thompson, this time for pointing me in the right direction, and to Ember Phoenix and Nathan from West Camp for all the right words.

DCS Neil Hibberd was as patient and helpful as ever, though I *did* need to go elsewhere for advice on the matter of police officers working while pregnant. I am hugely grateful to Sergeant Georgina Barnard for her expertise in this, and many other areas. I must also thank Jane Maier who, as luck would have it, was two weeks away from giving birth at just the right moment and was thus able to provide some timely heartburn, nausea and leakage-related information.

Thanks, obviously, to Sasha for causing all the trouble.

I would also like to thank Frances Fyfield for saving some procedural bacon, Jane Doherty for her wonderful moderation, John Brackenridge for help I could not have got anywhere else, and Mike Gunn for the best – if not the *only* – joke in the book.

And, of course: Hilary Hale, Wendy Lee, Sarah Lutyens, and David Shelley, who has *never* eaten in Chicken Cottage.